To Carol,
May yo... ...
...
Much ...
Jasmine Wallace

Demon's CHOICE

JASMINE WALLACE

ISBN: 9798857463413

Cover design by: Olivia (Fiverr.com: @oliviaprodesign)
Library of Congress Control Number: 2018675309
Printed in the United States of America

DEDICATION

To all the women who dream of being whisked away by a handsome gentleman who is a demon in the sheets.

This is for you.

Contents

FOREWORD

Dear Reader,

Demon's Choice is a supernatural romance with some dark topics. It contains content and situations that could be triggering for some readers.

This book is explicit and has explicit sexual content. It is intended for an 18+ audience.

Trigger Warnings include but are not limited to:

- Explicit Language
- Alcoholism
- Anxiety
- Death
- Suicide
- Murder
- Graphic Violence
- Physical and Sexual Assault
- Child Neglect/Abuse

Despite that, I really hope you enjoy my book!

If you do, I would be so grateful if you would review it on Amazon or Goodreads.

Much love,
Jasmine

INTRODUCTION TO DEMONS

In this book the order of Hell is a culmination of different believe and classification systems.

The inspiration of the seven Princes of Hell has been taken from "Lanterne of Light", an anonymous English Lollard tract often attributed to John Wycliffe. In this the Princes are all assigned to one of the seven deadly sins, with each demon tempting people by means of those sins. This system was also used later in history in the works of John Taylor, the Water Poet.

Lucifer: The Prince of Pride
Satan: The Prince of Wrath
Abaddon: The Prince of Sloth
Asmodeus: The Prince of Lust
Beelzebub: The Prince of Envy
Mammon: The Prince of Greed
Belphegor: The Prince of Gluttony

Other Classifications:
Incubi and Succubi: Demons of Desire, born of and overseen by Lilith (Consort of Lucifer)
Cambions: Half-demon, half-human
Natural Born: Demons born of Succubi or spawn from the lower pits of Hell
Reaper Demons: Those charged with the management of condemned or sacrificed souls
Dealer Demons: The faces of Hell, summoned accordingly to trade with mortals for their souls
Rouge Demons: Those that have abandoned the call of Hell, refusing to engage in the collection of power
Imps: Little creatures subservient to their masters, whoever they may be

PROLOGUE

The air was thick with palpable tension as it hung heavy over the fields either side of the converging roads. A storm was building on the horizon, its dark clouds rolling over each other, threatening to release the rain within. Lightning splintered in the sky with jagged flashes against the faded dusk red sunset.

In contrast a small man knelt in the middle of the crossroads, his hands clasped together in prayer.

A limp cat lay at his knees, its throat slit. The man had used its blood to draw ritual runes on a stone slab mixed with black ash and rosemary twigs. The smell of impure death permeated the unmoving air.

"Prayers are usually reserved for angels and the repentant," a deep gravel-like voice travelled across the distance startling the man who scrambled to his feet at the sound. "Consequently, by summoning me, I highly doubt angels or repentance are of any use to you now."

The man strained to see in the fading light but caught the unmistakable silhouette of a demon stepping towards him. "Which one are you?" the man asked shakily.

The demon sneered in amusement. "You summon without knowing who you are going to get? Summoning demons is dangerous at the best of times, but that's just foolishness."

"I didn't have much choice," the man admitted. "I could barely bring myself to kill the cat. Killing a woman..." the man shook his head sadly

"I couldn't do that. It would defeat the purpose."

The demon tilted his head in curiosity. "Intriguing statement. What do you want, Matthew?"

The man startled. "You know my name?"

"Of course. You summoned me, baring open your soul, so I know a lot about you. Not all, but enough," the demon took another step towards him and sighed. "What do you want in exchange for your soul?"

Matthew swallowed, fear building in his chest. A metallic taste clung to his tongue as he took in more of the demon's features. Dark red skin covered large toned muscles, rippling as he walked, exuding strength and power. The demon wore no shirt leaving his broad shoulders and chest bare. A long clean-line tattoo started in the centre of his chest plate spiking out towards his shoulders along his collar-bone. Loose trousers draped from his waist before they tucked into knee-high boots that were a matt black apart from a gold trim along the sole of the boot. Long black hair was swept back from his face and bound in a single braid down his back resting at the start of the trouser band. His eyes glowed black complementing the black horns that protruded from just above his temples, sweeping and twisting back over the crown of his head, almost touching at their point. Two talon-like horns grew from his shoulders, smaller ones trailing down his biceps finishing at his elbows. He stood a good two feet taller than Matthew's own five-and-a-half-foot frame. Everything about the demon screamed dangerous to the mortal man.

"Save my wife," Matthew croaked, his skin shivering as the demon stopped suddenly, a few steps from him.

Silence fell between the pair.

"She's dying," Matthew continued. "I can't lose her. I can't! She's everything to me. I don't know what I would do, or how I would live, without her," he shut his eyes to push back his dread before continuing. "She's pregnant and is refusing treatment because of that. She doesn't want to risk the baby. I can understand that, but not at the expense of her life!" Matthew ran his hand through his hair. "We can have more kids later. But not if she's dead."

"So, you would take the choice from her?" the demon asked.

"No... no..." Matthew said, shaking his head weakly. "I suppose... yes. I don't think she's thinking clearly because of the baby. I don't want to lose the baby either, but I don't want to lose her even more."

The demon pinched the bridge of his nose. The foolish sentiment of humans was exhausting at the best of times.

"Look," Matthew said, "I know a deal with you comes with a catch, more than just you claiming my soul. But I don't know what else to do. I'm desperate."

The demon looked at Matthew, placing his hands on his hips. "Alright, fine. I dislike these kinds of deals, but if your soul wasn't worth it, I wouldn't have come in the first place. Your wife will be healed. Call it a 'miracle' remission if you want. She won't lose the child and the pregnancy will be relatively normal."

Matthew shifted his weight uncomfortably as the demon paused. The demon seemed to be wrestling with himself, the muscles on his jaw pulsing with each passing second. Finally, he continued speaking.

"Your child however, will be born on the 29th of March next year—"

"But that's too soon!" Matthew interrupted. "It will barely be seven months by then!"

"They will be exactly seven months by the time they are born. Your child will bear the full weight of this deal. Whatever fate awaits it, cannot be changed," the demon continued. "However long its life, it is destined for Hell to stand as a powerful force within its ranks. And as for you..." Matthew swallowed hard. "You and your wife will have no other children. You will have seven years with your family and then I will come to claim your life and your soul," the demon took another step towards Matthew and held out his hand. "Agreed?"

"My wife... she will be fine though?"

"Yes."

Matthew stared at the demon's hand. Black talon-like nails extended from long red fingers. Slowly he extended his arm and clasped the demon's hand with his own. A small, curt shake and Matthew felt a sharp pain in his chest. His free hand flew to his chest, gasping at the pain. He looked panicked at the demon.

"Don't worry, that's just my brand on your soul. It belongs to me now," the demon said casually. "See you in seven years, Matthew."

The demon turned to leave and Matthew stared at his hand, letting the reality of his situation sink in. He looked up at the demon and called out, "Wait! Will you tell me your name?"

The demon looked over his shoulder at Matthew, the last of the light shifting across his angular features. "Ambrose," he said. Then with a flourish of flames, the demon was gone.

CHAPTER ONE

25 Years Later...

Soft morning light streamed through the sage green curtains of the apartment window, settling across Lena's face as she lay in bed, still curled up under the covers. Slowly she opened her eyes, welcoming the warmth of the sunlight in contrast to her cold apartment.

Lena looked at the clock on her bedside table, noting she'd woken up almost twenty minutes before her alarm. She squeezed her eyes shut, trying to force some last moments of sleep before she had to get up. After a moment she sighed heavily, realising the uselessness of her struggle. Gingerly, she stretched beneath the covers before forcing her body to sit up, keeping the duvet tucked under her chin to the best of her ability.

Although, she had been working steadily for the last few years since she moved to town, she was barely making ends meet, so paying for heating was not always a priority. Small towns and cities meant small wages which, unfortunately, utility companies didn't tend to adjust for. Waitressing was not the most lucrative of jobs even in the larger areas, but she liked the work and, sometimes, she even liked the people. However, with winter in full force, she could see the steam of her breath highlighted in the sunlight bouncing off her apartment walls.

Rubbing her eyes, she fought against the stiffness of her limbs in the cold before flinging the covers off her. Racing quickly to her bathroom, internally denying that she was cold, she turned on the shower, running the water as hot as she could manage. She stripped off and stepped into the shower letting the heat of the water warm her body, carefully keeping her hair out of the way. Although she wanted warmth, she didn't have time to let her hair dry, and getting sick from wet hair in the middle of winter was not on the cards for her that day.

Once feeling had returned to her extremities, she washed herself quickly before turning the water off. Faintly, she could hear her alarm going off from her bedroom. "Right on time," she said to no one in particular, wrapping her towel around her. She darted around her bedroom to turn off her alarm before grabbing the clothes she had laid out on her chair the night before and retreating to the steamy warmth of her bathroom. Drying herself as fast as she could before pulling on the plain black trousers and long-sleeve top, hoping from one foot to the other in an attempt to keep her blood pumping the warmth of the shower around her body. After wiping a small window in the fogged-up mirror, she pulled her reddish-brown hair up into a sleek ponytail. Her hair usually hung just past her shoulders, as its thickness provided a natural warmth around her neck, but when she would be working all day, she found the pieces of her hair that would fall in front of her face insanity inducing. Up was better for a day in the cafe.

She finished up by brushing her teeth and putting on a small amount of mascara. She thought of putting on some more makeup to smooth her complexion, but anything other than mascara would end up blotchy by the end of the day. The heat of the cafe would see to that. Deciding to brave some eyeliner kohl along her top lid to frame her dove-grey eyes, she inspected her work, satisfied that it should last the day with minimal fallout. Puffing out her cheeks with a firm exhale, she squared her shoulders bracing herself for the cold of her apartment as she left the bathroom.

"Flaming hell!" she cried tip-toe-ing across the wooden floor to the plush rug she had surrounding her bed. "I wonder if Marie will give me an extra shift so I can turn the heating on." She almost jumped back onto her bed tucking her feet under the covers whilst she leaned across a small expanse to her dresser to find some socks. She grabbed some thick black ones which she hastily pulled onto her feet. Rolling over, she climbed over the other side and reached for her favourite jumper that was hanging on the bed head. It was a deep purple with small white stars dotted randomly on the sleeves. The best part, it was thick woollen fleece inside and kept her unbelievably warm. "Much better," she muttered to herself as she finally got off her bed, pushing her feet into soft brown ankle high boots for the day.

Grabbing her bag, coat and scarf, Lena left her apartment and headed out into the snow. A fresh layer had fallen during the night, that now crunched underneath her boots with each step. She loved the snow and the quiet that lingered in the air as it clung to the streets. The cold bit at her cheeks but she smiled as she walked towards the street bakery on the corner of her block. She bought an apricot pastry and a hot latte before walking into the town's square.

The main square was fairly large for the size of town. There were two cafes that operated on opposite sides of the square. They were generally the busiest of the shops during the day until they shut around 3pm, then the restaurants would take over. Bakeries were dotted along various alleyways that trailed out from between the square's terraced buildings.

In the middle of the square was her favourite structure. A fountain that depicted a battle between angels and demons. The angels' wings were outspread as they descended over a field of demons who were surrounded by flames. Each figure was uniquely and intricately carved into the white and grey-veined granite, each with their own features and expressions. Above all was a gothic basin from which water trickled over the sides and the varying figures. The water was turned off for the winter, but in the spring, the trickling water sounded like small bells as it fell into the pool below.

She brushed off some snow from a bench at the base of the fountain and placed the paper bag her pastry had come in on the stone before sitting down. Her coat was long enough it would soak up and residual snow before her trousers did. Silently, she ate her breakfast and sipped her coffee whilst she watched the shops and cafes open, ready for the new day.

The town was large enough that you could keep to yourself, but you did become familiar with the faces that populated the streets. Lena had moved there just over four years ago after ageing out of foster care and spending almost two years living on the streets of the large city further south. Her old social worker pulled some strings, helping to buy her a train ticket and landing her a job at Café Marie. She scraped together enough money for two nights' stay as a small bed and breakfast on the outer parts of the town and then convinced Marie to pay her a month in advance so she could put a security deposit down on a studio apartment.

She had never looked back.

Trying her best not to attract too much attention, she had blended in fairly well to the town. Rumours travelled around for a bit but then about a year later a wealthy businessman had moved to the area and diverted all attention off her. She was happy enough to simply fade into the background.

She watched as a disjointed group of men and women started to walk across the square, effortlessly navigating the cobblestones and snow, heading for the train station down the hill. Some would leave the group momentarily to grab a coffee from the kiosks or a paper from the stand, but all eventually made their way to the south entrance. Trains only tended to pass through the town in the morning and afternoon to pick up and drop off local commuters.

Finishing her pastry, Lena downed the last of her coffee, before throwing the empty cup in the bin next to her. She checked her watch and saw that it was almost 7am. Looking towards Café Marie, she saw her boss just opening the shutters. Marie waved at her as she opened the cafe doors. She rushed in, kicking off the snow on her boots first.

"Hey Marie," she said cheerfully, shrugging out of her coat and heading into the kitchen to hang it up with her jumper and bag. She grabbed her apron and wrapped it around her waist, double checking her notepad, pen and change purse were securely tucked inside the pockets.

"Morning, Lena," Marie said with a warm smile. "Early as usual."

Smiling in return, she walked over to Marie and hugged her from the side. Marie had become like a mother to her since she moved there. The middle-aged woman ran the most popular cafe in town for the last two decades after introducing her famous apricot and mango tart. She had long auburn hair that over the years had become more and more interwoven with grey strands. No matter the day or season, Lena had never seen Marie with her hair down. It was always piled neatly on top of her head and held in place with a long golden pin. Marie's face was weathered but soft, with eyes that held warmth and kindness within their green depths. She could easily kiss the top of the older woman's head as she stood in height just short of Lena's shoulder.

"Only for you, Marie," she said, turning on the coffee machine.

The pair busied themselves for a period, organising the displays, cups and plates. Marie cooked all the cakes and pastries for the day the night before and Lena placed them now within the displays. Customers started to trickle in, ordering coffees and pastries before continuing on their way. It was too early yet for the customers that would usually sit at the tables for a leisurely breakfast, so Marie and Lena were managing on their own for the moment.

An hour after opening they were joined by Sarah and Michael.

"Hi you two!" Sarah said in her bubbly tone. She dashed into the kitchen to put away her things before joining them behind the counter.

Sarah ran the coffee machine and all things behind the counter for the rest of the day. Lena liked her well enough, but found outings with her on a personal basis to be exhausting, having attempted a few when she first moved to town. Sarah was constantly on the move, and with her champagne personality, she outshone anyone near her. Complimenting her personality, Sarah was gorgeous, with thick blonde hair that grouped in natural ringlets, and blue eyes that shone like diamonds in the right light. Next to her, Lena felt like a wallflower.

"Morning Sarah," Marie replied, handing a box of pastries to a waiting patron. "Thank you, see you again soon!" the matron said, waving after the customer before retreating to the kitchen where she would start baking bread rolls for the lunch period.

"Morning," Lena said with a smile before turning to greet Michael. "Morning, Michael."

"Good morning, Lena," Michael responded warmly, tipping his hat to her. He ambled his way to the kitchen where he would remain for the day. Michael was their chef for any hot food. He was Sarah's twin brother so his complexion was almost identical to hers, except he kept his hair short. In contrast to his sister, his personality was much more subdued, preferring to keep to himself and stay at home or work.

Lena remained behind the counter for a while working around Sarah, helping with the take-away orders until the floor tables started to fill up. She then moved to the floor taking and delivering orders, ensuring used tables were cleared down quickly ready for the next patron.

In this way the morning went quickly, as Lena ensured to make time for small talk with Sarah, although she tended to listen to Sarah, and with cafe regulars.

Checking her watch, she saw that it was almost quarter to nine. She smiled absently, knowing that *he* would be arriving sometime within the next hour. The traffic in the cafe had started to calm down so Lena swept through the floor ensuring all tables were cleared and placed a reserved sign on his favourite table. She doubted that he was aware she took such extra measures for him, but it made her inexplicably happy to see him so she didn't mind.

Two of her tables left moments later. She made her way to them, collecting her tips and placing them within her purse. She gathered the dirty plates and cups and took them to the kitchen, before returning to the table to wipe them down.

As she straightened the chairs, she smiled softly as the smell of sage and cedar wood wafted through the cafe. Turning, she watched the black-haired gentleman make his way to sit at his usual table in the corner, with his back to the wall. As usual he was dressed impeccably in a navy-blue suit with a white button up shirt underneath that always had the top button undone. A dark grey scarf hung casually around his neck, his matching coat already on the rack to his left. He caught her gaze and offered a warm smile and nod of acknowledgement.

Quickly, Lena tapped on Sarah's shoulder pointing at the man. Sarah smiled knowingly and moved away from the coffee machine granting ger access. She busied herself in making his coffee, whilst Sarah put through his food order for her. Without fail, the man had ordered smoked salmon on a brown bagel with cream cheese and chives for the last two years. His coffee was a pot of rich black espresso and hazelnut infused milk served separately. Lena would always put an extra biscuit on the side for him. He tipped well and she admittedly found him very attractive. She cared for all the regulars, but she wouldn't deny she went above for him. The casual flirtations were an added bonus, even though they only served to fuel her dreams with unobtainable desire.

Careful not to spill, Lena grabbed the daily newspaper and walked over to his table and set his coffee down for him, cup handle to his right, newspaper on the left.

"Thank you, Lena," the man said, nodding with approval. "Efficient as always."

"You're welcome, sir," she said, holding her tray to her side. "You're earlier than normal."

"Had some early morning business," he began as he opened the paper to wait for his food. "And besides, I was eager to see my favourite waitress." He looked up over the paper and smiled at her in the way that always made her blush. She had to remind herself to breathe as she was caught up in the depths of his deep hazel eyes. Although his shoulder length hair was always pulled back into a tie at the nape of his neck, a small strand brushed teasingly against his cheek, almost begging her to reach out and brush it behind his ear.

"You really are a blatant flatterer, sir. Anyone would think you're trying to get free coffee," she teased with a small nervous laugh.

"How many times do I have to ask you to use my name, Lena?" The man tilted his head to the right, his eyes bright with amusement, presumably at her reaction to his compliment.

"At this rate, I'm afraid you'll stop coming here if I call you by your name," she chuckled, hugging the tray to her stomach.

The man returned her laughter, taking a tentative sip of his coffee. "And deprive myself of your beautiful smile? Never," he lifted his gaze, locking with hers. His eyes always had a warmth to them, but today they seemed slightly dulled.

Lena smiled at him, tilting her head to the side, studying him. "Are you okay this morning? You look more tired than usual."

"I feel like I should take offence at that," he replied warmly, "but as it's you, I'll let it slide. I'm fine, thank you for asking. Working late last night then up early this morning is not conducive to a good night's sleep."

"I'll be sure to bring you an extra coffee then," she said. Glancing quickly to the side to make sure no one was watching, she leant forward slightly, closing the distance between them. "On the house."

"Ah, you see, my flattery was successful," he whispered, winking at her.

The kitchen bell rang and Lena excused herself quietly to retrieve the man's food. She placed it on his table, next to his coffee cup. Hesitantly, she smiled at him before saying: "Enjoy your food... Ambrose."

CHAPTER TWO

Ambrose read his paper whilst casually sipping his coffee. After he had finished his breakfast, Lena had brought him a second cup, smiling that radiant smile that he was sure was reserved for him. Every now and then, he would look over his paper to watch her move around the cafe, captivated by her grace and exuberance.

Almost a year after he had moved to the town, Ambrose had been sitting in the square people-watching. Back then he received a number of odd looks from people having caused quite a stir after purchasing the broken-down manor near the north gate. The manor had been built into the stone wall surrounding the main part of town before the residents had expanded further down the hill. It had been abandoned for over a decade before he bought it after the old owner died, but it had started to go to ruin before then due to the owner's inability to continue to care for the upkeep.

Using the wealth he had built up in his many centuries as a demon, he managed to have the manor fully renovated in less than a year. Although he also used some of his power to enhance certain aspects of the building, the amount of activity that he had been bringing to the house had not gone unnoticed by the town's inhabitants. Rumours spread quickly about his wealth and both men and women vied for his attention in the hopes of charity.

As he looked over the square, he found his gaze had been drawn to Café Marie. It was mid-autumn at the time, and although it had been getting colder, the cafes and restaurants were still serving tables outside. He'd felt a pull towards the cafe before, but had generally ignored it as he had other things occupying his time. On that day, he had nothing pressing to drag him away so decided to watch the cafe for a while to see if he could figure out what it was that had been calling to him.

Then he saw *her*.

Lena had walked out of the cafe doors, holding a tray full of coffees and cakes resting on her shoulder. Her hair had been pulled up in her usual ponytail, but she had wrapped a red polka scarf around the tie, the corners of the scarf hanging down, brushing enticingly along the curve of her shoulders. Ambrose could see her smile from the other side of the square and his eyes became intoxicated by the sight of her. She moved gracefully among the tables, stopping here and there to set down the orders before continuing to the next table. He noticed how the patrons would smile at her warmly as she walked past them.

As she had headed back inside, he found his legs started walking towards the cafe without any conscious effort from him. Ignoring the people around him, he crossed the square in a matter of seconds and strode through the cafe doors.

Oblivious to the sudden onslaught of whispers of the cafe's patrons as he stood in the door, he stared at Lena. Her back was turned to him as she picked up the next round of orders from the counter, neatly arranging them on her tray. Deftly, she lifted the tray onto her shoulder and turned around, her eyes locking with his.

What was only a second in reality, felt like an eternity to Ambrose, as he looked into her dove-grey eyes. Quickly, Lena dropped her gaze and turned, still holding the tray, and dashed through the kitchen doors.

Reality crashed back in on him, as he noted the eyes that turned his way from within the cafe. He looked around to take in his surroundings before quickly purchasing a pastry from the counter, desperately hoping that would allay any new rumours. Cursing himself, he dashed from the cafe and half-walked, half-ran back to his manor where he locked himself in his office for the rest of the afternoon.

It had taken him three days after that to gather the courage to go back.

Even now, Ambrose found himself enchanted by her, as she almost floated across the cafe floor attending to her customers. He had spent nights thinking about her, dreaming about her, but every time he had thought of possibly acting on those thoughts, fear would paralyse him. He had dated humans in the past, but they were never anything other than a distraction from immortality and the relationships never lasted long. The sight of Lena made him want to forget he was a demon and that was a dangerous thought to have. At any moment he could be summoned away, and to date he had yet to think of a plausible reason why someone might spontaneously combust and disappear for brief periods. To top it off, he doubted she would be receptive to his nature as a demon.

But today, something was different. He had not planned on coming to the cafe today after spending the night in Hell sorting through records. After nights like that he preferred to hole up in his library, avoiding human interaction and escaping into a book he hadn't read yet. He had even made it to his library, but as he opened his book, his mind drifted to Lena. Although not an unusual occurrence, the thoughts were overwhelming, and he couldn't concentrate on the book at all. Shortly after he admitted defeat and made his way to the cafe.

"Can I get you anything else, sir?" Lena asked, pulling him from his thoughts. He looked at his cup noticing he had finished his coffee.

"Lena," he said pointedly, raising a brow at her.

"Sorry," she said with that radiant smile of hers. "Can I get you anything else, Ambrose?"

He smiled at her, giving himself a moment to back out of what he planned to do next. Unfortunately, or fortunately, his mouth had other plans.

"Just one thing," he said. "Say 'yes'."

Lena narrowed her eyes, but her smile didn't leave her face. "Yes?" she queried, raising her brows in puzzlement. "Why do you want me to say 'yes'?"

Ambrose got to his feet, placing money on the table to cover both his bill and tip before folding his paper under his arm. "Say 'yes' to dinner," he said, keeping his eyes locked with hers, "with me."

Lena's eyes widened in shock and he was nearly undone by the flush of rose that crept across her cheeks. Her lips parted as she sucked in breath making him want to take her face in his hands and kiss their pink softness. She blinked rapidly as his question sunk in.

"Y- you want... to take me... out for dinner?" she stammered.

Ambrose nodded in response. "If you want—"

"Yes!" she interrupted quickly. A wide smile spread on her lips, a smile that travelled across her face and illuminated her eyes.

Ambrose chuckled at her eagerness, a gentle warmth flooding his chest, like the winter sun breaking through snow-filled clouds. He took hold of her hand and brought it to his lips, kissing her knuckles tenderly. He knew some of the other patrons had turned their heads to look at them, but he didn't care. "Alphonso's at eight?"

"Tonight?"

"Would another night suit better?"

"No," Lena blurted, still smiling. "No, tonight is fine. See you then."

"Until tonight," Ambrose kissed her knuckles again before dropping her hand and grabbing his coat. As he left, he allowed himself a moment to look back at her, as she was starting to clear his table. Their eyes met briefly, before she returned to her task and bustled off into the kitchen. Once she was out of view, he headed back to his home. Hopefully, now he could relax. At least, until dinner.

He made his way slowly uphill until his front door came into view. The exterior of the manor was mainly darkened stone work, but had parts of off-white render underneath the five windows that faced the street and on the surround of the doorway. He had the front door replaced with a solid oak one that had black iron hinges and knocker. Two smaller wings of the building started a few feet back from the front face of stone with render only surrounding the windows. The whole building melded into the town wall which was thicker here than anywhere else allowing for part of the manor to actually be within the wall. Of all the places he had lived in as a demon, this was one of his favourites.

Inside the front door was a generous sized entrance hall, clad in mahogany skirting against cream paint, with the grand dark-oak staircase sweeping from the centre of the room to the upper floor. Four doors branched off the hall, two for the front rooms and two either side of the staircase that lead to the smaller wings. Upstairs were three bedrooms and his office, built either to the front of the manor or into the wall.

It was his office that Ambrose headed for now, after hanging his coat next to the front door. He made his way up the stairs and turned left, heading for the second door down the hall. His office was built into the wall and didn't have any windows, which he was more than happy with, as it allowed him to carry out as many spells and power rituals as needed without having to worry about anyone seeing what he was doing.

He opened the door and was surprised to see that his fireplace already had a fire within it. As far as he remembered, he had not left a fire burning. Ensuring his power was ready to use, he pushed the door open fully and stepped inside.

"Finally. I've been waiting for almost twenty minutes."

He turned to the voice and saw his friend standing next to his desk. Marcus was generally the opposite of Ambrose, with a slightly shorter, stockier frame that implied lesser in strength to him. Despite this, Ambrose knew the fellow demon could throw his power around without any issue having been on the receiving end a number of times in the training pits. Marcus kept his longish blonde hair swept back off his face, although small strands would occasionally fall in front of his green eyes. Eyes which were now filled with mischievous intent as he stared at Ambrose.

"I wasn't expecting you," he said, walking over to his desk.

"When do you ever expect me?" Marcus said with a grin.

Ambrose looked up at his friend through his lashes. "You didn't have to wait around when you realised I wasn't here."

"Ah, it's no trouble," Marcus said, moving to one of the chairs Ambrose had placed in front of his desk and taking a seat. "Besides, I figured you were out watching that little waitress of yours and I wanted an update."

Marcus had been the only one he had talked to about Lena in the past. He trusted no one else with his feelings about her.

"She's not mine," he replied flatly.

"Only because you won't do anything about it," the demon wagged a finger in his direction as if chastising a child. "Very unbecoming, a demon who doesn't make the first move. She'll move on to a nice, boring mortal if you don't act soon."

Ambrose smiled at his friend before sitting down. The leather office chair squeaked slightly as he lowered himself into it, as he again silently reminded himself to oil the swivel hinge. "Well, you can amend that assertion of yours," he sighed, leaning back in his chair. "I asked her out for dinner."

Marcus' jaw dropped, shock evident on his face. "I am so glad I decided to hang around now." He grinned at Ambrose before leaning back in his chair and folding his hands over his stomach. "Well, it's about time, my friend."

He threw his friend a dubious look. "You and I both know this has every potential of not going well."

"Whilst true, if it does go well, then great. If it goes really well, you might even produce a cambion with her. But then," Marcus sighed, "if it goes badly... well, hopefully it gets her out of your system at least."

The mention of a cambion made Ambrose's skin crawl. He detested those creatures, present company excluded. Offspring produced between a demon and a human, but inherently evil to the point that their demon parent can barely control them and more often than not, they kill the mother at birth. If the father is human the resulting nature of the cambion is even worse. The production of one was not something he ever wished to entertain, but as they were seen as a status symbol among demons, he kept that opinion to himself. Marcus was different from most, as his mother had survived his birth, helping to quell any evil impulses in him as they arose.

"She could die," he said quietly.

"Yes, well, all humans die eventually," Marcus shrugged. "You could offer her a deal."

Ambrose nodded absentmindedly. He had thought of offering her deals in the past, but he could never imagine her accepting one.

Marcus sighed heavily, drawing Ambrose's attention back to him. His eyes were shut with his hands held in front of his face so each index finger was pressed against the sides of his nose. "That said," Marcus started, "you do have to be careful. The speculative relationship and related teasing were one thing..." He stopped for a moment as if trying to find the right words for what he needed to say next.

"But?" he prompted.

"But..." The demon leant forward resting his elbows on his knees. "If it gets back to... you know... that you are interested in a human woman, and that you might be interested in her, in more than just a physical gratification sense... he will cause trouble. You know he will."

He was talking about Zagan. Another cambion. Someone that Ambrose used to be intricately involved with but now they despised each other beyond comprehension. It had become Zagan's mission to destroy Ambrose, much as it had become Ambrose's mission to avoid Zagan. As Zagan couldn't actually kill him without causing issues that would directly affect himself, they kept a tense amicability for the moment. Marcus was right, Lena would be a prime target for Zagan if he found out about her.

"You tell me that now," he scoffed good-naturedly, "after months of pestering me to make a move."

"Honestly, I never thought you actually would," Marcus laughed before sighing softly at his friend. "I'm glad you did though. You were becoming insufferable."

Ambrose rolled his eyes at the demon but admitted to himself he was glad too. Her reaction to him asking had been one of the sweetest things he had ever witnessed, confirming his belief that she was as attracted to him, as he was to her. It made him wish he had asked her out months ago.

Marcus stood and walked around the desk to place a supportive hand on Ambrose's shoulder. "Just be careful," he said.

"Always am," Ambrose said, nodding his thanks. "So why else are you here?" he asked pointedly.

"Oh, um," Marcus dropped his hand quickly and laughed nervously, "I need your help."

He shut his eyes and took a deep breath. "How much?"

"Now before you berate me, I want you to know that I really thought this would pan out. I had no idea that Jorge would make a deal that would work against me," Marcus said quickly retreating back to the other side of the desk.

"How much?" he repeated.

Marcus shrugged whilst running his hand through his tousled hair. "It was a weapon's shipment. Difficult to put a figure on it really."

Ambrose got to his feet and placed his palms flat on the top of his desk leaning towards the nervous demon. "How much did you lose, Marcus? Do not make me ask again."

"Equivalent of two million euros..." the demon finally replied, his face falling flat.

Ambrose sighed and hung his head dramatically. He wasn't upset at his friend by any means, but he enjoyed their exchanges about managing Hell's finances. Lifting his head, Ambrose was smiling.

"Not your worst financial error," he said, sitting back in his chair. "Sit down. Let's see what we can do to minimise the fallout."

CHAPTER THREE

Lena practically skipped across the square after the cafe closed. She had a few hours before her date with Ambrose and whilst she planned on using most of that time to get ready, she thought she would walk around the town first to try and burn off some of her excitement.

Pulling her coat close to her body, she made her way down a side alley to the town's edge.

It was only a few minutes' walk from the square, but shortly she came to the gate built into the western wall. She walked through before turning to the right and headed towards the river that ran along the wall. She liked it here. It was quiet and few people walked through here at this time of day. The path that ran between the river and wall was more suited for morning walks for people with dogs, if at all, as halfway along it rose steeply up the hillside.

Small bridges were dotted along the river, despite the fact that it was narrow enough for most people to be able to simply jump across it. Lena noted that the movement of the river had stopped the snow from sticking along its edge, keeping the river stones exposed to the cold winter air. Behind the river was an evergreen forest that expanded up the hill ranges. Its trees stood tall and proud against the evening mist that was starting to descend.

She liked to walk along the forest edge, but rarely ventured within it, especially not when the mist made it impossible to see more than two metres of ground in front of you. Jumping over the river, she smiled at the crunch of the stones beneath her boots.

Regardless of the cold in her apartment getting the best of her most days, she loved winter. The smell of moisture on the air, the cold biting at her cheeks giving her more colour in them than she had naturally, and the soft quiet afforded by the layers of snow. She had never seen snow until she moved to the town, but she had instantly fallen for its magical qualities.

Taking in the stillness of the forest, Lena walked up the hill towards a small lookout she had found two years ago. From there she could look over the town all the way down to the train station at the bottom of the valley. Panting against the cold air, she welcomed the burning of her lungs. The exertion warmed her body, although she made sure to keep her coat on as she reached her destination. There was a metal bench at the lookout and she gratefully sat upon it, after brushing off the snow, letting her legs rest. From here she could see the roofline of Ambrose's manor.

Even though her heart was racing from the climb, she was elated. She knew the smile that had been on her face since Ambrose asked her out had not left her face for the remainder of the afternoon. Since moving to the town, she had not formed any relationships with anyone that could have developed into anything romantic. Sarah had set her up with Michael a few months after she started at the cafe, but they mutually agreed there was no compatibility there. She had started to think she would spend the rest of her life single and she had been fine with that. She liked her solitude and ability to do what she wanted, when she wanted, without having to worry about someone else.

That all changed when she met Ambrose.

The rumours that surrounded him had been intriguing but she had mostly ignored them. She had wanted to be ignored when she moved to the town, so she felt inclined to provide him with the same courtesy. The first time he came into the cafe, she almost dropped the tray she had been holding. He was gorgeous and he'd been staring right at her. Her breath had caught in her throat as she felt a magnetic pull towards him. Her mind had instantly thought of what it would be like to feel his arms around her, his lips on hers. She knew who he was and she couldn't fathom why he would be looking at her so intently, but it made her stomach flip with excitement. At the time, she had practically run into the kitchen, trying to hide her embarrassment at her reaction to him. Michael had looked at her confused as she hid in the staff closet briefly.

After gathering herself, she had made her way back into the cafe and was disappointed to note he had left. It was a few days after that he had returned and took up residence at his favourite table. At first, they had exchanged small talk here and there, but nothing much beyond that. Lena thought there was an attraction between them, but she always put it down to simple flirtations to entice good service, not something that would, or could, develop further. Then he started coming more frequently and the flirtations increased. His visits to the cafe had become a highlight of her day, to the point she often found herself wandering by his manor on days he didn't visit, wondering if he was okay. She was also certain that on days she wasn't working, she had spied him following her, watching her as she walked through town.

With her breathing returning to normal, she stood up and bounced on the spot for a moment, giggling to herself in excitement. She turned to make her way back down the hill, but paused briefly looking into the woods. The hairs on the back of her neck stood on end as she had a sudden feeling like she was being watched.

She shook her head, murmuring to herself that she was being ridiculous and stepped onto the path. She still had a couple of hours before the date so she wanted to head back to her apartment to start getting ready.

Having barely taken a few steps down the path, her stomach dropped as she heard footsteps behind her. She turned her head slightly, but before she could see who it was, a hand with a rag or napkin in it covered her mouth and nose. Crying out, she tried to push the hand away, but within moments her world went dark.

She was late.

Ambrose looked at his watch again as he sat at the restaurant. Well, not late... yet. It was still a few minutes to eight. To his surprise he arrived almost twenty minutes early, eager to see Lena again. He had already ordered a bottle of wine for them and sipped slowly on his own glass as he waited for her. Any time the bell over the door rang, he raised his head in expectation, and to his chagrin had been disappointed every time.

He sighed heavily as he looked out the window at the street. It had been decades since he last went on a date with a human, and back then they met at dances or he would collect them from their home, so only his punctuality had ever mattered. But then, he never remembered being as excited to see someone as he was Lena. He would happily give her the grace of waiting another fifteen minutes considering a fresh layer of snow was, yet again, starting to fall outside.

"Can I get you anything else whilst you wait, sir?"

He looked up dubiously at the waiter who now stood next to the table. Ambrose knew what he wanted, but he doubted the waiter could make her walk through the door. "I'm fine, thank you," he replied, turning back to the window.

The waiter walked off quietly, leaving him once again to his thoughts.

He didn't think there would be any reason Lena would not come. He was sure she liked him, and when he asked her face had lit up with the most adorable smile. He rolled his eyes at himself. *You're a demon, Ambrose,* he reminded himself. But there was no denying it, he had been enchanted by her since he first saw her. The pull he had felt towards her that day had only intensified as time went on. He wanted to get to know her, more than just the side she showed within the cafe. He knew there was more to her than a simple waitress. There was a deep intelligence in her eyes that was beyond intriguing, suggesting a breadth of life experience more suited to someone twice her age. Her beauty was simple, yet elegant and always unassuming. Unlike most women her age now, she didn't try to overstate her features with too much makeup. Having lived through many a fashionable era, from the French Revolution to Victorian Delicacy to Fifties Glamour, regardless of the progressions in feminine identity those eras were responsible for, he found natural beauty more enticing than anything.

He looked at his watch again, noting she was now indeed late.

Suddenly, he felt the familiar pull of a summoning. Sighing in annoyance, he realised dejectedly that he was going to miss dinner with Lena. Of course, she was already late, but only by a couple of minutes. He doubted she would wait the two hours it would take for him to revert to human form after this. Quickly, he got to his feet and threw some money down on the table. He walked out of the restaurant as quickly as he could, voicing his apologies to the host as he went, and making a quick dash to an empty alley.

Accepting the inevitability of the summoning, Ambrose made a mental note to take flowers the next time he went to Cafe Marie. He could foresee lots of apologising in his near future.

Flames covered his body as he was forced to transform into his demonic self. Over the years he had become accustomed to the pain as his horns broke through his skin and his limbs stretched and lengthened. His nails extended into talons and his skin darkened as the flames licked over his body. His clothes burned away and were replaced with his usual chosen attire for such events.

As the flames dissipated, he noted that he had been brought to an abandoned warehouse somewhere downtown in the city. He raised his brows surveying his surroundings. The building was dark except for some lamps that had been set up in the four corners, but to avoid detection, black paint had been splattered on the windows stopping the light from reaching the outside. Overall, the room wasn't very large, seemingly more suited for small-scale production with the floor space being less than ten metres wall to wall.

Summoning runes had been painted on the floor with the sacrifice's blood. White ash, cat bones and off cuts of the flower, Immortelle, had been placed in a circle around the makeshift pyre made from pallets and black fabric. Three men stood in awestruck shock near the pyre.

Ambrose froze as he took in the view of the pyre. Ice washed through his limbs and his breath caught in his throat as he looked over the woman atop it. Her wrists had been slit, fastened to the pyre by strips of fabric and positioned above two bowls that now held her life-blood. His body shuddered as he recognised her face, her dove-grey eyes staring at him blankly, dulled by death.

Lena...

Moments before...

Her eyes blinked open. Everything was dark so she couldn't see anything anyway. She groaned as the pain in her head throbbed behind her eyes. Suddenly, her body jolted and hit something hard above her.

She was in a trunk...

"Shit," she whispered to herself.

Lena tried to move her body but realised her hands and ankles had been tied together, the former behind her back. Fear and panic washed over her as she twisted her limbs trying to free them. The jostling of the car shot jolts of pain throughout her body as she was thrown around within the trunk. She tried to note which way the car was turning, but every time they hit what she could only assume was a speed bump, the throbbing in her head made her forget everything.

Suddenly the car came to a stop and she was slammed against the back of the trunk with a cry.

"I think she's awake." She heard the muffled voice from the front of the car.

"Doesn't matter. This won't take long."

She heard the car door open and shut, rocking the car. Frantically, she looked towards where the trunk would open, her eyes wide with fear.

Light streamed into the darkness as the trunk opened, forcing her to shut her eyes against the sudden illumination. Two pairs of strong hands grabbed her, one under her shoulders and the other her ankles.

"No!" she screamed, tears suddenly streaming from her eyes, as she contorted her body trying to break from their grasp.

"Shut up!" one ordered. The tone in his voice was terrifying and her mouth clamped shut involuntarily as icy fear constricted her chest.

She looked around at the men noting they all had similar features, although, one had dark hair whilst the other two were fair. The dark haired one ran over to a warehouse door and opened it, quickly ushering the other two carrying her inside. Somehow, she knew if she went inside, she would not be coming out. With renewed panic, she twisted her body causing the man holding her ankles to drop her.

"Oh, come on!" the other shouted at him.

"Sorry, she's stronger than she looks," he replied, moving to grab one of her shoulders as the men changed to dragging her behind them.

"Please don't do this," Lena pleaded, fresh tears pouring down her face as the men dragged her into the room and the door shut behind them.

"Why did we not bring a gag?" the dark haired one said. "Get her on the pyre."

"Please!" she screamed as the other two lifted her between them. They dropped her on the pile of pallets they had stacked in the middle of the room. The wood cracking beneath her. She twisted her body trying to break from the hands on her.

"Hold still," one shouted at her. "Keep her legs still, would you?"

She cried out in terror as hands grabbed her ankles pulling her legs straight, forcing her lower body to lay still. The grip was strong despite her efforts to pull free. "No," she whimpered as the other men forced her arms against the wood and they tied strips of twisted fabric around her wrists. "Please let me go, I won't tell anyone!" she begged trying to look at them through her tears.

"Shut up!" the one holding her legs shouted. He yanked, hard, on her ankles and Lena yelped as her knees and hips jarred with the sudden movement. The two by her arms took over, placing one of their hands on her elbows and the other pushing on her hips. Her mind, overrun by fear, barely registered one of them saying; "Start the chant."

The two holding her started whispering something under their breath as the dark-haired one let go of her ankles. She saw him bend down to grab something before he made his way to stand by her head. He knelt down placing whatever he was holding either side of the pyre. As he raised his hand, she choked on a sob as she saw the metallic glint within it, noticing the curve of the knife in the lamp light.

"No, please," she tried to plead with him one last time, her eyes desperately searching his face for something.

He seemed to pause for a moment, staring at her. "I'm sorry," he said softly, but there was nothing in his eyes, their blue tones devoid of any feeling. Looking away, he grabbed her left hand and, digging in the point of the knife halfway up her forearm, sliced a long single line straight down to her wrist. She screamed as pain ripped up her arm and watched in horror as her blood pooled from the cut and flowed down her hand before falling out of her line of vision. The man turned to her other arm and made a similar cut on her right wrist. Her screams seemed distant to her ears, no longer feeling like they were coming from her throat.

Lena struggled against the hands holding her, but they bore down on her, pushing her arms and hips painfully into the wood. She barely noticed as the man dropped the knife and started moving around the room, stopping to bend down for a moment before moving to another spot. Her eyes were locked on her wrist, watching as her blood left her body.

"I'm sorry... Ambrose..." she whispered as her vision started to blur. At least the pain had stopped.

"What did she say?" the one to her left asked.

"Ignore it, keep chanting!"

She could no longer determine who was speaking. Her body felt heavy and numb even as she vaguely noted the men were no longer holding her. Their words sounded muffled and far away. Her vision darkened even as a sudden glow like fire-light seemed to ignite in front of her. She managed to turn her face towards it, her mind blank, until finally, everything faded to black.

CHAPTER FOUR

Ambrose gritted his teeth as white-hot anger flushed through his body replacing the icy dread. He watched as the men looked at each other nervously, silently egging the others to speak first. They were worried and he was in no hurry to alleviate them of this affliction.

Looking at Lena's face, he stepped towards the pyre, surprised by his desire to take her body into his arms, take her away from here and simply leave the men behind. If he wasn't bound to at least hear them out he would have. He raised his hand and hovered it over her face, longing to touch her.

"Um..."

One man evidently found enough courage to make a sound. He dropped his hand by his side and looked up through his brows at the man on the left.

"Are you Ambrose?" the man asked, his voice filled with fear.

He contemplated ripping out the man's throat. It was incredibly tempting to visualise him bleeding out on the floor. But his obligation to the potential of a deal overwhelmed this possibility. He drew in a deep breath before raising his head to look at the men properly.

"Is the sacrifice not enough?" the man on the right asked. "Finding innocence now isn't easy. We did our best."

"It worked, didn't it?" he said flatly.

"So, you are Ambrose?" Again, the man on the left spoke.

He simply nodded in answer, taking a step around the pyre, making his way towards the men. It gave him immense satisfaction to see them take a step back in fear as he got closer.

"Don't leave the rune circle," he said, a wicked sneer forming on his lips. "Leave and any deal is off." The men quickly looked at the floor to make sure they were still standing within the runes, only for a moment before they locked eyes back on him.

"St- stay there," finally the man in the middle spoke. "Please?"

Ambrose stopped his advance and licked his lips. One man audibly swallowed.

"You three don't seem to have prepared yourself for this," he said, folding his arms in front of his chest.

"Ah..." the man on the right, "you are bigger than we were expecting."

Lifting a brow, he looked at the man. "You were expecting, what exactly? An imp?"

The men looked at each other again. He was growing impatient.

"What are your names?" Despite already knowing their names from the transference during the summoning, he was not sure which name belonged to which man.

"I'm Stephen," said the man in the middle. "Jason," pointing to the left, "and Lucas," pointing to the right.

Studying them, he determined they had to be brothers. Jason and Lucas were definitely twins having the same complexion and fair coloured hair. Stephen looked to be slightly older than them, his dark hair standing out in stark contrast, though his facial features were very similar.

"You have one minute to make your offer in exchange for your souls. One minute," Ambrose said, holding up one finger to impress his point.

The men on the edge waved their hands at Stephen, ushering him to speak.

Stephen swallowed and blinked rapidly before speaking. "Right, okay... um... we know we only get seven years, but... I... ah... that is... we... we need our father out of the way. He's the owner of Carter Enterprises and he's going to run it into the ground. We want the company transferred to our control. We could build it to what it could be, but he won't give us a chance."

Ambrose blinked slowly at him. "Are you sure you've thought this through fully?" he asked. "Forty seconds left."

They hesitated slightly, wasting precious time.

"What do you mean?" asked Lucas.

"What happens to the company once you die in seven years?" Ambrose sighed. "Thirty seconds."

"Well, our sister will get it then," Jason said hurriedly. "She's too young at the moment, but we'll set it all up so she's taken care of."

"And you thought, having all three of you make the deal was in her best interests? Take away her father, and then her brothers in seven years' time? Fifteen seconds."

"What happens at the end of the minute?"

"You'll see. Twelve seconds."

Stephen spoke again. "We don't want our father killed, just removed."

"Good, specifics are important. Six seconds."

"Can you just remove him from the company, but not from our lives? Or not from his life? Don't kill him."

"If that's what you want. Time."

Silence fell over them as Ambrose looked at each of them in turn.

"So... do we have a deal?" Lucas asked hesitantly.

"To be clear," he sighed. "You want your father out of the way, but not killed. Additionally, you want control of the company transferred to you. In exchange you will give me all three of your souls." Stephen nodded when Ambrose paused. "Hardly seems fair," he said as he looked over his shoulder back at Lena's body. "Tell me something," he started, "you have a sister, an innocent herself, and had no issue in killing this woman?"

The men seemed hesitant to answer. Ambrose looked back at them awaiting an answer. Jason spoke first.

"We did what we had to," he said. "You made a deal with an old family friend last year. He told us what we had to do."

Ambrose tilted his head. "How did you pick her? As you said, innocence is hard to find." The men look at each other, their fear once again spiking.

"Why?" Jason asked.

Ambrose shrugged. "I'm just curious."

"Ah..." Lucas spoke, "my girlfriend's mother is... *was*... her social worker. I went through her records one day. Not the most innocent of childhoods, but she kept herself out of trouble, mostly," he shrugged. "Importantly for us, she seemed like the type of person who wouldn't be missed."

Looking back at Lena, Ambrose decided he'd had enough of this.

"You know," he said, raising his chin to look at the ceiling, "the summoning only requires that I listen to your proposal. I do not need to accept." He scratched his cheek with a single talon turning back towards the men. They fidgeted in their places, darting their eyes to the floor to ensure they were still within the runes. "On top of that, the innocent you chose," he paused momentarily to ensure that all three men were looking at him, "I was meant to go on a date with her tonight."

Ambrose could almost taste their fear in the air. Panic washed over their faces and Lucas took a step back, leaving the runes.

"I wouldn't," he said darkly, locking eyes with Lucas. "You can try to run, but I promise you, you won't get far." Glowing red tendrils of raw power licked from his fingers and up his arms, flaring out into the surrounding air like flames of fire.

"Oh god," Stephen said, falling to his knees.

"He can't help you now," Ambrose snarled and lashed his arm out, power rippling from his hand and hitting Stephen in the chest, sending him flying and crashing into the wall behind him.

Lucas spun on his heel and attempted to get to the door. Ambrose snaked his power out and around Lucas' ankle. The man cried out as his feet were wiped from under him and he was slowly dragged back towards the demon. He turned his head back, utter terror within his eyes.

Ambrose turned his gaze on Jason, who stood rooted to the spot, frozen in fear. In a flurry of flames, Ambrose was in front of him, wrapping his taloned fingers around the man's neck. Suddenly, he could smell ammonia and looking down noted that Jason had wet himself. "Pitiful," he growled and tightened his hand around Jason's throat, his talon's easily piercing the soft flesh. Jason's eyes widened as he coughed and spluttered, crimson blood pooling from the corners of his mouth. Ambrose threw him aside and turned back to the other two.

"No, Jason!" Stephen cried, trying to get to his feet.

Lucas was screaming as Ambrose's power constricted around his ankle. Ambrose pulled him closer and picked him up by the back of his neck. Placing a hand in the middle of his back, he used his power to drill through Lucas' spine to his chest, severing the spinal column and spraying blood across the floor. Lucas fell silent and his body went limp, as Ambrose dropped him unceremoniously.

"Oh god, please stop!" Stephen begged huddled by Jason's now lifeless body.

"I told you," Ambrose said, walking slowly to the snivelling man. Slowly he bent down until his eyes were level with Stephen's. "He can't help you now."

Ambrose stared at Stephen, his jaw clenching with unbridled rage.

"I'm sorry," Stephen cried. "I'm sorry."

He narrowed his eyes at the man in disgust. "For someone who summoned a demon, you are pathetic."

"You killed them. You were supposed to help us and you killed them," the man sobbed, holding his dead brother.

Rolling his eyes, Ambrose extended a hand and placed a single talon under Stephen's chin raising it so he could look him in the eye. "Your brother's held her down. You slit her wrists. I can smell her essence on your hands."

"We didn't know," Stephen pleaded. "We didn't know who she was to you."

"I know," Ambrose said, nodding. "How could you? After all," he leant forward until his face was mere inches from Stephen's, "she was just a name in a file to you."

In the blink of an eye, Ambrose's tendrils of power sharpened and slashed at Stephen's wrists. The man cried out recoiling and pulling his arms to his chest. "No, no, no, no!" he screamed, falling to the ground and pushing away from Ambrose with his feet. "Please don't do this. Please!" he begged.

"That's right. Beg for your life. Beg, like she begged. Then die, like she died." Ambrose rose to his feet and stared emotionless as Stephen's whimpering and thrashing slowly grew weaker and weaker until finally his body stilled.

"And look at that," Ambrose said to the room, "I still get their souls."

With a sigh, he shut his eyes and pinched the bridge of his nose. This was not going to be good for business. Especially if he had indeed dealt with their family friend. His anger had gotten the better of him, but he would deal with that later.

A pit formed in his stomach as he turned to face the pyre. Solemnly, Ambrose walked over to Lena's body, trailing the back of his hand along her arm. He untied the fabric on her wrists, freeing her from the pyre before kneeling down in front of her body, never taking his eyes off her face. Fear and pain were etched across her features. Her beautiful grey eyes were dull and lifeless. "What a waste," he said as he rubbed some of the white ash on the floor between his fingers. "Lena, if you are still around, hold on..."

Running a sliver of power through his fingers, he traced the ash along her forehead in the shape of an inverted crucifix. The ash glowed for a moment before it seeped through her skin, her body absorbing the power he gave it and running it throughout. If her soul was nearby and had not yet moved on, there was a chance she could be reborn as a demon.

He took a deep breath waiting for the power to finish its work. Taking a moment, he brushed his fingertips along her cheek, looking for any sign of her soul returning to her body.

"Come on, Lena," he said under his breath. "Please come back."

Suddenly, her chest rose, arching her back as her body sucked in air with a loud gasp. Ambrose watched fascinated as her eyes glowed black for a moment before returning to her normal dove-grey. Colour flushed in her cheeks and her arms and legs curled as her soul settled back within her. She blinked a few times as her vision returned.

He slapped his hands over his ears as a blood-curdling scream ripped from her throat. The scream was over as soon as it had begun and when he looked again at the pyre, Lena had retreated across the room to the left and pushed herself up against the wall. Sitting on the floor, she curled her body up, keeping her knees in front of her chest. Her hands were pressed over her mouth as she looked at him with horror written all over her face.

"It's alright, Lena," he said softly, keeping his body as still as possible so as not to startle her further. "You are safe now." He heard her whimper as she tried to suppress her cries at his voice. Holding up his hands, he slowly got to his feet and walked backwards until his back was on the far wall from her. "I'm not going to hurt you."

He saw her take a few deep breaths from between her fingers. Her eyes were locked on him but he thought he noticed her body start to relax. Slowly, she lowered her hands from her face, keeping them locked together just under her chin. Her eyes were wide with fear as she opened her mouth to say something, but no sound came out. She coughed slightly and took a shaky breath.

"A- Ambrose?" she stuttered.

With as much warmth as he could muster in the moment, he smiled, pleasantly relieved that she recognised him.

"It's me," he replied.

Dropping her eyes from him, Lena started to look around the room. He followed her gaze, pressing his lips together as he noted the scene he had created was possibly not the ideal introduction to him as a demon.

"Um..." he started wanting to explain.

"Did you do this?" she asked before he could say anything further.

Ambrose contemplated how to answer. "Ah, well... yes." The ability on how to explain further suddenly eluding him.

"And they..." she looked at her wrists, furrowing her brow as she saw the cuts and blood on her arms. "I'm dead, aren't I?"

"Yes," he said simply. "I've brought you back for now, but it's only temporary. If–"

"What are you?" she interrupted. She seemed to be processing the situation rather quickly, but her voice was shaky and had an air of uncertainty to it.

Ambrose sighed. Her reactions thus far were expected. But he wasn't sure how she would be going forward. "I am a demon," he said. "I know this is a lot to take in, but you don't have a lot of time before your soul will leave your body again. If you come with me to my home, I can explain what happens now. We can't stay here," he said, sweeping his hand over the room. He waited for a moment to see if she comprehended his words. "May I come over to you?" he asked tentatively.

Lena was staring at her wrists, all emotion having left her face as a sober expression formed upon it. She nodded her assent.

Walking over to her slowly, he held out his hand, careful to keep it relaxed. "Lena?" he said to gain her attention. "Take my hand."

She looked up at him apprehensively, eyeing his hand with suspicion. After a deep breath she cautiously placed her hand in his and Ambrose helped her to her feet.

"Hold on," he said. "This may be disconcerting."

Flames gathered around them, dissolving the scene around them and transporting them to his office. He would have to go back to clean things up, but he had to focus on Lena first.

She swayed slightly, twisting her head to look at the room. "What the–?" she started, but couldn't seem to finish her thought.

"I'm sorry," he said, dropping her hand quickly. "It might be best if you sit down." He waved to a chair by the fireplace.

"I'd rather stand," she said sharply.

"Alright," Ambrose said, retreating to his desk to give her space. "I'm sorry, Lena, but you are dead." He looked at her trying to assess her reaction. If she was scared or confused it didn't show. She just stared coldly at him, like she was trying to decide what to make of him. "Even more so," he continued "you were sacrificed in a ritual to summon a demon. To summon me. Unfortunately, this means that your soul... is bound for Hell or Purgatory. Where you end up depends on you." An eyebrow raised but no further emotion showed on her face.

After about a minute, she spoke. "So, what now?" Lena asked, her voice now calm and steady. "Do you open a gateway or something?" A snide grin appeared on her lips but no light or humour touched her eyes. Ambrose smiled at her bravado.

"No gateway... or highway." His amusement grew as he watched her try to suppress a smile. Finally, some good emotion from her. "You now have a choice, a luxury only afforded to sacrificed souls."

"Lucky me," her voice dripped with sarcasm.

"I appreciate the ironic nature of that statement. But your choice in the final moments of your life was taken from you, and as such, we give that back to you in your first moments of death," Ambrose said with as much empathy as a demon like him could muster. "Hell is not as bad as the Church and superstitious groups would have you believe. It's not exactly a nice place either, hence why higher-level demons tend to choose to live top-side." He decided he could take a few steps closer to her. He had no inclination to deny the attraction he felt for her even now. They had lost their chance whilst she was alive, but perhaps he could give them another chance in death. "There are three choices; one, go to Hell and live whatever life awaits you there. You may be turned into a demon or find your soul used to feed the fires. You may be taught to torture or be tortured. Some go on to become guardians of Hell or war mongers. Some simply join the legion as a lower rank servant of sorts. Everyone's time there is different and no one can predict the outcome." He took another step towards her closing all distance. He could easily reach out and touch her cheek should he wish to. Lena had to crane her neck to keep looking at his eyes, but he noted that she did not step away from him.

"The second option is Purgatory," he continued. "Essentially, this is oblivion. Your soul will go into a kind of endless sleep, mixed in with other souls until such time as it is recycled. Reincarnation of sorts. But you will not be aware of it."

"And the third choice?" Lena whispered.

"Finally, you can stay here. With me," Ambrose said. "You would become my assistant of sorts. An immortal demon with initially limited powers, although, depending on how long it takes for demonic transformation to kick in, there is room for growth. You would be bound, and only answerable, to me. I will take care of you, as long as you follow and do everything I say. Do that, and you get to stay top-side. Unfortunately, you cannot return to your old life. And, you would have to live here, with me, where I can keep an eye on you. The first few days, even weeks, can be disorientating. We must always keep what we do here a secret, so you would have to stay close to me."

"So, the choice is potential torture in Hell, unaware oblivion in Purgatory, or whatever may come with you?"

Ambrose only nodded in response.

Lena's gaze dropped. He watched her face as she caught her bottom lip between her teeth in contemplation. Surely, she wouldn't choose Hell. Why would anyone choose Hell? He couldn't imagine her choosing Purgatory. Surely, she would choose him. But why was she taking so long to answer? He hated the tightness in his chest and the uneasiness that washed over him as he imagined her choosing Hell over him. He wanted her to choose him.

"I–" Lena started, but her voice broke. She coughed slightly to clear her throat. "I missed our date."

Pity whelmed in his chest as he looked at her, tears brimming in her eyes. He sighed heavily. "Technically, we both missed it," he commiserated.

She pressed her lips together as the corners of her mouth turned down. Taking a shaky breath, Lena raised her chin and looked him in the eye. "Alright," she said, "I choose you."

Ambrose smiled and stepped around Lena to stand behind her. He clasped her wrists in his hands and brought them up to her eyes, the cuts facing her. She trembled under his touch and he felt an immense sense of satisfaction at her reaction to him, despite what she had just been through. He leant down, placing his lips next to her ear.

"Good girl," he growled.

He tightened his grip on her wrists as she gasped. Glowing red tendrils of power flowed from his hands snaking onto her skin before they seeped into the cuts. The two long slits that caused her death closed up becoming instead deep red lines. The blood on her skin darkened to black and formed tattoo-like bindings of interlocking chains of thorns encompassing each wrist. The thorns spread down the inside of her forearms snaking up to the inside of her elbow where they ended in a point like an arrow. He noted with appreciation the beauty of her bindings.

"Now," he said softly, still holding her wrists, "you belong to me."

CHAPTER FIVE

Lena's mind raced as she felt Ambrose's power coursing through her body. He was so close, and even in his current form, she could smell his scent of sage and cedar washing over her. For a moment she wanted to lean back in his arms and pretend that all of this was a dream. Some sick, twisted dream that she would wake up from in a minute. But a small voice in the back of her mind told her that this was all real regardless of her denials.

Ambrose let go of her wrists and she stared at the new... she didn't know what to call them. Markings? Tattoos? *Bindings?* Not that it really mattered she supposed, but bindings felt like the most appropriate word considering what they represented. They spread from the lines that marked where the men had cut her as small flicks of black that spiralled around each other but never touching another mark. In some ways they looked like the sparks of fireworks that separated from the main source of fuel. Harsh spikes that seemed to bite into her skin.

Slowly, she touched the fingers of her right hand to her left wrist, feeling along the line. It was not a scar. It was not raised or indented, but more like it was drawn on. She let her fingers trail up the bindings until their point in the crook of her elbow. Admittedly fascinated by them, she turned her arm back and forth to inspect them fully. The marks near her wrist wrapped round and met on the opposite side like a full cuff around her arm.

"How do they feel?"

Ambrose's question bought her out of her trance, but she hadn't comprehended his words.

"What?" she said in surprise.

He was looking at her intently, having walked back to his desk to lean against it. "How do they feel?" he nodded towards her arms.

"Uh," she started looking back at her bindings. "Fine, I guess. They don't really feel like anything."

"Good. That means your soul isn't fighting them," he said with a soft smile. "It wants to stay."

"Well, I suppose that's something."

"Are you okay?"

She blinked at the question and the sincerity behind it. "I don't know," she answered truthfully. "I can't keep a straight line of thought at the moment."

Ambrose sighed. "I know this is difficult. I've been where you are now." She looked up at him. Seeing him in demon form she had difficulty imagining him as the man she'd served in the cafe.

"You haven't always been..." she waved vaguely, not able to finish her question.

He chuckled softly and folded his arms. "No, I was human once. And I was sacrificed and made the same choice."

"But you don't always look like..." she waved again, her voice trailing off.

"You can say the word. Nothing bad is going to happen," he said with a warm smile.

Lena exhaled sharply in annoyance at herself. "I know, I know... I just..." she sighed further looking up at the ceiling.

"Demons that were human can retain their human form. You may notice you have not instantly transformed," he said, nodding towards her.

She looked at her arms again. "You know, actually, that had not crossed my mind."

"Transformation comes later, once you settle into your new life," he explained. "It doesn't usually take long, a couple of weeks generally. It depends on how powerful you will become."

"How do I find that out?" she asked, taking the time to finally look around her.

The office was exquisitely decorated with landscape paintings hung on almost every free space of wall. Despite the generic nature of the paintings, they seemed to move and breathe with life as her eyes shifted over them. The desk was placed in front of the right wall, two large bookcases lining the wall behind it, each one filled with matching collections of leather-bound books and the occasional bronze bust or sculpture. The two chairs in front of the desk were dark-wood with red cushioning and gold studs. The floor was oak parquetry and a deep red rug spanned the space between the desk and the fireplace on the left wall. In front of the fireplace were two wing-back leather seats that faced the other. The feel of the room matched the demon she had just bound herself to.

"Lena?" Ambrose said, pulling her attention back to him.

"Sorry," she said quickly. "The room suits you."

He smiled warmly. "Thank you. As I was saying, you find out by training. That is what we will focus on for the next few weeks."

"Right, sure," she said, dropping her gaze. "Ah, not to be... indelicate, I guess, but can I take a shower?"

"Yes, of course," Ambrose said, pushing off from his desk. "I'll show you to your room."

"My room?" she asked, tilting her head. "Oh right, I have to live with you now."

He sighed as he walked to the door to open it. "It's easier if you do. We'll talk later about what to do with your apartment."

"It's rented," she said flatly, following him out of the room. "I can put my notice in easily enough. Just need to figure out what to do with my stuff."

"We'll sort that all out over the next couple of days," he said. "This way."

They turned left down the hallway and Ambrose led her to a door that opened to a room towards the front of the manor. Peering quickly down the stairs, she was shocked at the enormity of the entrance hall. "Holy crap!" she said louder than she meant to. "My apartment would fit twice into that!"

Ambrose looked over his shoulder at her and laughed at her reaction. "Is your apartment a box?" he queried.

Lena poked her tongue at him. "No," she retorted, placing her hands on her hips. "But it is a studio so it's not much bigger than a box, I suppose."

Ambrose opened the door to the room that was now going to be hers. There was no decoration on the walls, but that didn't detract from the elegant beauty of it. The carpet was plush mauve with golden oak skirting to frame it. The walls had been painted cream, and the outside facing wall had been decorated with a gold filigree mural. Two windows faced the street outside and the four-poster bed sat between them. Cream and gold bedding was already on it as if she had been expected.

"This is a guest room," he said standing to the side to let her pass. "I didn't really have any use for it, so I keep it like this in case it is needed. And to appear normal. It will be yours now. You can decorate it how you wish. Whatever you want, I can arrange it for you."

Lena walked past him in awe of the luxury before her. The bedroom was almost the same size as her studio, but there was no open kitchen or squeezed in dining area. She couldn't remember ever being in a room like this before.

"It's beautiful," she said softly as she slowly walked into the middle of the room.

"There is a bathroom through that door," Ambrose said, pointing to a door in the right corner of the room. "Take as long as you need. I'll find you some new clothes."

She looked down at her clothing, for the first time noticing the state of her. She'd lost her coat and favourite jumper somewhere in the events of the night. Her trousers and top had small tears and smears of grease from the car trunk in various places. Not to mention the sleeves of her top had been torn and were now crusting with remnants of her blood. In addition to everything, she realised she no longer had any shoes on.

"The jumper I could get over, but the boots?" she said dismayed. "Took me months to break in the leather on them. We can burn these clothes, right?"

Ambrose pressed his lips together in a sympathetic smile. "Yes, if you want. Just leave them by the door for now. Come back to my office when you're ready." With that, he bowed his head and pulled the door shut, leaving her alone.

Lena just stood there for a moment staring at the door. She found herself wanting him to come back and just hold her. But his demonic form was rather imposing so she was also glad to have some space for now. Sighing she rubbed her face before running her hands through her hair. The tie had broken at some point and her hair was matted with dirt, grease and blood.

"Great sight I must make right now," she sighed to herself. She walked over to one of the windows and looked out to the street. Everything looked normal. People walked past as usual, the street light illuminating the pathways. She unhooked the curtain ties and pulled the golden fabric shut, moving to the other window to do the same before finally peeling off her ruined clothing and leaving them in a heap by the door as instructed.

The bathroom was just as luxurious as the bedroom. White and cream tiles along the floor and walls complemented by the gold trimmed mirror and basin. A copper rolled top bathtub and shower stood proudly against one wall with a white shower curtain that reached the floor. Childhood excitement took over as she almost jumped into the tub, reaching to turn on the water. Once the water had reached the desired temperature, she put her whole body within the stream, letting the warmth permeate her hair, face and skin.

Bottles of shampoo, conditioner and soap lined a shelf along the wall which she now used generously, scrubbing her body raw with one of the cloths. She paused momentarily as she rubbed the cloth over her bindings. For a moment she thought if she scrubbed hard enough, she could get rid of them. Realistically, she knew that was not possible, but her reality was changing, and quickly.

Instead, she sunk into the tub, looking at her arms and letting the water run over her shoulders.

"What have you gotten yourself into, Lena," she murmured to herself. Earlier that day she had been imagining what her date with Ambrose was going to be like. What she was going to say. What he was going to say. What food she would order and which wine they would share. Now, her image of him had been permanently altered to include the large, red-skinned demon who had just claimed her soul as his.

Her body shivered remembering how he had stood behind her, holding her wrists. His voice in her ear had awoken something deep inside her that had made her want to launch herself into his arms and kiss him until she forgot everything. No one had ever made her feel like that.

Suddenly, she gasped as images of the face of the one who cut her wrists flashed in her mind. She hugged her knees tightly, dropping her head onto them as powerful sobs racked her chest.

After a few minutes, her breathing returned to normal. She pressed her palms into her eyes as if she was trying to push the images away.

"I'd say I've lived through worse, but as the events of tonight actually killed me..." she said, leaning her head back to let the stream from the shower hit her face. "Come on, Lena, buck up."

She turned off the shower as she pulled herself to her feet. There was a large soft towel on a rail which she gratefully wrapped around herself. She wiped her hand over the mirror so she could look at herself. Thankfully, she had managed to wash off all her makeup, glad she hadn't looked at the state of her face before she got in the shower. Her eyes were red from crying but otherwise she looked like herself again.

Sighing heavily – she foresaw a lot of that in her future – Lena finished drying herself and wrapped her hair in a smaller towel on top of her head before stepping back into the room. She noted that her old clothes had been removed and new ones had been laid carefully on the bed.

Making a mental note to both thank Ambrose for the clothing and question where he got women's clothes so quickly, she lightly trailed her fingers over the clothes noting how soft the jeans felt. The underwear was plain black with a matching bralette which she pulled on surprised that they fit perfectly. The faded-grey jeans and black top were similar, fitting along the lines of her body comfortably. She raised her eyebrows, impressed at Ambrose's eye.

Looking around she noted the absence of socks and shoes, but as her feet didn't feel cold, even after standing on the tiles in the bathroom for a while, she concluded she was probably fine without them.

Taking a deep breath to steady herself, she made her way back to Ambrose's office, pushing her wet hair off her face and twisting it into a makeshift plait that would have to do for now until she got some new hair ties. Reaching the door, she knocked politely, thinking it better to wait to be invited in rather than just enter.

"Come in, Lena," Ambrose said from the other side of the door. She wondered what he would look like as she opened the door, and was mildly dismayed to see him still in demon form.

"Hey," she said quietly, stepping inside, keeping her eyes on the floor.

"Feeling better?" he asked. Despite him being sat behind his desk, the sheer size of him as a demon was intimidating. He looked up at her. Although his eyes were pools of black, she had no trouble in figuring out what he was looking at. She merely nodded in response to his question. "Are the clothes, okay?" he asked, nodding towards her.

"Yes, thank you," she said hurriedly. "Not sure if I should ask where you got them from though."

He smiled at her. A smile that, despite the demonic features, set off a flurry of butterflies in her stomach. "I made them. As demons, we have a range of powers and magic accessible to us. There are limitations, but clothes are easy enough to conjure up."

Whatever she had been expecting him to say, that was not it. "Oh..." she said in response. "Thanks."

"Not a problem," Ambrose said, getting to his feet. "Lena, we—"

Before he could finish his sentence, a ball of fire erupted between the two chairs in front of his desk. As the flames dissipated, they were replaced with a large, blonde man dressed in an impeccable tan suit.

"Ambrose?" the man said tilting his head. "I thought... why are you... your date?"

Lena stared in shock at the man's sudden appearance. Ambrose merely pinched the bridge of his nose, placing his other hand on his hip.

"What are you doing here, Marcus?" he asked impatiently.

"I was just going to wait and avail myself to some of your brandy until you got back," the man named Marcus replied. "But why—" he stopped suddenly before turning his head towards the door, locking eyes with Lena. "Oh my..."

She turned her head to look at Ambrose, her eyes wide. "Is this a usual occurrence?"

"It has been today," Ambrose said flatly, staring daggers at the man.

"Oh my!" the man repeated, almost running over to Lena and pulling her into a tight embrace.

"Hey!" Lena exclaimed as she was pulled off her feet. The man smelt like burnt sugar but she found the eager embrace rather comforting.

"Sorry!" he said, putting her back on the floor. "Truly sorry. You must be the infamous Lena." His smile was full of warmth and amusement. She couldn't help but return the gesture.

"Infamous?" she queried.

"Ambrose has talked so much about you," Marcus said, putting his arm around her shoulders and pulling her closer to the desk.

"Shut up, Marcus," Ambrose threatened although he made no move towards the man.

"Oh, really?" she teased looking at Ambrose, a smile plastered on her face.

"Yes, but I want to hear it all from you now. Sit, sit," Marcus gestured to one of the chairs.

"Marcus," the demon growled.

"Oh, hush Ambrose," Marcus said, waving his hand at him dismissively. "Although," he said, turning his head slightly towards Ambrose, "why is she here and why are you like that?"

An uncomfortable silence fell over the room as Marcus looked back and forth between Ambrose and Lena.

She looked at her hands, before extending her arm and pulling the sleeve up slightly. Marcus' eyes widened at the sight of the red line and black markings.

"Oh, my dear," he sighed, taking hold of her hand. "I'm so sorry."

"Thank you," she said quietly.

Marcus squeezed her hand reassuringly before turning back to Ambrose. "What happened with the deal then? Did you make it?"

"No," he sighed, sitting back down, folding his hands on the desk in front of him. "I killed them."

"Ambrose..."

"Don't, Marcus," Ambrose snapped menacingly. "Not now. I need to go back to clean up as soon as possible. Lena, you should go to bed. Try to sleep."

She nodded absently. "I was just about to ask if it's normal to feel tired?"

"It is, yes," Ambrose replied softly, turning his head towards her.

"You will need to rest for the first few days as your body heals, or recovers, from the things done to it during your life. Especially the sacrifice itself," Marcus explained.

"Have you been through this too?"

"No, but I've had boundlings under my care."

"Boundlings?" Lena asked, raising her brows.

"We've tried thinking of a better name but, honestly, it's one of the best ones," Ambrose sighed.

"My mother was human. My father was a demon," Marcus said, still looking at her. "I'm what we call a cambion, or changeling."

"Oh... There's a lot to learn isn't there," she said, turning her gaze to her free hand on her knee. She opened and closed her fingers, in her usual way, trying to sort out her thoughts.

"Yes, but that is all for another day," Marcus said, getting to his feet and helping pull Lena to hers. "Right now, you need to try and get some sleep."

She hesitated for a moment. "I'm not sure I'll be able to sleep. I barely made it through a shower before seeing... their faces."

"Unfortunately," Marcus said, placing a comforting hand on her shoulder, "that may not go away any time soon. But nothing will happen to you whilst Ambrose is here."

"I promise, Lena," Ambrose said, standing himself.

"But you said you have to leave?" she said, looking at him.

"Only for a short while. I'll be back before you wake up."

Marcus looked back and forth between the pair. "I'll stay here with you," he suggested. "I can hole up in the library until Ambrose gets back. Nothing will happen to you."

Lena looked at Marcus for a moment and decided that she liked him. She felt like she could trust him and was touched by his offer. "Alright. Thank you," she said with a small nod.

"Don't mention it. Now, off to bed," Marcus smiled as he ushered her out of the office.

Without really thinking, she turned and walked to her new room, her mind already fogging with the need to sleep. She pulled her jeans off and hung them on the end of the bed, before crawling under the covers. To her surprise, sleep came easy, and soon her eyes closed and darkness settled in.

Then, the dreams began...

CHAPTER SIX

Ambrose stared dubiously at the back of Marcus' head after Lena had left the room.

"Will you really stay with her until I get back?" he asked.

Marcus sighed and hung his head before turning back to face Ambrose, his hands on his hips.

"Yes, I will," he said with a curt nod. "If only to berate you when you get back."

Ambrose dropped his gaze, shame washing over him. "I didn't have a choice," he said quietly. "I couldn't let her pass on."

"I'm not talking about binding her to you, although that has its own issues, it is your right," Marcus said walking back to the desk. "Killing the ones who sacrificed her..." he stopped his thought, simply shaking his head. "You better head off to clean it up. Make sure there is nothing left for human or demon to find."

"When I get back, can you at least wait until I revert to human form before you tear me a new one," he said, moving round to stand next to his friend.

Marcus nodded. "Yes, I can do that," he said calmly. "I'll be in the library. May feel the need to shout at you and don't need her hearing that. Not tonight."

Ambrose held out his hand as a peace offering. Marcus sighed but with a smile grasped his hand. "Thank you, my friend," he said before he disappeared in a flurry of flames.

Appearing back in the warehouse, Ambrose noted thankfully that no one had come across the scene as yet. He looked around to see what else occupied the room apart from the sacrificial pyre. There were scraps of paper, fabric and twigs scattered along the walls, coated with a thick layer of dirt and dust. Evidently it had been a long time since anyone set foot within here. Until tonight at least. Walking over to one of the walls, he touched some of the twigs and paper, surprised to note they were mostly dry. He could smell the salt in the air from the nearby harbour. That at least made one part of his job easier.

Walking to the door, he opened it cautiously to check if there was no one outside. Confident no one was going to see him, he opened the door fully and walked over to the car. They hadn't shut the trunk and he could smell Lena's scent of soft citrus coming from it. Anger boiled anew within him as he thought of her bound within. He looked inside the trunk and saw that it was empty apart from some engine oil and washer fluid bottles. The oil was a welcome sight and he picked it up. It wouldn't burn well, but it would corrupt any scents from demons and DNA from humans. He emptied the bottle over the trunk, pausing at points to see if he could still pick up Lena's scent. Once satisfied that it was all gone, he moved to one of the doors to look inside the car.

Behind the driver seat he found Lena's bag, boots and jumper. Ambrose smiled happily as he picked them up and placed them carefully on the ground beside the car for now. He poured the remaining oil over the floor mat getting rid of the last of her scent from the car.

He re-entered the warehouse and picked up the bodies of Stephen, Lucas and Jason, taking them out to the car in turn and placing them within the car. He used his power to heal the wounds he had inflicted on each of them. He wasn't the best of healers so it wasn't perfect and a keen eye might notice the repair job, but he hoped that enough time would pass between now and the bodies being found for decomposition to hide it sufficiently. Above all he hoped the bodies would never be found, but anything was possible.

Closing the doors, he caused a spark within the engine, igniting a fire that travelled into the cabin. He would let that burn whilst he sorted the inside of the warehouse.

Back inside, he walked back to the pyre and bent down to collect the two bowls that held Lena's life-blood. He poured one into the other so he could stack the bowls without spilling. The blood had started to congeal but it was still fresh enough for his purposes. He moved to outside the rune circle before dipping two fingers into the blood. Holding them in front of his face he whispered an incantation under his breath and watched as the runes burned away. There had obviously been blood on the pyre as it caught alight under the spell. Similarly, the blood on his fingers smouldered away.

Throwing some of his power at the lamps in the corners, he caused them to fall and spark as they hit the ground, allowing the dried paper and twigs to catch alight and burn. He sent another wave at the pyre, exploding the pallets to splinter across the floor, adding more fuel to the immediate flames. He nodded to himself approvingly.

"That should do it," he said, noting as the paint that blocked the windows started to bubble and drip having only been half dry earlier. By the time the fire was spotted, and someone got there, there shouldn't be anything for humans or demons to find.

Still holding the bowls, he walked back to the car and rested his hand on the hood. It was warm beneath him as the fire spread within the cabin. He flowed his power over the car body, keeping the fire contained and focused on destroying the bodies. He looked to his right and saw that the harbour was closer than he expected. The warehouse they had chosen was only a few lengths from the end of the pier it was built on. Overall, it had been a good location.

Ambrose placed the bowls next to Lena's things before heading to the back of the car and placing his hands on the top of the trunk. He pushed, rolling the car forward slowly. Once the car had started to move, he blasted power through his hands, accelerating it towards the end of the pier. It drove off the pier having reached an adequate speed to throw it a metre or so into the water below. The water would extinguish the fire, but it would have had enough time to burn by now. If anyone noticed the car tracks, it would look like they drove off the pier on their own.

Picking up Lena's things and the bowls, he walked over to the end of the pier, where he knelt down and washed the bowls in the sea. He watched with reverence as her blood mixed with the salt water. Once the bowls were clean, he pooled his power within his hands and melted them, letting the molten metal drops fall into the sea with satisfying sizzles.

Finally, everything should have been covered. He held Lena's items close as he stood and walked back slowly to the warehouse, the flames steadily growing and causing the metal of the walls to creak and groan with the increasing heat. Checking the ground around him, he could not detect any of Lena's scent anymore. With that, he gathered his flames and transported himself back to his office.

He placed Lena's bag and jumper on a chair, tucking her boots beneath it. As he did so, his demonic form started to recede, his clothes from before the summoning reforming against his skin. He shrugged out of his suit jacket and threw it at his chair, before grabbing a bottle of brandy from his side table and two glasses. Taking a deep breath to prepare himself, he left his office and made his way to the library. He headed downstairs and walked through the door to his right.

"Everything sorted?" Marcus asked as he walked inside. He was stood by one of the bookshelves, perusing the spines of the books.

Ambrose nodded, placing the glasses and bottle on the table in the middle of the room. "The warehouse will look like an accident. The car and the bodies may look suspicious, but a few days within the sea and it should be fine."

"Should be?" Marcus said, turning round and walking over to the table.

"Well, sufficient enough for humans. Can't imagine why any demons would poke around but you never know," he said, opening the brandy and pouring the red-golden liquid into the glasses.

Marcus chuckled slightly. "I promise I won't tell."

Ambrose smiled at his friend.

"What is it about her, Ambrose?" the cambion asked as he took a sip of the brandy.

"What do you mean?" he asked. "I've told you how I've been drawn to her for the last two years."

Marcus nodded slightly as he sunk into one of the chairs by the table. Ambrose followed suit sitting opposite. "You have. But meeting her tonight, I get it."

He tilted his head at Marcus. "You get what?"

"She pulls you in," he explained. "Not even five minutes with her in your office, and I felt protective enough to offer to stay. There's something about her."

"You're not developing feelings for my girl, are you Marcus?" Ambrose teased.

"And this morning you said she wasn't yours," the other demon laughed. "No, don't worry my friend. I have no interest in her, not like that anyway. But I am interested *about* her." He leant forward and poured himself more brandy. "Her energy is different to any I've felt before."

"How so?" Ambrose asked, finishing off his glass.

"As yet, unclear."

"What's that supposed to mean?"

"I don't know," Marcus sighed, shaking his head. "She seems too calm. Almost like death is not the worst thing she's been through. Now, I know there are plenty of souls where death is not the worst thing. But... she was innocent enough for a summoning ritual for you to work, and she's not freaking out?"

Ambrose was silent for a moment as he looked into his empty glass. "They said something about that," he said eventually. "One of the men. Something about not that innocent of a childhood. She had a social worker, so... foster care?"

"Maybe," Marcus mused. "But somehow, she kept innocent enough to work. Being a virgin at her age seems unlikely in this day and age. Or something else is at play."

"These three were not the sharpest tools in the shed," he chuckled. "They may have thought they were but their fore-planning was incredibly lacking."

"I'm not talking about them," the cambion said softly. "But we might as well get on to them. You know it's bad news to kill the summoners."

Ambrose sighed heavily, pouring himself more brandy. "I was starting to wonder when we would get to that."

"Anything could have happened, Ambrose," Marcus chastised. "You could have been seen; exposed. Not to mention it meant you had to go back, in demon form, I might add, to clean up. Thus, doubling the chance of being seen."

"Being seen hardly feels like an issue when you are literally being summoned to be seen."

"You know what I mean," Marcus said, rolling his eyes. "Summoners want to see us, they expect to see us. We are both fully aware of what governments get up to these days. You want to be caught and experimented on?"

"I can literally flame out of any situation like that. I'm not exactly worried, Marcus."

"Okay, so that's a bad example. Except you can't flame out if you are unconscious. We may be immortal and we may not need sleep very often, but living top-side, you can still be affected by a sedative."

Ambrose looked at his friend with a pit in his stomach. Marcus was right of course. There are a lot of risks in what he did tonight. Generally, demons needed neither sleep nor food, sustained by the souls not worthy of becoming demons that instead fuelled the fires of Hell. Living on earth and in human form meant that human needs occasionally needed to be met. But it also meant they could suffer human downsides, such as hangovers, if they overindulged in liquor.

"If I say I've learnt my lesson, can we let this go?" he asked with a smile.

Marcus scowled. "I shouldn't, but I will. On one condition," he said, holding up a finger.

"Name it."

"I want to help with Lena's training."

Ambrose stared at Marcus puzzled by his request. "Not that I would say no, but why?"

The cambion shrugged. "As I said, there is something about her. I want to find out what."

Raising his eyebrows, Ambrose nodded slightly. "Alright," he said slowly. "Sure, why not. As long as you keep it to training. I will use the 'I saw her first' card if I have to."

Marcus laughed heartily. "Deal," he said, wiping a tear away. "She's too young for me anyway."

The pair settled into a comfortable silence for a while as they sipped on the brandy between them. Eventually, Ambrose spoke.

"If there really is something about her, something truly different," he said softly, "we'll need to be careful Zagan doesn't find out about her. I won't allow her to be manipulated by him."

Marcus sighed heavily. "He's not the only one we'll have to worry about. But yes, you're right."

"I know thi–" Ambrose started but stopped turning his head sharply to the door, getting to his feet in a swift movement. He was barely aware that Marcus had done the same. "Did you feel that?" he asked, trying to focus on the tense energy that had suddenly washed over him.

Marcus nodded. "Could it be?"

"Lena!"

Ambrose and Marcus burst through the library doors and raced up the stairs to Lena's room. Ambrose threw his shoulder into her door, quickly forcing it open. The men stared at the scene before them, frozen in shock.

The bed was on fire, flames licking up the posters, the canopy smouldered and bits fell off into the source below. Lena lay in the middle of the bed, tossing and turning within the flames, her face a picture of fear and agony. Her shirt had burnt away along the arms as her bindings glowed white hot, instantly combusting anything they touched. The heat from the fire made Ambrose's skin prickle as all moisture in the room evaporated.

"Lena!" Ambrose shouted, racing over to the bed. "Lena, wake up!" The bindings should have forced her to follow his command, but instead red lightning shot from her hands, colliding with the walls and ceiling.

Marcus rushed inside pulling his jacket off as he transformed into a demon. His skin turned black as silver-grey markings appeared on his chest wrapping round to his back which now sported two black and grey bat-like wings. His golden hair turned silver and grew in length until the tips touched his shoulders. Horns sprang from his temples curving over his ears before looping back towards his chin like ram-horns.

"Stand back," he barked at Ambrose, before stepping towards the flames and holding his hands up against the heat. Black smoke-like power billowed from his arms mixing with the flames and cutting off the air. Marcus bent the smoke to smother the fire in most places as it acted like a dome in which neither flame nor air could pass through. He wrapped his power around Lena's arms, stopping the bindings from making contact with anything else.

Lena woke suddenly and screamed as she sat upright. She screamed again at the sight of Marcus.

"Lena, it's alright!" Ambrose cried hurriedly as he crawled onto the bed and pulled her into his arms. She clung to his shirt and buried her face into his chest. "Shh," he soothed, "it's alright."

Marcus raised a brow at Ambrose as he looked over the damage to the bed. The fire was out, but the bedding and frame smouldered in the aftermath. Ambrose pressed his lips together in response, as Marcus reverted to his human form, retrieving his jacket from the floor.

"I'm sorry," she cried, shaking her head. "I'm so sorry."

"It's alright Lena. It was a dream. You're safe now," Ambrose said, stroking her hair. "Sleep now," he commanded.

Her bindings glowed for a moment before she slumped against him, her body limp. Ambrose picked her up in his arms, holding her against his chest, resting her head on his shoulder.

"You can't compel her to sleep forever," Marcus said after pulling his jacket back on.

Ambrose looked at Lena's face. At least now it looked peaceful.

"I know," he said, shifting her weight slightly. "She shouldn't have been able to do this," he continued looking around the room.

Marcus merely nodded. "I'm going to the Repository. I'll be back tomorrow. I'd stay with her if I were you. Don't want her burning your whole house down."

Ambrose laughed slightly. "I'm sure I've got a spell somewhere that can repair this. But yes, the whole house would be difficult to explain." He turned back to his friend. "I'll send you a message when she wakes up."

"Fair enough," Marcus said, patting him on the back. "Good luck, my friend."

With that, the cambion disappeared.

Holding Lena close, Ambrose walked to his room. As gently as possible, he laid her down on his bed, pulling the covers over her. Carefully, he cut away the burnt sleeves of her top, telling himself he would fix it in the morning.

Watching her sleeping face, he tried to sort through his feelings for her. Something he had tried to do a number of times previously, but there had never been any urgency back then to do so. Now she was going to be living with him, he needed to figure it out. Before he'd reasoned there had been a sexual attraction, or at least that was what he called it in the beginning. As time moved on, he realised he had a warm affection for her, looking forward to their interactions in the cafe. He'd become protective of her, almost possessive and he'd tried to pull away a few times, not wanting to raise unwanted attention or jeopardise her safety in any way. But anytime he tried, he found himself inexplicably pulled back to her.

Something was so different about her compared to other mortal women he had dated in the past. Something that he found so incredibly endearing, so attractive, and he wanted to find out what it was. Acting on the impulse he'd resisted when seeing her on the pyre, he reached out and brushed the back of his fingers along her jaw. Her skin was soft and smooth, its creamy whiteness bright against his sun-kissed tan. Her soft-pink lips were parted slightly and the desire to kiss her suddenly became overwhelming as he quickly dropped his hand and stood up beside the bed.

Although she was compelled to sleep, she looked so peaceful, despite the events that had unfolded tonight. With a sigh he bent over her and kissed her gently on her forehead. "Sleep well," he whispered against her skin, grabbing a book he had left on the bedside table and heading to a chair by the fireplace.

Every now and then Lena would stir and Ambrose would look towards her to check she was still sleeping. Occasionally he would command her back to sleep when he thought she might be waking. She needed rest, and right now he didn't care how she got it.

He kept his vigil of her until the sun started to touch the walls of the town.

CHAPTER SEVEN

"Lena, it's time to wake up."

The voice gently pulled her from sleep. She stretched her arms above her head before slowly opening her eyes, pleasantly surprised that the air above the covers was warmer than she expected. The golden canopy above the bed was lit like glowing amber by the sun that streamed in through the windows. The scent of sage and cedar washed over her as the events of the night before suddenly came back to her.

"Oh shit!" she exclaimed, sitting bolt upright in the bed.

Ambrose stood at the foot of the bed, a soft smile on his lips.

Lena looked around herself at the room she was in. The room was similar to the one she had gone to sleep in last night, but with rich burgundy carpet rather than mauve. Cream walls with gold trim reflected the warmth of the carpet giving the room a golden amber glow. The bed was larger than hers had been and the bedding was crushed burgundy velvet with cream sheets. The frame and posters were made from a rich mahogany with the golden drapes tied to each corner. She could only assume this was Ambrose's room.

"Oh my god," she said, dropping her head into her hands. "The fire. I'm so sorry, Ambrose."

He laughed softly, moving to sit on the edge of the bed by her feet. "Please, Lena. Don't worry about it. A lot happened to you yesterday. There are bound to be a few... bumps... along the way."

She felt the mattress dip as he sat down but didn't raise her head.

"Saying that is not going to stop me from apologising. I am well aware, you just had this whole place redecorated."

"Lena, look at me," he said firmly.

With a deep breath, she looked up at him. She was glad to see him in human form again, her affection for him rekindled instantly. He was close enough to touch if she stretched out her hand, but she just hugged her knees to her chest, keeping her legs under the warmth of the covers.

"I don't care about the room," Ambrose continued looking into her eyes. Her body tingled under his gaze and warmth spread through her belly. She had always thought he was gorgeous, but looking at him now in the morning sun and the warm glow of his room, she was stunned by him. "I can fix the room no problem. My focus now is you. Making sure you are okay. You gave Marcus and I quite a scare last night."

She dropped her gaze, focusing instead on his hand resting on the mattress. "I'm fine," she said softly. "I'm sorry for any trouble I caused."

"Lena, it's no trouble," he emphasised. "I know you were dreaming. What did you see?"

Dropping her head back to her knees, she tried to curl up into as small a ball as she could manage. Her body felt frozen as she tried to push the memories from the night before out of her mind.

"What is it, Lena?" Ambrose pressed. "I can feel your fear."

Lena looked up surprised. "You can?" she asked, her voice barely louder than a whisper.

"The binding is fresh. There is a link between us that, although it will always be there, will settle with time. But for now, I can sense you and your emotions very clearly," he explained. "It's how I knew you were in trouble last night."

"I'm sorry."

Ambrose gave a small smile. "Please stop apologising. As I said, it will settle with time. I was expecting this." He titled his head and his gaze grew concerned. "What did you see?"

"I don't know," she said quietly. "It was just flashes. Nothing in particular. I just remember being so afraid."

"You have nothing to fear now as a demon," he said gently.

"You say that like it just automatically fixes everything," she sighed. "Until yesterday, I thought demons were just made-up concepts by the church for the purpose of scaring the masses into compliance. In less than twenty-four hours, I have been kidnapped, killed and turned into a demon, bound to a man... or demon," absently she waved towards him, “that I was supposed to be going on a date with. I don’t know how to be a demon. Not yet anyway... and saying I have nothing to fear does not magically get rid of it! It may seem like a simple concept to you, but it’s not to me.”

To his credit, Ambrose remained silent, but his brow furrowed with concern.

“But I feel safe with you,” she continued, her voice growing softer with each word. “I remember waking up. I remember... Marcus?” Ambrose nodded in confirmation. “And I remember you holding me. I don’t remember anything after that. I don’t remember any dreams, and I’m assuming I’ve been here since then,” she said looking around the room.

Ambrose sighed and he seemed to be deep in thought. Lena glanced at him through her eyelashes but tried to avoid looking at him directly. His mere closeness made her heart race, although she was puzzled as to how it was still beating considering her recent death.

"Well then,” he said suddenly, making her jump slightly, “you can sleep in my room for as long as you need. As long as I am not called away, I will watch over you at night." He gave her a warm smile. “It will be about two weeks before you don’t need to sleep every night.”

"Called away?" she asked, lifting her head to fully look at him.

"I could be summoned at any time. And I can't always control it," he explained.

"Right, of course," she responded quietly. "Thank you."

They fell into a comfortable silence for a moment, simply looking at each other. Eventually, Ambrose tore his eyes away much to her disappointment.

"We should get going. Marcus is waiting downstairs for us," he said, getting to his feet. "I've made some new clothes for you. They look the same as the ones from yesterday, but less charring."

Although Lena laughed, she buried her face again into her knees in embarrassment. "Why is Marcus here?" she asked into her lap.

"He is going to help with your training as a demon."

Lena lifted her head in puzzlement. "Do you not do that?"

Ambrose smiled and nodded. "Yes, I do. But Marcus has offered to help, and it would be unwise to decline. He knows far more than I do. That and, I think he's fond of you," he chuckled.

"Must have been everything you told him about me," she teased.

Ambrose starred in abject horror. "I really wish he hadn't said that.

Is there any chance you can just forget that?"

She shook her head enthusiastically. "Never."

"I was afraid of that," he sighed. "Oh, I have something for you," he said as he dashed over to a chair by the bedroom door. Turning back round, Lena could see what he had found.

"My boots!" she squealed in excitement.

Ambrose smiled at her reaction.

"I also found your jumper and bag. They're in my office when you want them."

"Thank you," she said with genuine joy in her voice.

"I'll be outside whilst you get dressed. I'll wait by the door, so just come out when you're ready."

She watched as Ambrose walked out of the room.

"For a demon, he is a gentleman," Lena said to herself as she swung her legs over the edge of the mattress. She pulled on the jeans and socks before slipping her feet into her boots with a grateful sigh. She changed her top, leaving the burnt one folded neatly on the chair. Dashing quickly into the bathroom, she checked her hair and smoothed it slightly with some water. Using her nails, she teased some of the knots out as best she could. Once satisfied with how she looked, she left the room almost running into the back of Ambrose.

"Oh," she cried softly, stopping herself short of colliding into him. "Sorry."

Ambrose turned and smiled at her, making her heart skip. "You're going to give me a complex if you keep apologising over everything."

She laughed sheepishly. "Sor- uh... childhood habit. Hard to break."

"We'll work on it," he said, starting to head down the hall. "Follow me."

She half jogged behind him as they made their way down the stairs. Halfway down, she stopped dead in her tracks. "The cafe!" she exclaimed. "Marie..."

"Lena," Ambrose started, sadness on his face. "I'm sorry, but you can't go back to the cafe. Not to work anyway."

"But I need to let them know."

"And you will," he said, stepping towards her and taking her hand in his. His warmth was comforting as she looked into his hazel eyes. "But not today. You need to get a handle on your powers first. We can't risk something like last night occurring in front of mortals."

"Marie will send someone to my apartment if I don't show up or at least call today," she said earnestly. "I've never taken a day off."

Ambrose sighed and looked at the floor. "I've already called her for you. I told her you were sick."

"Oh," she sighed.

"And tomorrow the cafe is closed so we have a couple days to sort things out," he continued giving her hand a squeeze.

She knew she should have been annoyed that he took that upon himself, but was in some ways grateful as she knew she would not have been able to make that call herself. "Yeah, you're right... thanks."

"I can feel your upset. I'm sorry I didn't wait to speak to you about it," Ambrose almost pleaded with her. "I was trying to make things easier for you."

"I know," she said sadly. "And I mean it; thanks. I'm just not looking forward to saying goodbye to them."

He dropped her hand. "Come on. First day of training will distract you from that. Small steps, Lena."

She nodded before continuing down the steps. Ambrose ushered her to the right and opened the door for her. Stepping inside, Lena instantly forgot her sorrow as her eyes widened in awe at the library.

The dark oak parquetry flooring from the entrance hall extended into the library complementing the bookshelves that lined each wall. The room was larger than she had been expecting as she viewed the large rectangle table that stretched down the length of the room, eight chairs a side. Each chair was cushioned with emerald green fabric and black anodised studs, contrasted against the warm grey wood. Light-coloured leather wingback chairs were placed in each corner of the room, each with their own side table and lamp. The bookshelves were filled with... well, books... much like Ambrose's office, but there was a mix of all kinds, not just leather-bound. One shelf to her left had been dedicated to numerous scrolls and parchments stacked on top of each other.

Among some of the collections were random displays of geodes, models and artefacts. Her eyes were drawn to a book that was open, raised on a wooden stand in one of the far wall shelves. It was covered in clear crystals across both its pages and cover, forever freezing the book in time. A few of its pages were curled up in random patterns, crystals holding them in place within the air. She wanted to pick it up and study it, but Marcus' voice pulled her from her trance.

"Good morning, Lena," Marcus said, getting up from one of the wingbacks. "How are you feeling this morning?"

Lena found herself unexplainably happy to see him, as she bounded over to him to give him a hug. Ignoring the surprise on his face, Marcus opened his arms to embrace her.

"I see you are feeling better then," he said with undertones of laughter.

"Much," she said, giving him a warm smile as she released him and took a few steps back. "And, good morning. It's nice to see you human again after last night. The wings, however, were a nice touch."

He smiled warmly at her. "Well, thank you."

"So, I hear, you will be one of my teachers," she said, turning her head to further take in the wonders of the library.

"If you don't mind. Although I was already intrigued from when I first met you, your display last night was very impressive, and I would be honoured to help guide your growth," he said, walking over to the table and pulling out a chair.

"I destroyed the room, Marcus," she sighed, turning towards him. "Not exactly what I would call impressive."

"On the contrary," Ambrose said, coming to stand beside her. "It is exceedingly rare for a newly made demon to access their powers on the first night. No matter the reason for why you accessed them."

"He's right," Marcus confirmed. "Come sit."

Lena walked slowly towards Marcus, lowering herself onto the chair he held out for her.

"Today, we need to focus on accessing your power at will, and by extension to control it," Marcus said, sitting next to her. Ambrose sat opposite.

"Ordinarily," Ambrose explained, "we would go through this after tying up loose ends from your life, but after last night, we don't think this can wait."

"From what we saw last night, your power manifests as lightning," Marcus said. "Powerful, but difficult to control."

"Also desirable," Ambrose added, his brow furrowing.

"Desirable?" Lena queried looking back and forth between the men.

Marcus nodded. "Hell works on power. Demons feed on and use that power to survive. Likewise, demons that can live on earth work to increase that power. This does lead to some creating factions, or their own power bases. Demons that can manifest lightning are highly sought after."

"You are newly bound," Ambrose continued. "To me, by your

choice. But similarly, by your choice, you could divert to another demon, and there will be those that seek to persuade you to choose them. There may also be those that will seek to take you by force, overriding your binding to me with their own."

"Is that really possible?" she asked, staring at him.

"Unfortunately, yes," he said with a slight nod. "In time as the binding settles, it will be harder for another demon to overcome my binding, but for the first few weeks, it's best to be careful. I can't keep you a secret forever," he said with a rueful smile. "We will need resources in Hell that we cannot replicate top-side."

"But for now, we will train here," Marcus said.

Lena leant forward, placing her elbows on the table and her head in her hands. "I'm going to have a killer headache by the end of the day."

"Unfortunately, aspirin doesn't tend to help demons in the same way as humans," Ambrose said with a soft laugh. "But we have herbs that we can make a tea from, which will help."

"Let's begin," Marcus said. "Hold out your hands, palms facing each other. You are going to try and create a spark between them."

Lena took a deep breath and straightened her back, holding her hands out as instructed.

They spent hours in the library, Ambrose and Marcus instructing her in various power control methods. She found herself able to access her lightning almost effortlessly, but keeping it between her hands only was a struggle. More times than she cared to count, her power would escape and attempt to land on the bookshelves or either man. Diving out of the way of a stray lightning bolt became its own exercise for the men, much to Lena's frustration. Thankfully, Marcus had some foresight and had placed protective sigils around the room which prevented her lightning from actually hitting anything of consequence.

"You're using your power like it's going out of style," Marcus said around lunchtime. "It's not infinite and you send it out in concentrated waves which is why you are already starting to feel exhausted."

Lena looked at him haughtily, but couldn't deny that she was panting from the exertion of the morning.

"You need to refine the way you use it, pulling it out slowly rather than just throwing it around."

"That is the second time you've said that but you've not told me how!" she snapped, her frustration growing.

"Visualise it," Ambrose said calmly, picking himself up off the floor from the most recent power burst. "Your power is an extension of you but it also exists as a separate entity within you. You should be able to, for lack of a better word, communicate with it. See it and persuade it to do what you want it to."

She took a deep breath and closed her eyes. Holding her hands out in front of her again, she tried to focus on finding her power centre that Marcus had told her about earlier. She had found it deep within her core, as if it rested just under her heart, between her lungs. It crackled with dangerous and almost painful energy that sought to escape. Trying to visualise it as single strands of electricity, she grabbed hold of just one, stretching it out in small waves so as not to break the thread which would cause another explosion. But her concentration and energy were waning.

Unable to prevent it, the power snapped and a large bolt escaped her hands, making its way for Marcus' head. Eyes wide he dropped to the floor and the lightning instead collided with the protective barrier over the table.

"Sorry!" she cried as her legs gave out beneath her and she fell onto her hands and knees.

"It's okay," Marcus sighed. "That seemed better. At least only one bolt came out of that."

"You almost had it," Ambrose said, rushing over to help her to her feet. "I could feel it within you. Your focus slipped, just for a moment. That caused the bolt."

Lena shrugged his hand off her arm before storming over to another corner of the room. "You keep talking like lightning can be manipulated like fabric, but it doesn't feel like that inside. It feels volatile and... angry. Concentrated in a singular ball like a bomb wanting to explode. It wants to escape and no matter how much I hold on it fights me the whole time," she said, placing her hands on her hips as she turned to face the men. "What does your power feel like?"

The men were silent for a moment contemplating her question. Ambrose answered first.

"Mine feels like string throughout my entire body," he said slowly. "It pulls and flows depending on what I want it to do. It is like another limb, calm and familiar." He held up his hand and allowed tendrils of his power to rise from the centre of his palm in demonstration. "I can use it like another hand, or sharpen it to act as a weapon. But it didn't always feel like this. In the beginning it almost hurt, like it was ripping through my skin, whenever I tried to use it. That pain was because subconsciously I was rejecting it. Fighting it. Fighting the demon I had become." His hand dropped and Lena thought he looked sad. Ambrose sighed before lifting his gaze to look at her. "We are not expecting you to master your power in one day, Lena. It takes time."

"Even natural born demons and cambions need time to learn how to control their powers," Marcus said stepping forward. "It's easier, because as children we are naturally curious to explore our powers, but we are rarely in control of them until much later. Mine was more straightforward than others. It is fused with my blood, flowing effortlessly around my body. It fills me completely. It manifests as smoke, but it's more than that. I can compress it to act like a blanket or a wall, or expand it like... well... smoke."

Lena tried to suppress the laugh but failed miserably, a small chuckle escaping her lips. She sighed heavily, her body almost aching from the morning's exertion and her sudden realisation that she had not eaten anything since yesterday. As if on cue, her stomach growled.

"Perhaps, we should get you some food before continuing?" Ambrose said with an amused smile. Lena popped her tongue at him, but nodded in agreement. "Come on, I'm sure we can find you something in the kitchen."

"I could eat," Marcus said, his serious mood turning buoyant as he turned to the door.

She smiled, with genuine warmth, and followed the men out of the library.

CHAPTER EIGHT

Although Ambrose had the kitchen renovated when he moved into the manor, he had hardly used it. He kept a general stock of tinned and other non-perishable items for as and when he needed them, but otherwise he stored potion and spell ingredients there which did not always lend themselves to edible cooking. If he needed food, he preferred the cafe or a restaurant.

Thankfully, Marcus proved himself quite adept at throwing together a decent meal. Ambrose and Lena stood around the stove watching the cambion cook as the trio traded in pleasant conversation. Ambrose found himself enjoying the effortless exchanges, stopping short of being thankful for the circumstances that led to this moment. But as Lena glided around the kitchen passing ingredients to Marcus as she went, he found himself yet again enchanted by her. If only Marcus had not been there, he would have lifted her onto one of the counters and claimed her as his.

Shifting uncomfortably as his body heated, Ambrose tried to push his desire for her out of his mind and focus on the topic of conversation currently flowing between them.

"So, you said your mother was human last night," Lena said, passing a shaker of salt to Marcus. "Did she know your father was a demon?"

Marcus shook his head solemnly, tossing the contents of the pan in front of him. "Not straightaway. He told her when he found out she was pregnant with me. Demon pregnancies progress quicker than humans, so he had to come clean when she started asking questions." He poured a tin of bean sprouts into the stir fry before continuing. "At least with my parents, unlike some human-demon relationships, they genuinely cared for each other. My mother actually survived my birth which is unfortunately uncommon. She and my father were very hands on with raising me. As the mothers don't generally survive, cambions tend to be raised within the barracks in Hell so aren't the most pleasant of demons to be around. Even for ones that have been a demon for as long as me."

"Oh," Lena said, absolutely enthralled at the information, as she leant forward on her elbows and rested her chin in her hands. Ambrose tried to ignore the stab of jealousy he felt seeing how she looked at his friend. "So cambions should be avoided?"

"As long as you don't class me in that assessment, yes, if you can help it," Marcus said with a slight laugh. "They don't tend to play nice with others and are more focused on gaining power than other demon's might be."

"So are cambions the natural born demons you've talked about?"

"No," Ambrose said, leaning forward and resting his elbows on the counter. "Cambions are naturally born, but natural born demons have two demon parents or are spawned from somewhere within the depths of hell. They are usually born to succubi and incubi and cared for by Lilith and her subordinates."

"Oh, I know that name," Lena interjected with her face lighting up.

"Most do," he said with an amused smile. "They come in a number of different forms, but because they were never human or do not have a human half, they only live within Hell."

"Right, you've said that before," she said with a sigh. "There's so much to remember."

"You'll get there," he said softly. "You've got plenty of time now to learn everything."

"Yeah... demons are immortal right?"

"Just as long as you are aware, immortality does not mean invulnerability," Marcus chimed in. "You can be hurt or killed by other demons. Humans can kill us but it is a lot harder for them to do so. A knife or gun won't do much, but poisons will."

Lena pressed her lips together and nodded absently as she took in the information. "What happens to a demon if they die?"

"Unknown," Ambrose said as he pulled out some plates and cutlery to serve up the stir fry Marcus had made. The trio made their way to the table in the corner of the kitchen to eat. "Or at least unclear." he continued, pulling out his chair. "Supposedly, their energy reverts to power Hell or moves on to Purgatory. But as none ever come back, we don't know for sure."

"Well," Marcus said, sighing as he sat down. "I've had enough of talking about Hell and power. Tell us about you, Lena."

She shook her head. "My life is not interesting."

"I don't believe that for a second," the cambion wagged his finger at her with a teasing smile.

Ambrose watched her face change, furrowing his brow, as she pushed the food around her plate with her fork. Something was off. Her mood had changed and the smile that had brightened her face was gone. Her dove-grey eyes darkened to a midnight storm. Then and there he knew someone had hurt her and he was surprised at his sudden desire to hunt down whoever it was.

"What about Ambrose?" Lena said with a coy smile that didn't reach her eyes.

"I already know his story," Marcus replied, waving his hand at Ambrose dismissively. "Not interesting."

"Geez, thanks," he said, rolling his eyes. Lena chuckled at his reaction and he felt warmth spreading through him as she looked at him. Everything in him wanted to be alone with her now, such that he found himself regretting that he had agreed to Marcus' help, despite the advantages it would provide.

Lena inhaled sharply and dropped her gaze to look at the table. "I don't like to talk about it," she said calmly before taking a mouthful of food. "And if I do talk about it, there is no cliff notes version."

"Well," Marcus started, quickly swallowing his first mouthful of food. "I'm interested in the full story. You are remarkably accepting of your fate as a sacrifice and demon, which I find incredibly intriguing." Ambrose nodded his agreement as his friend's assessment.

"I've known true demons in my life and honestly, I can't bring myself to place Ambrose or you in that category." The tone in Lena's voice was both heartbreaking and full of sincerity. Ambrose pulled his brows together, curious as to her meaning.

There was an uncomfortable silence for a while, disturbed only by the sound of forks on porcelain as they ate their food. Lena finished her meal first but she continued to stare at her empty plate. Ambrose noticed that she was opening and closing her fists in her lap as if she was trying to grasp something that wasn't there. She'd done something similar the night before. It appeared to help her sort out her thoughts. He and Marcus had seen many a new boundling close up about their human life and they knew not to push.

Suddenly, she sighed before raising her eyes to the ceiling. "I don't remember much of my early years. I can remember my father's voice, his eyes, the song he used to sing to help me sleep... but his face is a blur. He died when I was six. Six and a half. Something like that. All my memories of my mother before then are gone..." she trailed off, her eyes glazing over as her memories took over.

Ambrose looked on quietly, waiting to see if she would return to them, then reached out and took her hand in his. She looked at him quickly as he squeezed her hand slightly in reassurance, ignoring the look that Marcus shot his way. "What happened to your mother?" he asked, encouraging her to continue.

"She, uh..." Lena turned her gaze back to the table and her face became unreadable. "She became an abusive alcoholic who blamed me for my father's death."

Ambrose heard Marcus exhale loudly before shifting in his seat. He knew that Marcus would be angered by Lena's statement. The cambion had known such a devoted mother who accepted his demon half without question. He found abusive parents intolerable.

"When my father died, he left a fairly substantial life policy to support my mother and I," she continued leaning forward and resting her arms on the table crossed in front of her. "My mother used most of it to drink and gamble herself into oblivion. It became anyone's guess what would set her off on one of her alcohol fuelled rages in which I would hear in great detail how I ruined her life. Social services got called more than once, but nothing ever happened. I was placed in foster care shortly after I turned ten. The dislocated shoulder and broken collar bone from when she threw me down a set of stairs were too much for them to ignore."

Ambrose glanced over to Marcus cautiously. His face had become one of anger mixed with sadness, green eyes fixed on Lena's face. Unlike Marcus, Ambrose had his own history with an abusive parent, and his heart ached that he and Lena should share such a tragic upbringing.

"The first family I was placed with were relatively lovely people, but I was damaged goods and so I was only there a month before I got moved to a group girls home. I was there for three months, then I was sent back to my mother after she attended some classes and stopped drinking for a month. I was removed again after two weeks when I landed in ER with fractured ribs, a punctured lung and internal bleeding. A week after that, she drank so much she killed herself," Lena shrugged as if the way her mother died was just a side note in her story, which Ambrose assumed for all intents and purposes, it was.

"I went from foster family to group home but didn't stay anywhere longer than six months at a time. Some were ok, others were almost as abusive as my mother. One tried to sell me for drugs when I was fourteen."

Ambrose inhaled purposefully at that information trying to control his anger. Marcus was not doing much better, having laid his hands flat on the underside of the table to prevent them from shaking. Humans thought demons were evil and yet were themselves capable of abusing children in such a manner.

Lena continued seemingly not noticing the reaction of the men before her. "But stroke of luck in a ton of shit and the police raided the drug den as they were making the deal. I aged out of the system and with no family to help, I ended up either couch surfing with the few people I did know or on the streets. My father had thankfully made an account in my name which my mother couldn't touch. It had a small amount of money in it which I used very quickly just to survive. Finding work in the city that wasn't prostitution, or something else equally life-threatening, without a stable education history wasn't the easiest task in the world."

She leant back in her chair and Ambrose was shocked to see an almost relieved look on her face, as if recanting her life had been physically painful. Similarly, he was in awe of her. She had been through so much, well aware himself of how hard it is to feel unwanted by a parent or anyone, and yet all he had seen of her was a bright and positive young woman.

"I fell in with the wrong crowd for a bit. Needed out of the city so I begged my old social worker to help me get here and she did what she could. Helped me get the job at the cafe and she paid personally for my travel here. I had to find my own accommodation. Marie, bless her, took me under her wing and, while I say I had to convince her, it didn't take much. She paid me a month in advance so I could pay my security deposit and first month's rent." Lena fell silent for a moment, her brow furrowed. "Then I was sacrificed, so now I'm here with you two, telling you in too much detail the fucked-up history that is, or was, my life," she finished pressing her lips together and crossing her arms in front of her chest.

It took every ounce of Ambrose's self-control to not pull Lena into his arms, his desire to take her away from everything almost overwhelming him.

Marcus managed to speak first. "I'm sorry, Lena." He made as if to say more but seemed unable to find the words.

"It's fine," Lena said flatly. "Can't change what's happened. I am..." she paused momentarily, contemplating her next words. "Yeah, I am happy with where I am, even with the circumstances that led me to sit here now, so I don't regret any of it."

"That's a very sage viewpoint to have," he said, nodding his head slightly. "Still, for what it's worth, I am sorry."

"Thanks," she offered Marcus a small smile before grabbing the empty plates and getting to her feet. She dropped them in the sink as the men just sat silently at the table. "Can we stop for today?" she asked, standing by the sink. "I'm exhausted. And I'm still trying to process everything that happened last night."

"Yes, of course," Ambrose said, standing up and walking over to her. "I haven't had a chance to repair your room yet, but if you want to be alone, you can use my room for now."

"Thank you," she said softly, turning to the door to leave. "See you later Marcus."

"Goodbye, Lena," Marcus responded with a nod in her direction.

"Call for me if you need anything," Ambrose said as Lena opened the kitchen door.

After she had left, Marcus got to his feet with a heavy sigh. "I'll be going too then. Let me know when she's ready to continue."

Ambrose nodded and shook Marcus' hand before he vanished in flames. He stood there for a moment, replaying the events of the morning and the recent discussions. Even before seeing her on the pyre, he had felt very protective of Lena, and hearing her story had only served to intensify that feeling.

His mind elsewhere, Ambrose made his way up to Lena's room to begin repairs. He stopped by the final room on the top floor, which he kept as an altar room of sorts. Over the months, it had become more useful as storage and was where he kept his ritual artefacts and conduits.

Grabbing what he needed, he thought about how to help Lena

progress in her training. Guiding her in the way that he and Marcus had been didn't seem to be working, and maybe her past had something to do with that. He didn't need further details of her life to know that it will be affecting her even now. Her rebirth as a demon would dig up a lot of old memories as if they were happening to her all over again. Not to mention the memories of her sacrifice playing fresh and likely on repeat in her mind.

It didn't take him long to repair the room. Once he was finished, he returned to the library to pour over some books to see what he could find to help Lena. He decided it was best to leave her alone in his room for now. When she was ready to come out, he would speak with her.

Setting up at the table with a few books, Ambrose tried to set his focus to the words in front of him. He had managed only a few pages before his mind turned to Lena, picturing her within the library as she tried to gain control of her power. Even when her brow had been furrowed with concentration, he found her beauty enthralling. Her cheeks had been flushed with pink and her eyes, those dove-grey depths, had sparkled with pride the first time she had made an intentional spark.

He shook his head slightly and returned to the books. He had pulled out an old manuscript written in the early 1100's that had been written, as far as he was aware at least, by a natural born demon who studied different manifestations of power. He found passages here and there about lightning, but nothing was consistent. Where calmer, less volatile, forms of power seemed to manifest in similar ways across different demons, manifestations of lightning and certain forms of fire, such as lava and explosions, proved too dangerous to study in great detail.

He raised his brows upon reading a study about a demon who had essentially blown themselves apart when they tried to compound their power internally in the supposed aim of creating an increased single discharge. He decided that was something Lena didn't need to learn about.

Sighing heavily, Ambrose let his head fall back to stare at the ceiling after realising he had read the same passage three times. Shutting his eyes momentarily, he let his mind wander up the stairs and into his bedroom. He imagined Lena lying on his bed, much as she had been the night before, leaning over her and kissing her cheek. His mind's eye watching as he brushed a strand of hair away from her face, running his fingers along the line of her jaw towards her chin so he could tilt her face towards his. Her pink lips enticing him to taste her, her eyes drawing him closer, until he pressed his lips to hers, drinking in her scent of citrus.

His eyes snapped open as he shifted uncomfortably in the chair, his body hard and hot for hers. He had dreamed of her before, of laying her beneath him and stripping all clothes from her body, slowly baring her beauty to his eyes. The dreams had been increasing and were driving him to the point of distraction. He knew he needed to get her out of his system, but that was not what he wanted. She had become a reason for existing the last few months. Her smile had bought him untold joy, especially when he saw he was the cause for it. And Ambrose wanted to give her every reason to smile.

Lena had agreed to dinner with him, so he reasoned there must be something there. She must feel some portion of what he feels for her. Some portion of desire.

"You're just torturing yourself at this point, old boy," he chastised himself before pushing the chair back and abandoning the reading. He decided to at least check on her, to make sure she was okay.

"Lena?" he called as he knocked on the door to his room. He felt silly knocking to enter his own bedroom, but he knew it was better to be cautious about potentially startling her at the moment. "Lena?" he repeated after a moment with no answer.

Concern growing, he opened the door slowly and looked within. She wasn't there. Walking into the room, he checked the bathroom without success. With long, deliberate strides, he walked back out and checked his office and Lena's room. Unable to find her, he practically ran down the stairs and checked the library despite having just come from there. The kitchen and the other wing were also devoid of her presence. Now panicked he checked the front door and noted that it was unlocked.

She was gone.

His heart racing, he looked around the entrance hall trying to think about where she might have gone. Commanding her to return wouldn't work unless she was close enough to hear him. Running around the town looking for her would cause too much of a scene. He raked a hand through his hair and exhaled sharply trying to force his mind to focus, cursing that he didn't know where her apartment was. On some level he doubted she would go there, and he desperately hoped she wouldn't have gone to the cafe.

"Shit! Think, Ambrose," he said, placing his hands on his hips and closing his eyes. He took a deep breath to calm his mind, trying to picture where she might have gone. Their bond was fresh so he could feel her emotions, but it was still forming so finding where she had gone was difficult. He saw glimpses of the roof of his house and the wall as if looking down from above. He could smell the snow and hints of pine from the surrounding woods. Exhaling with relief he realised where she was and grabbing his coat, plus a spare one for her, he rushed out of the front door and headed for the north gate.

CHAPTER NINE

Fresh snow had blanketed the area covering all of the footprints from the events of the day before. Lena sat on the bench overlooking the town, simply allowing flashes of her memory to invade her mind. She had picked up a stone from the river on her way up to the lookout which she now turned over in her hands, focusing on the small imperfections across its smooth surface to help keep her emotions in check. This was something one of the multitudes of court appointed therapists had taught her. It allowed her to review her most traumatic memories, completely detached from the emotion of them. Something she desperately needed to do now. If panic, fear or sadness started to rise within her, she would press the stone into her palm, as if to push her emotions into it.

After leaving the library, she had fully intended to go up to Ambrose's room and sleep, but seeing the front door she was overcome with the need to leave. She knew that it would cause issues, but in that moment she didn't care. She needed to breathe fresh air and feel the cold bite at her skin as it had before. Disappointment had washed over her as she realised the cold meant nothing, and whilst she was aware of it, it didn't cause her to shiver or shy away from it. She was truly dead, regardless of if she breathed or could feel the beating of her heart.

What a mess we're in, huh?

Straightening quickly, Lena looked around her. Someone had spoken, but it hadn't quite sounded like it was a physical voice. But she had heard *someone*. It wasn't her voice. Had it come from her mind? It was silky and alluring, but had an undertone of primal fierceness that scared her. Closing her eyes, she took a deep breath, trying to push away the fear that had washed over her at the sound of it.

"Lena?"

That voice was familiar. Ambrose had found her, quicker than she had expected. She didn't turn to look at him, but nodded in acknowledgement. Feeling his warmth getting closer to her, she was surprised when he laid a coat over her shoulders.

"I know you don't need it," he said softly before moving around the bench to sit next to her, "but to avoid unwanted questions it's best to get in the habit of taking a coat with you when you leave the manor."

She stayed silent, but slowly she pulled the coat tighter around her body.

"Are you okay?" Ambrose asked. She knew he was looking at her, but she couldn't bring herself to return his gaze. She just shook her head in response. "Do you want to talk?" Again, she shook her head. She saw him nod from the corner of her eye as he leant back on the bench and fell silent.

They sat there for almost an hour, unspeaking and unmoving, simply watching the sun move closer to the horizon, as she turned the stone in her hands under the coat. Eventually, Lena started to speak.

"I have never been in control of my life," her voice was barely more than a whisper, but she knew Ambrose heard her when he turned his head towards her. "Not until I moved here. It was always up to others. Adults, who thought they knew better, telling me where to go. What to do. Who to be. I never had any choice. And even when they asked what I wanted, more often than not I was simply ignored." She licked her lips and sniffed slightly before continuing. "I'm not even upset that I died. I'm more upset that I didn't get to choose how I died. With everything my mother put me through, I would tell myself, in some morbid sense of humorous irony, that if she didn't kill me, then at least I could choose how I died. But even that was taken from me."

Lena felt Ambrose place his hand on her back and she shut her eyes, finding comfort in the warmth of it. "I know it may seem stupid to someone like you, but you told me last night that I had a choice. A choice that was truly mine. And yet... it's led to something that again takes my choice away." Her brow furrowed as she tried to continue. "You haven't explained how this works fully, but... I can feel that being bound means I don't have a choice now. Or at least, not completely. I can feel that you are in control. And yet I'm surprised and confused by the realisation that," she finally turned her head to look at him, "I'm okay with that."

Ambrose's face was unreadable, but he kept focused on her, simply allowing her to speak. He spoke now.

"You still have choices. Choices that no one, not even myself, can make for you," he said softly, moving his hand to stroke her cheek. Lena closed her eyes and leant into his hand. "Come back to the manor, get some sleep, and, although it will take time to explain everything, I will explain how the binding works tomorrow."

"Just us?" she asked leaning into him to rest her cheek on his chest. She wasn't sure why she had made such a move, but joy flooded through her body as he placed his arm around her shoulder drawing her closer to him.

"Just us," he confirmed, a smile in his voice.

Together, they stood and with Ambrose's arm still around her shoulders, they made their way back to the manor. She still felt uncertain about everything, but at least with Ambrose, she knew she would be okay.

"It is not often that sires need to compel their boundlings, but it is worth knowing what it feels like," Ambrose said to Lena, as they walked into the library the next day.

"Compel?"

"Command might be a better word," he replied. "Essentially, you are forced to do what I tell you through the binding between us. Eventually you will break from the bond, but only once you have learnt enough, or become powerful enough to act in your own right as a demon."

"What are some reasons you might need to compel me?" she asked, looking up at him.

"Security is the main one. Sires tend to confide in their boundlings and may compel them to silence. Boundlings are one of the few that sires can truly trust to keep a secret. Safety is another possibility, either to protect the sire or the boundling depending on the situation. Or defiance to follow orders," he said with a coy smile. "I compelled you to sleep on your first night after you destroyed your room."

Lena dropped her gaze to the floor with a nervous laugh. "Yeah... I'm still really sorry about that."

Ambrose chuckled. "As I've said, don't worry about it. Shall we begin?"

She nodded hesitantly.

"I'm going to tell you to do something. Don't fight it," he said, folding his arms and leaning his hip on the table next to them. "Pick up that book," he said, nodding towards it.

Lena watched as her bindings glowed and her hands moved on their own picking up the book in front of her. Once the book was in her hands her bindings faded to black.

"Good. Now, try to fight against the order," Ambrose said, "and I apologise in advance. Put the book back down."

Again, her bindings glowed and she felt her muscles try to place the book back on the table. She fought against it, gripping the book tightly, trying to pull it to her chest. Instantly, pain shot through her arms causing her to cry out and slam the book on the table. Her knees buckled and she started to fall to the floor. Ambrose caught her arm holding her up until her vision stopped spinning.

"That," she said through gritted teeth, "was unpleasant."

"Quite," he chuckled, still holding her arm as Lena steadied herself. "Compelling is a battle of wills. Opposing wills causes pain, aligned wills don't."

"So, breaking from a bond requires the boundling's will to become greater than the sire's?" Lena asked curiously.

Ambrose smiled approvingly. "I thought you would figure that out. And yes, that's a part of it. Not just your will though. Your strength and power needs to be equal or greater than your sire. Or at the very least sufficient to support your own will." He paused for a moment, seemingly contemplating his next words. "Each bond has its own unique qualities as well which can affect when it comes to an end. For example, bonds that are fraught with tension often don't last long, but they also rarely result in powerful demons. Complimentary bonds can last for decades, even centuries. No two bonds are the same."

Lena smiled, a wicked thought popping into her mind. She looked up at him, her eyes sparkling with mischievous intent and asked, "So, do you think we will be fraught or complimentary?"

Ambrose raised his eyebrow in response and titled his head, a grin spreading across his lips. "Well, let's find out, shall we? Kiss me," he commanded.

With no pain, she leant forward and pressed her lips to his. But, compelled or not, the small kiss wasn't enough for her. This man... demon... or whatever he was... who she had dreamed of kissing for months now, wanted her to kiss him. And she wasn't going to let the opportunity pass.

Raising to her toes, Lena placed her hand on the back of Ambrose's neck to deepen the kiss. He seemed surprised but didn't pull back. Instead, he wrapped his arms around her waist pulling her closer to him. She held onto his shoulders as he lifted her in his arms and forced her back against the bookshelf. Her legs hooked over his hips as his hands now gripped beneath her thighs, holding her firmly in place. She ran her fingers through his hair, drinking in his scent and taste.

Ambrose brought up his knee to support her weight, freeing one of his hands and moving it to her jaw. Using his thumb he pulled at her chin, opening her mouth and slipping his tongue inside to lick and circle with her own. She moaned against his mouth, letting her hands roam from his neck to his shoulders. She felt like she couldn't get enough of him, wanting simply to melt into his warmth and lose herself to his kiss.

She cried in protest as Ambrose broke the kiss, his chest heaving as he regained control of his breathing. Likewise, Lena had to remind herself how to breathe as she fell into the bright sparkle of his hazel eyes. He smiled as he rested his forehead against hers. "Definitely complimentary, I'd say" he whispered. "As much as I would like to continue this, unfortunately, we have a lot to get through today."

Lena laughed breathlessly. "Sorry for jumping you like that."

"Don't be. I have been wanting to do that since I first saw you," he said slowly, setting her down on her feet, but keeping his hands on her hips.

"You have?" she asked surprised, leaning into his chest.

"Mm-hm," he smiled at her in a way that made her stomach somersault. "Why do you think I came to the cafe almost every day?"

"So why did it take you almost two years to ask me out?"

Ambrose sighed and placed a soft kiss on the top of her head. "Relationships between a demon and a human are complicated. Not impossible, but complicated. And they usually don't end well. I've felt lust over humans before but the feeling usually faded once I got to know them more. I wanted to see what would happen. Although, I do wish I hadn't waited so long, I'm not entirely upset at this outcome."

"What was different with me?" she asked, snaking her arms around his waist, deciding she never wanted to let go.

He was quiet for a moment, lifting his head to look at the bookshelf, before answering. "Most humans have an element of shallowness to them that I cannot stand. Couldn't stand it when I was human and still can't stand it after centuries as a demon," he said, an air of irritation in his voice which sent a shiver down her spine. "I know the rumours that spread through the town about my wealth, so I'm certain you knew about them as well."

"Yeah..." she said sheepishly.

"But you never asked," Ambrose looked back at her and lifted one hand to stroke the back of his fingers along her jaw. "You didn't seem to care what I was worth or what I did. You never asked about my business, you only ever asked about me. If I was okay. You would comment on when I looked tired, telling me to rest or take it easy. Or say how good it was to see when I was in a good mood. And I noticed when you convinced Sarah to start letting you make my coffee." Lena could feel the heat rising in her cheeks as she realised just how much attention he had secretly paid her. "You genuinely cared about me, and you barely knew me. That quality I found irresistible."

Lena felt a stinging in her eyes as tears threatened to form. She dropped her head quickly so he wouldn't see and shut her eyes tightly. She had never had someone speak to her so kindly before. And now it came from a demon of all beings. She coughed slightly as she loosened her arms from his waist.

"You said we have a lot to do today..." she said softly, trying to ignore the disappointment that washed over her when Ambrose pulled away completely.

"Yes," he said, "we need to sort some things out. Tie off some loose ends from your life so you can fully embrace being a demon."

She nodded. "Right, yes, makes sense."

"Come here," Ambrose said, pulling out a chair for her at the table. Almost instinctively, she looked at her bindings but noted they were not glowing. He laughed. "I won't compel you to sit at a table, Lena."

Irritated at his reaction, she pressed her lips together giving her best deadpan expression she could muster before moving to take the seat. "Thanks," she said sarcastically.

"You're welcome," Ambrose said, matching her energy as he moved to take the seat next to her. "I'm afraid I will need to compel you now though," he leant forward resting his elbows on his knees as he looked intently at her. "This is a security and safety matter and it is something that we do with all new boundlings."

Holding his gaze, Lena understood the seriousness of the situation. "Alright," she said. Unfortunately, her need to make light of serious events decided to kick in. "H- uh... I was going to say 'hit me', but I'm afraid a demon might take that literally. And 'lay it on me' also doesn't feel appropriate."

Ambrose dropped his head into his hands. "You could have just left it at 'alright'," he sighed looking at the floor.

She bit her bottom lip desperately trying not to laugh at the awkwardness she caused. "Right, sorry! Uh... 'compel me'? No, that's worse."

"Oh hell," he said quickly, leaning back in the chair and hanging his head back so he now looked at the ceiling. "You just made it weird."

"I'm sorry!" Lena laughed as she slapped her hands over her mouth. "I'm so sorry!"

Ambrose pinched the bridge of his nose. "It's fine," he said, his voice strained. She sucked in some air before slowly blowing it back out through pursed lips. He raised his head to look at her. "You done?"

She nodded slowly. "Yes," she said finally.

"Good," he leant forward again, shaking his head at her. "Now listen, because there are some things you, or we, need to do." He looked at her for a moment as if expecting her to say something, but she decided it was best to remain silent. He nodded approvingly before continuing. "First, we are going to go by your apartment and pick up whatever you want to keep. Don't worry about furniture as there should be everything you need here. If there is anything you want in particular, I will arrange for it to be collected later on. You will give notice to your landlord, I will give you enough money to pay out the remainder of your lease. Second, you need to go to Marie's and quit."

At the mention of Marie, Lena dropped her gaze, sadness washing over her. Quietly, Ambrose took hold of her hand and squeezed supportively.

"I know this is going to be hard. I can see and feel how much Marie means to you. But we cannot risk exposure. This is a necessary step," he said reassuringly.

She drew in a deep breath. "I know. I do understand. What should

I say to her?"

"It doesn't really matter, as long as you don't tell her the truth. I would recommend you say I offered you a job as my assistant and you accepted. If you need, or want, to work another shift you can, but it would be better to just cut ties now," he gave her a small smile and she knew he was right.

"Does that mean we will be moving from here?" Lena asked.

"No," Ambrose said hesitantly. "We possibly should, but no. I don't think we need to unless people start asking too many questions. It may not be a normal perk these days, but if you say the job comes with lodging then that should suffice. We will have to move eventually once people start realising we don't age, but we have some time before that happens."

The gravity of the situation started to sink in as a heavy pit formed in her stomach. Lena hadn't even thought of that, but it made sense. "Of course," she said, remembering that Ambrose had mentioned centuries earlier. "How old are you?" she asked suddenly.

Ambrose blinked in surprise. "Ah..." he started, "I've forgotten the exact number but, around six hundred years as a demon, give or take a decade. I was close to thirty when I died."

Lena stared at him in disbelief, her eyes wide. "Not the figure I was expecting."

"No other comment?" he asked, raising his brows and smiling warmly.

"Nothing I'm going to say out loud," she said, pressing her lips together.

"Wise choice," he said. "Now..."

"Now, comes the command, right?"

"Yes. Ready? This shouldn't hurt, but it's not a simple command so it may not be exactly comfortable either," he said, squeezing her hand again.

Lena nodded. "I'm ready."

Ambrose took a deep breath and locked his eyes to hers. "Lena, you can never tell anyone about Hell or demons. You can never tell a mortal that you are a demon. You can never tell a mortal about the offer I made to you. You can never bring a mortal to the house or any house in which we might reside. You can never repeat to a mortal any of the things you will learn during your time as a demon. You are here to serve Hell, to serve me, and as such, your priority is to protect our secrets here. If you are ever summoned by a mortal these rules do not apply, but in those instances, you must only present yourself in demon form. You must never let a mortal see you transform. Do you understand?"

Her bindings glowed brighter than before and seemed to almost constrict at his words. There was no pain, but heat spread from her wrists throughout her body. Her head spun and she clutched at the sides of the chair afraid she might fall off. Something within her told her that no matter what, this was not a command that she would ever be able to overcome.

"Whoa," she said, dropping her head into her hands, desperately wishing it not to explode as it throbbed from the instant headache. "Flaming hell that was intense."

"Are you okay?" Ambrose said, rubbing her arm.

Lena tried to nod but the slight movement made her want to hurl. "Yes," she said weakly. "And yes, I understand." She sighed heavily trying to clear her head. "Please make the room stop spinning." Ambrose chuckled at her comment and rose to his feet, walking away. When he came back, he placed a warm hand on her back and held out a glass of water. She took it gratefully and sipped the cool liquid slowly. "Thanks," she muttered. "That was more than a normal command, wasn't it?"

"Yes," he answered, sitting back down. "It's an ancient command passed down for centuries. My sire did it to me, to similar effect. Only natural born demons don't receive it, but they also don't have a human form so rarely venture outside of Hell."

"So, you had a sire?"

Ambrose nodded.

"Did you get along with them?"

"Decidedly not," he sighed. "My sire is not someone you want to meet either. Despite that, it took me almost a century to break from him."

"I'm sorry."

"Thank you, although not necessary," Ambrose said with a smile. "We should get going. Best to get this out of the way so we can focus on the rest of your training."

Lena nodded, forcing air out with puffed cheeks to steady herself. Once she was sure her legs would not give way, she got to her feet and followed him out the door.

CHAPTER TEN

The next few days passed quickly for both Ambrose and Lena as they settled into their new normal. Ambrose had been surprised at how well Lena leaving her old life behind had gone. It had turned out that Marie's niece, Rachel, had been looking for a job, so although Marie was sad to see Lena go, it was fortunate timing.

The apartment had also been as fortuitous. Her landlord had been thinking of selling and thought it would be better to sell vacant rather than with a tenant. Ambrose had paid out the two months' notice on the apartment as Lena packed up some of her personal items. She hadn't been interested in any of the furniture and the landlord had been happy for it to remain. It took a couple of trips, but together they got all of Lena's things up to the manor.

Lena was still struggling with control of her power, but she excelled quickly in other areas of her training. Spell work and rituals she picked up within a day and now if Ambrose was looking for her, he could be certain to find her in the library, pouring over grimoires and ancient scrolls. Her control over summoning and scrying rituals quickly outpaced his own. With only a little over an hour of instruction, she had picked up transporting herself through the fires of Hell.

Although he knew Lena held a warm affection for Marcus, she had started to over-dramatically despair when he would arrive much to his amusement. "Must we destroy more furniture today!" she would cry, throwing herself into a chair.

Marcus would ignore her theatrics for the most part, but would occasionally match her energy, using his own power to pull the chair out from under her. "Less yapping, more zapping."

Ambrose could see that, ultimately, Lena enjoyed her sessions with Marcus. He easily answered any questions she had about how Hell worked, other kinds of demons, and demonic history. Ambrose would answer what he could when they were alone, but Marcus had been born almost fifteen hundred years ago, so his wealth of knowledge was far more encompassing. That and any time he and Lena were alone, they tended to devolve into sessions of kissing and exploration that were rather detrimental to conversation.

They were cautious when Marcus was around, as Ambrose was unsure of what his reaction would be, and they were both still unsure of what to call this attraction between them. Through their bond, he could feel the desire Lena held for him, which only served to heighten his for her, to the point where he now felt addicted to her scent and touch.

When they were alone in the manor, they settled into a routine of keeping within easy reach of each other, moving what they needed between rooms to simply be together. If Ambrose needed to work in his office, Lena would gather some books from the library and curl up in one of his armchairs. If she wanted to test some spells in the altar room, he took the opportunity to sort items within that he had allowed to clutter the corners. He had been surprised at how much peace and joy Lena had brought to his life. Things he hadn't realised he had been missing until now. He had taken to calling her 'dove' in endearment of this quality.

The nights, however, were difficult. Lena was still plagued by dreams as she rested. Memories of not just her sacrifice, but her mother and some of her foster placements had resurfaced. She had tried to return to her room one night, but the screams that echoed through the house brought that to a swift end. Ambrose then insisted she sleep within his room, where he could watch over her as needed. She had not protested against it, but they agreed that he would only compel her to sleep if it looked like she was about to destroy the bed in her sleep. Otherwise, they thought it would be best for her to sort through her dreams as they came. Ambrose would sit close by to soothe and comfort her as needed. He was thankful that for now he had not been summoned away from her, afraid of what would happen if she woke up alone.

One night, Lena had been tossing and turning in the bed, distress clear on her face, but, as they had agreed, Ambrose hung back to see if she could sort her way through it without his help. Suddenly, she had sat bolt upright, screaming and with tears streaming down her cheeks. He jumped up from the armchair and started to run towards her when flames covered her body and she disappeared.

"Shit!" he cursed. She had yet to transform into her demonic form so she couldn't have been summoned, if she was going to be subject to summonings at all. He closed his eyes, trying to find her through their bond, when he heard her flame back behind him. Spinning on his heel, he found her standing in front of the fire, dripping wet, her eyes wide in shock, thunder in their depths.

"The *fuck* was that?" she cried, flinging some water off her hands.

"Where did you go?" he asked, quickly racing to the bathroom to grab a towel.

Lena grabbed the towel from him, wrapping it around her shoulders. "The hell should I know?" she said, her expression that of pure annoyance. "Middle of the ocean for all I can tell. Pretty sure I saw a shark."

She stormed to the bathroom as he grabbed another towel to pat away at the puddle she had left on the floor.

"Sorry about that," Lena said softly as she returned from the bathroom, having changed into dry clothes and patting her hair with the towel.

"It's fine," he replied. He stood and looked at her. "Are you okay?"

"I would think you'd be sick of asking me that by now," she said sitting on the edge of the bed.

Ambrose smiled sympathetically at her as he walked over to sit next to her. He wrapped his arms around her waist, pulling her closer to him and letting her rest her head on his shoulder. "What happened tonight?" he asked, rubbing his hand over her hip.

Lena sighed heavily, closing her eyes. "I saw my mother," she started. "I had tried to run away one day, but the police picked me up and took me back before I could get far enough away. She beat me black and blue over that. Broke a couple of ribs, if I remember correctly. Guess I was trying to run away again."

"Not from me, I hope," he teased, pinching her side. She twisted in his arms with a small laugh, before pulling her legs up to hang them over his lap, turning her body towards his so she could wrap her own arms around his waist. They had held each other like this before and he loved it, placing his hand on her thigh and resting his chin atop her head.

"Not from you," Lena sighed, letting her body relax into his. "That was not a new dream, but it's not one I've had in a long time." Her voice was barely louder than a whisper and was mixed with sorrow and fear. "I know Marcus said I would likely see, or relive, moments from my life, but I wasn't expecting them to be so vivid."

Ambrose rubbed his hand along her thigh comfortingly. "My father used to beat me as a child. His way of toughening me up," he said softly. Lena raised her head at his statement, shock evident in her eyes. "It's okay," he assured her, placing his hand on her head to bring it back to his chest. "It was a very long time ago and I am very much over it now. I'm telling you this, because I've been where you are now. I never really had nightmares about my father when I was alive, not that I can remember anyway, but I do remember suddenly having dreams about him after I became a demon. It's difficult, but it's all part of the process of becoming a demon. You need to come to terms with your life, accept it and desensitise yourself to it. That helps you to come to terms with what happens in Hell."

Lena was silent, softly running her fingers over his arm. "When will I go to Hell?" she asked finally.

"Today actually," he replied. "You've made a lot of progress lately. We need to start the process of finding your design."

"My design?"

"Your purpose or what you do for Hell. The Repository has all of the information you will need to find it and is also where you can test things out," he said, pulling her closer to him. "I would have liked to keep you away from there longer, but there are others that know of your existence now, so there shouldn't be any harm in taking you there today if you like."

"What do you mean by others?" Lena asked, lifting her head again.

"Other demons. Marcus and I have kept you an express secret, but there are demons who keep track of rebirths so word inevitably gets around." Ambrose paused for a moment taking a deep breath. "Due to the relationship I had with my sire, I am not an overly powerful demon. I am by no means weak, and I have built a reputation which protects me for the most part. That said... I cannot defy the order of Hell. In time, you will be tested within the pits, against other demons, to determine the extent of your powers. If you are very powerful, which with lightning manifestation you should be, you will be afforded great respect, but additionally that extends to the demon you are bound to. I am happy with what standing I have, but there will always be some that wish to increase theirs."

"You said that some may try to take me from you?"

He nodded. "That's why I've kept you away from Hell for the moment. Letting our bond settle and strengthen makes it harder for demons to take you. They could literally override my binding with theirs. The longer you are bound to me, the less likely they would be successful. You can always choose to go to another demon and then it doesn't matter how long we've been bound, your choice overrides."

"But it takes more than my choice to break from the bond?" Lena huffed but nestled her head into the crook of his neck. "You demons sure make things confusing."

A soft chuckle rose within his chest as Ambrose contracted his arms around her, pulling her closer, eliminating all space between their bodies. "You are not wrong there."

Lena sighed, running her hand over his chest. He welcomed the warmth that spread across his skin under her touch, closing his eyes and leaning his head against hers.

"You said that your bond with your sire was... rocky," she said, her warm breath sending shivers across his skin. He simply murmured in affirmation. "So why didn't you choose another demon to bind to? Like Marcus?"

Ambrose smiled ruefully, rubbing his hand up and down along her spine. "I didn't know Marcus back then, and I decided it wasn't worth the risk to try someone else. Better the devil you know." Lena laughed softly, tracing circles with her fingers over his chest. "And my sire had... *has* great power, and is not afraid to use it. No one would have dared take a boundling from him." He paused for a moment, contemplating if he should ask the question that just invaded his mind, not entirely sure he wanted to know the answer. "Would you..." he started with a sigh, "do you think you would consider binding to someone else?" He could feel her smile into his neck.

"Better the devil you know," she teased. Ambrose surprised himself with a snort which caused Lena great amusement, laughing at his reaction. With a wicked grin, he tickled her sides, keeping her body pinned to his so she couldn't escape him. "Stop!" she cried, a wide smile plastered across her face, desperately trying to get her breath in between fits of laughter. "Ah, stop! No! I'm not choosing someone else!"

Letting up, he placed a soft kiss on her forehead as she cupped her hand to his cheek. Her eyes sparkled with joy and he wanted to get lost in their grey depths, content in that moment to take in all of her beauty.

Lena sighed heavily before breaking their gaze and dropping her eyes to her hand now on his arm. "I have never felt like I belonged anywhere," she said, her tone shifting to one of solemn thought. "My mother didn't want me. My foster placements seemed like they couldn't get rid of me fast enough. Until I came to this town, I always felt like I was imposing on everyone. Coming here and getting my own place I didn't have to worry about any else. I only had to worry about myself."

He watched her face as a range of emotions mixed over her features.

"I... I don't feel that way with you," she said leaning her head into his shoulder again. "I don't feel like a burden or like I'm not wanted. I feel comfortable and safe, and as long as you are happy for me to be here, I plan on staying."

Silence fell over them as Ambrose simply held her, enjoying the feel of her body against his, breathing in her scent of citrus, now mixed with a hint of sea water. Nothing else needed to be said for now. Perhaps later, but not now. After a moment she lifted her head to look at him, her eyes darkening with desire.

"Kiss me," she requested softly.

He gladly obeyed, moving his hand from her thigh to cup her cheek, and lowered his lips to hers. They met slowly at first with soft, warm and comforting kisses, simply enjoying the feel of the other. Lena moved her hand to his chest, bunching his shirt within her grip, pulling at the fabric, encouraging him to deepen the kiss. Hungrily, he crushed his mouth to hers, almost desperately, wanting to taste every part of her.

Pulling her atop his lap, Lena straddled his hips, wrapping her arms around his shoulders. Ambrose pinned her body to his with one arm, placing his free hand on the back of her head, burying his fingers into her hair. A primal need hardened his body as Lena moaned into his mouth. Pressing his tongue to her lips, a wave of pleasure washed over him as she responded so readily, parting them to allow his tongue to explore the warmth of her mouth. Their tongues met, dancing with the other, in a frenzied passion.

Unsatisfied with their position, he flipped Lena onto the mattress underneath him, smiling as she cried out with surprise at his suddenness. He nuzzled at her neck, as his hands ran down the length of her body, cupping the roundness of her bottom and pulling her hips up against his. She tangled her hands through his hair, sighing with pleasure as he kissed and nibbled along her jaw. Her legs wrapped around his waist, pulling him to her. He felt her body shiver beneath him, exciting his desire for her further. Fully aware, she would be able to feel the hardened length of him, he pressed his hips forward, pushing hers into the mattress, silently cursing the barrier of their clothing between them.

Lena's soft moans beside his ear fuelled him as he cupped the mound of one her breasts, running his thumb over the hard peak of her nipple underneath her shirt. Despite the fabric, he moved his head to capture the other between his teeth, nibbling softly as she dug her nails into his shoulders. He wanted more, he needed more, as he slipped his free hand between them. She only wore her shirt and panties when she slept, so he easily gained access to the warmth of her core as he pushed the fabric aside. His fingers found their mark and he growled with satisfaction noting that her entrance was already slick with her desire.

"Ambrose," Lena moaned, her nails almost painfully ripping at his shirt. His mind went blank at the sound of his name pouring from her lips like a sensual whisper. All that existed to him now was her, and her pleasure.

Slipping a finger within her wet channel, her warmth and silkiness drew him in. As he sought to explore her depth, he couldn't deny the anticipation now building within his gut. She had cried out, almost in surprise, when his finger had entered her, something he would usually have put to the initial sensation of something going inside her, but it caused him to pause. Feelings of hesitation radiated through their bond. Nerves and anxiety mixed with her desire, but he felt them all the same. She had just dreamt of her mother, a mother who made her feel lesser than and unwanted. He couldn't fight the pit in his stomach now forming that he had been convenient to make her forget those feelings.

Ambrose squeezed his eyes shut, taking a deep breath to steady himself as he withdrew his hand and lifted his head to look at Lena. Her face was flushed and her eyes were filled with confusion as she stared at him.

"Ambrose?" she queried. "Is something wrong?"

His stomach plummeted knowing what he was about to say could go very badly. "No, nothing is wrong as such. I just..." he hesitated for a moment and sighed before continuing. "I don't want to rush into anything with you."

Hurt spread across her features and Ambrose cursed his lack of eloquence, wanting to take it back. It took everything in him to push himself off her, sitting back on the mattress, hating himself for causing her pain. Lena pushed herself up onto the bed, resting her back against the headboard and hugging her knees to her chest. He felt more like a demon that he had ever before, seeing how she shrank from him now.

"What did I do wrong?" she asked meekly.

"Nothing," he said panicked, looking at her desperately pleading with her to believe him. "Lena, you did nothing wrong. I'm just afraid that this is a reaction to your dream. I want you, Lena. Desperately, I want you. But I don't want you to do something you might regret in the morning."

Lena looked down at the mattress. "What makes you think I would regret it?"

He shook his head slowly. "You might not. But if you did, I would never forgive myself."

They fell into an uncomfortable silence, as Ambrose felt Lena withdrawing further from him, guilt pervading every part of his body. He sighed heavily before finally speaking.

"Lena, I'm sorry," he said softly. He looked at her, regretting it instantly as he saw tears beginning to form in her eyes. He needed to get out of there. Put some distance between them so he could breathe. So he could figure out what to say. "I- I have to leave for a little bit. I need to sort some things before I take you to Hell."

"It's fine. Go," she said sharply.

Ambrose nodded as he got to his feet. "We'll talk more in the morning."

"Sure," Lena sighed as she pulled the covers over her and turned her back to him.

Fuck, he thought to himself as he ran his hand through his hair, summoning his flames around and letting the process draw out his demonic form.

CHAPTER ELEVEN

Lena lay in the bed for a while after Ambrose had left. This was the first time she had been alone in the manor since she became a demon. It suddenly felt huge once she could no longer feel the warmth that generally radiated from him within the room.

Turning onto her back she looked up into the canopy above her and sighed in annoyance. Giving up on the idea of getting anymore sleep, she pushed her body up to sit in the bed. She took a deep breath before throwing her legs over the side and getting to her feet. With no conscious intent, she pulled on some leggings then made her way to the kitchen and began to clean, regardless of the counters and floors already sparkling shine. Despite the fact she had been forced on many occasions to clean her foster homes from top to bottom, she found cleaning soothing and a calming way to silently seethe away her anger.

As she walked into the kitchen, she felt a deep sense of loneliness wash over her. She had just been rejected by the man she felt so incredibly drawn to, in a way that no man had ever made her feel before. Replaying moments of the last few days, she analysed their stolen kisses when Marcus' back was turned and their less secretive embraces when they were alone. Did Ambrose really reject her or was there another reasonable excuse for his hesitation? She began to wash down the island counter, but her movements were slow and lethargic, as if she was going through the motions without really being present.

Logically, she understood why Ambrose had pulled away. They had both shared something deeply personal about themselves and she knew she had been feeling vulnerable in that moment. Emotionally, she wanted to kiss him, to touch him, to feel him against her, desperate to feel needed and wanted by him. His seeming rejection of her hurt, creating a deep pit of longing within her core. But more than anything, she hated how angry she felt that he'd left.

Filling the sink, the sound of the water filled the silence of the room, but it only made her feel more alone. She had opened her body and soul to him, feeling safe within his arms, hoping that he would reciprocate her feelings. The rejection had not been outright, but seemingly after he had toyed with her like some twisted game in which only he understood the rules. She had never been like that with another man. Of course, she'd been nervous, she was still a virgin after all. Despite all efforts, advancements and intentions of others, she had managed to keep that piece of herself. Ambrose had no way of knowing of course, but his pulling away made her feel like she wasn't good enough, like she was unwanted. Like something was wrong with her.

Rejection was the staple of her history. Constantly moving from one family to the other with only a trash bag to carry what little possessions she had. Scraps of clothes, a small necklace her mother had given her and a letter her father had written before he died. She had lost the necklace – although she had always suspected it had been stolen by her foster placement at the time – two years before she aged out of care. She had read her father's letter, but it always caused her such pain she couldn't bring herself to look at it too often. Everyone had left her. Every placement, every friend, every other child she had met in the system had left. Even her own parents. She couldn't shake the feeling that she was unlovable, that no one would ever want her in the way she needed. She wanted to scream, to let out all the hurt and pain that was inside her, but she couldn't even summon the energy for that.

Instead, Lena sighed in frustration, throwing her cloth onto the tap and pulling out the plug from the sink. Watching as the water swirled around the sink in its vortex, emptying into the pipes, she tried to imagine that her anger was flowing with it. Mentally pouring her emotional turmoil into the sink, a singular tear fell from her eye creating a trail down her cheek.

A prickling feeling began to crawl over her skin as the salt from the sea water started to pull all moisture from her. She grabbed a cereal bar from the pantry which she munched on as she headed back up to

Ambrose's room. Briefly contemplating if she should instead go to her room, she reasoned that in terms of taking a shower, she had moved all of her soaps and lotions to his bathroom so it didn't make much sense to use the other one.

Stripping off her clothes, she ran the shower as hot as she could manage. She dimly noticed that it didn't seem to matter anymore how hot she ran the water, but she found the temperature she used to like when she was alive. Stepping into the water, she let the heat run over her body, soaking into her skin and muscles. Sighing with contentment, she lifted her face into the stream, welcoming the cleansing feeling it gave her. After washing her face, she kept her shoulders and back within the water and stared at the exposed pipework running up the wall to the shower head above her.

Tilting her head slightly, she tried to recall her limited knowledge of high school science when they studied electrical circuits. It occurred to her in that moment, that electricity flows through wires like water flows through pipes. If the pipe is narrowed, the flow is concentrated and with enough pressure the stream from the end of the pipe increases in range and force. Widen the pipe and you can increase the pressure to get the same force, but the range is affected by the less concentrated exit. The water would spray out creating more coverage and where it landed would be less predictable.

Ambrose and Marcus had been trying to get her to increase the pressure of her power, growing it inside her, like they do for their power. But like water, this made it uncontrollable. Looking at her hands, Lena focused on them as the ends of the circuit. Keeping them close together made a predictable circuit, but even a predictable circuit could be thrown off by too much electrical current being forced through. Maybe, rather than trying to hold on to the lightning and building on it, she needed to let it out in small bursts, keeping the pressure within her lower, and hopefully, more manageable.

Taking a deep breath, Lena reached inside herself and with her mind pulled a small spark of lightning to the surface, instantly releasing it rather than trying to hold on. The spark shot across her hands, pride swelling within her chest, before it travelled up her arms and over her body, painfully electrocuting her. The shock pulled an intense bolt from her core, covering her body and launching at the shower head exploding it and the majority of the pipes.

"Oh shit- fuck- dammit- flaming- *FUCK!*"

As she screamed, her body slammed into the bottom of the tub, a loud crack echoing through the bathroom as her head collided with the rolled rim. Squeezing her eyes shut as her vision started to blur like the static of an old out of tune television, she barely noted as the water splashing over her increased in coverage. With what little part of her brain that was still functioning, she assumed she had managed to destroy the shower head completely, causing the water to simply spray randomly throughout the room. With a groan, she forced one of her eyes open trying to locate the taps, but realised she wasn't able to move her body to reach them anyway.

"Shit," she sighed in defeat.

Well done...

Rolling her eyes, Lena tried to block out the voice. She didn't need her own mind berating her at a time like this.

"Lena?"

Her eyebrows shot up in shock. "Oh no... Marcus?"

"Lena!" he shouted, his voice getting closer.

"Wait! Marcus, don't come—" The door to the bathroom flew open and Lena could just make out the cambion's frame from the corner of her eye. "In... too late..." she sighed.

Marcus' hand shot up to cover his eyes, although his body seemed frozen in place in the doorway. "I am *so* sorry," he cried, flailing his other hand in front of him trying to find the door handle without his vision.

"It's fine," Lena said, a hint of laughter in her voice. "You might as well help me. I can't feel, or move, my limbs at the moment."

"Uh..."

She smiled at his hesitation. "Take a step forward then two steps to your left. Grab a towel and hold it in front of you. Then you can place it over me without looking at me. But first, *please*, turn the water off."

Marcus shuffled as instructed and she sighed in relief as the water finally stopped beating down on her body. He laid the towel over her body, and despite that it was already soaked from the rainstorm she had caused, she was glad for the feel of it.

"What happened?" he asked, looking around the room as he went to gather more towels. She turned her gaze as best she could without the full use of her neck. The mirror had been shattered and she could hear the crush of the shards under Marcus' feet as he crossed the floor. The shower curtain ripped from the rail, now lay half in the bath underneath her and half blown towards the sink. Some tiles that had been behind the pipework had suffered a similar fate to the mirror, cracks evident across their cream surface.

"You know, we really need to put power protections in all the rooms at this point," Lena said with slight amusement at the destruction she had caused.

"Please don't tell me you were practicing your powers in the bath."

"Shower actually."

"Lena..." Marcus sighed in exasperation.

"What?" she replied innocently, raising her eyebrows. At least she still had control of her facial features. "It's not like I did this on purpose. Didn't occur to me that just because my power manifests as electric lightning that it would actually behave like electricity. I seriously can't move my body."

"You have just electrocuted yourself," Marcus returned to the side of the bath with more towels, although all were as thoroughly soaked as the one already covering her. "Your body has gone into shut down. It should pass."

"Should?"

"Well, I've never known anyone to do this to themselves so... unclear."

Lena sighed as Marcus attempted to tuck another towel around her body. "Fair enough." She winced as he brushed a hand past her neck. "I hit my head pretty hard."

"I'll have a look once I get you out of the bath," he said before standing up. "Hang on, I'll just grab some dry towels from your room."

"I assure you, I am not going anywhere."

Marcus rolled his eyes then turned on his heel and walked out the door. Lena kept track of him as best she could from her peripheral but she could barely see the door so lost sight of him quickly. She smirked to herself thinking that at least with a power blast in the bathroom, she hadn't set anything on fire. Although, she doubted that Ambrose would see it like that. This was going to be interesting to explain.

She heard Marcus come back into the bedroom, but he seemed to pause just outside of the bathroom. "If I laid the towels on the bed, do you think you could flame over to it?" his voice came through the doorway.

"Unfortunately, no," she called back. "I've already tried."

"Okay. Uh... okay, I'll get you out first," he said walking back into the door frame and placing the dry towels on a chair next to it in the bedroom, "then try to swap the wet towels for the dry ones." He walked back to the bathtub and crouched down beside it. "Apologies in advance, if I see or touch anything I shouldn't."

Lena chuckled slightly as Marcus hooked an arm under her knees and behind her shoulders. "You know for demons, you and Ambrose are politer than some humans."

"I'll try not to take offence at that," he smiled teasingly as he shifted his feet slightly to gain better leverage. "Ready?"

"Go on," she groaned, preparing for the possibility of pain.

Marcus began to lift her up and had almost stood fully when flames appeared in the doorway. Lena tried to look towards it but without the use of her neck could only make out the general shape of the figure who now stood between them and the bedroom.

"What is going on?"

Marcus startled and his arms flew to his sides, dropping Lena back into the tub. "Ambrose! Hey, uh..." he turned quickly towards the door frame as she cried out at the fresh jolt of pain that rocked through her body. At least the towels had cushioned her lower body a bit but her head bounced off the rim, increasing her headache tenfold.

"Jesus Christ, Marcus!" she shouted. "Did you have to fucking drop me?"

"Shit! Sorry!" He turned back towards her and lunged to pick her back up.

"Don't touch her!" Ambrose roared, stepping forward and grabbing Marcus' upper arm pulling him away from the bath. Lena could now see his features, despite the white lights that danced across the edges of her vision. She had never seen him so angry and for the first time since she met him, she felt truly afraid of him. He was in human form, his eyes dark pools that made her skin shiver and a cold sweat break out across her forehead. She could only imagine what the scene looked like to him, flaming in to see Marcus holding her rather intimately, and she couldn't blame him for that.

"Ambrose, wait, let me explain," Marcus cried, holding up his hands and taking a step back.

"Get out," her sire growled, his voice deathly quiet as he stared at his friend.

Lena swallowed before speaking. "Ambrose, I appreciate this is an awkward situation to walk into, but I can't move my body." His gaze shot to her, surprise mixing with the anger. "So could someone, I honestly don't care who right now, get me out of the tub. It is not as comfortable as it looks."

"What?" Concern suddenly washing over his features, softening his gaze, Ambrose immediately crouched down and lifted her into his arms effortlessly. "Why can't you move?"

She sighed immediately, forgetting her fear as she felt warm and secure in his arms. "Can I explain later please?" she said breathing in his scent as he manoeuvred her head onto his shoulder. "I really don't want to have this conversation whilst only covered by a towel."

"Wait," Ambrose said as he now took a moment to look around them. "What happened to my bathroom?"

"Um... it was an accident," she said sheepishly.

"An accident?" He strode out of the bathroom heading towards the bed. Marcus followed picking up the dry towels which he hurriedly flung over the bed before Ambrose placed her down on the mattress. With purposeful movements, Ambrose deftly wrapped the warm dry towels around her, casting aside the wet ones, never exposing her body. "What the hell did you do to my bathroom?"

"Ah..." she contemplated her fate, trying to focus on the softness of the mattress under her. "I figured out my power control."

"At the expense of my bathroom?"

"Well... yeah."

Ambrose pinched the bridge of his nose for a moment taking a long steadying breath before he pulled the covers over her. "Lena... please elaborate," he sighed.

"Um... well... I was in the shower and I thought to myself that electricity is kind of like water."

"Explain."

"You know, my head just slammed into the side of the tub twice in the last ten minutes or so. It's throbbing," she shut her eyes as if to drive home her point. Ambrose looked at Marcus who immediately turned on his heel and left the room. In his absence, Ambrose checked over her body, feeling along her arms and legs checking for anything potentially broken. Gently, he felt around her neck, his eyes shut, concentrating on what his fingers could feel. Lena winced every now and then as small shoots of pain sprang from his touch, but she kept her eyes locked on his face, trying to determine what he was feeling.

"Ambrose..." she started but he shook his head.

"Shh, not now," he soothed, pulling his hands away and opening his eyes to look at her. "We'll talk later."

Marcus returned with a cup of tea, in which a mix of feverfew, butterbur and peppermint were steeping. Ambrose took the cup and gently lifted Lena up so she could sip gingerly at the tea. The herbs took a little longer than aspirin used to but slowly the throbbing in her head subsided and she sighed with relief.

"So?" Ambrose asked pointedly.

"So," she started to explain, "I was thinking about how water is like the electric charge. Pressure is voltage. And flow is the current. And I figured that if I am holding on to the charge that is increasing the pressure and as such, I am increasing the voltage. So, when I then let the charge flow, the current comes out a little overpowered. But if I release in small bursts, then the pressure remains low and the current is controllable."

"And my bathroom was the test subject?" Ambrose said, raising his eyebrows at her.

"Ah... note I said I figured this out in the shower."

"Oh hell..." he ran his hand through his hair as he stared at her in disbelief. "Lena, you do know that water and electricity generally don't mix well."

"Yeah, I know. Figured that out real quick," she retorted, rolling her eyes. "It's not funny Marcus!"

The cambion, who had been silently chuckling in the corner of the room, clamped his hand over his mouth and took a few deep breaths to steady himself.

"Why are you here anyway?" Lena asked.

Marcus shrugged despite the dark look her sire shot his way. "Ambrose asked me to hide out in his office whilst he was away, to make sure you were alright by yourself. Looks like he made the right call," he said with a smile, his gaze moving between them. "Well, I'm going to leave you to it. I don't think today is a day for training anyway." And with that he flamed out.

Ambrose sighed before turning back to her and slowly extracted one of her arms from under the covers and towels. "Are you okay?" he asked as he started to rub her hand and arm in circular motions.

Lena sighed at his touch, warmth spreading from where his fingers met her skin. "I'm only just starting to feel my fingers again, so... I will get back to you on that." She paused briefly. "Thank you."

"For what?"

"For still caring enough to ask Marcus to look after me."

"I never stopped caring, Lena."

Ambrose carried out his work silently as he massaged her limbs trying to ease the pins and needles that painfully indicated the return of sensation to her body. Slowly, she tested her ability to move and found she was able to open and close her hands and curl her toes. He initially helped her move her legs and arms until enough strength returned for her to move them on her own.

All the while, Lena kept at least one towel wrapped tightly around her body. She wanted to say so much to him. To tell him she was sorry for getting upset, but at the same time she didn't feel like she needed to apologise. The care he directed towards her now, made her question the need for her concerns this morning. He was so gentle and cautious with his movements, apologising quickly if anything caused her pain. She wanted to pull him into her arms, to feel his warmth against her, to press her lips to his and never let go. She wanted him to want her in the same way.

Gently she twisted her hand and caught hold of his wrist. His eyes shot to hers, their hazel depths earnestly searching her face. Slowly he leant forward and pressed a gentle kiss to her head. Lena closed her eyes and sighed almost in relief that he was so close. Ambrose placed his hands either side of her face and lifted her chin up before brushing his lips over hers. Her desire for him rekindled brighter than ever.

"I'm sorry," he said softly against her mouth. "I'm sorry I hurt you this morning." He pulled her into his arms, pressing their bodies together. Still shaky, she wrapped her arms around his waist and buried her face into his neck. Ambrose sighed against her, the tension she could feel in body easing as he did so. She felt his breath against her ear, her skin shivering with desire. "You are mine," he whispered into her ear. Lena gasped silently at the declaration and her arms contracted around him, her stomach tightening in anticipation. "I don't care what I said or did this morning, you are mine. And I am yours. And I will spend eternity making sure you, and everyone else, knows that."

She didn't say anything. She couldn't say anything. She simply pressed her face into him, squeezing her eyes tightly shut to prevent the flood of tears that now threatened to flow. Revelling in his warmth and strength, she stayed still within his arms, refusing to be the first to break the embrace. Ambrose seemed like minded in that regard, his arms tightening around her back. Silently they stayed like that until the sun started to peek through the edges of the curtains.

CHAPTER TWELVE

Ambrose had never felt such jealousy as he did when he saw Lena in Marcus' arms. Looking back, he recognised he had jumped to a conclusion that the scene did not ultimately warrant. But he had felt her pain through their bond and on his return his fear mixed with shocked anger had taken over his rational thought. He knew in that moment, as far as he was able to, he would never let another man, demon or otherwise, touch Lena. She was his, she was meant to be his, and likewise, he would give everything he was to her.

It took everything in him to let go of her earlier, but he kept his gaze on her now as she slowly walked around the room testing out the stability of her legs. He had helped her to get dressed at her request, before aiding her to her feet.

"I think," Lena said cautiously as she turned on the spot, "that everything is working again. Hopefully, no lasting effects." She beamed at him, her beauty catching him once again off guard.

"Promise me, you won't try using your power in the shower again," he sighed with a soft smile on his lips.

"No problem," she said, poking her tongue at him. "My fear now is getting caught in the rain."

Ambrose laughed and got to his feet. "As long as you don't take any more impromptu visits to the ocean you should be okay."

"Ha! You're hilarious," she scoffed.

"Alright, show me what you can do," he said, putting his hands in his pockets. "Spark it up."

Lena raised her eyebrows in surprise. "Are you joking?"

"Nope," he shook his head. "You said you figured it out. Show me."

With a sigh, she rolled her shoulders, small clicks coming from her back and neck. "Okay," she said softly. Closing her eyes, she held her hands in front of her chest and a small spark shot between her hands. She took a deep breath and with her exhale the spark grew and maintained a steady arc between her hands. Grinning at her accomplishment, Lena opened her eyes and looked at her power. The red glow of the lightning lit up her features and Ambrose was mesmerised by her. He smiled with pride and watched silently as she increased the space between her hands lengthening the arc until it started to crackle and spark in various directions. When the sparks looked like they were going to connect with other objects she retracted her hands reducing the spark to a more controllable level. Slowly she placed her palms together, extinguishing it completely.

"Not bad," he said, walking over to her. "Target practice is next."

Lena laughed. "Not today though, right? I may be standing, but I'm not entirely steady."

Ambrose nodded in answer and pulled her into his arms, resting his chin atop her head. "Not today, my dove. We go to Hell today." He gave her a tight squeeze before letting go. "Get some shoes on and we'll head down. I'll transport us as you don't know where to go yet." He watched as she walked over to the chair and pulled her boots out from under it. "By the way, have you noticed that your bindings have grown?"

"What?" her back straightened and she looked at her arms. She had pulled on a tank top so her arms were fully exposed. She traced her fingers up the black marks which used to stop within the crook of her elbow. Now, they snaked halfway up her biceps. "No, I didn't. Are they meant to?"

He shrugged. "Not generally so noticeably, but yes. Whilst you are bound, they may grow in response to your growing power, compensating to keep you bound. For peace of mind," he said quickly as she looked at him curiously, "it's not something I am doing. It's a natural process of your transformation."

"Did yours grow?" she asked, returning her gaze to her arms and continuing her inspection.

"Yes," he nodded. "By the time I broke, my bindings covered my arms and shoulders. It will be worth keeping track of how quickly they are growing."

"Right," she whispered, before she finished putting her boots on. Getting to her feet she made to grab a cardigan.

"No," Ambrose said quickly, shaking his head. "You need to keep your bindings exposed. Only demons are allowed in Hell and until you transform, your bindings are the only indication of what you are."

Lena had startled at his abruptness, but let her hand drop to her side. She walked back to him and Ambrose held out his hand for hers. Interlacing their fingers, he caught hold of her chin and pressed a tender kiss to her lips.

"The journey will make me transform, but hold on. Ready?" he asked looking into her eyes. Lena nodded, never looking away as he gathered the flames around them and directed them to Hell.

Heat and the smell of sulphur and brimstone bore down on them as they appeared within an empty cavern carved out of black stone. Lena coughed slightly, letting go of Ambrose's hand and covering her nose. He smiled, his demonic fangs poking through his lips slightly.

"You'll get used to that," he said softly.

"Geez, I forgot how tall you are as a demon," she coughed, craning her neck to look up at him. "Like, you're already a foot taller than me as a human, but this is ridiculous."

Ambrose laughed and placed a hand on her lower back, gently directing her along a corridor. "I'll give you a little tour before we head to the Repository. Obviously, Hell is a massive place so we won't be able to see everything today, but you shouldn't need to venture out of this area too much for now."

"I think the smell is worse this way," she gagged, scrunching her nose against it.

"More than likely. As I said, you get used to it."

They headed down the corridor before it opened up into a larger cavern. The walls were the same red and black rock, however red dust was scattered across the floor, piling in some areas and disturbed by footfalls in others. Lines of lava snaked through the rock, dimly illuminating the rough surfaces with its golden-red glow. There were a number of other demons within the room and Ambrose could feel the tension rising in Lena's body. He kept his hand reassuringly on her back, pushing her forward.

Some of the demons looked at them as they entered, but then turned back to their companions, continuing their conversations with little care.

Two smiled at them and started to make their way over.

The first was a male demon with dark red skin covered with faded tattoos across his shoulders, chest and hips. Two black and red bat-like wings hung casually from his back, the tips dragging on the ground behind him. Four red horns protruded from his shaved head curling towards the nape of his neck with a simple elegance. His black robe draped loosely over his shoulders, just barely touching the tops of his boots.

In contrast, his female companion had pale red skin, tinted with undertones of grey. Two black horns sat above her temples rising up over her head. A trail of smaller horns sprung from the crown of her head to halfway down her spine, mostly covered by her long black hair that hung loose around her shoulders. Instead of feet she had hooves that poked through from beneath her skirt as she walked.

"Ambrose!" the male cried, stepping forward and shaking his hand.

"Xavier," he nodded. "Pasha," he acknowledged the female demon who stopped just behind the winged demon.

"Who is this?" Pasha asked softly, completely ignoring Ambrose.

"This is Lena," Ambrose said, instinctively stepping closer to her. "My new boundling."

"I heard you had gotten one," Xavier said, turning his gaze to Lena. "Hello, my dear. Ambrose has certainly done his best to keep you a secret, but there are many secrets in Hell and almost all of them are known to someone," he smiled at her in amusement, taking her hand in his and kissing her knuckles. Ambrose swallowed his annoyance at the gesture.

"Are all demons such gentlemen?" Lena smirked, raising a brow.

"Most of the older ones are," Pasha answered, returning the smirk with her own. "Remnants of humanity that manage to cross the divide between life and death. Is this your first time in Hell?"

Lena nodded. "It is."

"How long have you been a demon now?" Pasha asked.

"Uh... almost two weeks," she replied.

"And yet to transform, I see," Xavier exclaimed. "My, my, could our Ambrose have found a boundling of greater power than him?"

"Don't tease, Xavier. Ambrose has served you your own arse a number of times within the pits," Pasha sighed, rolling her eyes in annoyance. Unlike some demons, Pasha had kept the white of her eyes, but her irises were enlarged and a deep, striking black.

"What is two weeks long?" Lena asked, looking up at Ambrose.

"Weakling demons would have transformed by now," Xavier answered. "Average transform within three weeks. Rarely do transformations take more than four."

"The last demon who took longer than four weeks was Amicus. He's now an apprentice under Abraxas, a lord within Lucifer's inner circle," Pasha explained further.

"And it was nearly four hundred years ago he became a demon," said Xavier.

Ambrose sighed. He liked Xavier and Pasha well enough but they knew how to command a conversation. "I'm taking Lena to the Repository," he interjected.

"Ah, time to find your design then," Xavier cried excitedly, his red eyes brightening at the idea.

"I'm still unclear on what that is," Lena said, shifting on her feet and crossing her arms in front of her chest.

"Think of it as a job," Pasha replied. Xavier started to speak but Pasha grabbed his arm, silencing him. "Your sire will explain it further to you. It's not our place," she said pointedly, staring at her companion who merely nodded at her instruction.

"What do you do?" Lena asked.

"I work within the nurseries," Pasha answered. "Natural born demons need someone to look after them whilst they grow. Xavier is a record keeper. You'll find a number of things he has written within the Repository."

"To which we must be getting," Ambrose interrupted, his patience exhausted. "Until next time," he said, placing his hand on Lena's back and guiding her towards a passage on the other side of the cavern.

"I hope to see you again Lena!" Xavier called after them. Pasha shook her head at him before practically dragging him in the other direction.

Once they were in the corridor, Ambrose took a deep breath, calming his mind.

"Well, they seem nice," Lena said, shooting him a knowing glance. He pressed his lips together and looked ahead of them.

"Don't trust Xavier," he cautioned. "He always has an angle and writes everything down, so don't tell him anything you don't want to be forever recorded. Pasha is alright, I think. She and Xavier are usually together, but otherwise she likes to keep to herself so I don't know much about her."

Lena nodded, starting to skip alongside him as she tried to keep up with his long strides. Ambrose noted her efforts and slowed down, a small smile on his lips.

"Sorry," he said softly, rubbing his thumb across her back. They rounded a corner and came to stand in front of two large black doors. "If you don't mind, we'll skip the tour today. The sooner I can get you back to the manor the better." Stepping forward he pushed open the doors for her and showed her inside.

Lena smiled, her grey eyes bright with amusement. "Fine by me," she said softly, trailing her fingers across his stomach as she walked past him.

"Hm, you're going to get me into trouble one day," he growled, following close behind her.

"What," she said, turning back to look at him, "do demons not have relationships?"

Ambrose smiled at her. "They do," he replied. "Some have very long lasting and stable relationships. But for their own safety, they don't usually display them publicly, lest someone else use it against them. And at any given moment, I want to push you up against a wall." He couldn't help the sense of satisfaction he got as he saw her blush at his comment.

"Well, then, we could get in trouble together," Lena sighed, desire filling her eyes.

With a growl, he caught her waist and pulled her towards him, claiming her mouth with his. Due to his increased height he had to bend at the knees to accommodate her. His other hand snaked behind her neck, entangling in her hair as if to pull her closer. He drank in her citrus scent wanting to devour her completely. Lena was panting when he finally pulled away, her eyes half closed.

"You have no idea how tempting you are," Ambrose whispered against her mouth. She smiled, her fingers softly trailing across his chest.

"I'd prefer you in human form, but, right back at you," she teased, poking her tongue out and running it across his bottom lip. He moaned at the gesture before crushing his mouth to hers again. Her tongue slipped inside his mouth and met with his own.

"Hell, woman," he sighed into the kiss. "You are going to drive me insane."

He finally ripped himself from her and took a deep breath, before grabbing her shoulders and turning her round to face the room.

"Life as a demon is not just one where you can do what you like, despite what humans may have imagined," Ambrose explained as he stepped around her and walked into the room. "Hell is a kind of business where demons keep the wheels turning, and every demon does their own thing. The benefit you have, is that no one determines what you do, that is for you to decide." He looked over at Lena as she stared in amazement at the large room filled with books, scrolls and various artefacts from across all periods of time. He smiled softly at her rapture. "Lena, are you listening?" he asked in a half-hearted attempt at berating her.

"Huh?" Lena said, looking at him. She suddenly smiled and laughed nervously. "Sorry, yes! I get to choose what 'job' I do for Hell," she said, making air quotes with her fingers. "What kind of jobs does Hell need its demons to do anyway?"

"Anything that serves to increase the power or reach of Hell. For example, bringing in more souls, which is like power production. Some, like Pasha and Xavier, work within Hell in what might be called supportive roles. It's up to you to figure out where you want to fit in, and as you are now immortal, I would recommend you find something you like doing."

"Okay... what are some ways that others work?"

"Well..." he contemplated her question for a moment. "For example, I make deals. There are those that sow conflict in varying ways generally resulting in disastrous events such as war or genocide... or both. Some work in tandem with others such as succubi and incubi demons, who, uh..." he paused for a moment unsure how to describe them, "they create condemned souls for lack of a better description."

"How do you choose?"

"Well, this is where you figure that out," Ambrose said, waving his hands towards the contents of the room. "This is the Repository."

The room was large and filled to the brim with books and other objects. Six desks lined the floor between the door and the back of the room, facing each other in pairs. Each desk had its own stool and various writing implements stored at the top. Light emanated from stone pillars that had deep running cracks reaching from the floor up to the ceiling in which liquid lava flowed. The bookshelves were carved out of the walls that seemed to breathe with their own life. Small bits of paper flitted around the room, stopping at various bookshelves to touch different spines of books or scrolls of paper. In response the books or scrolls would disappear in flames, transporting either to a different shelf or to one of the desks. At random intervals around the room, tables were set up with various objects and mechanisms to be used for testing newborns to aid in finding their design. Small black winged creatures scurried around the floor, grabbing items much like the enchanted papers and running off with them to one of the other rooms behind the various doors that were scattered around the walls.

"Wow," Lena breathed quietly.

Ambrose smiled at her. "To start, you'll stay in the main room, studying all forms of designs. The adjourning rooms are practice areas. Once you've found something you want to try, the Keeper can help you set up in one of them to test it out."

"The Keeper?"

"Think of her as a librarian," he said walking further into the room. "She can help you find anything in here."

Lena followed him, hopping over one of the creatures as she walked down the steps. "What are those?" she asked curiously as one hoped up onto her arm to look at her. It flapped its tiny wings and tilted its head to the side. Its face was pixie like, with large black eyes that took up most of its face. A small red slit served as its mouth. "It's kind of cute," she said with a smile. The creature flew away to the top of one of the bookshelves.

"They are imps," he replied. "Harmless enough. They work for the Keeper."

"Try to steal anything from here and they become not so harmless."

Lena spun on her heel, almost falling over, towards the voice at the back of the room. Ambrose chuckled silently as her eyes widened in awe at the demon that now walked towards them.

The Keeper was huge even for demons, towering almost two feet above Ambrose in demonic form. Four large leather wings spanned from her back which she held close to the body, the bend of her wings held proudly behind her head. Her skin was a dark charcoal that shone from the lava as she walked past the pillars. Two black horns protruded from behind each of her ears circling behind her head in sharp points. Black hair fell over her shoulders barely hiding the two horns that grew from her shoulders. A loose black robe draped over her body, flowing effortlessly with each step, her cloven hooves echoing loudly across the stone floor. She had a terrifying aura to her, mixed with an intelligence that warned all of her ability to tear them apart with both her hands and her words. Her size and form effortlessly managed to make any mortal tremble at the sight of her. A reaction that was also common even in older demons.

"Lena, this is Morgan," Ambrose said with a bow to the demon. "The Keeper of the Repository."

He watched as Morgan stopped a few steps away from his boundling who was opening and closing her mouth, seemingly unable to form words. The Keeper raised her brows and looked at him in amusement. He smiled at her knowingly. Morgan usually had that effect on newborns, and it was always fun to see.

"You're..." Lena started almost forcing the word out. "You're hot," she finally choked out, much to Ambrose's surprise as he stifled a laugh.

The Keeper smiled warmly and held out her hand for Lena's. "Thank you, child. I will admit, I don't hear that often."

Lena took hold of Morgan's hand, allowing herself to be led towards a desk in the middle of the room, her eyes still fixed on the Keeper's face, despite having to crane her neck back at an unnatural angle to do so.

"This will be your space, whilst you are learning," Morgan said, her voice echoing through the room. "You should have been here a week ago. Ambrose has been avoiding me."

"You knew about me?" Lena asked, her eyes still locked with Morgan's.

Morgan nodded in response. "Here within the Repository, we have a book that records any time a new demon is born or made. Only myself and the Princes of Hell have access to it. I keep track to make sure that sires aren't hiding their boundlings."

"Morgan, she has lightning manifestation," Ambrose said, stepping forward. "She accessed them on her first night. She had to gain control before coming here."

Straightening her back, Morgan stared at Ambrose for a moment, exchanging a knowing look without words. "Interesting," she said softly, turning her gaze back to the boundling. "Do you have control now?"

"We think so," Lena answered.

"Well, then we shouldn't waste any more time in finding your design. You will come here every day for the next week for at least four hours to study and practice. After then, you will have freedom to read and practice at your leisure, and I will act as more of a guide," Morgan moved over to a shelf and pulled a number of books from it, returning and piling the books on the desk. "You will start with reading these. Once you understand their contents, we'll move on to some practical tests. Ambrose, it's time for you to leave."

"Wait, what?" Lena startled, a brief look of panic crossing her features.

"It's alright, Lena," Ambrose reassured her. "I have to leave. I'm not meant to influence you finding your design in any way."

Morgan hummed in agreement at his statement. "Sires are not allowed to interfere in the process. He will be back in a few hours to collect you. You are not allowed to take anything from the Repository, so you must study here." She turned her head slightly to one of the adjourning rooms. "I will be back in a moment. I must see to another student." As elegantly as ever, Morgan strode off to the room, ducking her head to pass through the doorway.

Lena stared at Ambrose in a way that made him want to take her away with him. He sighed heavily, walking over to her and pulling her into an embrace. "You are safe here," he whispered into her ear. "Morgan's imps serve more than just to protect the books and objects. And she is feared among all demons. Nothing will happen to you here under her care."

"You trust her?"

"Yes. She has no desires, or time, for a boundling of her own. I promise, you are safe here."

"You'll be back soon?" she asked, holding onto his arms.

He nodded. "In a few hours." He took hold of her chin and lifted her face to his, placing a gentle kiss on her lips. "See you soon," he kissed her again before tearing himself from her and walking out the doors.

CHAPTER THIRTEEN

Again, Lena felt very much alone after Ambrose left the Repository, but the feeling was different this time. At least in the manor she was in a relatively familiar place. The Repository was huge and moved around of its own accord like a living, breathing thing. In here, she felt like a child who had only just learnt how to walk and was now expected to run.

She sighed heavily before taking her seat at the desk Morgan had piled the books upon. Pulling the one from the top of the pile, she laid a large, ancient-looking tome bound in black leather in front of her. Running her fingers over the rough surface of the book, she couldn't help but feel a sense of foreboding. The title of the grimoire was written in a language she didn't recognise but after staring at it for a moment she found she understood it. *Daemons and Demons.*

"That seems redundant," she muttered under her breath.

With a deep breath, she opened the book and began to read. The words on the page seemed to pulse with an otherworldly energy, and as she read on, she felt a sense of wonder building within her. The contents of the grimoire were dark and twisted, filled with spells and incantations that promised mortals power beyond imagination. For demons it seemed to serve merely as a historical guide. But, as she determined eventually, definitely not redundant.

Whilst daemons and demons were similar entities, they served drastically different purposes. Daemons were benevolent, guiding spirits that helped form personalities or shape advancements in nature and history. Demons on the other hand were generally seen as malignant and evil creatures set only to amass power and aid in the downfall of Heaven. However, neither description was totally accurate to the actual nature of both.

She read about the seven Princes of Hell, and how each one presided over a different sin, tempting mortals to give in to their most base desires. Lucifer, the first to fall from Heaven, but not the first demon, was said to be the most powerful of the seven. His domain, pride. The grimoire described him as a beautiful and charismatic creature, capable of seducing even the most devout of God's followers. Mammon, the second prince, was the lord of greed said to be surrounded by riches and temptations, encouraging others to acquire more and more wealth, even at the cost of one's soul.

Lena found the knowledge contained within the grimoire to be alluring, tempting her to delve deeper into its pages. She didn't even hear Morgan return to the room or walk up behind her.

"Glad to see a student with an appetite to learn," Morgan said, stopping beside the desk.

"Holy freaking—" Lena cried falling off the chair and landing on her bottom with a loud thump. Her hands sparked with electricity which fizzled out quickly.

The Keeper simply raised her brows as Lena scrambled to her feet, brushing dust off her jeans. "I didn't mean to startle you," Morgan said, her velvety voice sending a shiver down her spine.

"It's fine," she said quickly. "I don't... or didn't... tend to read often for the reason I get too engrossed and lose track of what's happening around me. Got me in a lot of trouble when I was younger."

"I'm sorry to hear that," Morgan sighed, wandering over to a bookshelf. "Reading is an essential path to gaining knowledge. You may not take anything from here, but you are always welcome to come here whenever you want."

Lena took her seat again, looking at the grimoire. "Morgan, may I ask you something?" she asked, continuing when she heard the Keeper hum in acknowledgement. She wanted to ask so much about Ambrose and that moment he and Morgan had earlier, but she lost her nerve. Coughing slightly, she asked a different question: "Is your name really Morgan? Seems so ordinary for a demon like you."

"My name is actually Morganoth. As time has moved on, I find

Morgan is less intimidating," she answered, giving Lena a warm smile over her shoulder.

"Sure, because your name is the most intimidating thing about you," she chuckled to herself.

Morgan laughed, turning towards her. The laugh sent shivers down her spine, its frivolity barely covering the underlying menacing nature of it. Lena smiled, almost out of fear, but utterly charmed by the monstrous demon in front of her, who suddenly seemed so... *normal.*

"You are going to fit in well around here," Morgan sighed breathlessly as she wiped a tear from her eye. "Keep your mind as sharp as your tongue, and you will be fine. But that's not the question you wanted to ask, is it?"

"Ah, yeah," Lena sighed, absently flicking at the edge of one of the pages in front of her. "It's not really fair of me to ask you though so..."

"This is Hell, my dear," Morgan said, moving to the desk in front of Lena's and sitting down, resting her arms on the table, her wings rising into the air. "Fair is what you make of it."

Lena stared at the Keeper from under her brows. "If you want to go for less intimidating, that," she motioned with her hand to Morgan's current posture, "is not it."

The demon smiled and nodded knowingly. "Ask me," she pressed.

With a deep sigh, Lena carefully picked out her next words. "Ambrose has been telling me who to trust and who to avoid. This is my first time here, but he's told me some names and given general descriptions," she sighed, staring at her hands. "I saw that look between the two of you, so I'm guessing you've known him awhile. I know I'm bound to him and I like him generally, but... can I trust him?"

Morgan tilted her head to the side, studying Lena. "Do you have any particular reservations about him?"

She shook her head. "No, not really. I feel like he's not telling me something, but I know better than most that it's human, and I suppose, demon nature to keep secrets. And that's fine, he's entitled to keep secrets." Taking a deep breath, she looked up at one of the shelves watching an imp scurry across its surface. "I had a shit life. The last few years were okay, but I learnt not to trust anyone. I feel safe with him, but..." she paused briefly, wondering if she should be this open with Morgan for having only just met her. "But," she decided to continue, "is that enough reason to trust him?"

The Repository was silent for a moment, broken only by the sound of the imps running about. Morgan sat back in the chair, seemingly contemplating her answer.

"Safe is a rarity here, so if you have it, hold on to it," she answered finally. "But it can also be dangerous. Sires can trust their boundlings implicitly because they can force you to tell them everything. Side note, don't trust other boundlings for this exact reason." Morgan pointed a finger at her like a mother telling off a child. Lena chuckled slightly but smiled gratefully. "Boundlings cannot always trust their sires, and as the eventual goal is to break from their bindings, they tend to be quite reserved from their sires anyway. The only person you can truly trust as a boundling is yourself. That said," she said pointedly, leaning forward again and lowering her voice, "Hell is a game of politics and Ambrose knows how to play it. He was one of my favourite students and he keeps his hands, relatively, clean. If there is anyone down here you can trust, it's him."

Lena stared at Morgan, the tightness in her chest easing slightly. Pressing her lips together, she nodded slightly, looking down at the desk. "Thank you," she said softly.

The feet of the chair scraped across the floor and Morgan got to her feet, walking past Lena and patting her on the shoulder. "Finish the grimoire. I have to see to other students."

Lena looked around the room. "What other students?"

Morgan chuckled, making her way to one of the doors. "The Repository exists across a number of realities. We layer them atop the other so that students can study undisturbed. Otherwise, you would be tripping over each other. This is your Repository and although you may share it with one or two other boundlings in time, for now it is yours." Morgan opened one of the doors and ducked her head, pausing halfway through the doorway. Looking back at Lena, she smiled. "The best thing you can do is trust your gut. Once you make a decision, trust that it is right for you and stick to it."

Lena nodded in gratitude as Morgan disappeared through the door.

Turning back to her desk, she began to read again. It took her a while to wrap her head around the contents of the grimoire, but she found herself yet again thoroughly enthralled by it. Imps would occasionally scurry across the desk surface, checking on her, or so it seemed, but she paid them little mind. She was just finishing the last page when Ambrose returned, almost reaching the desk before she noticed him.

"Miss me?" he smiled at her before placing a gentle kiss on her cheek. Lena nodded as she returned his smile, taking hold of his hand.

"How long has it been?" she asked, sliding off the stool.

"Almost five hours," Ambrose said, running his hand over the cover of the grimoire. "I remember reading this," he chuckled.

Lena's eyes widened. "Five hours?" she queried. "Geez..." Rotating her shoulders, eliciting further cracks from her joints, she sighed heavily. "Time flies."

"That it does," he smirked. "You can leave the books on the desk. You'll come back to them tomorrow after all. Come on," he said, tugging her along behind him, "I want to show you something."

"Okay," she laughed, allowing him to lead her away. "Wait, should we tell Morgan?"

"She can flay me later," he said, looking over his shoulder at her with an eager smile. "You can't miss this."

Utterly bewildered at his enthusiasm, Lena practically ran behind him trying to keep up with his pace. They had started heading back to the cavern but took a turn down a corridor just before reaching it. She became aware suddenly that she had indeed become used to the smell that had offended her on first arrival. It was still there if she concentrated, but it no longer bothered her, even as the corridor headed downhill and the smell intensified.

"Stay close, okay," Ambrose said suddenly, giving her hand a squeeze. "It will be busy."

"What will be b—" her words were halted as they rounded the corner and she saw a wall of demon backs in front of them. "Whoa. That's a lot of demons."

He smiled at her, pulling her into the crowd. "Come on, it's happening."

"What's happening?" she asked as he managed to get her in front of him, pushing her closer to the front of the crowd. As she was still in human form, the surrounding demons towered over her, so she could easily stand at the front without bothering anyone around her. All were talking in hushed tones as if they didn't wish to disturb the scene that now laid out before them.

Blinking in vague disbelief, Lena tried to comprehend what her eyes were seeing. Large beasts walked across the cavern that had been transformed into a den-like abode, recessed into the floor in front of her. They looked like dogs, but easily three times the size of an average large-breed. Black, shaggy fur spanning across their bodies. On some, their coat was mixed with grey colouring over their snouts, back and upper flanks. Their eyes glowed like shifting pools of fire. Lena almost gasped at the sight of their long fangs when one nearby yawned lazily.

"Are these... hellhounds?" she whispered over her shoulder.

"Yes," Ambrose replied. "And one is about to have pups." He bent closer to her to point towards the back of the den where she could see one hound in particular lying on their... *her?*... side, supported by two other hounds behind her. A demon knelt next to her, keeping her head on his lap as he stroked her neck comfortingly. "Seeing a hound give birth is said to be good luck down here," Ambrose explained quietly. "Their numbers have been declining. That demon by her, he's been the one looking after this den for the last decade. He's helped birth more pups in that time than in the last century. There are two other hounds currently pregnant, but we don't know when they'll give birth yet."

"So, we just wait and watch?" she asked.

"Yep," Ambrose nodded. "She's been in labour for the last two hours though so shouldn't be much longer."

Lena fell silent, simply studying the creatures before her. One in particular caught her interest, towards the right side of the den. It was larger than most of them, although definitely not the largest. Its body reminded her of a greyhound, in some respects, although its snout was not as pointed. Defined muscles rippled under its skin as it made its way across the den, making its way to a bed of straw laid out in an alcove within the walls of cavern. It seemed to have trouble lying down, and even more so in getting comfortable. Lena assumed this was another pregnant female.

"Look," Ambrose said suddenly.

She turned her gaze back to the centre of the den, just in time to see the first pup born. Happy whispers rose from the crowd as the demon by the hellhound, pulled the pup closer to its mother's face, allowing her to lick the pup clean. The demon checked over the pup carefully as all whispers silenced around her.

"It's a girl," the demon announced to the crowd, enticing a hushed cheer from them. Lena smiled at the beauty and absurdity of it.

It wasn't long before two more pups joined their sister. Another girl and one boy. Sadly, one pup did not make it, despite the best efforts of the demon. He wrapped it in a cloth, before tending to the mother, ensuring her pups latched properly for their first feed.

"That's it everyone," he said, turning to the crowd. "No more pups for today." With hushed murmurs, most of the crowd turned to leave. Others hung around to watch the new mother hound with her pups.

Lena felt rooted to the spot, as her appreciation for the simple elegance of the creatures before her sunk in. "Thank you," she whispered to Ambrose. "Thank you for bringing me here."

Ambrose moved beside her and lowered himself to sit on the ledge, hanging his legs over the side. She followed suit, remembering to keep a small distance between them considering their conversation earlier.

"I used to love coming here," he sighed, resting back on his hands. "It's nice now there are more hounds, but that also means that it's busier than it used to be. It's not as quiet a place to retreat to anymore."

Lena nodded absently, her gaze wandering over the den and its inhabitants. What she assumed was a male, laid beneath their feet, stretched lazily with its back pressed against the wall, its long legs sprawled across the floor. She smiled at it, wondering if it was at all aware of what had just happened within its den.

The demon who had now finished cleaning up the mother hound, started to walk to a ramp off to the side of the den, making his way up the ledge and towards Ambrose and Lena. As he drew closer, Lena managed to get a better look at him.

His skin was an ashy red and his bindings, the standard black, wrapped in angular spirals along his forearms before fading just past his elbows. A small crown of horns ran from his temples to the back of his head but his dark blonde hair almost completely covered them. Lena thought generally he looked quite handsome for a demon. There was something eerily familiar about him. Sharp jaw, high cheekbones, a dimple on only one cheek...

"Cyrus?" she asked, her eyes wide with surprise. "Cyrus Tanner? Is that you?"

The demon stopped in his tracks, his head snapping towards her. He was silent for a moment, seemingly studying her face before answering. "Lena?" the demon replied, tilting his head in confusion. "What? How did you..."

She could see Ambrose's head looking back and forth between her and Cyrus from the corner of her eye, however, her gaze was fixed on her childhood friend.

"What in the world?" she started, getting to her feet and walking towards him. "When did you become a demon?"

Cyrus glanced over to Ambrose briefly before looking back at her. "Ah, well, about ten years ago now. You?"

"Two weeks."

"Oh shit, I'm sorry."

"Me too."

They simply stood in front of each other for a moment, studying the other. Lena could scarcely believe that her childhood friend now stood in front of her. Confusion mixed with bittersweet joy sent butterflies through her stomach as she searched for the right words to say to him.

"Does someone want to explain to me what is going on?" Ambrose snapped, getting to his feet. "You obviously seem to know each other."

Lena looked at him in surprise, feeling slightly guilty for essentially forgetting about him. "Cyrus and I were in foster care together," she explained. "Wait, you said you became a demon ten years ago?" she turned back to Cyrus who nodded in answer. "You aged out then, right?"

The demon sighed and again nodded. "Yeah, sort of. Do you remember, I moved to a new placement just before aging out?" Lena nodded. "I moved counties last minute. My new foster parents used me as a sacrifice just after I turned eighteen."

"Damn, that's rough," she sighed, folding her arms in front of her. "I'm sorry, Cyrus."

"Ah, don't worry about it. I'm okay," he said softly. There was an uncertainty to his voice that gave her pause. Was he really okay? "I'm sorry I couldn't keep in touch like we'd promised. How'd you get on after I left?"

"Well," Lena smiled and shook her head, "they tried to sell me for drugs."

He chuckled slightly. "No rest for the wicked then. But I'm sorry. That sucks."

"Don't worry about it," she said looking back at him with a smile.

Cyrus smiled back and she could see the remnants of her old friend in his eyes, despite their demonic black form. With a slight cough, he spoke, "Ah, look, I have to... ah, no nice way of saying this... I have to dispose of the pup that didn't make it, then get back to the hellhounds. I'll see you round, yeah?"

"Sure," Lena nodded as her friend hurried off. She could feel Ambrose's eyes on her as she pressed her lips together, purposefully keeping her gaze away from him. "Are you going to say anything, or just stare a hole through me?"

He clicked his tongue loudly. "I'm deciding whether I should command you to stay away from him."

"Jealous?" she turned to look at him, a teasing smile on her face.

"Hardly," he pursed his lips and took a step closer. "Cyrus is bound to someone worth avoiding. Someone I actively avoid," he explained, his eyes growing dark. Her smile dropped as she understood the gravity of his words. "I can see you're friends, so I'll allow this for now."

"Allow this?" she scoffed. "Ambrose–"

He held up his hand to silence her. "But... if it comes to protecting what I've built, even more so, if it comes to protecting *you*, I will stop you from seeing him. I'm sorry, Lena. But there are certain things I cannot risk."

She stared at him, letting his warning sink in. She nodded slowly. "Okay," she said finally. "I understand." Dropping her gaze from his to stare at the floor, a heavy indescribable pit formed in her stomach.

Ambrose sighed, closing his eyes. "Let's go back home," he held out his hand for her. After a moment, she stepped towards him placing her hand in his, as he transported them back to the manor.

CHAPTER FOURTEEN

Lena had made great strides since going to the Repository. She had passed all practical tests that Morgan had thrown at her with flying colours by the end of the week. Most days, Lena spent much longer than the Keeper's required four hours there, coming back to the manor exhausted at the end of the day. She and Ambrose had only passed the odd pleasantry between each other before she would either retreat to her room for sleep, or, now that she no longer needed to sleep every night, to the downstairs sitting room to relax. Her dreams had lessened in intensity and she said she wanted to see if she would be okay on her own now. He'd wanted to convince her to stay in his room, but could see and feel that it would have been a futile argument.

He missed her terribly when she was away, waiting in eagerness for her to return, only to be racked with guilt when she avoided conversation with him. He knew he had upset her with his comments about Cyrus, but he was at a loss as to how to resolve the issue. Cyrus was bound to Zagan. As far as Ambrose was aware, Zagan did not yet know about Lena, or at least didn't know that she was bound to him. But as Cyrus now knew about her being in Hell, Zagan would definitely find out from him shortly.

Sitting in his office, Ambrose sighed as he leant back in his chair. He had been trying to reshuffle some investments all afternoon, but couldn't stop thinking about Lena to the point of painful distraction. Anytime he had tried to connect with her over the last week she had pulled away from him. He had even gone to the cafe to pick up some of her favourite treats from Café Marie, which she had been thankful for, and yet the cakes still sat in the kitchen untouched. He wanted to make things right with her, but feared that boat might have sailed. At this point he could use a summoning to distract himself.

A knock on his office door made him sit upright.

"Come in," he said.

The door opened slowly and Lena stepped inside. He sat forward in his chair, a tentative joy crept over him that she had come to see him.

"Lena," he sighed, "welcome back. Is everything ok?"

She nodded slowly, her eyes fixed on the floor. "Can we talk?" she asked.

"Of course," he replied quickly. "Please, sit," he motioned to one of the chairs. He got up from his chair and moved to the other side of the desk, taking the seat opposite her.

"Thanks," she said softly, sitting down.

She didn't say anything further, silence falling over them as she twisted her hands in her lap. He felt her uneasiness pulsate through him, causing him to shift in his seat, unsure of what she was going to say.

Lena took a deep breath, blowing it out through puffed cheeks, her eyes remaining on the floor. "I miss you," she said finally.

Whatever he had been expecting her to say, that was not it. He wanted to reach out and take her hand, but thought it might be better to let her expand further before acting on anything. "I'm always here for you, Lena," he settled on.

"I know," she started with a steadying sigh. "I just... I keep... ah, I keep replaying what you said about Cyrus. And anytime, I want to see you or talk to you, I go back there and..." she paused briefly, opening and closing her hands in her lap, "and, I get so annoyed."

Ambrose slumped back in his chair, his eyes locked on her face, noting the confusion and pain that furrowed her brow.

"I get it," she continued, finally lifting her eyes to look at him. "I really get it. If I've learnt anything in life and in this week with Morgan, it's that trust is a commodity that should not be overlooked if you have it. Especially, when there are those at every corner wanting to abuse it or take it from you." Lena pressed her lips together, looking back to the floor. "I just, I need you to understand something. About Cyrus and I."

She fell silent, uncertainty written across her face. He pushed himself to lean forward, resting on his elbows, trying to show that she had his undivided attention. "I'm listening, Lena," he whispered.

She tilted her head and looked him in the eye. There was a deep pain rooted within her grey depths that he wanted to extinguish in any way that he could.

"Cyrus and I... we depended on each other for a long time. Or, really, I depended on him," she bit her bottom lip before continuing. "We were in three of the same homes together. I hadn't had anyone in my life, up until that point, that had been around for as long as he had. He looked out for me. He beat one of our foster dads into a pulp because he tried to climb into bed with me when I was twelve. That was just our first placement together."

Ambrose shifted in his seat, anger washing over him for what she had endured. He sighed forcibly trying to control himself for her.

"When he was moved, the last time I saw him, he promised that if he was able to set up okay, he would come back for me. Take me away from everything. I was devastated when he left," she said softly, tears starting to form in her eyes as she looked away from him. "Seeing him again, it was nice. It was nice to know he hadn't just forgotten me. That there was another reason why he didn't come back."

Her voice broke with the last sentence, a tear escaping from her eyes. Despite his previous judgement, Ambrose quickly reached towards her, taking one of her hands in his. He remained silent but wanted to provide her with comfort. With a heavy sigh she looked at him, her eyes swimming with emotion.

"I know I can't ask you to not take him away from me again, and I'm not going to. I understand the need to protect what you built. And as a fellow boundling, I know to be reserved around him. As I said, I get it," she sniffed. "I can be careful. Growing up in foster care, you learn how to keep secrets. But I need my friend. Someone who knows what I've been through. What I'm currently going through. Who is going through the same thing as me."

"I know–" Ambrose started.

"No, you don't," she interrupted. "Not really. Not in the way he does. You haven't been a boundling in over five hundred years, Ambrose. Cyrus is one now. And he knows what happened to us in foster. You and Marcus, you're great. But it would be nice to have a friend that is just mine."

He hung his head, taking a deep breath. She was right, but he didn't like it. But he supposed he didn't have to like it. Not really. Not if he wanted to salvage whatever relationship he had, or hoped to have, with her.

"Do you love him?" he asked softly, unsure he wanted to know the answer.

"Yes," she answered, "but not like that. May seem juvenile but, he became like my big brother." He could tell through their bond she meant what she said.

Rubbing the back of her hand with his thumb, Ambrose allowed her words to settle over him. He nodded slowly. "You're right," he said. "You deserve to have your friend." He took a deep breath and looked up at her, happy to see a small glint of joy in her eyes, hoping he wasn't about to extinguish it again. "But first, you need to know about Cyrus' sire."

Lena furrowed her brow but nodded, indicating that she was ready to listen.

He let her hand drop and leant back in his chair. "Cyrus is bound to a demon called Zagan. He's a cambion, and one of the ones truly not to be trusted. He has a sick, twisted moral code and an over inflated ego. He doesn't care who he hurts or steps on to get what he wants. And he will want you. More than anyone else, he will want you."

"Why?" she asked with a small shrug.

Chewing the inside of his cheek, Ambrose simply replied; "Because you are bound to me."

Her eyes filled with confusion, but she remained silent allowing him to continue.

"Zagan, was my sire," he said. "And, ever since I broke from him, he and I have been lockstep in trying to destroy the other. I've grown tired of it, so I have simply been avoiding him and protecting what I've built. He, as ever, still tries to bring me down. Taking you," he paused to look at her, hoping she would understand the gravity of what he was about to say, "well, he would see that as a great triumph. You would become his trophy, and he would use you against me at every turn." He sighed as he pressed his hands together in front of his chest. "I don't want to see you get used like that. I know from experience that Zagan forces all his boundlings to tell him everything. Cyrus will not be able to keep your secrets. So don't tell him any."

Lena let out a shaky breath, before pushing off from her chair and kneeling between his legs. She placed her hands on the top of his thighs, her chin tilted up to him. He stared at her, studying every feature of her face. Her long brown lashes perfectly framing her beautiful eyes. Creamy white skin only marked by a soft rose blush across her cheekbones, complimenting the pinkness of her lips. He raised a hand and placed it on her cheek, indescribably happy to be touching her again.

"You said, that day, that I am yours," she whispered, leaning her head into his hand. He furrowed his brow wondering where she was going with this. "And I want to be," she continued. "I want to be yours. More than anything. But I need you to promise me something?"

He raised an eyebrow at the question. "If it is within my power, anything."

Lena hesitated for a moment, simply staring at him. Slowly, she leant forward, lifting on her hands and placed a soft kiss on his lips. Ambrose closed his eyes, breathing in her scent as if he had been starved of it.

"Can I ask," she said against his lips, "that you don't compel me when it comes to whatever relationship may develop between us? For any of the other reasons you stated the other day: security; safety... fine. I promise, I will understand. But," she took a deep breath, pausing for only a moment, "most... well, pretty much all... of my previous relationships have been... *controlling*. It's taken me a long time to stand up for myself and for what I want. I wanted a relationship with you when I was alive, and I still want one, so... please don't take that from me. Don't take my ability to be with you... willingly."

He brought his other hand to her face, holding it tenderly between his grasp. Dropping his head, he brushed his lips across hers slowly and deliberately, trying to evoke her attraction for him again. "I promise," he said against her lips, before smiling wickedly. "Unless you ask."

Lena laughed breathlessly, slapping him on the thigh despite the smile that now crept across her face. "Thank you," she sighed. Pushing up on his thighs, she climbed onto his lap. Ambrose eagerly opened his arms for her, helping pull her legs over his until she straddled him in the chair. He sighed with relief as she rested her forehead on his, revelling in the feel of her body against his. "I'm sorry," she whispered, wrapping her arms around his shoulders.

"For what?" he asked, letting himself fall into her eyes.

"For being so distant."

He shook his head, running his hand up and down her back. "Don't be. I seem to have picked up a habit of hurting you. Of jumping to conclusions when it comes to you. I want to stop doing that."

She placed a finger under his jaw, angling his face upwards, as she pressed her lips to his in a long, drawn out kiss. He felt his body react instantly, his stomach tightening with desire. His arms contracted around her waist, pulling her closer to him, as much as the confines of the chair would allow. She broke the kiss, tracing his lips with her fingers and sending shivers of anticipation down his spine.

"Do you trust me?" she asked, her eyes burning into his.

He knew his hesitation in answering her question would be unwise, but he wasn't sure how to answer. "Lena, I..." he started. "I have trouble trusting anyone. I'm sorry. I know that's not what you want to hear. It took decades for me to start trusting Marcus. I want to. I really want to. And I do to an extent. I just..." he trailed off, wondering how many more times he would have to go through moments like this. Just when they were getting close, he had to push her away again.

To his surprise, she smiled. "It's okay," she whispered. "I understand. Probably better than most."

"Do you trust me?" he asked, touching the back of his fingers to her jaw.

Lena kissed him before answering. "I trust that you will do everything you can to keep me safe. But beyond that, I'm not sure yet. We have plenty of time to figure it out though."

He laughed quietly, as they shared a smile. She hadn't pulled away. *Maybe*, he thought to himself, just maybe, they could make this work.

"So," she said, lifting her head whilst keeping her arms around his shoulders. "In the interests of trust, it's been three weeks. Well, three weeks tomorrow."

Ambrose tilted his head in confusion. "What's been three weeks?"

"Me as a demon," Lena replied with a slight huff. "And, I've still not transformed." She coughed uncertainly before shifting her arm so that her cardigan dropped off her shoulder. Ambrose's lips parted in shock as he looked at her arm. Her bindings had grown further since he saw them a week ago. Now they enveloped her arm, the trailing end of thorns just starting to sprawl over the curve of her shoulder. "They've grown five inches in a week," she sighed.

Staring at them, he lifted his hand to touch her bindings. It was almost like he could see them growing under his fingertips. All that in only a week? It hardly seemed possible.

"Do they feel different?" he asked softly.

"No," she replied. "I don't even notice them growing. But it seems like every time I look at them, they've expanded. The looks and whispers in Hell are getting hard to ignore."

His gaze snapped to her face, noting the concern that washed over her. "What whispers?"

Lena shrugged. "I don't hear what they're saying. A new boundling has come into the Repository. His sire," she pursed her lips and her brow furrowed, "Titus, I think his name was, but I can't really remember, just stared at me. Like he knew something I didn't."

Sighing heavily, Ambrose pulled her cardigan back over her shoulder. "Okay," he said, leaning his head back on the chair. "Not to be controlling, but no more tank tops in Hell. Something with sleeves so we can hide the growth, but keep your forearms visible. And we need to get you into combat training, sooner rather than later. So, you can fend off any unwanted advances."

"Why do you sound like that's a bad thing?" she asked with a soft smile.

"Because," he replied, "Zagan works the training pits."

"Oh..."

Lena leant forward, resting her head against his shoulder. He wrapped his arms around her, closing his eyes to try and think through their next steps.

Zagan was not the only demon in charge of the pits, so maybe they could work it that they only went there when he wasn't. But Ambrose was sure that their presence there would get back to Zagan who would then show up regardless. He could start training her here, with Marcus even, but the pits were made to accommodate resulting damage. It wouldn't make sense not to utilise that. The pits also had other newborn demons who Lena could practice with. All were still learning their powers, so she would be less likely to suffer any real harm that way. Additionally, medic demons hung around the pits to tend to any serious injuries inflicted during training.

He chewed his bottom lip, unsure of what the right move was. The pits would ensure that everyone knew what her powers were. She would be known to all of Hell. But he doubted they could avoid that much longer anyway. Especially if whispers were already circulating. Rumours were far more dangerous than the truth in most cases.

Three weeks. Lena had been a demon for three weeks. Which also meant that he had not slept in over a month. Living top-side so much definitely had its disadvantages sometimes.

"How are you getting on at the Repository?" he asked, defeated by his own thoughts. He was too tired to work it all out today.

"Fine, I think," she replied, nuzzling her face into his neck. He smiled at her affectionate gesture, happy to let her continue without input from him. "Morgan seems happy with my progress, despite not yet finding my design. I need a break from reading though."

He chuckled, tightening his embrace around her. "Understandable."

She kissed his neck, sending thrills across his skin. Her hand trailed up his chest, until it rested on the side of his neck. He sighed as her lips travelled over his neck and jaw, a soft smile on his lips. A low growl pulled from his chest as she shifted over him, her hips grinding against his lap. She was intoxicating, and he was pretty sure she knew it. Her mouth came to rest beside his ear. "Want to help me relax?" she whispered, the warmth of her breath causing the hairs on the back of his neck to stand on end.

Slowly he opened his eyes as she moved her face in front of his, a sly smile brightening her face. "Where have you been my whole life?" Ambrose asked rhetorically as he lifted his head to claim her mouth with his. He grabbed the back of her neck to deepen the kiss, placing his other hand on her hip, pulling her against him.

She ran her fingers through his hair, as she nibbled at his bottom lip. With a smile, he opened his mouth for her, allowing her tongue to meet with his. He wanted to devour her, to take everything she had to offer him. Grabbing under her thighs, he made to stand, intending to carry her to the bedroom, but his legs had other ideas.

Unfortunately, now that he had acknowledged his exhaustion, it had become overwhelming. His knees buckled underneath him, barely keeping her in his arms as he grabbed for the other chair to steady himself. Lena quickly put her feet on the floor and pushed against his chest, helping to hold him up.

"Ambrose?" her voice was panicked. "What's wrong?"

He shook his head and pressed his lips together. "Nothing. I'm just tired," he sighed. "I'm sorry, Lena. The weeks are catching up with me. I think I just need to go to bed."

"No need to be sorry for that," she said quickly, placing her arms around his waist as she helped him to his feet. "Can you walk?"

He gave her a dubious look, feinting offence at her question, despite feeling very unsteady on his feet.

"Sorry for asking," she jeered, rolling her eyes at him. "Come on, I'll help you."

Gratefully, Ambrose hung his arm over her shoulders as she led him out of the office and towards his room. He kicked off his shoes once he was sitting on the edge of the bed. She helped him out of his jacket and shirt, placing them neatly on a chair by the door. Once lying down, he managed to wriggle out of his trousers, before climbing under the covers. He apologised to Lena as she picked them up off the floor and placed them with his other clothes. She simply hushed him with a wave of her hand.

"You've been taking care of me for so long now, let me return the favour," she said sitting on the edge of the bed beside him. "I'm guessing it's been a long time since you've slept now."

"You're not wrong," he chuckled, taking hold of her hand. "Will you stay here tonight?" he asked, his eyes pleading with her, not wanting her to leave again.

Lena smiled and nodded. "I need to take a shower," she said softly. "But, yes, I'll sleep here tonight."

"Okay," he sighed as his head sank further into the pillow. He felt her get up from the bed and place a gentle kiss on his cheek as he drifted off to sleep.

CHAPTER FIFTEEN

Lena woke to find herself pinned to the mattress by a warm weight across her chest and hips. She smiled softly as she turned her head to look at Ambrose's sleeping face. Evidently, he had rolled during the night and had draped his arm and leg over her in a half-embrace. His scent, warmth and the steady sound of his breathing excited her soul as she twisted her body to turn towards him. Gently, she laid her hand on his bare chest, over his sharp tattoo, feeling the slight rise and fall of his steady breathing.

Watching him sleep, she studied his features, noting how thick his black eyelashes were as they fanned across his cheeks. His usual angular expression was softened by the calmness of sleep. A few strands of hair had fallen over his face, barely touching his nose. She traced her fingers across his jaw towards the small cleft in his chin. Keeping her touch as feather light as possible so as not to wake him, she touched her fingers to his lips, their smooth surface depressing slightly under her touch.

What was it about him that drew her in so much? He was so kind and caring, something she had not experienced at the hands of a man before. Something she thought she would never get to experience. Yet, here was someone who readily gave her all of his attention. Someone who seemed to want her in the same way she wanted him. And she wanted to experience everything with him.

Slowly, she leant forward and pressed a soft kiss where her fingers had been. Ambrose sighed softly in his sleep, his arm contracting around her, pulling her body closer to him. Lena smiled and kissed him again, firmer this time.

He smiled against her mouth as his eyes fluttered open. "Good morning," he said sleepily.

"Good morning," she said with another kiss.

"Although I am not complaining about the wake up," he said softly, "I feel I need to apologise for trapping you." He started to let go, pulling his leg off her hips, but stopped when she pressed herself against him.

"Don't," she said, snaking her arms up between them to wrap around his neck. She pulled him close, claiming his mouth with hers, opening her lips to allow his tongue to meet with hers. After a moment, she pulled back, moaning softly as she did so. "I want you."

Eyes wide, Ambrose only hesitated for a moment, before bringing his hand up to cup the back of her head and crushing his mouth against hers. He pulled her close as he propped himself up on his elbow and nudged his leg between hers. Lena thrilled at the gesture as she manoeuvred her body to lie beneath him, bringing her knees up either side of his hips. She couldn't help but notice that his body moulded perfectly to fit between her thighs.

Warmth spread from her core as she arched her back to keep her body pressed against him. Ambrose ran his hand down her spine until he hooked his fingers under the hem of her shirt and pulled it up, exposing her upper body to his gaze. He leant back on his knees, helping to pull the shirt over her head. She laid back against the pillows, her hands holding on to his forearms, feeling completely at ease as his eyes travelled over her body.

"You are so beautiful," he said as he trailed a hand down her side and over her stomach. She shivered under his touch, her back arching as if to provide him with a better view. "The most beautiful thing I have ever had the pleasure of seeing. Are you sure about this, Lena?"

"Yes," she said breathlessly, her body aching for his touch. "Yes, Ambrose. I want you. I need you."

With no further encouragement needed, he pulled back enough to help pull her panties off, before tossing his own briefs aside. Covering her body with his again, he kissed along her jaw and neck, his hands exploring her body. He found the firm peak of her nipple and caught it between two of his fingers giving it a small, gentle tug. Capturing the other in his mouth, he flicked his tongue over it causing her to gasp with pleasure, running her fingers through his hair as if to hold him there forever. He suckled and licked her nipple whilst rolling the other between his fingers. A low growl pulled from his throat as she squeezed her thighs against his hips, her core quivering in anticipation of his attention.

Leaving his mouth where it was, Ambrose ran his hand down her side, brushing lightly over the curve of her hips causing her to squirm. She felt him smile against her breast as he found her ticklish spot. Catching hold of his jaw, she firmly pulled his face up to hers. Obediently, he brought his lips to hers, his eyes sparkling with delight as he looked at her. She felt treasured under his gaze, his hazel eyes almost glowing as she let herself fall into their brilliance, never wanting this moment to end.

His hand continued down her hip, slipping it between them and making his way to her already slick entrance. She shifted her hips slightly, allowing him better access, as he ran his fingers over her clit. Her mouth opened and her head dropped back as a wave of pleasure washed over her. Ambrose dropped his mouth to her neck, kissing and biting lightly as his fingers paid intimate attention to the sensitive bud.

"Ambrose," she said breathlessly, her nails digging into his shoulders. If he minded, he didn't say, but simply pressed on with circling her clit with his thumb. She moaned loudly as he slipped a finger and then two inside her wet channel, stroking and stretching as they explored her depths.

Suddenly, Ambrose caught her jaw with his free hand and angled her face back to his. Her mouth already agape, he delved his tongue inside meeting with hers in a frenzied dance. Her mind went blank with his kiss, her desire for him increasing as his hand remained against her neck, holding her jaw in place for his intentions. She cried with disappointment as he pulled his mouth away.

"You are so wet. So ready for me," he whispered against her mouth, removing his hand from between them. He raised his arm to rest his elbow beside them before popping his fingers in his mouth to taste her on them. Lena almost moaned at the sight, her hands gripping the top of his arms as if to steady herself. Her breath quickened at the thought of him inside her, but a seed of anxiety grew within her belly.

She felt Ambrose's body stiffen above her, his eyes locking with hers and filled with concern. *Oh no...* both she and the voice said simultaneously in her mind, remembering the emotional link between them.

"Lena, what's wrong?" he asked softly.

"Nothing," she replied quickly. "I'm fine. Don't stop." She cupped his jaw with her hand and smiled.

He kissed her gently, but more reserved than before. "I can feel your hesitation."

"Ignore it, please," she pleaded against his lips.

"I can't," he said, lifting himself onto his elbows, placing his hands either side of her face and brushing the back of his fingers along her jaw. She pressed her cheek into his hand, feeling secure and safe under his weight, despite it pinning her to the mattress. "Lena, talk to me. Are you sure you want this?"

"Yes," she said without hesitation.

"Then why are you anxious?"

"Ambrose, please..." she sighed, holding his wrists as she looked up at him, hoping to convey her desire for him through her eyes.

"Lena, all I want is to bury myself within you. To feel your warmth around me. But I don't want to do anything you're not sure about. Was it something I did?"

She shook her head fervently, her body burning knowing now that her desire was mirrored within him. "No. It's just..." she exhaled sharply before continuing. "I've never... uh... oh god, you're going to make me say it," she covered her face with her hands in embarrassment. "I've never had sex before."

There was a long silence between them as Lena shifted uncomfortably beneath him. Ambrose was frozen in place, his eyes wide with shock.

"Ambrose?" she asked tentatively, noting he had stopped breathing.

Well done, you broke him...

Oh, shut up, she told the voice.

"You're a *virgin?*" he blurted finally.

She rolled her eyes dramatically. "You don't have to say it like that..."

"Not sure how else I'm supposed to say it? You've never had sex before?"

"No."

"But you... ah," he started his eyes glancing towards his hand in confusion.

"Oh god, I'm not a prude, Ambrose," she said, slapping him

teasingly on the arm. "I've fooled around, I've watched porn and had my fair share of toys. I know what sex is, I just never had any desire to go all the way with anyone."

"Not with anyone?"

"No," she laughed.

"May I ask why?"

"The answer to that will almost certainly ruin the mood."

Ambrose smiled warmly at her before placing a tender kiss on her cheek and whispering in her ear, "We have eternity to rekindle it."

She rolled her eyes at him but couldn't suppress the small laugh at his comment.

"Okay, well in the interest of not completely ruining the mood, I'll give the watered down version. Um... growing up the way I did, with my mother and then foster care, experiencing and seeing how children in the system were treated, I..." she paused for a moment, reflecting on her words. "Look, I know not all children in foster care have a bad time or are treated badly, but my experience wasn't great, so, I decided I never wanted to have kids. I didn't want to risk any children of my own ending up in the same situation. And, no birth control is one hundred percent effective, *and*... no doctor will perform a tubal ligation or hysterectomy on a single twenty-four-year-old with no children. So, the best thing was just to... not," she said with a shrug. "And then once I moved here, there wasn't anyone I was even remotely interested in, until you, obviously, so it never came up. And this is not exactly something I thought I would ever say with a naked man between my legs!"

Ambrose laughed and pressed a gentle, drawn out kiss against her lips. Her body responded instantly, as she wrapped her arms around his neck, never wanting to let go.

"Completely understandable," he said, resting his forehead against hers.

"I can't get pregnant as a demon, right?" she asked, unsure if she really wanted to know the answer.

"It's possible, but very unlikely. Usually, only succubi can get pregnant," he said truthfully. "But if you want, we can perform a ritual that will stop you from ever getting pregnant. If we perform it immediately after, you should be safe. Or, do you want to stop until after we've done that?"

Lena cupped his face between her hands and kissed him gently. "No,

I don't want to wait anymore," she whispered against his mouth. "Ambrose, I want to feel you inside me. Please," she begged.

He smiled and claimed her mouth with his, shifting his hips between hers. Pulling back slightly, he looked between them, using his hand to position the head of his cock at her desperately aching opening. Once in position he returned his arm to hold his weight above her. "Ready?" he asked, dropping kisses on both of her cheeks.

Her face flushed at his tenderness, as she held onto his neck and shoulders, lifting her knees instinctively to hook over his hips. She nodded, all speech stolen from her as she revelled in his warmth.

Slowly, Ambrose pressed his hips forward, the head of his cock entering her pussy. Lena dropped her head back at the sensation. She had used dildos in the past, but this felt different as he inched forward, stretching her walls around him with no input from her. He was larger than any toy she had used, but she was not uncomfortable or in any pain. Warmth spread from her belly throughout her limbs as she squeezed her thighs against his hips, pulling him deeper within her.

He dropped his head into the crook of her neck and moaned against her skin. "Oh god, Lena. You feel amazing. So warm and tight, I've never felt something so wonderful."

She moaned loudly into the room, as the full length of him filled her completely. "Ambrose," she cried, "I need you."

As if commanded, he pulled his hips back, before pushing forward again. She gasped as the movement coursed another wave of pleasure throughout her body. His pace increased as her channel walls relaxed slightly, growing accustomed to his size, until he found a steady rhythm that pulled moan after moan from her throat. He kissed her neck, his warm breath almost burning against her already flushed skin. Lena drank in his scent of sage and cedar that mixed with the light sweat that now coated their bodies.

With a swift movement, Ambrose took hold of her knee, bringing it up and pinning it to the mattress, giving way to greater depth. She felt desperate to pull him closer still, lifting her free leg higher to hook over his back, using what strength she had left to pull his hips to hers. Her arms wrapped around his shoulders and she moved her mouth next to his ear.

"Ambrose," his name falling like a sensual whisper from her lips, "take me. Make me yours." He growled against her neck, vibrations coursing from his chest, his pace quickening at her statement. She felt intoxicated, even addicted to him, wanting more yet unable to get enough.

"Lena," he rasped, his fingers digging into her knee almost painfully, but she didn't care. "I can feel your pleasure." He lifted his head, nuzzling against her jaw. "Kiss me," he growled against her skin.

With what little self-control she had left, she turned her face towards him, his mouth covering hers as he drank in her moans. Trailing one of her hands up over his neck, she tangled her fingers through his hair, desperately holding on to him like a lifeline, afraid if she let go, he would disappear, that the magic of this moment would disappear. His tongue danced with hers, his scent overwhelming her, pushing her closer and closer to the edge. She had never imagined such an experience could be so beautiful, so perfect. Electricity danced across her skin as his hand cupped her breast, tweaking her nipple in time with the movement of his hips.

Lifting his mouth from hers, Ambrose stared into her eyes, a soft smile on his lips. "Feeling a spark, my dove?" She could see reflected in his eyes, the electricity she felt was her lightning as it arced around them, harmlessly connecting with the bed posters and canopy in slow, fluid-like movements. Unable to speak, she pulled his lips back to hers, nibbling his bottom lip, gasping silently as he shifted his hips, increasing the pace between them. "Lena," he moaned into her mouth, "your pleasure is overwhelming. I'm so close. Come for me, my dove. I need you to come."

Her back arched and her toes curled at the endearment. Her core started to clench and pulse as pressure built within her belly. Shifting her hips slightly, the pressure broke and waves of ecstasy caused her body to spasm with joy, her cries echoing through the room. Ambrose followed suit as he growled into her ear and his own climax rocking his body against hers. She thrilled at the feeling of his hot release filling her and heightening her satisfaction, prolonging her pleasure. Lightning crackled around them, lighting up the room with its red aura before fading as their bodies descended from the heights of their passion.

As they stilled, they remained entwined letting their breathing return to normal. Lena turned her head and kissed his cheek, smiling with pure joy and contentment. "That was incredible," she whispered.

Ambrose lifted his head to look at her and brushed a light kiss across her lips. "You were incredible, my dove," he said, his voice full of sincerity that made her heart swell with happiness. He rolled to the side, shifting his weight off her chest, pulling her leg with him so that it was draped across his waist. She rested her head on his chest, feeling at peace in his arms. "No drifting off, my dove," he whispered, kissing the top of her head. "I'm not done with you."

Lena laughed against his chest, trailing her hand over the soft bed of hair covering it. "Is it always like that?"

"I'd say yes, but as it was the most beautiful thing I've ever experienced, I have nothing else to judge it by," he answered her, running his hand up and down her back as she nestled into his side. "Give me a minute to recover and we could see if it is."

"Should probably go do that ritual first," she said, lifting her head onto her chin to look at him, shivers running across her skin as he smiled at her with such warmth and affection, taking her breath away.

"You really don't want kids?" Ambrose asked, the question genuine with no judgement behind his eyes. "The ritual is not reversible."

Nodding, Lena propped herself up onto her arm to look at him better. "I really don't. And no offence, I really don't want a demonic baby. Especially if, as you've said, natural borns have no human form." She looked away briefly before asking; "Do you want kids?"

He chuckled. "No," he said, shaking his head. "Same reasons."

"Well, then," she smiled, "let's go scorch that earth."

Returning her smile, he pulled her close for a kiss. "Go, clean up. I'll get everything set up in the altar room."

Dropping a final kiss on his lips, she rolled over and off the bed. Euphoria flowing through every inch of her body, she smiled with joy as she felt Ambrose's gaze follow her across the room until she entered the bathroom.

Once inside she fell back against the door, sinking to the floor and hugging her knees to her chest. Her body was buzzing from the morning's events. Yes, she'd never been with anyone else to make any sort of comparison, but she could feel deep within her, that she would never be satisfied with anyone else. Ambrose had awoken something inside that now craved his body, his touch. His kiss. Closing her eyes, she remembered the feeling of him entering her for the first time. The thrill and the sensation. She'd felt complete, like at last she'd found some semblance of belonging, perverted as that might be.

She'd been truthful with him the night before. She wasn't sure she could trust him. If what he and Morgan had said was true, then her growing bindings indicated a strength in her that she was yet to tap into.

Something that others had always made her doubt was possible. If that power was really as great as the books she'd been reading had implied, Ambrose could easily use her to protect himself as long as she remained bound to him. In her gut she didn't think he would, but the voice in her mind told her to be careful, that he wasn't telling her everything. The majority of her life she had been subjected to the manipulations of others. It would take more than one morning of bliss to overcome the scars that had left behind.

But Ambrose had relented to her desire to see Cyrus. So maybe, just maybe, he really did have good intentions, and genuinely cared about her. That's what she thought when she was alive. Why did becoming a demon have to change her view on him?

Taking a deep breath to steady herself, Lena got to her feet and cleaned up. Ambrose was not in the bedroom anymore when she went back. She pulled on some clean underwear and a short sleeve shirt. The sheets on the bed were still strewn across it, half on the floor. With a soft smile, she placed her hand flat on the mattress, where she could still feel the warmth from their bodies. Her smile growing, she turned on her heel and left the room, eager to be with Ambrose again.

CHAPTER SIXTEEN

"So, what are the pits like?" Lena asked, half jogging beside Ambrose as they walked through the corridors of Hell.

"Like... pits," he said, soft laughter in his voice.

She scoffed at him. "Thanks captain obvious."

He smiled at her. "Remember what we talked about?"

"Yeah, yeah," she sighed. "Do what I'm told. Answer questions only when asked directly. Keep my head down."

"And, use your powers sparingly, if you can. Don't exhaust yourself," he continued. "Marcus is tracking down Zagan. Hopefully, he can keep him away for now. Won't work forever, but we'll cross that bridge when we get to it."

They rounded the corner entering an expansive cavern that had large circular pits recessed into random spots along the floor. Walking across the floor were a number of demons, each looking into the pits, barking orders and instructions to those within. The sound of grunting demons filled the air as they trained under the watchful eyes of the demons above. Above their heads, near the roof of the cavern, a group of winged demons sparred with each other. They moved with inhuman speed and agility, their wings flapping as they leapt and dodged their opponent's attacks.

"Just when I think I'm getting used to it down here," Lena said, her eyes darting throughout the room. "How freaking big is this place?"

He chuckled at her reaction. "As big as we need it to be," he replied.

"Come on." He led her over to the pit in the centre of the cavern. It was the largest one in the room, used to train newborns or host sparring matches worth watching. "Hey, Archie!" he called out, waving at one of the winged demons standing next to the pit.

"Archie?" Lena asked under her breath. "The demon you are going to get to train me is called Archie?"

Tossing her a discrete smile they walked up to the red-skinned demon. Ambrose shook his hand warmly.

"Ambrose," Archie greeted him with a nod. "So, this is Lena then?" he said, turning to her.

"Hey," Lena smiled with a small wave.

Archie bowed his head slightly in greeting, jet-black hair that blended in with his horns almost perfectly, falling in front of his eyes that glowed like red pools of fire. He crossed his arms in front of his chest as he looked Lena up and down, appraising her. "Not transformed yet," he said walking around her.

"No, not yet," Ambrose replied, giving Lena a reassuring nod, as she shifted on her feet.

"Age?"

"Three weeks."

"Manifestation?"

"Lightning."

"Interesting."

Lena rolled her eyes and pressed her lips together. Ambrose knew she was desperately trying not to snap at the inspection, feeling her annoyance vibrate within his chest. He raised a brow at her, willing her to remain silent.

"What's her control like?" Archie asked, rolling his shoulders as he stood behind Lena, studying her.

Ambrose had to force himself not to laugh as she opened her mouth to say something before snapping it shut with a loud click of her teeth. "She's got the fundamentals."

"Turn around," Archie said to her. Even Ambrose bristled at the command towards his boundling. Lena looked at him from the corner of his eye, indicating her patience was wearing thin. He nodded, telling her to comply, as he tried to convey his sympathy for the situation with his eyes. She huffed and turned on her feet to look at Archie, who smirked at her. "You may be bound to Ambrose for now, but you serve Hell. Get used to taking orders from demons more powerful than you."

Lena's face relaxed along with her shoulders as she looked at the ground. She nodded in understanding before looking back at Archie.

"Good," Archie said, stepping towards her. "Now, follow me."

She let out a long sigh before turning on her heel and following the demonic trainer into the centre pit. Ambrose pressed his lips together, walking behind them to sit at the edge of the pit and observe, well aware she was going to be pissed at him when they got home. Archie was a good trainer, but he had no people-skills.

"No point pitting you against transformed demons yet. They'd destroy you," Archie explained as he and Lena descended into the pit. "With lightning manifestation, you might accidentally kill another newborn, so for now, you'll train with me until we see what your capabilities are."

Ambrose kept his gaze on them, only looking away to quickly scan the faces of other demons who ventured close to the pit. So far, no one that he was worried about, but he would consult with Marcus later just in case.

"You're transformed though," Lena retorted, although Ambrose noted she kept emotion out of her voice. *Clever girl*, he thought.

"True, but I won't accidentally kill you," Archie said with a smile.

Archie and Lena stopped in the middle of the pit. Unfortunately, Archie was removing her from training with other newborns, thus removing the possibility of her training in obscurity, as Ambrose had hoped. But they couldn't go back now. He witnessed what Lena had talked about regarding the whispers as soon as they arrived in Hell today. Boundlings were more of a commodity than he had let on to her as yet, and if one showed true potential, even more so. The current growth of her bindings had not gone unnoticed.

"Alright, show me what you can do," Archie said, standing in front of Lena and pointing towards the dummies lined up along one of the walls. "Throw your power at one of those. And if Ambrose told you to hold back, don't. I will be able to tell."

With a slight huff, Ambrose tilted his head to the side, curious to see the outcome of this. Lena had been training in the Repository with Morgan, but he hadn't been privy to any of that. Their sessions with Marcus had been focused on containing the lightning, or using it as an extension of herself rather than as a weapon.

Lena nodded and rolled her shoulders as she turned to the dummies.

Ambrose watched her carefully, sensing a calmness wash over her. Red lightning crackled from her hand and travelled up her arm, dancing over her skin as she focused it into a singular point. Throwing up her arm, the lightning shot from her hand in a fast and explosive arc, slamming into the centre of one of the dummies. It exploded under the force of the blast, ripping apart and sending charred remnants into the air. He straightened his back in surprise at the power behind her attack.

"Impressive," Archie said, looking at the damage. "Very impressive. Again, dial back the power though. Hit the target, but don't destroy it, if you can."

Ambrose saw her shoulders rise as she took a deep breath. His eyes darted around the edge of the pit. As suspected, the blast drew attention and more faces appeared to watch her. He made a mental note of the names he knew, but for now he wasn't worried.

Another arc of lightning sped towards the neighbouring dummy, again hitting it dead on. This time only a black scorch mark could be seen, the dummy was left otherwise intact. Ambrose smiled with pride. *Not bad, Lena.*

"Well done," Archie walked over to the dummy to inspect it. His black claws scraped over the surface of the scorch mark, the damaged area crumbling under his touch leaving a small caved in crevice. "Maybe still a little overpowered, but reasonable."

Turning back to Lena, Archie gathered his own power in his hands. Blue flames licking up his arms, lighting his red skin up with an eerie glow.

"Ah..." she remarked softly, taking a step back.

"Now we test your reactions. Don't worry, I won't throw anything at you that will hurt. Much," he said with a sneer. Ambrose shifted, unsettled by the statement. "Flame out of the way, or simply dodge. I don't care what you do. The aim is to not get hit. Feel free to try and hit me, if you can. Ready?"

"Do I have a choice?" she asked, raising her brows.

"No."

Without another word, Archie threw a fireball at Lena, who gathered her flames and disappeared just as the attack neared her. She appeared to Archie's right, sending an arc of lightning towards him. He twisted on his heel, easily dodging the bolt causing it to hit the wall behind him. Another fireball sped towards her, as she ducked to the ground and rolled out of the way, the fire extinguishing on the floor where she had been. Ambrose was surprised to see how quickly she moved, how fast she anticipated the attacks. Not something he had expected her to be able to do so readily.

Lightning coursed up her arms as she slammed her palms into the floor sending sparks like waves across the ground towards Archie's feet. Morgan had to have taught her that, Ambrose mused, impressed at her quick thinking. Archie spread his wings and jumped into the air before the electricity could reach him.

"You would have been better, keeping me on the ground. Now I have the advantage," he jeered, sending two fireballs towards her.

Lena flamed out of the way at the last minute. It looked like she was slowing. Ambrose was sure that last move would have used a lot of energy. With a sigh, he risked looking around the room again. Cursing under his breath for getting caught up in the spar below, he noted with annoyance that a small crowd had gathered. The other trainers all seemed to have abandoned their pits, more interested in the fight between Archie and Lena instead. Some fully fledged demons had also amassed, whispering to their boundlings or between themselves as the events progressed. Two caused him possible concern, but at least he couldn't see Zagan. *Yet.* Hopefully, Marcus was succeeding in keeping him occupied.

Reappearing in front of the dummies, Lena sent a wave of lightning out from her hands. It was spread out but moved faster than one of her concentrated bolts. She wrapped it round Archie's ankle like a snake and pulled him back to the ground. With a cry, Archie's back slammed into the floor, the lightning enveloping his body momentarily before dissipating. Ambrose's mouth hung agape at what he had just seen. Where had she learnt that?

Archie laughed as he rolled over and propped himself up on his elbows. "Not bad, Lena. Not bad." Lifting to his feet he looked over to where she was panting heavily. "You're nearly spent though."

As if on cue, Lena's knees gave out and she fell onto her hands, her shoulders heaving as she tried to regain her breath. Ambrose bit his lip in annoyance. She had exhausted herself.

"You are certainly creative in strategy," the trainer complimented walking over to her. "Did you fight in life?" He held out his hand for her. Glaring at him through her lashes, Lena sighed, grabbing hold of his hand as he helped her to her feet.

"When I needed to, which was more than I care to admit," she said, brushing the dirt off her knees. "Living on the streets you pick up a thing or two. Managed not to get hit though," she smiled cockily at him.

Archie tilted his head, before dropping to the ground and twisting on his foot, kicking out one leg to try and sweep her legs out from under her. She moved quick though, despite her exhaustion, placing her hands on Archie's shoulders and jumping onto his back. Her additional weight threw him off balance and they fell to the floor. Lena rolled to the side, quickly scrambling to her feet as Archie tried to follow suit. Racing towards him, she landed one hand flat on the middle of his back between his wings and sent lightning through her fingers. Archie convulsed under her touch, his head thrown back, mouth open in a silent scream. She kept him like that for a few seconds before pulling back and flaming to the other side of the pit, out of his immediate reach. Falling to one knee, she kept her eyes locked on the winged demon who groaned as he pushed himself into a kneeling position.

Hushed whispers rippled through the crowd and Ambrose was sure he heard one or two demons clap. He looked around, noting that there wasn't any spare space around the edge of the pit anymore. Maybe this had been a bad idea.

"Where'd she learn that?"

Ambrose startled to hear Marcus' voice, turning his head to stare as his friend sat down beside him.

"What are you doing here?" he whispered angrily.

"Sorry," Marcus replied. "I lost track of Zagan."

"Fuck!" Ambrose scanned the crowd, trying to see if he could spot him.

"Words getting round already, anyway," the cambion said under his breath. "The boundling who knocked Archie onto his arse."

"That was less than five minutes ago," he said, panic rising in his chest. He couldn't see Zagan, but that didn't mean that he wasn't watching.

"This is Hell, Ambrose," Marcus shrugged as he too scanned the room. "Word gets round quick. Nothing we can do about it now. Even if he's not here, she's going to be a hot topic of conversation for a while."

Ambrose sighed, resigning himself to the inevitable. Marcus was right. Lena was showing impressive skill for her first time in the pit. There was no keeping her secret now.

Beneath them, Archie shook his arms out, recovering quickly to throw a fireball towards the said boundling. With the distance she had given herself, Lena launched herself to the side, just as a second fireball closed in on her new position. She threw up her arms, throwing a bolt of lightning to crash with the fire. The blue and red energies clashed in the air, sending out a shockwave that pushed her back into the wall behind her.

Archie had gotten to his feet, spread out his wings and rushed towards her, flames building in his hands. With a cry he threw a punch at her chest. She ducked last minute causing his fist to connect with the wall beside her head. Shards of rock covered them, smoke and dust filling the air. Holding up her hands, Lena caused an explosive spark that pushed him back just enough for her to slip to the side. She balled her fists as they crackled with red energy and jabbed at his ribs, connecting both times. Wincing at the punches, Archie shuffled on his feet, trying to turn to meet her.

"Are we sure that's our Lena?" Marcus said, tilting his head. "She can move."

"Unclear. This is making me wonder how three guys managed to jump her," Ambrose mused.

"Three versus one is very different."

"True."

She flamed to Archie's other side, just as he got his footing, and jabbed at his opposite ribs. He was getting frustrated and if Ambrose could see it, so could Lena. Ambrose noted she was using her small size to her advantage. Archie was nearly three feet taller than her in demonic form. Swinging his arms out was essentially useless as she could duck under them without losing her footing.

Suddenly, Archie pushed out his wings, clipping Lena's shoulder and sending her to the ground. Ambrose swore he heard some of the demons around him gasp in surprise.

Barely having touched the floor, Lena flamed to the centre of the pit, distancing herself again from the winged demon. He spun around as she reappeared, sending a large fireball in her direction. Ambrose held his breath as he realised she didn't have time to avoid the attack. She managed to throw up her arms to cover her centre, but to the audible shock of the crowd, the fireball connected with her, sending her flying into the wall at the opposite end of the pit.

Her cry echoed through the pit as she slumped against the wall, trails of smoke rising from her body. Ambrose's jaw clamped in anger and he felt Marcus' hand on his arm, ready to hold him back if needed. He breathed out heavily as pain radiated over his back. "She's hurt," he whispered to Marcus, who merely squeezed his arm reassuringly.

A medic quickly dropped into the pit next to her, bending down to check her injuries. Ambrose noted part of her shirt had burnt away, but thankfully, her bindings had not been exposed. They had a hushed exchange as the medic checked over her, coursing some of their power over her back.

Archie walked over to them, exchanging a few words with the medic before they left. He held out his hand for Lena, who took it with a dubious scowl on her face.

"So much for not getting hit," she said, annoyance dripping from her voice. Ambrose breathed a sigh of relief at the sound.

"You did very well," Archie commended her. "Not many first time boundlings can bring me to my knees." He bent down to whisper something in her ear. She smiled at whatever it was before thanking him. Ambrose watched curiously, mentally noting to ask her about that later. "Enough for today. You well exceeded my expectations. Rest up. Come back tomorrow," Archie said, patting her on the back.

Lena nodded before looking up at Ambrose. Her eyes widened to see the crowd that had gathered.

"Get out of here!" Archie barked at the crowd who quickly scrambled to disperse.

Getting to his feet, Ambrose made his way towards Lena as she exited the pit. He stilled suddenly, turning his head to look at the opposite side of the pits edge, icy dread washing over him. His eyes locked with the demon opposite who smiled cruelly at him before turning and disappearing into the crowd. *Zagan...*

"Shit," Marcus cursed, standing next to him. "I'm sorry, Ambrose."

Ambrose shook his head. "It's fine," he said quietly. "We just adapt."

"Hey," Lena said cheerfully as she walked up to them.

"Hey, Lena!" Marcus said, smiling at her. "Impressive display. Well done."

"Thanks," she grinned at him.

"Excellent work," Ambrose placed a hand on her arm, giving her shoulder a squeeze. Sending his power over her shirt, he discreetly repaired some of the damage to it. "Ready to go home?"

Lena hesitated, biting her bottom lip as she looked at the floor. "Ah, do you mind if I go see Cyrus?"

"Cyrus?" Marcus asked, confused. "What, the hellhound keeper?"

"Yeah, he and Lena knew each other in life," Ambrose explained to his friend. "Ah, Lena, I know we talked about it, but I'm really not sure it's a good idea..."

The hurt in her eyes was instant, sending a dagger of guilt into his gut. "Ambrose, you said—"

"I know what I said," he interrupted. "It's not about that, Lena, it's..." he trailed off not wanting to have this conversation now. Not here.

"Don't do this, please," she pleaded with him.

"Lena..." he sighed heavily, placing his hands on his hips. "Dammit, okay!" he relented. "Okay. You're right, I know. No talking about me or Zagan though, okay?"

She beamed at him, hopping from one foot to the other in excitement. Ambrose rolled his eyes and shook his head in defeat. "I promise," she said.

"And do not tell him about your bindings."

"Got it."

Looking at her, Ambrose realised that regardless of their bond, he was going to have to make more concessions in the future for her. Especially considering her recent display of power. "Okay," he said softly. "Go see your friend. Do you know how to get there?"

"I can backtrack from the Repository," she said looking towards the cavern entrance.

"If you head back to where we arrived, take the first corridor on your left then the second right," he directed her.

"Thank you," Lena touched his arm briefly, as she started to walk past him.

"When you're done, head straight back to the manor," he called after her. "If you're not back in two hours, I'm coming to get you."

"Got it. See you later!" she cried over her shoulder waving at him and Marcus.

They watched Lena disappear through the entrance to the cavern, before Marcus turned to Ambrose. "Cyrus is bound to Zagan, right?" he asked, raising his brows.

"Yep," he replied, making his own way out the cavern.

Marcus sighed and followed his friend. "This is not a good idea..."

"You don't need to tell me that," Ambrose retorted as they walked into the corridor.

"Then why are you letting her go see him?"

Ambrose rounded on his friend, knowing he was directing his annoyance at the wrong person but unable to stop himself. "Because if this is going to work between her and me, I need to trust her," he said, his voice deathly quiet. "Sure, I could compel her, but one day that's not going to work anymore. She needs a chance to make her own alliances. I can't take this from her, Marcus. I can't," he said, pulling back slightly and folding his arms in front of him. He looked at the floor with a heavy sigh. "Not unless I really have to."

Marcus nodded and patted him on the back. "Alright. Well, at least we know she can handle herself," he consoled. "I hope you know what you're doing, though."

"Yeah," Ambrose said dejectedly. "So do I."

CHAPTER SEVENTEEN

The whispers had certainly increased, Lena noted to herself as she made her way to the hellhound den. As soon as she had made her way back to where she and Ambrose had arrived, the demons in the junction had fallen silent to stare at her. Dropping her gaze, she hurriedly ducked down the first corridor as Ambrose had directed. Their whispers erupted as soon as she had gotten out of the line of sight. Sighing in annoyance she took the second corridor on her right, happy to realise she recognised the area. Picking up her pace, she quickly rounded into the den, thankful to note that it was absent of other demons except for the one she wanted to see.

Cyrus was fussing over the new pups who were now running around his feet, falling over him and each other as he tried to inspect them. He was chuckling softly to himself as he tried to pick up one of the errant pups, a sound that made Lena's heart sing with joy. A sound she had once thought she would never hear again. Hearing her enter he looked up to the entrance and smiled.

"Hey, Lena," he greeted her with a small wave. "What brings you here?" Hopping over the pups whose mother now came to corral them to an alcove, he made his way over to her. "Whoa, you look like Hell. What happened?"

Lena rolled her eyes but smiled at the remark. "Geez, thanks," she scoffed. "First time through the training pits." Cyrus hissed at the explanation, giving her a commiserating grin. "I wanted to see you," she continued. "Thought we could catch up a bit."

His expression fell slightly, an odd sadness filling his eyes. "Ah, Lena... you know I... I'd love to, but I'm not sure that's wise," he said, crossing his arms in front of him.

"I know you're bound to Zagan," Lena sighed. "And I know he and Ambrose don't get along. But as long as we don't talk about them, I don't see a problem."

Cyrus looked at the ground shaking his head. "It's not just them, Lena."

"I haven't seen you in ten years, Cyrus. To the point where I thought you forgot about me. You were my only friend in foster. I'd like to get my friend back. Come on," she pleaded.

He chewed his bottom lip, looking at her, his eyes conveying the conflicting feelings within. "Alright fine," he sighed, a soft smile forming on his face. "You always could twist my arm. I have to check in on one of the mothers. We can sit in her alcove."

Lena beamed and clapped her hands together, following him down into the den. Some of the hellhounds lifted their heads to look at her as she and Cyrus made their way across the floor. He led her into an alcove on the far wall. She noted that they were no longer visible from the entrance once they made themselves comfy on the floor. Leaning back against the wall, she stretched her legs in front of her as she watched Cyrus check over the hellhound currently sleeping on the bed of straw strewn over the floor.

"So, who's this?" she asked.

"This is Zamira," Cyrus said softly, running his hand over the fur on her neck. "She's a little over a month pregnant. Should be around four or five pups."

"She's beautiful," she sighed, smiling as Zamira stretched out with a lazy yawn, her long tongue unfurling from her mouth as it opened wide, woken by their presence.

He looked at her, mild surprise on his face. "Most new boundlings are creeped out by them."

"Don't get me wrong, they are intimidating at first glance. But then so was Morgan..."

"Ha! I'm more scared of her anyway."

"Completely valid," she chuckled, remembering her recent lessons with Morgan and the numerous clips over the back of the head she received in the process. The laughter seemed to have caught Zamira's interest, who rolled over within the alcove until her head landed on Lena's lap. Cyrus took the opportunity to rub over Zamira's belly, pressing in here and there, gently checking on the pups. She watched him for a while as she stroked along Zamira's snout, before asking him; "How'd it happen for you? Your sacrifice?"

"Oh hell, Lena," Cyrus huffed as he fell back against the opposite wall, resting his elbows on his knees. "You really want to talk about that?"

"Why not?" she shrugged.

He sighed, his head dropping forward. "The last family I went to, they were okay. Positively nice compared to what I left behind. No offence," he finished quickly looking up at her.

Lena grinned, understanding what he meant. "None taken. Remember they tried to sell me for drugs."

"Yeah," he chuckled. "But something was off. I just couldn't put my finger on it. I put it down to only being there a month whilst waiting for the apartment our social worker organised for me." He paused for a moment to pick up a piece of straw from the ground, twisting it between his fingers. "Just under two months of living on my own, the family broke into my apartment and knocked me out. I know I got stabbed," he sighed, indicating to the red star in the middle of his chest. His death mark, like the lines on her wrists. "But, I woke up dead, Zagan standing over me. I don't remember what actually happened, and Zagan has never told me. Not that I've asked either." Lifting his head, he looked at Lena. "What about you?"

"I was jumped," she said, scratching behind Zamira's ear. "Three guys. I think they drugged me, but I don't know. I blacked out for a bit. Woke up in the trunk of their car moments before killing me."

"Wait, you were awake for it?" Cyrus asked, shock evident in his voice.

"Yep," she sighed as she looked at her wrists. "Saw their faces. Felt the knife as it went into my skin. Felt my blood leaving my body. It's all kinda surreal now."

They were silent for a moment as Zamira snored softly in her lap. "Shit, Lena," Cyrus said with a heavy sigh. "I'm sorry. At least I don't remember my death."

Lena shook her head before looking back at her friend. "What made you choose to become a demon?"

"Ah, not sure really," he shrugged. "It felt like the right choice to make at the time."

"Yeah, I get that. Same for me." Lena bit her lip, wondering if she should tell Cyrus that she knew Ambrose before her death. *Bad plan...* the voice, that was now becoming annoyingly familiar to her, cautioned. Ignoring it, she ran the conversation through her head. Reminding herself of Ambrose's warnings about Zagan, she determined it was better that it remain a secret. She couldn't see how it could be used against them, but it was better safe than sorry. "Hey, can I ask you something?"

"Sure, shoot."

"Why the hellhounds?" she asked, looking at Zamira. "How'd you figure out they were your design?"

"Ah," he sighed, looking up to the roof of the alcove, seemingly contemplating what to say. "Well, Zagan brought me here one day, just in passing," he explained. "I was fascinated by them, and it just kind of... clicked. They listened to me, accepted me. The previous keeper of this den died a few years before I got here. The other keepers tried to help out, but the packs are very selective of who they allow in. There should be a number of keepers to a den, to provide round the clock care, but I'm all this den has for now. You any closer to figuring out yours?"

"Ha! Good one," Lena chuckled, shaking her head. "Nah, not really. I'm pretty good with spell craft and even potion making, but I'm not settling into any one thing. I don't want to work deals. I haven't seen enough of the pits to decide on that yet. Artifice eludes me."

"Yet, you always had such a sharp tongue."

She poked said tongue at Cyrus. "I hate manipulating people. I'd rather avoid a design that involves people at all. Might end up just helping Morgan out in the Repository at this rate."

"Oh, the horror!" he mocked.

"I know right," she laughed with him, enjoying the relative normality of the exchange between them, despite the topic of their conversation. "I've missed you," she said softly.

"Yeah," he nodded, rubbing his fingers over his cheek. "Me too, little mouse."

"Hey," she scoffed, wagging her finger at him. "Just because you're in demon form and therefore still tower over me, does not mean I'm still little," she scolded him. "Older than you in human years."

He smirked at her. "Still beat you in demon years."

Again, they fell silent, just looking at each other. "Are you okay?" Lena asked after a moment. "With Zagan?"

Cyrus shook his head emphatically. "Lena... I'm not going to talk about him."

"No, I know," she said hurriedly. "Sorry, that's not what I meant. I just... I mean, it's weird, isn't it? We bind ourselves to someone we've only known, what? Five or ten minutes? After going through a seriously traumatic event. How do we know we made the right choice?"

"We don't," he sighed, looking at her sympathetically. "And you've got to come to terms with that. It's a long time, but being bound isn't forever."

"Yeah... you're right," she said with a small nod. "Did..." she started before trailing off. Coughing slightly, she tried to restart her question. "Did you think of me... after..." Her voice broke, unable to continue.

Cyrus sighed heavily, drawing her gaze back up to him. He had a pained look on his face, his eyes squeezed shut as he rubbed his temple. "All the time," he whispered finally. "I wanted to come find you. But the command to not expose ourselves to mortals stopped me. I even considered asking Zagan or another to find you, to make you a deal." He shook his head softly, looking at her with sadness in his eyes. "Some days, I thought you might be better off in Hell than in the environment we lived in. But mostly, I hoped you would never come here. I hoped that you would find some peace after ageing out. Some place where you could be free of everything we went through." He smiled ruefully at her, his head tilting to the side. "Imagining you moving on and making something of your life, helped me through my transition here."

Looking up and swallowing, Lena tried to push back the tears that were forming in her eyes. "I was angry at you for a while, thinking you had abandoned me. I needed you. I tried looking for you, but even with Tracey's help, I couldn't find you. After a while I thought maybe, if I couldn't find you, you couldn't find me. So, I let the anger go and moved on," she sighed, resting her head back against the alcove wall. "Unfortunately, I got myself into a fair bit of trouble after ageing out," she smirked, rubbing the back of her hand over her forehead. "The last four years were okay though. I moved to a small town, worked in a cafe. Even made a couple of friends." She was happy to see him smile, genuine happiness in his eyes.

"I'm glad to hear that," he whispered, warm emotion filling his voice.

Zamira shifted again, completely pinning Lena's lower half to the floor. She raised her brow at the hellhound, whose eyes were now open and fixed on hers. "Comfy?" she asked, tilting her head to the side.

Cyrus chuckled softly. "She likes you. Zamira, get off," he commanded. Zamira yawned but made no move to obey. "Zamira? Get off," he repeated, his brow furrowing. "Huh..."

"What's 'huh'?" she asked, looking at her friend.

"She's not listening to me," he laughed. "Tell her to get off."

"Why me?"

"Just try it, Lena," he sighed at her.

"Okay..." Uncertain as to the point of this exercise, Lena looked at the beast before speaking. "Zamira, get off."

With a slight huff, the hellhound rolled to her other side, freeing Lena's legs which she now stretched out, relieving the stiffness of them.

"Interesting," Cyrus remarked with a smile. "Say 'stand up'."

"Stand up?"

Zamira huffed again, as she pulled her paws underneath her and pushed herself up. The sheer size of her made the alcove suddenly feel very small. Lena smiled nervously, noting that she had to crane her neck to keep looking into Zamira's eyes.

"She's yours now."

"What?" she asked, her gaze snapping to Cyrus through Zamira's legs. He was grinning uncontrollably at her.

"All hellhounds are meant to eventually find a demon they imprint onto," he explained. "Not every demon gets a hellhound, but all hellhounds get a demon. If they imprint, they do so for life. She won't listen to anyone else now."

The information took a moment to sink in. Her mind still processing the news, Lena scrambled to her feet, coming face to face with Zamira. "What am I supposed to do with a hellhound?" she exclaimed.

"Beats me," Cyrus said, getting up to stand beside her. "That's your problem now, little mouse. I just look after the unbound and pregnant ones."

Zamira stretched out her snout and licked Lena's check. "Ah... thanks girl," she said hesitantly, raising her hand to scratch under Zamira's jaw. "Um... lay down," she ordered, needing to gain some distance from the hellhound. Zamira seemed relieved as she laid back down on her side, rolling over the hay contentedly. Lena smiled at the creature, realising she was not entirely upset at the prospect of caring for her. "Not sure Ambrose will appreciate me taking her home."

"Probably not," Cyrus laughed under his breath. "You've got time to warm him to the idea though. She can't go with you whilst she's pregnant. She'll need to stay here until she gives birth. Should be in the next few weeks."

"Well, I always wanted a pet," Lena smiled softly. "So how does it work? Her being mine and all?" she asked, turning towards Cyrus.

"Ah, well, not entirely sure," he replied, scratching his cheek. "Not my area and never looked into it. As a keeper, I'm unlikely to have a hellhound imprint on me so..."

"Cool," she said, pursing her lips. "But she stays here for now?"

"Yup," Cyrus nodded. He looked at her and smiled. "You may have to tell her to stay though if she tries to follow you out. Come on. We should let her sleep." Taking a final look at Zamira, Lena followed Cyrus out of the alcove and back towards the den entrance. "Might want to break it to Ambrose soon though. Give him as much time as possible to adjust," he said as they walked. "You'll need to sort a den for her near you once she's had her pups. She won't be able to stay with the rest of the pack."

"Great, can't wait to have that conversation," she huffed, rolling her eyes.

"Good luck."

"Cheers."

They made it to the entrance, turning to each other, unsure of what to say or do now. Lena wanted to give him a hug, but thought it might not be a good idea. If they'd still been in the alcove, maybe, but risking anyone else seeing them would only serve to fuel the whispers that were already driving her insane. Even as she contemplated this, Cyrus looked down the corridor before stepping forward and pulling her into his arms. She gasped at the suddenness of it, but wrapped her arms around his back as best she could, joy spreading through her chest at the familiarity of him.

"I really have missed you, little mouse," Cyrus said into her ear. "I'm sorry you're here, but I'm happy to have seen you again."

"Ditto," she sighed, tightening her grip on him slightly.

"Hey, Lena?" he asked, finally letting go and taking a small step back.

"Yeah?"

He smiled at her, a melancholic sadness in his eyes. "This was nice," he said after a moment. "I agree we shouldn't talk about our sires, but otherwise, I'd like to be friends again."

"It's a deal then," she smiled, folding her hands over her heart. "Sires are out of bounds."

Cyrus laughed and mimicked her action in the way they had done when they were kids. "Deal. Maybe one day I'll see you again top-side."

"It would be nice to see you in human form again," she teased.

"See you round, little mouse." He reached out and nudged his fingers against her jaw affectionately.

"See ya," she said, quickly looking down the corridor to make sure it was still empty, before bounding off in the opposite direction she had come. Glancing over her shoulder, she saw Cyrus grin at her before turning round and heading back into the den.

She still had some time before she had to go back to the manor and contemplated if it would be worth passing by the Repository to see if Morgan had anything about hellhounds she could read. Stopping at a small junction, she bit her bottom lip. Ambrose had not been entirely okay with the idea of her seeing Cyrus so perhaps pushing the boundaries today was not a great plan. He had told her to go back to the manor as soon as she was finished, after all.

Turning her head to the side, her thoughts were interrupted by the sound of footsteps coming down the corridor. Deciding she didn't want to deal with whoever it was, she gathered her flames and transported herself back to the manor. Her curiosity, and the Repository, could wait until tomorrow. Additionally, the aches from her round with Archie were starting to catch up with her.

She reappeared in the entrance hall and made her way up the stairs to see if Ambrose was back yet. Determining that he would likely want to ask her about her conversation with Cyrus, she thought it would be better to go to him rather than the other way round. She didn't want to hide anything from him, lest he stop her from seeing her friend again.

CHAPTER EIGHTEEN

"You have a hellhound?" Ambrose cried as he jumped up from his desk in surprise. Lena sat opposite him, her elbows on the arm rests as she pressed her fingers to her temples, her lips pressed together in a thin line. "Lena! Where in the hell are we supposed to put a hellhound?"

He wanted to grab her shoulders and shake her as she shrugged in response. "You could have warned me they imprint on demons," she said under her breath, rubbing her temples slowly. "How was I supposed to know this would happen?" She lifted her gaze to look at him, giving him a meek smile. "Anyway, we've got time to figure something out. She's pregnant."

Ambrose pinched the bridge of his nose and breathed out heavily. "You do know you get her pups too. Until they're old enough to live in the den on their own."

Lena placed her fingers over her mouth and shook her head. "Nope. Didn't know that," she huffed, annoyance clear in her voice. "Because all of this is completely new to me, Ambrose. I'm going to kick Cyrus' arse." She turned her gaze to the ceiling. "Sorry," she sighed. "It's not like I meant for this to happen."

"I know," he breathed as he returned to his seat, placing his head in his hands. "Did you at least have a good time with him?"

He heard Lena get up out of her seat but kept his head bowed. "Yes, I did." She placed her hand on his shoulder, causing him to lean back to look up at her face. Her smile was breathtaking as she leant down and placed a soft kiss on his forehead. "Thank you, Ambrose," she whispered to him. "I know you have your reservations about this. Cyrus was worried about it too. We promised not to talk about our sires."

"Okay. Good," he nodded. Wanting to hold her, he pushed his chair back and placed his hand on her hip. As if knowing his intent, she lowered herself to sit on his lap, wrapping her arms around his neck and leaning into his body. "I'm glad you had fun," he said as he snaked his arms around her waist, pulling her close.

"No, you're not," she smirked.

He chuckled at her remark. "I am," he assured her. "Really, I am. I'm just cautious. I don't want you getting hurt."

"That's why I have you, right?" she asked, gently brushing her lips over his. Ambrose felt warm relief wash over him as she did so, relishing the feeling of her softness.

"Do you have any idea how tempting you are?" he asked, tightening his grip on her waist.

Smiling, she placed repeated kisses against his lips, running her fingers along his jaw with a featherlight touch that made his skin shiver with desire. "I'm getting the idea with how many demons stare at me in the corridors," she teased him, licking her tongue over his bottom lip.

"Maybe I should lock you up," he growled, smiling against her mouth.

"Oh, that could be interesting," Lena purred, pressing her body against his.

He sighed before pulling back slightly, his gaze becoming serious. "Lena, about Cyrus—" he started.

"I know," she interrupted, placing her hands either side of his face. "I get it, okay? I'll tread carefully. I didn't mention anything about us or what's happened since I became a demon. I promise."

Ambrose sighed, well aware that she was really trying to show him that she could be trusted. That she knew what she was doing. He was beginning to understand just how intelligent she was. Added to that she had street smarts, her display in the pits against Archie proved that. "I know I've been telling you who to trust and who not to. I am also fully aware that you need to figure out who you want to trust, on your own terms." He rubbed his hand over her thigh before continuing. "However, regardless of our attraction for each other, or the sex, we are a bound pair until you break your bindings. Your actions could affect me."

"I know," Lena said, tracing her fingertips along his jaw. "I do really appreciate everything you are doing for me. I don't want to cause you any trouble."

He smiled, enjoying her small attentions. "A hellhound might..."

"I'm sorry!" she cried emphatically, rolling her eyes.

"It's fine," he said, laughing internally at her reaction. "Probably not a bad thing overall. Hellhounds are fiercely protective. They're guard dogs essentially. There may be times, she can get to you faster than I can."

"Does she feel things like you do?"

"No, not as we understand it," he answered, shaking his head. "But you are linked in a way. Hellhounds have no powers until they imprint when they start to share the power of their demon. Now she can do everything you can do. You can call her from wherever you are and she'll flame to you."

"A hellhound with lightning powers," she sighed looking over his shoulder. "What could go wrong?"

"So much..." he chuckled.

Lena chewed the inside of her cheek for a moment. "Maybe a faraday cage would be a good den?"

Ambrose let out a full belly laugh at the comment, the imagery she evoked coming to the forefront of his mind. "I'll look into it." Reaching up he took hold of her hand, placing it between both of his and kissing her knuckles. "There's something else you need to know Lena. The relationship between a sire and boundling is uniquely symbiotic."

"It's definitely something," she said, giving him a wicked grin.

He closed his eyes, trying to keep his thoughts on track. If only she knew how distracting she could be. "Lena..." he sighed.

"Sorry, sorry," she chuckled. "I'm listening."

Checking that she was actually listening, he looked up at her, keeping his expression devoid of emotion. "Boundlings need their sires. I've told you before that you remain bound until your power is sufficient to support you as a demon."

"I remember," she nodded.

"Well, it's a bit more than that," he explained. "My power sustains you, until your power can do it on its own. It's why I can feel your emotions, your pain, everything."

"Okay..." she said, her voice barely more than a whisper. She straightened, her body leaning away from him slightly as she focused on his face.

He sighed, hoping she wouldn't react too badly to the next part. He'd been trying to find a way to tell her this for a while now, but the right words had always eluded him. If she was going to have a friendship with someone close to Zagan, however, he wasn't left with any choice. He had to tell her. "But it also means that if anything happens to me... well," he braced himself for her reaction, "essentially, if I die, so do you."

Lena's face went blank and her eyes dulled as his words settled in her mind. He felt her withdraw emotionally from him, even before she pulled her hand from his and got to her feet to walk back to the other side of the desk. He watched her carefully, wishing he had found a way to tell her sooner. "You know," she whispered, her back to him as she stared into the fireplace. He barely heard her speak. "That's probably something I should have been told earlier."

Her emotions were running wild and he had difficulty sorting through them as they coursed through his mind. He could only stare at her back as she stood rooted in the middle of the room, fiddling with her necklace. He desperately wanted to say something to her, but could feel that she wouldn't hear him. Not right now. It was best to wait for her to speak.

After a moment, she inhaled sharply and turned to face him. Her face was unreadable, but she nodded as she exhaled. "Okay," she said softly. "Okay. Well, I've already died once, so... fine." She looked at him, an odd sadness filling her eyes. "You should have told me."

"I know," Ambrose said, getting to his feet and walking around the desk to lean against the front, his hands in his pockets. "I didn't know how to tell you. I'm sorry, Lena."

She rubbed her hands over her face, pressing her fingers against her temples as if to stem a building headache. "This changes everything," she sighed.

"It shouldn't," he said. "It's not up to you to keep me alive. I'm only telling you to make you aware of it."

"Are you kidding?" she cried, stepping towards him. "With everything you've told me about Zagan, of course it changes things."

He shook his head, looking at the floor. "I don't want you to worry about that, Lena. That's my problem."

"It is my problem, Ambrose!" she yelled at him, a desperate pain etching into her features. "It's my life too! Jesus Christ!" Throwing her hands in the air she turned away from him, her breathing hard and fast. "I want to trust you, Ambrose, but I constantly have this feeling that you're not telling me something. Low and behold, I'm fucking right!" She placed her hands on her hips, keeping her back turned to him.

The pit in his stomach felt unbearably heavy, realising he didn't know how to make her understand. He wanted to tell her everything, but he was too afraid she would choose to leave him, or another demon would take her from him, and then all his secrets would be exposed. He had even considered suggesting she bind to Marcus, thinking she possibly would be safer with a more powerful demon than him, but selfishly he didn't want to lose the feeling of the bond with her. Swallowing hard against the intrusive thoughts, he finally mustered the strength to speak. "After we talked about Cyrus—"

"Forget Cyrus, for fucks sake!" she interrupted, shouting at him, her eyes bright with anger as she turned back to him. "Cyrus does not factor into this equation."

"But you were right, Lena. You need your own alliances. Your own friends," he said, folding his arms in front of him, wishing he could turn back time to when she told him about her hellhound. Wishing he could take everything back, approach it differently.

"I need you more!" she yelled, red sparks firing from her arms, dissipating immediately into the surrounding space. Ambrose's breath caught in his throat, his chest tightening as he looked at her, eyes wide with shock. "Screw Cyrus! Until a week ago, as far as I was aware, he disappeared off the face of the earth ten years ago. I haven't known him for the last decade. Yes, it was nice to see him again, but who knows what he's like now. If it came down to you or him, I'd choose you. Every time." Her voice grew soft, her chest heaving as her eyes bore into his. "You are the one I've known for the last two years. You are the one I've wanted to be with. Fuck everyone else!"

He knew he needed to respond in some way, but he found himself frozen, in awe of her fury, shocked at her declaration. His mind wasn't working, only hearing her words on repeat. He barely registered as she rushed towards him, throwing her arms around his neck. Opening his arms, he caught her body as it collided with his, her mouth claiming his in angry passion.

Lena pulled back from the kiss, holding her hands either side of his face, her dove-grey eyes brimming with tears as she looked up at him. He tightened his grip on her waist, keeping barely enough space between their faces for air to move between them. He didn't want to speak, too afraid to move, lest she leave him.

"You are the only one I need," she whispered against his lips.

Nothing else mattered now as he crushed his mouth to hers, one of his hands flying to the back of her head, trying to pull her closer. Lena moaned into the kiss, running her fingers through his hair, seemingly also unsatisfied with the current level of contact. Reaching down, he grabbed her thighs as she jumped up into his arms. She held onto his shoulders as he carried her to his bedroom.

They fell onto the bed, Ambrose pinning her beneath him, his hands roaming every inch of her body, unable to get enough. She pulled at his shirt, undoing the first few buttons before he pulled back, ripping it over his head and throwing it to the floor. Lena propped herself up, tossing aside her own shirt and bra, clawing at his shoulders to pull him back to her.

He caught her jaw with his hand, opening her mouth so his tongue could delve inside to taste her. She was so sweet, her citrus scent washing over him in waves. And he wanted more. Tears ran down her face from the corner of her eyes. He wiped them away with his thumbs, cradling her face with as much care and affection as his current state of mind could convey. He was hungry for her, his body hard and hot, ready to claim her over and over.

"Ambrose," she moaned as he moved his mouth to her neck, nuzzling against her soft skin. She lifted her knees, squeezing her thighs around his hips.

Encouraged by her reaction, he trailed his mouth down her body, stopping briefly at her breasts, capturing one of her hard nipples between his teeth. He growled with desire as he felt her skin shiver under his touch. Her cries echoed through his mind as he laid soft kisses down her supple belly, his hands brushing over her waist and hips. He wanted to claim every inch of her body as his. To mark her as his so that no one would touch her and all would know she belonged to him.

Pushing back onto his knees, he grabbed the seam of her jeans, tugging them down as she lifted her hips to aid in their removal. He threw them aside, dropping back to focus his attentions on her abdomen. Lena ran her nails over the skin on his shoulders, leaving red lines in their wake, her body writhing beneath him. Smiling into her skin, he breathed in the scent of her desire, placing his hands under her thighs to angle her hips up to his mouth.

Her moan was like music to his ears as he lapped at the cream already pouring from her, dipping his tongue inside to taste all of her. He had never tasted something so delicious. She tangled her fingers through his hair, as if she was trying to prevent him from ever stopping. Moving his mouth to cover her clit, he licked and swirled his tongue around it, enjoying how she seemed to hunger for his touch. He placed one of his hands under his jaw, sliding two fingers inside her. Her walls were already pulsing, clenching around his fingers as he pumped them in and out in time with his tongue on her clit.

"Ambrose!" Lena screamed, throwing her head back and arching her spine as her climax took over her body. He grinned wickedly against her, savouring the flood of release that now coated his hand and tongue.

As her convulsions eased, he pulled his trousers off before moving himself over her, pressing her body into the mattress. She held onto his neck, her eyes closed as her breathing started to return to normal.

"You're so beautiful," he said softly. "Irresistibly exquisite."

Lena opened her eyes and smiled at him, her beauty stealing what little self-control he had left. Claiming her mouth with an impassioned kiss, he shifted his hips until the head of his cock rested at her entrance. She sighed into his mouth, arching her back so her breasts pressed against him. Bracing his hands on the mattress, he pressed his hips forward, sheathing his cock inside her warmth.

Ambrose moaned at the feeling of her enveloping him, breaking their kiss and burying his face into her neck. She was so tight and wet, he had to fight to not come as soon as he entered her, her pleasure vibrating through their bond, pervading his own senses. Nothing would ever compare to how she felt around him, her walls clenching with every movement. He began to move his hips, eliciting further moans of pleasure from his bed-mate. His dove. *His.*

She was perfect. Everything he needed. He wanted to tell her everything. Give her everything. And he would. He knew he would. No matter how long it took, he would find a way.

Slamming his hips forward, he wrapped his arms under her shoulders, pulling her tightly against him. Her breathing ran rapid, sending waves of warmth over his neck, as she nuzzled her nose against his jaw. Turning his face, he captured her kiss, immense pleasure building within him as she moaned into his mouth. Everything about her drove him closer to the edge, wanting nothing more than to jump from it, pulling her with him. Sensing she was close, he found the pace that seemed to best build her desire, keeping it as steady as possible, focusing on her need over his own. Her hips shifted, enticing a deep growl from his chest, as she wrapped her legs around his waist, pulling him deeper into her.

"Lena," he moaned against her lips, "I–" Suddenly, he stilled, despite her protests, his body racked with a familiar, yet unwelcome, feeling. He was being summoned. "Fuck! No, not now!" Ambrose closed his eyes as the pull of the summoning coursed through his body. "Lena, I'm so sorry!" He quickly looked at her face, agony gripping his chest to see the distressed look in her eyes, as the flames overcame him and he was summoned away. "No!" he roared as her face disappeared from his view.

As the flames subsided, he was at least grateful for the clothing that appeared during the summoning. His body had transformed into his demonic self which had also wiped away the scents and sweat from their lovemaking. His cock, however, still stood firm and twitched, longing to feel Lena wrapped around it again. He shut his eyes and sighed to calm himself before turning to the middle-aged woman who had summoned him.

"This," he said, the strain dripping from his voice, "had better be good."

CHAPTER NINETEEN

Lena sat up in the bed and pulled her knees to her chest, as she realised that Ambrose must have been summoned. It was the first time he had been specifically summoned since her death, so she had never really thought of the inconvenience of it until now. Her body was still hungry for his touch and warmth, but her mind now raced with a million questions and concerns.

She knew that for him to be specifically summoned that an innocent had to be sacrificed, and due to human's lack of imagination, more than likely it was another girl. Not likely they were sacrificed in the same way as her exactly, but their life-blood had to be used in the summoning runes. That also meant, as Ambrose had explained to her, that their soul now belonged to him as payment for the summoning. Would he now bring them here and offer them the same choice of binding to him? And was she *jealous* about that?

Lena threw her legs over the edge of the bed and grabbed her robe pulling it around her. It would be a little while before Ambrose got back, so she might as well do something rather than sitting around for him. Especially if he was going to be giving another girl's soul the same introduction as he had given her. If she was really feeling jealousy, she wanted to keep her mind busy. She considered having a shower, but that would leave her alone to her own thoughts, which she decided was better to avoid.

Not really caring where she was going, she found herself in the library.

Feeling some comfort within the room, she grabbed a book she had left on the table and crawled into one of the armchairs, pulling her feet under her. Laying the book open over her lap, she tried to ignore her racing mind by focusing on the words within. Perhaps she'd have been better to go to the Repository. She knew that at least Morgan would be able to find something to occupy her.

Her earlier conversation with Ambrose played on her mind. She had opened up to him in a way that she had never allowed herself to do with anyone else before. She never allowed someone to know how desperately she needed them. How afraid she was of losing them. Afraid that they would use that information against her, to manipulate her. It had happened only once before and she'd been left devastated in the aftermath, barely surviving the subsequent pain and loss. She knew she wouldn't survive it happening again, so why did she so readily let herself depend on Ambrose?

It wasn't his fault being pulled away like that, she reasoned with herself, but for some reason it still hurt. That it would happen whilst he was inside her, whilst she opened everything she was to him, made it all the more painful.

Anxiety grew within her, realising that she had more reason than before to be worried by his absence. What if something happened to him? Would she even be aware of it?

Would a new boundling feel the same way?

Lena swallowed hard and shook her head, trying to ignore the thought. What right had she to be jealous, after all? Ambrose had been around a lot longer than her. He, himself, had told her, he didn't trust her yet. She had responded the same so that didn't matter. But would he still want to carry on their relationship if he had someone else to mentor as well? Alone, they could easily get caught up in each other. Someone else would divert his attention. What if he preferred the new one?

With the book now laying forgotten in her lap, she looked up at the shelf beside her. Her gaze settled on the crystallised book that was displayed as a prominent centre piece to the shelf. Not the first time she had been fascinated by it, she had asked Ambrose what it was.

"It was fished from the Dead Sea, cased in the salt crystals," he had explained to her. "It's a copy of the '*Lemegeton Clavicula Salomonis*', the lesser key of King Solomon, detailing spells, curses, rituals and conjurings."

She had looked over it a number of times, trying to read anything through the crystals, mere curiosity as to if she could than actually trying to learn from it. The Repository had other copies of King Solomon's works and she had read a handful of them. But the crystals felt so delicate under her touch, despite Ambrose's assurances she wouldn't, she worried about damaging it, so tended to leave it on its stand to look at it.

Lena sighed, letting her head fall back against the chair. No matter what she did, her thoughts would turn to Ambrose. She wanted him back. She wanted to forget everything and just return to how they were a week ago. Forget Hell, forget Cyrus, forget Zagan… none of it mattered to her.

But what would she do if Ambrose did bring back a new boundling. The soul might not choose to be bound of course, but it was far too easy to imagine that they would. After all, she knew firsthand how alluring he could be, even in demon form. She knew deep down she would be heartbroken if she had to share his attention.

Buck up, Lena.

Oh, shut up, she responded to the voice. She hated hearing it. The fear it evoked in her had lessened since she first heard it, replaced now with annoyance. But she couldn't deny it was sometimes nice to… *converse* with.

What makes you think he would seek someone else?

What makes you think he wouldn't?

Do you honestly believe he would be with someone else in the same way he was with us just now?

Closing her eyes, she remembered how passionate he had been with her. The feel of his hands on her body, the heat from his fingers branding her skin with his touch. She could still pick up undertones of his scent as she took a deep, steadying breath. His mouth and tongue had felt so warm and perfect between her thighs, her core still aching for him even now. She didn't want to lose that. She didn't want to lose him.

It seemed she was destined to lose everyone she cared about. If her life had taught her anything, it was that everyone leaves, eventually. Her father died, her mother killed herself, her family abandoned her to foster care. Although not his fault, Cyrus left, or was taken from her. Would Ambrose be taken from her as well? Just when she started to feel secure with him. Just when she started to believe she'd found someone she could truly care about.

"Lena?"

Sitting upright, she heard Ambrose's voice, but it was distant. He probably was looking for her in his room. She didn't call back as fear washed throughout her body. She had lost track of time, realising that it had been almost an hour since he'd been summoned. Had he brought the sacrifice's soul back? Was it a girl?

"Lena!" His voice was closer now and with a faint rising panic in it. Lena hung her head, closing her eyes and took a deep breath as she got to her feet. "Lena!" he called again. "Where are you? Answer me!" There was definitely panic in his voice.

His command didn't compel her. He wasn't using their bond to force an answer. She took some solace in that. "I'm in the library," she eventually called back, placing the book back on the table and turning towards the door. It took all her resolve not to run into his arms as he opened the door and walked in, his eyes fixed on hers. The longing she had felt for him earlier immediately returned, but her fear at being replaced froze her to the spot. "Welcome back," she said as calmly as she could.

Ambrose took a couple of steps towards her but still kept a small distance between them. He tilted his head studying her face. She turned away from him, focusing her gaze instead on the floor. He was still in his demonic form which she no longer found to be as intimidating as she used to, but in the moment, he was rather imposing.

"Did the deal go okay?" she asked.

"Lena," he said, completely ignoring her question, "are you alright? Why are you in here?"

His voice washed over her adding to the growing warmth between her thighs. All she wanted was for him to hold her, to tell her how much he wanted her, like he did when they were in bed together. But the contrasting icy grip on her chest made it difficult for her to breathe.

"I'm fine. I didn't know when you would be back," she said. "Thought I might as well distract myself. I'm fine." Lena steeled her resolve and turned back to look at him. She was not prepared for the fact that he had moved closer to her. If she wanted, she could reach out and lay her hand on the broad expanse of his chest. Warmth radiated from him and she wanted to melt into it.

"Well, I'm back now," he said, but the concern didn't leave his eyes even with her assurances. "Shall we go back to bed?" he asked, extending a hand towards her.

It would be so easy to just take his hand and forget about her fears. But she would only be lying to herself and putting off the inevitable. "Aren't you busy?" she asked stepping away from him so the pain in her eyes wouldn't betray her. Fully aware he was feeling everything from her through their bond, she tried to empty her mind, to stop her uncertainty from travelling to him.

"Busy? Lena... what's wrong? I know being summoned in the middle of sex is not ideal, but why do I feel like I am being punished for it?"

She could tell he was frustrated at her reaction, especially considering how they had been just before he left. Was she wrong for not wanting to just go back to bed and pretend like nothing had happened? No, she didn't think so. If there was going to be another woman bound to him then things were different. The dynamic had changed and that needed to be sorted out first.

Lena focused her gaze on a geode collection in one of the bookshelves. They glittered in the lights like deep amethyst pools. "Busy with the sacrifice," she said coldly. "My introduction took longer than an hour."

She heard Ambrose sigh heavily but couldn't bring herself to look at him. "So that's what this is about," he said. There was relief and humour mixed within his voice. A pang of anger at his response coursed through her chest, tightening the already growing tension in her gut, but she kept it in check willing to let him explain further. There was a long silence before he spoke again. "I didn't bring her back here, Lena."

Shocked, she turned to look at Ambrose. He had a soft smile on his face as he leant against the table and folded his arms.

"You didn't?" she asked, her voice barely louder than a whisper.

"No," he said, shaking his head. "I don't have to bring every sacrificed soul back here, and I don't have to offer them the same choice I gave you. I choose who I have bound to me."

She stared at him in disbelief. "So where is she?" she asked hesitantly.

Ambrose shrugged. "Hell or Purgatory. I don't know and I don't care. What I do care about is why you were worried about it?" He pushed off from the table and walked over to her. Pulling out a chair next to her, he sat down so she didn't have to crane her neck to look at him. Slowly, he took hold of her hand and brought it to his lips. He kissed her knuckles softly, carefully avoiding brushing his fangs against her skin. Warmth radiated from her hand up her arm, washing over her chest. Lena sucked in her breath as he so easily turned her attraction for him back on.

"I thought... I thought all sacrificed souls got a choice as to where they go?" she said, blinking rapidly, trying to sort out her thoughts.

"They do, but I don't need to be the one to take them through that," Ambrose explained, his lips remaining against her hand. "I only do if I want to offer the chance to be bound to me. Otherwise, a reaper demon will deal with it."

Lena fell silent and merely stared at the demon in front of her. He had chosen her, much in the same way she had chosen him. That thought echoed around her mind growing louder and louder in tandem with the almost pleasant ache of her heart.

"I... I was afraid," she said softly, her voice unsteady. "Afraid, that... you wouldn't want me anymore." All her life she tried to be strong, to show that she was in control. She never let anyone get close to her for fear that they would hurt her in the same way her parents had. In the same way everyone had. But Ambrose was different. The only times he had hurt her were is some way or another linked to his desire to keep her safe. He had never hurt her physically or even intentionally. She had felt drawn to him in life. And she was still drawn to him in death. She had even imagined being with him when she thought he was just a man. With him, she felt safe. She had felt safe with him from her first night as a demon. To her own stark surprise, she felt safe enough with him to show her true vulnerability now.

Ambrose turned her hand over and kissed the red line on her wrist put there by her sacrifice to him, holding her fingers firmly between his. "I'm sorry I got pulled away from you. I'm sorry if it hurt and I'm sorry that it caused you to worry." The sincerity in his voice made her throat catch with the sweetness of it. "I didn't offer for you to be bound to me because I had to. I offered because I wanted a chance to be with you, to see what you could become. To see what *we* could become," he looked up at her, his eyes full of warmth and longing. "Our chance to be together during your life was taken from us, so I brought you here as a second chance. I have been so happy with the time we have spent together over the last few weeks and I wouldn't jeopardise that for anything." He smiled softly, as his gaze searched her face. "You are the only one I need, Lena."

A single tear began to fall down her face as he repeated her earlier declaration and Ambrose reached up to brush it away with his thumb. Any remaining resolve she had, or desire to protect her heart, crumbled at his touch and she threw herself into his arms. He caught her and pulled her firmly against him. She felt him bury his face in her hair and his fingers pressed into her sides as if he couldn't pull her close enough. Wrapping her arms around his shoulders, she pulled her legs into his lap, falling into the warmth and firmness of his body. Her fears had been swept away by his words, her heart beating furiously, as if it wanted to explode from her chest. Her shoulders heaved as choked sobs pulled from her throat and tears flowed freely from her eyes.

Ambrose began to rub her back letting her cry into his shoulder. "Hush, my dove. It's alright. I'm here." She revelled in the tenderness of his touch, breathing in his scent of sage and cedar. She never wanted to leave his arms.

They held each other for what felt like an age to Lena. Slowly, she lifted her head to look into his eyes. She smiled at him then leant towards him and pressed her lips to his. He held her face between his hands, his talons tangling in her hair, deepening the kiss between them. Her body burned with desire for him and she felt him harden beneath her.

"Shall we go back to bed?" he said, pulling away, his chest heaving beneath her hands.

She nodded, climbing off his lap and pulling his arm to bring him to his feet. She kept close to him as she looked up into his eyes, which was an effort in his current form. "We'll have to wait a bit before we start up again. I may want you more than anything, but even I will admit, in demon form, you are too big for me," she said with a smile. Ambrose burst out with laughter as he pulled her closer to him, draping his arm over her shoulders. "Hey, how come you can so easily transform when travelling to and from Hell, but you can't transform back to human now?"

"Transforming voluntarily is easier on your body," he answered. "You are mentally and physically prepared for it. During a summoning, you are forced to transform. It rips through you and takes time to recover from." He kissed the top of her head as she leant her cheek into his chest. "Well, I think the mood tonight has been thoroughly altered anyway so I propose we simply return to our room and be together. Sleep if needed. But I am not letting you go." As if to drive home his point, Lena felt his fingers press into the top of her arm. She wrapped her own arms around his waist and let him guide her back to his... *their*... room.

She was right. The dynamic had changed. But not how she thought it would. Now she felt secure, safe and more importantly, wanted.

CHAPTER TWENTY

They didn't sleep. Lena had opted for a quick shower to finally get rid of the aftermath of the pits. After Ambrose reverted to his human form, they rested together against the headboard, as he held Lena's hands between his. Running his thumb over her knuckles, he sighed heavily trying to sort out his thoughts.

"I want to tell you everything, Lena," he said softly. "I don't want you to think I'm hiding anything from you. But I've been around a long time, so there might be things I miss, but that doesn't mean I'm intentionally keeping anything from you."

Lena nodded, shifting on the bed slightly and giving his hand a reassuring squeeze.

"This is all new to me too, you know?" he continued. "I've never had a boundling before."

"You haven't?" she asked, surprise evident within her voice.

He shook his head in response. "Nope, you are my first. That's partly why I accepted Marcus' offer to help train you, to also help me figure out what I'm doing. I know roughly how it works, from my own experience, but I've never helped in the moulding of a boundling." He looked at her. She was staring at their hands, a soft smile on her lips. She really was the most beautiful thing he had ever seen, the soft glow of the fire providing a warm halo behind her. "I need you to understand why Zagan gets to me so much. Why I am so overly cautious when it comes to him. But it doesn't start with him.

"I've told you about my father before. Not in great detail, as I don't remember much about him anymore," he said, drinking in the sight of her next to him. "His wife tried to protect me from him as much as she could, but there was only so much a woman in the fourteen hundreds could do."

"His wife?" Lena asked, raising her eyes to look at him. "Not your mother?"

"No, although I called her my mother," he replied. "My birth mother was one of her maids that had an unfortunate encounter with my father. He would remind me that I was just an accident of his any chance he got."

"Oh, Ambrose. I'm sorry."

He smiled at her. "It's alright. My birth mother's pregnancy was kept secret until she gave birth to me. My mother pretended to be pregnant so it wouldn't raise any questions when I suddenly turned up. She and my father had tried to have children of their own but it didn't work out, so she gladly took me in. Something not many mistreated wives would have done back then. I'm still incredibly grateful for the compassion she showed me."

"She sounds like a wonderful woman," Lena said, interlacing her fingers with his. "Did you know your birth mother at all?"

"Unfortunately, not," he said softly. "She was sent away when I was one, or so I was told. I don't know anything about her. I thought about looking after I became a demon, but the command not to reveal anything to mortals prevented me from trying."

Ambrose sighed, pushing himself to continue. "My father, once I was older, arranged a marriage for me. I was sixteen, she was twelve." Lena gasped but he continued without pause. "I was married for a month when she died from some kind of fever. Before you ask, no, I never slept with her, much to my father's displeasure." He heard her sigh with relief, and he tugged at her hand. "You didn't really think I would have, did you?" he asked in mock offence.

Lena pressed her lips together in a guilty smile. "I don't have any understanding of what it was like back then," she responded. "I'm not in a position to judge."

He nodded pensively. "It was very much expected that I would. But she was so scared that first night. I'll never forget the fear in her eyes. I swore I would never be like my father. I would never force myself on someone. Unfortunately, it was that trait that means it takes someone of innocence to summon me." She shifted closer to him, so that her thigh pressed against his, pulling his hand against her stomach as comfort. "I also had younger half-siblings by that point. My sisters were an absolute joy in my life. I could never hurt someone who reminded me of them.

"That didn't stop my father though. He quickly arranged another marriage for me. Thankfully she was a bit older, sixteen, but I still couldn't do what he wanted. I was pulled away by the trailing end of the Hundred Year War over Normandy shortly after getting married to her. My father took it upon himself to 'comfort' my wife. She died giving birth to his child, who sadly also passed, before I got back. I nearly beat him to death once I found out what happened."

"Oh, Ambrose," Lena sighed, rubbing her hand up his arm. "That's horrible."

He smiled at her briefly, silently thanking the stars for her patience and empathy. And for whatever fated design brought her into his life. "My mother, with her family's influence, was able to prevent my father from making another arrangement until I was older. Much to my father's annoyance, families also did not want to give their daughters to me, worried they would suffer a similar fate to my first two wives. I didn't blame them. I would have been happy remaining single for the rest of my life by that point." Ambrose paused for a moment, looking away from Lena, focusing on the feel of her hand encompassing his before continuing. "Her name was Margaret, the woman who was supposed to be my third wife."

"Supposed?"

"My father had organised a private ceremony in which, as far as I was told, only he, my mother, and Margaret's parents would be in attendance. Turned out it was just our fathers. Our mothers weren't even aware of the engagement. They gave us some wine telling us our mothers would be there soon. The wine was drugged. They killed us in a double sacrifice."

"To summon Zagan," Lena whispered.

Ambrose nodded. "Zagan's power is such, there is very little he cannot offer a person, but he does require two sacrifices to be summoned. I don't know what our fathers got in return, and I never cared about it either. At least I was out of my father's control." He sighed bitterly, forcing himself to continue. "Zagan offered to bind both Margaret and I to him and we accepted. We had no idea what he had planned for us. He seems to relish in the pain of his boundlings, even more so if he is the one inflicting the pain. It wasn't long before Zagan would compel Margaret into his bed constantly. It drove her insane."

He peered up at Lena from the corner of his eyes to gauge her reaction. She was staring off to one of the walls, her face expressionless. "What happened to her?" she asked. "Is she still around?"

"No," he shook his head. "She killed herself. There is a pit of fire in the centre of Hell that is fuelled by condemned souls not worthy of becoming demons. The Infernal Pit as we call it. It is what sustains all demons. But no demon can survive falling into it. She jumped into the pit. It was shortly after that I finally broke from Zagan."

"She was raped by him for almost a century?" Lena exclaimed, looking at him in shock.

He couldn't bring himself to meet her gaze. He still held on to a lingering guilt for what happened to Margaret, regardless of the rational thought that he had been as much under Zagan's control as her. "Zagan is extremely controlling of his boundlings. He kept her very close to him. We were just passing the Pit one day and she jumped in. Not a word or anything."

Lena sighed and rested her head on his shoulder. Relishing the closeness of her, he pressed a soft kiss to the top of her head. "I'm sorry, Ambrose," she said softly, gripping his hand tightly. "Did you love her?"

"No, not really. I cared for her. Zagan used this against me, forcing me to watch or join in his treatment of her. He would play us off against each other, forcing us to fight in the pits, mentally manipulating us until we couldn't tell what was real anymore. I feel guilty for what happened to her, but otherwise I barely even remember her now."

"It's not your fault," she said, lifting her head and looking into his eyes. There was no hurt, malice or pity in her eyes like he had been expecting to find. Instead, they were filled with warmth and caring. She looked at him the same way she had in the cafe on days when he had been exhausted. Their dove-grey depths illuminated with kindness and compassion. Ambrose felt a certain tightness in his chest ease under her gaze.

"Lena," he whispered, before leaning in to her and pressing his lips to hers. There was no passion behind the kiss. He just needed to feel her. She raised her hand and trailed her fingers over his jaw, the tenderness of her touch sending shivers across his skin. "How did I find someone like you?" he asked against her lips.

She smiled, kissing the tip of his nose gently. "I could ask the same thing," she said. Her smile faded as she looked into his eyes. "I can see why you and Zagan are so at odds. And I haven't even met him yet."

"Unfortunately, I think that will be an inevitability at this point. He was at the training pits yesterday. He'll be looking for any excuse to speak with you now," Ambrose sighed as he pulled back from her, resting again on the headboard. "Lena, I think you should keep your friendship with Cyrus."

"What?" she asked, her brows rising in shock.

He nodded. "I know what it's like to be in his situation. He needs his own friends as well," he said. "I'll be honest, I'm not overly happy about it, and maybe you could say I am a little jealous. But I'd be no better than Zagan, if I was the reason that stopped you from seeing Cyrus. Especially, whilst I'm sleeping with you."

Lena chuckled even as she slapped her hand over her eyes in embarrassment. Ambrose smiled at her reaction, gently taking hold of her hand and bringing it to his chest. She looked at him, affectionate humour on her face.

"I trust you, Lena," he said, touching his other hand to her cheek. "I truly do. I've never told anyone all of this. Not even Marcus."

Her gaze softened and her lips parted at his statement. "Ambrose..."

He placed his thumb over her mouth stopping her from speaking. "I'm not expecting you to trust me in return," he said softly. "I hope you will in time, but on your terms. Not mine."

She swallowed and closed her eyes, kissing the pad of his thumb, before lifting her head to look at the canopy. "I still feel like there's something missing. Something you're not saying," she sighed resting her head back against the headboard. "But I'm starting to wonder if I'm just projecting."

He watched the emotions play out on her face simultaneously feeling them unpack within him. "Well," he said, trying to help focus her mind. "I know one thing you haven't told me."

"Oh yeah?" she smirked, looking at him from the corner of her eye. "What's that?"

He smiled as the feeling of joy returned to her. "Where did you learn to fight?"

Lena laughed softly, her warm smile returning to her eyes. "I aged out of the foster system, but... I didn't really live with my last two families. I basically lived on the streets since just before I turned seventeen. I'd been in a group home up until then. Got mixed up with some people that, well, either you hit or you got hit. I was sick of getting hit, so I… I learnt how to hit back. Met a guy… ah…" her eyes widened with hesitation as she trailed off.

"Bad boy type, huh?" Ambrose said with an amused smile.

"Yeah, kinda," she replied sheepishly, peering at him from the corner of her eye. "I don't even know why I was drawn to him anymore. He was an arse. Controlling, manipulative. Constantly getting us into trouble. He called himself TJ," she chuckled almost fondly, shaking her head. "Stupid name. But he was relatively good looking, and paid attention to me, so I got swept up in the moment. I ran away with him more than once. Social services always found me one way or another. Cops would pick me up and deliver me back to the homes. The families I was placed with kept trying to get me back into the group home saying I was a lost cause. Did a week in juvenile detention at one point because of delinquency."

He laughed out loud, trying to picture his sweet Lena in prison. "Even as a virgin, you were innocent enough for a summoning?" he blurted.

"Yeah, go figure…" she replied softly, her expression saddening.

"Sorry," he apologised quickly. "I didn't mean anything by that."

"I know," she said, squeezing his hand reassuringly. "TJ taught me how to fight, until he realised that my knowing how to fight meant he couldn't hit me as easily. Then just after I aged out, he disappeared." Her brow furrowed as if her next memories still caused her pain. Ambrose rubbed her hand between his, hoping to give her some comfort as she had him. "The year before I moved here, I'd been living in a homeless compound. I used fighting as a method of staying alive. Underground cage matches were lucrative ways of getting money."

"I thought you said you avoided life-threatening endeavours?"

"It's only life-threatening if you aren't good at it," Lena said, pressing her lips together. He raised his brow in surprise, but realised he kind of liked this side of her. A side that knew how to survive, no matter what was thrown at her. "TJ showed up to one of the fights. Male on female fights didn't happen often, but when they did, they made the most money. I was broke and desperate. And I was angry. Sadly, my anger got the better of me and he put me in hospital. For a week.

"Apparently, my medical info still had my old social worker as contact. She came to the hospital and tore into me. Until then, I hadn't realised how much she actually cared about me." Pulling her hand away from him, Lena leant forward, wiping a stray tear from her face and wrapping her arms around her knees. "I promised her I'd stop fighting if she helped me get away. Start fresh. Her only condition was that I never speak with TJ again, or anyone else I used to get in trouble with. The rest you know."

Ambrose leant toward her, pulling her into his arms. She made no protests, resting her head on his chest. "Do you know what happened to TJ?"

She shrugged against him. "Died, I think. He got mixed up with hard drugs. Last I heard he OD'd in some back alley."

"What did Archie whisper to you?" he asked. "If you don't mind me asking."

He felt her smile. "Firstly, he apologised for hurting me. Apparently, I had also really hurt him when I electrocuted him. He said I earned his respect and that if I ever needed help, he would give it."

"What is it about you that just draws demons in?" he mused aloud. "Marcus was the same the first time he met you."

"Hey," she chuckled, "I'm a delight."

"That you are, my dove," he smiled, tightening his arms around her. Something occurred to him as she rubbed her cheek against his chest. "Hey, what was your social worker's name?" he asked, angling his head to look at her face.

"Tracey," Lena answered, "why?"

He sighed heavily. "I do have something else to tell you, but I'm pretty sure you're not going to like it."

She pushed herself off him so her eyes were level with his, but she didn't pull away, keeping her hand flat on his chest. "What?"

"Those men who killed you," he said softly, "one of them, dated your social worker's daughter. They got hold of your old file. That's how they found you."

"Oh," Lena said flatly. "And from my file they thought I was innocent? I highly doubt my social worker knew I was a virgin."

Ambrose chuckled at her mock-shock response. "They didn't seem very bright in all honesty."

"No kidding," she smiled, wrapping her arms around his neck and pressing a gentle, pleasant kiss to his lips. He pulled her close, shifting their hips lower on the bed and laying them down on the pillows. Lena sighed as she relaxed in his arms. "Doesn't matter now. In some ways, I'm happy they did pick me."

Definitely not something he expected her to say. "Why's that?" he said as he buried his face into her hair, breathing in her citrus scent.

"Because it meant I got to know the real you."

Happiness and relief spread through his chest as he tightened his grip on her. He felt her starting to drift off in his arms, as her fingers that had been tracing small circles on his chest started to slow and her breathing became soft and steady. Contentment washed over him as he allowed himself to find the comfort of sleep as well.

"Ambrose?" she said sleepily, shifting her head back to rest on his shoulder. Her eyes were glazed as she looked at him.

"Hm?" he replied, brushing a strand of hair off her face.

"I do trust you."

His eyes flew open as hers shut, a soft smile resting on her lips. His heart was racing, his chest burning at the sensation. "Lena..." he whispered knowing she wouldn't respond. Sleep now completely evading him, he spent the night, studying her face, praying he would never break her trust in him.

CHAPTER TWENTY-ONE

A few days after her fight with Archie, Lena was in the Repository trying to find some information about transformations. The whispering since the fight had become unbearably loud whenever she walked through the corridors. More and more demons were stopping her in her tracks, interrogating her for information about herself and Ambrose. If her sire or Marcus were with her, they were less bold with their approach, but some weren't even deterred by that. She hoped that by finding a way to transform, she might be able to more assertively dissuade demons from pestering her. Ignoring the voice in the back of her head that she couldn't force a transformation, she perused the shelves aimlessly taking solace in the peace the Repository provided her. Even going to the training pits when she wanted to let off steam was becoming more of a spectator sport with her as the main attraction. Her aim in moving to the town had been to disappear. This was her worst nightmare.

Sitting at her desk, she flipped through a book written by Xavier, making notes on a separate piece of paper. She hoped she might get a chance to speak with him again soon, and hoped further he would answer her questions rather than ask his own.

"So, you're Ambrose's new plaything?"

Lena startled as she lifted her head to face the voice. Her limbs ran cold as she saw the intimidating winged-demon standing in the doorway staring at her. His skin was black as night with bright red scars running across his arms, chest and back in angular tribal patterns. Four horns protruded from above his temples. His eyes glowed red and orange like flickering fire, with small horns adorning his cheek bones trailing up to his temples. Tight fitting leather trousers left nothing of his lower half to the imagination, despite the red sash messily wrapped around his waist. His whole body exuded a menacing and sinister power, like he didn't have an ounce of warmth or care within him. A seed of fear settled within her gut at the sight of him.

"Who are you?" she asked, pretty sure she already knew the answer.

"You first, beautiful."

Her skin crawled at the endearment. Whoever this guy was, she instantly didn't like him. Something about him felt wrong, dangerous, and the voice inside her told her to be careful.

"Lena," she said, although not completely certain why she complied so easily. "And I'm not Ambrose's plaything."

"Beautiful name for a beautiful woman," he said with a sneer. "And of course you are. His scent is all over you."

Her stomach churned and every instinct in her wanted to run far and fast. "Your turn," she said, swallowing the rising sense of unease.

"The name is Zagan."

Now her stomach dropped hard and fast, fear washing over her. This was Ambrose's old sire. "Unfortunately for you, I don't know if that name suits you."

Zagan smiled at Lena's remark. "Witty too," he said, "you are wasted on a demon like Ambrose."

"And what is that supposed to mean?"

"A bound demon for nearly four weeks and you haven't even found your design or transformed yet," Zagan raised an eyebrow as he placed his hands on the desk in front of her and leant in towards her, his wings rising proudly behind him. She forced herself not to recoil from him. "Despite your impressive display in the pits, the power within you is as yet untapped, and Ambrose has done nothing about that. I could help you release it."

She clenched her fists wanting nothing more than to connect one of them with his jaw, but she knew that ultimately, she wouldn't stand much of a chance against him. Demonic form or not, he towered above her and she got a feeling that her power would be nothing compared to his. Talking her way out of this was her only option now.

Witty, but not rude, Lena, the warm yet terrifying voice whispered in the back of her mind. *Or, at least, not outright rude.*

"And how exactly would you plan to do that?"

A smug smile spread on his lips. "Aside from making deals I also train unbound demons. I'm the best there is in Hell."

"Ah, well, out of luck there. As you can see, I'm bound," she said, pressing her lips together and holding up her arms showing off her bindings.

"But you could be bound to me," Zagan said, pushing away from the desk to walk around it, coming to stand next to her. He took hold of her chin to tilt her head up so she was forced to look at him. "Think of the fun we could have exploring your... *depths.*" It took all of her willpower not to throw up then and there at his words. "I could teach you things, show you things, Ambrose couldn't even dream of."

"Geez, you make a tempting offer..." she slammed the book she was reading shut before ducking her head and sliding off her stool as smoothly as she could. She retreated to the bookshelf to put the book away and to put as much distance between her and Zagan as possible without making it seem like she was scared of him. "But I'm afraid I'll have to pass. I'm fine where I am."

"Don't dismiss my offer so easily, beautiful. I am significantly older and stronger than Ambrose," he said, walking over to lean on the bookshelf. Lena bent backwards as far as she could without losing her balance. Any space between them was a blessing. Where Ambrose smelt like sage and cedar wood, Zagan had undertones of ash, brimstone and... *death.* "Just think of the possibilities as we opened you up."

"That sounds less like an offer and more like a threat," she said, desperately trying not to gag.

"Then here's my offer," he said, taking a step closer. "You bind yourself to me, come into my bed as you have for Ambrose, and I will give you power beyond imagining. Satisfy me, and you will want for nothing."

"You make it sound so fun."

"I know you are friends with Cyrus. I'd allow you to have him too if you so desire."

She swallowed against the metallic taste rising in the back of her throat. Anger boiled her blood hearing him try to use Cyrus as a bargaining chip.

"Come now, beautiful," he sneered when she didn't respond. "Join me."

"Okay, you have got to stop calling me that," she said, holding up her hand and stepping back in time with Zagan as he stepped closer.

"Think about it if you need. But don't think long," he lengthened his stride and came round on her, placing his arms either side of her shoulders, resting his palms on the bookshelf. "For now, I only want you in my bed. Tomorrow, I may want more."

"Can't wait to find out what that may be. The rest has been so enticing thus far." As she tried to duck under Zagan's arm, he caught her wrist forcing her back against the bookshelf.

"When you join me, I will find a better use for your mouth than your sarcastic remarks," he said, a cruel sneer on his lips.

"Oh joy."

"It will be. For me."

Lena knew she was in trouble, but no longer cared. This interaction had gone on long enough and she wanted to thoroughly scrub the top layer of her skin off. A dip into one of the lava pools sounded more inviting than Zagan's offer. "Let go of me," she said coldly, trying to pull her wrist from his grasp.

"I will make you mine," he said, bringing her wrist between them. She stared at his fingers as black sparks of power crackled from their tips and spread over her skin. The electric points pierced into her bindings like sharp needles and prangs of white-hot pain shot up her arm. Horrified, Lena watched as her bindings began to pulse and shift as their shape started to change.

"What are you doing? Stop!" she cried as the pain from her arm caused her vision to blur. "Please stop!" Images of her sacrifice flashed through her mind, seeing the knife sink into her flesh and the feeling of her blood leaving her body. Tears fell from her eyes as she blinked against the images, trying to focus her vision.

Suddenly, flames burst next to the pair. Ambrose stepped from them and grabbed Zagan's shoulder, twisting him away from her. With an explosion of red power, Ambrose punched the winged demon in the chest, sending him across the room and crashing against the opposite wall. Her sire stood in front of her, shielding her from the cambion, as she collapsed against the bookshelf clutching her wrist. Her vision started to come back into focus as she inspected her arm. The black power had dissipated and her bindings had returned to their familiar thorn-like pattern.

As the throbbing in her wrist subsided, Lena looked past Ambrose to see Zagan getting to his feet, a thunderous scowl on his face.

"Did you think I wouldn't feel that?" Ambrose said calmly. Despite his outward appearance, Lena could feel the waves of rage that poured from his body.

"Pity," Zagan spat, brushing some splinters of wood off his shoulder. "But it won't be long before you don't. You can't watch her all the time"

Ambrose took a step towards the other demon. "Back off, Zagan. She's mine."

"Or what?" The two demons stared at each other for what felt like an age. Lena realised she was holding her breath and tried to exhale quietly so as not draw attention back to herself. "You caught me by surprise that time Ambrose. Do not fall into the belief that you will be able to do that twice," Zagan said, puffing out his chest, but something was off. His shoulder seemed to wince from where it had collided with the bookshelf. "Not that it matters. Give it time, she'll see that she's better off with me." Lena shuddered with disgust at the prospect.

"And if she does that will be her choice. You cannot force that upon her," a voice said from the back of the room. Morgan stepped through a doorway, slowly approaching Zagan. Lena noted that all the imps that had been around had disappeared, evidently having scurried off to find their mistress. "Leave," she commanded, her voice dangerously calm.

"Stay out of this, Keeper. It doesn't concern you," Zagan spat, displaying what little bravado he had left as he stepped away from the intimidating demon.

"I will not allow my students to be disturbed," Morgan replied, spreading her wings and claws threateningly.

The sneer on Zagan's face was terrifying, but some relief washed over Lena as she saw him turn towards the door. "Fine," he said, distain dripping from the solitary word. He was almost out of the room when he looked back over his shoulder at Lena. "See you later, beautiful." And with that he was gone.

"Can't wait..." she said under her breath.

"Are you okay, Lena?" Morgan asked, looking at her. Lena nodded as she pushed herself to her feet, remaining behind Ambrose's frame. "Stay with your boundling, Ambrose. I need to speak with my council about this incident."

As Morgan left the Repository, Ambrose quickly turned towards Lena and took her wrist in his hands. He turned her wrist a number of ways inspecting her bindings as he went. Lena shivered at the tenderness of his touch. "Are you really, okay?" he asked.

"I'm fine," she said with a heavy sigh, trying to release the tension in her body from the encounter. "I see why you don't like him. What a dick. The term 'beautiful' and I are no longer allowed to be in the same sentence."

Although Ambrose smiled at her statement, his eyes remained dark and serious. "Stay away from him, Lena," he warned.

"With pleasure. You'd have to compel me to want to go near him," she pulled her wrist gently from his grip. She looked towards the door as her sire turned to assess the damage of the bookshelf that Zagan had hit. The bookshelf had started to repair itself and Ambrose knelt down to collect some of the books that had fallen. "Okay, so I know who he is now, but what's his game?"

"He likes causing trouble," he said, placing the books back on the shelf.

"You know, I figured that out on my own," she felt her irritation rising at his response. *Talk about stating the obvious*, the voice huffed with annoyance causing her to laugh internally. She walked back to her desk, her nose wrinkling as she picked up remnants of Zagan's scent. Regrettably, she knew she was not going to forget the nausea he caused her any time soon.

Ambrose sighed before turning back to look at her. He looked tired, almost like he had used too much energy getting Zagan off her. "He's constantly after power. Seemingly of the belief that he should have unfettered control over Hell. The more power he gets the more that belief grows. What did he say to you?"

"Only what we were expecting," she replied, fiddling with a piece of paper on the desk. "Told me to choose him, change my binding to him."

"What did he offer in exchange?"

"Him," she said, gagging slightly at the thought. Ambrose chuckled at her reaction. "And Cyrus."

Ambrose stepped towards her, placing a palm down on the desk. Like Zagan, he towered over her in his demon form. But unlike Zagan, she did not feel intimidated, but rather safe and protected. She wanted to lean into him and breathe in his scent forever. "I'm sorry to sound like a broken record, but stay away from him. I'm serious about this, Lena," he said, his voice filled with concern, "you do not want to get mixed up with him."

She looked up at her sire and shivered under his gaze as her desire for him increased. However, she needed to lighten the mood first and ease the tension that had built in her body. "Yes, sir," she said, allowing a mischievous smile to spread on her lips. She was relieved to see his face soften and a spark of desire light up his eyes.

Extending his arm, Ambrose took hold of the front her neck pulling her towards him and used his thumb to angle her face up to meet his. "How many times have I told you to use my name?" he teased as he lowered his head and brushed his lips along hers.

"Make me," she said, smiling against his mouth.

"Looks like I need to remind you who you belong to."

With that, Ambrose crushed his lips against hers with an almost desperate passion. Lena let her body mould against his, grabbing hold of his upper arms to steady herself as she parted her lips, allowing him to delve his tongue into the warmth of her mouth. He placed his other hand on the small of her back, pressing her stomach against his lower body. She could feel the hardening length of him on her thigh, straining against the clothing between them.

She snaked her arms up to wrap around his neck as he bent down and grabbed at the back of her thighs lifting her up into his embrace. She wrapped her legs around his waist, revelling in his strength as he held her. The tips of his fingers were only a breath away from the building warmth between her legs. Running her hands through his hair, she deepened their kiss as she shifted her hips to try and gain some satisfaction from his body. Her fingers brushed along the length of his horns, the smooth yet bumpy surface intriguing to her touch. Ambrose growled with desire as she held on to them, using them to pull him closer to her.

Crying out in surprise, she exhaled sharply as he laid her none-to-gently on the desk, his hand behind her head to cushion it from the impact. He again claimed her mouth with his own and pressed his body against hers. She kept her arms and legs around his neck and waist as he pushed his hips forward. She could feel every bump and curve of his firm body against her stomach. His other hand cupped her breast, squeezing tenderly as she gasped and arched her back under his touch.

Ambrose moved his lips to her neck, biting and sucking along her jaw to her collarbone, his fangs pleasantly scratching over her skin as Lena twisted beneath him. His hand trailed from her breast down her stomach before he slipped it within her leggings. She moaned with excitement as his fingers found their mark, tracing her slick crease with expert ease. Taking caution with his talons, he let one finger slide into her channel drawing a low moan from his own throat. She felt another wave of warmth bloom from her abdomen, inciting a wave of wetness to flow from her centre. Her mind went blank as her body surrendered to his fingers.

Pulling his head back slightly, he smiled wickedly at her whimpers of protest. "Say it," he whispered.

"Don't stop," she begged, having barely heard him. Her hips bucked trying desperately to find some form of release.

"Not until you say it," he said firmly, pressing his palm onto her mound, keeping his finger unmoving within her.

"Say what?" she asked, oblivious to his game.

"Say my name. Say who you belong to."

Reality crashed in on her, as she stared in shock at him, realising he had won. How easily he manipulated her body and mind and how readily she let him. She smiled as she squeezed her legs against his hips, no longer caring to deny or fight how much she wanted him to claim her. Grabbing his horns as he grinned at her, she pulled his face closer to hers. She managed to lift herself enough to gently kiss the skin on his neck just below his ear. "Ambrose," she breathed, "I belong to you, Ambrose."

She felt him smile against her cheek. "Good girl," he growled as he plunged another finger into her core.

Her head flung back at the immense wave of pleasure that rocked her body as he continued to leisurely pump his fingers, slickness coating the inside of her panties. She clung desperately to his shoulders, her nails digging into his skin. She was barely aware as Ambrose pulled up her top exposing her breasts to him. He took one of her peaked nipples into his mouth, biting lightly and causing shockwaves to rake over her skin.

Pressure built within her abdomen as he slipped in another finger, pressing within her as far as he could reach. Lena welcomed the release with a cry as the rolling waves of her climax washed over her body. Her hips bucked against his hand as her pussy clenched around his fingers. She felt his growl of satisfaction vibrate against her neck.

"Ahem..."

Her body froze at the cough, all pleasure immediately quelled as embarrassment took over. She hadn't even heard the door open. Or had it been open the whole time? Ambrose immediately shifted his body to cover hers completely before looking up at the door. Two demons stared either in shock or fascination at the scene before them. He scowled at them, but otherwise didn't move. Lena was acutely aware of his fingers still within her as the demons remained in the doorway.

"Get out," her sire growled, his voice dripping with a deadly threat that sent a fluttering warmth through her stomach.

As if compelled, the demons straightened and turned immediately. One fell over his feet as they scrambled to get out the door. She heard the door slam shut, but her body didn't relax.

Ambrose looked down at her with a warm smile. "You make for quite the show, my dove."

She hit him in the chest, but made little impact, before covering her face with her hands. He laughed at her attempt to hide before slowly withdrawing his fingers. She squirmed beneath him as he so easily reignited the flames of her desire, watching with rapt attention as he inspected her juices on his fingers and then sucked them into his mouth. Her heart beat rapidly within her chest at the sight of him savouring her taste.

Smiling with satisfaction, he placed his elbows either side of her head pressing his hips against hers. Her leggings were soaked but she didn't care. Ambrose had awoken something within her that she wasn't sure would ever again be fully satisfied except by him. And she wanted more.

"Shall we continue this at home?" he asked, placing a kiss on her forehead.

Lena could barely speak for the experience he had just given her. She nodded, bringing her arms up to wrap around his neck as he gathered his flames around them, transporting them to their bed with her still beneath him. Slowly his demon form receded, but the strength and warmth of his body remained. Pulling him closer, she kissed him as her excitement and anticipation for the night ahead grew.

CHAPTER TWENTY-TWO

"I think I've forgotten how to walk..."

Ambrose smiled as he watched Lena steady herself on the bedpost, a sheet wrapped around her, trying to make her way to the bathroom. "Do you need help?" he asked lazily.

"The help you provide, would have me on my back again within moments," she chuckled looking dubiously at him from the corner of her eye.

He laughed as he got up from the bed, pulling on his briefs and making his way over to her. "I promise, I'll be good," he said, kissing her on the cheek.

"Yeah, right," she smiled, elbowing him in the ribs.

"Take your time then, I'll go run the bath."

Kissing her again, Ambrose stepped around her and walked into the bathroom. He turned the taps, feeling the water for the right temperature, before grabbing a bottle of bubble bath and pouring some of it into the stream.

They had spent most of the night and early morning having sex. It had become his mission to overwhelm her body with passion, feeding his own with her endless moans of pleasure. He knew her body would be aching today, and he had to admit that even he was a little sore from his efforts. Their moments of rest had been filled with light conversation, kissing and gentle touching until their desire reignited. It had been a fantastic distraction from the interaction with Zagan the day before.

Remembering it now, he felt his anger rising. It had been such a blatant display, coming for her in the Repository, regardless of if anyone had been in there with her or not. Morgan's imps would have gotten her before Zagan could have completed taking over Lena's bindings, but it had still been too close for comfort.

The pain she had felt under his power had ripped through Ambrose as he'd been sitting in his office, waiting for her to get back. Fear had overtaken him as he raced to get to the Repository. He was not able to flame directly there, needing to get to one of the junction caverns first. Once in Hell, he could flame to the doorway of the Repository, where he saw Zagan holding her wrist as she struggled to pull away from him. He was by no means a match in power or strength for his old sire, so the element of surprise had been his only advantage as he jumped the final distance to them.

Taking a deep breath, Ambrose stopped the flow of water and returned to the bedroom. Lena had moved to the edge of the bed to sit on the mattress, an almost reproachful look on her face. Smiling warmly at her, he walked over and lifted her into his arms. She cried out in surprise, but readily wrapped her hands around his neck. Looking into her sparkling eyes, he captured her mouth with his, as he walked with her back to the bathroom.

"Hm, you're being really good," she teased against his lips.

"Aren't I just," he laughed, letting the sheet fall from her body. Gently, he lowered her into the bath. She sighed as the water enveloped her body, its warmth soothing her muscles and joints.

He knelt beside the bath, taking hold of her hand and lifting it towards him. Gently he rubbed soap into her skin, massaging her muscles as he did so.

"You don't have to do that," she said softly, twisting her wrist to lightly capture his with her fingers.

"I know," he smiled, leaning forward and kissing the top of her head. "I want to."

Nothing further was said for the moment, whilst he continued his work, massaging her other arm, tracing carefully over her bindings, discreetly inspecting them as he went. His intention was not to rekindle their passion from the night, but just to feel her, to remind himself that she was still there. That she was still his.

"Ambrose," she whispered. He knew she was watching his face, but he avoided her gaze for now as he moved to her legs. "Ambrose, look at me." Shutting his eyes momentarily, he sighed heavily before raising his gaze to look at her. "Are you okay?" she asked, her eyes filled with the warmth and care he'd come to yearn for.

Nodding absently, he made his way to the head of the bath and placed a soft kiss to her lips. "I'm fine," he assured her.

"You don't seem fine," she said, her eyes searching his face.

Brushing her hair back from her face, he looked desperately into her eyes, wishing to simply be lost in their dove-grey depths forever. "I..." he started, his voice barely louder than a whisper. "I have not felt fear before, like I did when I felt your pain yesterday. I thought I was going to lose you."

Lena shifted in the bath, pulling herself up on the rim to bring her face level with his. "I would think last night would prove without a doubt, that didn't happen."

He smiled at her, cupping her cheek with his hand. "And I am incredibly thankful for that."

"I'm not going anywhere, Ambrose," she stated, touching her fingers gently to his jaw. "Even if Zagan or someone else took me away from you, I would fight, tooth and nail, to get back."

Her sincerity and conviction stole all power of speech from him. Raising his other hand to capture her face, he kissed her, pouring as much affection as he could into the kiss. Pulling back, he smiled, seeing her eyes hooded with desire. She was beyond beautiful to him. Never in his wildest dreams had he thought they would be like this now. Together, with her fully aware of what he was, what his life was like. Sharing in his life. Thinking back to that morning he had finally asked her to dinner, it seemed like a lifetime ago now, but he still felt the same way. Utterly and completely captivated by her.

"Go out with me?" he blurted out before he could stop himself.

Lena burst out laughing, but he took no offence at it. "Ambrose, I think we're a little past first dates."

"I mean it, Lena," he said, rubbing his thumbs over her cheeks. "Let's go for dinner. Tonight. They way we were meant to before all of this. Let's do some portion of this, of us, right."

She shook her head at him, even as her eyes filled with mirth and her pink lips curved into a soft smile. "Okay," she said warmly, placing her hand on his wrist. "Okay," she repeated, "what do you want to do?"

"I'll book at Alphonso's for tonight," he smiled. "Archie is expecting you in the pits today, so just make sure you're at the front door by seven. Preferably not smelling like Hell."

"Ugh..." Lena sighed, leaning back in the bath. "I forgot about the pits. Not sure I'll be as quick on my feet today."

"You'll be fine," he said reassuringly. "From what you said the other night, I don't think Archie will let anything happen to you. I do think, however, that either Marcus or I should escort you when in Hell. No more going there on your own. At least until things settle down."

"If they ever settle down," she groaned. "Alright. Once I'm finished with the bath and can walk on my own again," she looked at him pointedly from the corner of her eye, "I'll call Marcus to take me to the pits. I'll see you at seven."

Smiling with pure joy, he placed a final kiss on her forehead. "I'll leave you to it, then." Pushing up from the tub, he turned to leave, glancing back at her as he started to pull the door to the bathroom shut. "Until tonight, my dove."

After he got dressed, Ambrose retreated to his office for the day. He had been neglecting to review some of the investment reports over the last few weeks, since Lena came into his world, but he would use them now to distract himself until dinner. Marcus came by briefly to discuss the logistics of escorting Lena when in Hell, but agreed it was probably for the best. At least for the moment.

With his excitement for dinner mounting, he found the afternoon passed relatively quickly. As it neared six-thirty, he found he was practically skipping back to his room to get dressed. The reports had not distracted him as well as he had hoped, so he'd spent a good portion of the day planning on what to wear. He'd decided to wear the same suit that he had worn on Lena's first night as a demon, when they'd meant to have dinner all those weeks ago. The light-grey panama suit had reminded him of her eyes when he bought it. Shiny black buttons adorning the jacket and waistcoat. He pulled on a white shirt, but left the top two buttons undone after deciding a tie would be too formal for such a night.

Absently, he wondered if Lena had gotten back yet and if she had, where she was getting dressed as he had not seen her since that morning. Cursing his eagerness, he waited by the front door checking his watch. Would she be late again? Not that it had been her fault for not showing last time. But what if something happened in the pits? He hadn't felt anything through their bond, so that seemed unlikely.

"Hey you."

His train of thought was interrupted by the sweetness of her voice. Turning around, his breath caught in his throat, leaving him awestruck as she walked down the stairs. "Wow," he breathed.

Her smile washed over him like the warmth of sunlight, as he took in the full sight of her from head to toe. She had left her hair loose, pushed back over her shoulders, a single strand curling over her collar bone. Its dark auburn tone, shining under the warm lights in the entrance hall. The dress she wore was a deep forest green with long sleeves that flared over her hands, perfectly covering her bindings. The neckline touched the nape of her neck before spanning out towards her arms to meet the sweetheart bust. Its tight fit hugged every curve of her body to perfection before draping gently over her thighs, stopping just past her knees. Her heels clicked softly across the wood flooring as she walked towards him.

"You're breathtaking," Ambrose said, placing a coat around her shoulders.

Lena raised on her toes and pressed a light kiss to his cheek. "You're not so bad yourself," she whispered into his ear.

"Careful, my dove," he warned, pulling her hand into the crook of his arm, "or we won't make it to dinner."

She chuckled slightly, but settled in at his side. "I'll behave."

Ambrose opened the door for them, helping her down the steps and across the street stones, all the while drinking in the sight of this woman by his side.

"When did you get back?" he asked as they made their way to the town square.

"About an hour ago. I went straight to the altar room to make this dress," she smiled.

"I was wondering if it was made or bought."

"I could never have afforded something like this in my lifetime."

"You have access to my accounts now, Lena," he said softly, placing his hand over hers as it rested on his arm. "You can buy whatever you want."

"I know," she nodded looking into the distance, "but that still feels weird. Besides, currently, it's easier to make something I know will cover my bindings, than search all over creation for something that might."

"Fair enough," he chuckled. "It's beautiful, just like you."

Lena pressed her lips together and shook her head slightly. "Yeah,

I'm still not okay with being called 'beautiful' again, yet."

"My apologies. Stunning then."

"That'll do."

They reached Alphonso's, where they were seated at a small table towards the back of the restaurant. Tucked away behind some fernery, they were afforded some privacy from the rest of the patrons. On arrival, the host had greeted them warmly, unabashedly voicing his joy that they had not let the failure of their first date prevent this one. He had even given them a bottle of red wine on the house as he eagerly escorted them to their table.

"Well, that was awkward," Lena sighed, her smile brightened by the candlelight.

"If only he knew the truth, huh?" Ambrose chuckled as they clinked their glasses together.

"If only," she said, sipping her wine.

The host had returned quickly to take their order. Once they were alone again, the conversation flowed freely, pausing only when their food and further drinks were delivered.

Ambrose spoke of his childhood and his mother, her compassion and gentle nature being the sole reason he attributed to not being more like his father. He described his sisters, three of them, who constantly fought with each other for his attention, wanting him to take them hunting or horse riding, anything that got them out of the house. Careful to check around them, ensuring no one was listening, he recalled some of his fellow soldiers from the war and the antics they got up to in France.

Lena told him about some of the other children she had met whilst in foster care and the families she had actually enjoyed being a part of. It always seemed to come down to some stroke of bad luck that resulted in her removal from them. She talked about meeting Cyrus and how initially he couldn't seem to stand her, calling her a mouse because she had been so quiet. Until, when he prevented their foster father from abusing her, he helped her find her voice, her ability to stand up for what she wanted.

"You've told me about your mother," Ambrose said, leaning forward in his chair after their plates had been cleared. "Will you tell me about your father?"

"I mean, what else is there to tell?" Lena shrugged, fiddling with the stem of her wine glass. "He died when I was six. I don't remember him."

He frowned slightly, feeling the sadness that washed over her in that moment. "Did no one tell you about him?"

Sipping her wine, she sighed heavily. "In some ways my mother did, I suppose. My extended family all lived overseas so once I went into foster care, I lost contact with anyone who could tell me about him." She paused briefly, looking into her glass, her brows furrowing together as she pulled at her memories. "My parents were very much in love. Whilst my father was alive, he and my mother were perfect parents. Doting on me and each other. I have this memory, we went camping, or caravanning... yeah, I think it was a caravan," she smiled fondly as the memory resurfaced. "I don't remember where it was anymore, but every morning, my father would take me for a walk through the forest. We'd go birdwatching, or explore the small creeks that ran through the trees. I remember him carrying me back to the caravan on his shoulders. My mother would make pancakes with bacon and sausages before we'd get back."

He studied her face as she closed her eyes, holding the memory in her mind. "That's a lovely memory," he said, reaching across the table and taking her hand in his.

"I don't even know if it's real," she sighed, running her thumb across the back of his. "But I don't have anyone to tell me otherwise. So, I like to think it's real. It made other things easier." Her eyes sparkled softly as she bit her bottom lip with an odd smile. "My father wrote me a letter before he died."

"What does it say?"

She shrugged with a soft laugh. "Not much really. It says that he loved me, more than he thought he would. My mother had just been diagnosed with cancer when they found out she was pregnant. I know it was advised she have an abortion so she could receive treatment, but I don't know what her or my father's thoughts were on that. It didn't matter in the end. She went into sudden remission and was able to have me without complications. Well, except for the fact I was born two months early," she chuckled, taking another sip of her wine. "It was a weird letter that left me with more questions than answers," she shook her head slightly. "It's painful to read. Don't really feel like repeating it."

"I understand. I won't push."

There was a brief silence between them, as Ambrose processed what she had just told him. Something about it was oddly familiar to him, but he couldn't figure out why. He wanted to ask her for more details, but decided against it, believing it could put an end to the niceness of the evening thus far.

"Hey, can I ask you something?" Lena said suddenly.

"Of course," he nodded.

"Why are deals seven years?" she asked, tilting her head to the side. "Seems like such an odd number to use."

"That's the thing you want to ask?" he scoffed, raising a brow at her.

"Okay, it's a topic departure, I'll grant you that," she chuckled, spreading her hands out in front of her, before folding them on the table. "But I've tried to research it and came up with nothing. It's driving me a little crazy."

He laughed silently at her, shaking his head. "Seven is just kind of our thing," he replied. "Seven realms for the seven Princes of Hell. It symbolises completion after the seven days in the week in which God made everything."

"And the seven deadly sins," she smiled.

"Exactly. Each one represented by a prince."

Lena fell quiet for a moment, her brows pulling together. An emotion he couldn't place flowed through him. But as quickly as he felt it, it disappeared as she coughed and straightened her back to ask, "Did God really make it all in seven days?"

"Six if you ask him, but no," he shook his head with an amused scoff. "His creation was merely the split in morality. Before then there were only daemons, beacons of fate, neither good nor evil. He made angels and demons and set off the whole power struggle between them. Or at least, that's what I've gathered. Record keeping back at the beginning was not as thorough as it is now so only the originals would know the truth of it."

Lena raised her chin at the term. "The originals?" she queried.

"God, Michael, Lucifer... the ones that were there before or immediately after the split," he explained.

"Have you met any angels?"

"No. They don't come down often. And when they do it's a big deal. Hell is buzzing for weeks after."

After they finished off their wine, Ambrose helped Lena to her feet, eager to get her back home. The host helped them with their coats before declaring them the most handsome couple of the evening. Lena blushed at the statement, ducking her head into Ambrose's chest as he wrapped his arm around her shoulders.

"Ambrose?" she asked as they lazily walked back to the manor.

"Hm?"

"Thank you for tonight," she sighed, leaning into his side. "This was wonderful."

He tightened his hold on her shoulders, pressing a kiss to the top of her head. "Anytime, my dove."

CHAPTER TWENTY-THREE

Almost a week after their first proper date, Lena was walking through the corridors of Hell. Already the practicalities of escorting her everywhere had fallen flat, with both Ambrose and Marcus being called away by summonings or reports to their superiors. She had learnt early on from Morgan that certain designs had things like councils to which demons with that particular design, or variations thereof, would report their recent acquisitions. But it had been something that slipped her mind until recently as Ambrose had never mentioned them himself.

"My only recent summoning, until now, was your sacrifice," he had explained to her. "And it didn't exactly go to plan. I couldn't risk reporting it until I thought of a reasonable lie to cover it up."

With the help of Marcus, they spun a story that the three summoners had tried to capture Ambrose, leaving him with no choice but to kill them. Carefully, he gave Lena small commands that would prevent her from telling the truth in such a way that should she ever be questioned by the council it would not be immediately evident she had been compelled. Marcus had tested the effectiveness of them until all three were satisfied that Ambrose was protected.

Thankfully, she had not seen Zagan since the day in the Repository, but she had taken to scanning a room before she entered it to check for his presence. She'd had to profusely apologise to a new boundling the other day, after they had flamed into the Repository unexpectedly and she had blasted them with lightning. Their sire, Titus, was none too impressed, but Morgan had helped her soothe the situation.

"Hey! Lena!"

Pulled from her thought, she turned her head slightly to look at the demon who called out as he ran over to her with a cheerful grin on his face. "Hey Cyrus," she said, returning his smile.

"On your way to the Repository?" he asked, pulling her in for a hug.

"As per usual." She was surprised at how happy she was to see him after her recent encounter with his sire.

Cyrus chuckled slightly as they started to walk along the carved-out corridor together. "I'll walk with you. I'm heading that way anyway. I need to stop by the Vault to collect a cursed object."

"Cursed object?" she asked, looking up at him.

"Yeah! Have you not seen them yet? Oh, you're going to love this! Come with me, you can go to the Repository later," he said excitedly as he grabbed her hand and started to drag her along after him. Lena couldn't help the light-hearted laugh that escaped her as they almost ran through the corridor. They passed demons who stared at them in either amusement or annoyance but she didn't care. She hadn't explored that much of Hell yet and she couldn't think of a better tour guide than her childhood friend.

"If Morgan comes looking for me, you can explain the detour to her," she teased although she gladly followed him.

They passed the Repository and turned left branching down a corridor that she was not familiar with. She knew that the hellhound den was down this way, but until she was finished with the Repository there hadn't been any need for her to wander this way too often.

Cyrus pulled her to a small offshoot alcove that housed two large ebony black doors. The handles were fossilised human spines that caused her to stop in her tracks as she stared at them.

"Lena?" he asked hesitantly.

"Huh?" she started looking at him. "Sorry... the spines are an interesting touch. I'm sure I say this every time I'm down here, but seriously... just when I think I'm getting used to things down here, there's another shock looming in the shadows."

"Oh, yeah..." he said, looking back at the door. "Poetically put though." He gave her a warm smile and she felt herself relax. "Come on, let me introduce you to the Caretaker."

Lena tilted head and a small smirk on her lips. "The Caretaker?" But she wasn't left to wonder long as a naga-demon with a deep emerald green and black serpent tail for the lower part of its body slithered up to her. Its hands were clasped together, fingers interlaced, in front of its chest. Lena could clearly see each rib as the naga's upper body was almost skeletal in nature, its grey skin pulled tightly across its rib cage like wet paper on a wire frame. Its face seemed normal, but was indistinguishable as to its gender, if it had any. Hollow cheeks and eyes that sunk into its skull like empty pools, gave it an eerie appearance that made her think of something akin to a grim reaper. Her eyes widened in both awe and tentative fear, heightened by the total silence in which it moved, graceful in its movements, as it crept closer.

"Oh... hi," she squeaked.

The naga smiled, or at least Lena thought it smiled. The tightness of its skin meant the movement of its mouth was almost imperceptible.

"Greetings, young one," its voice was like sandpaper in her ears and sent an involuntary shiver down her spine.

Lena blinked rapidly trying not to react further. It moved around her, encircling her with its serpent half. She could see the strength in the tail as its muscles rippled around her. The scales shone brightly even in the dim light of the vault. Her fingers twitched as she longed to touch them, wondering if they were as smooth as they looked. Swallowing hard, she fought against the temptation. Even demons have the right to personal space.

"Hey Caretaker," Cyrus started but the naga held up its hand to silence him.

"I will get to you in a moment, Cyrus," it said, still looking at her. "What are you called, young one?"

"Um... Lena," she stammered fascinated by the creature in front of her. "Do... do you have a name? Or are you just called... Caretaker?"

The naga blinked and tilted its head, its long black hair falling from its shoulders, as if taken aback by her question. "You may call me, Calza, if Caretaker does not suit you. That was the name given to me, although I have not used it in centuries."

"Never knew you even had a name," Cyrus said.

Calza whipped out its tail and swiped Cyrus' feet out from under him. The boundling landed on his back with a loud thud and sharp cry. "You never asked," it said almost coldly. "No one ever asks. And I said I would get to you in time." The naga moved away from them slightly as Cyrus pushed himself back onto his feet, rubbing the back of his head. "Lena," Calza said, drawing her attention back to it, "you must be very young to still be in human form here."

Lena shrugged. "Ah... well, I became a demon nearly five weeks ago, so young... depends on who you ask, I guess. I've been told I should have transformed by now"

"It is unusual for a demon to not have transformed by that time, but it is not unheard of," Calza said, once again clasping its hands before it. "You are bound to Ambrose, I see."

She blinked in surprise. "How did you know?"

"All bindings are unique in design. Yours are indicative of him."

"Oh," she said looking at her bindings. Furrowing her brow, an unsettled feeling formed in the pit of her stomach. "He said he's never had another boundling, so how do you know they're his?"

"He has not had another as far as I am aware. Bindings emit an aura of the sire's power. Not all demons will be able to pick up on it, but older ones like myself will." Tentative relief eased the tension in her gut before it dropped sharply at the sound of Calza sighing heavily as it turned its gaze to Cyrus. "I have told you before, Zagan is not welcome to the items within this vault."

Lena raised her brows and looked at Cyrus with amusement in her eyes. He suddenly looked very uncomfortable, shifting his weight from foot to foot.

"Ah, come on, Caretaker, have mercy on me," Cyrus pleaded. "Yours is the nearest vault to us and the other caretakers aren't as nice as you."

"You never return my objects. I no longer trust you, or Zagan, with them."

"Never again, scouts' honour," Cyrus said, holding up his hand to his chest.

"Were you ever a scout?" she asked, folding her arms.

"Well... no," he admitted.

She spun as she heard Calza laugh. It was an unsettling sound, almost like nails on a chalkboard.

The naga shook its head as its laugh subsided. "I like you, Lena. Your company is welcome here anytime," it said before slithering up to her. "Is Cyrus a friend of yours?"

"Yes," she answered with a nod. "He and I knew each other before we became demons."

"Do you trust him?"

"Ah..." she glanced at Cyrus over her shoulder, seeing him press his lips together, nodding his head, and gave her a knowing look. "Yes and no," she responded truthfully. "I don't trust his sire, so I am cautious when it comes to him. If not for Zagan, I would."

Calza stared at her for a long moment, studying her face, before it made its way over to Cyrus. Lena hadn't realised she was holding her breath until it moved away from her and she exhaled sharply. "As a friend of hers I will permit you, and only you, not Zagan, one last chance. If you do not return this object when the deal is over," it held up a finger as if admonishing the boundling, "it will be the last time."

Cyrus swallowed but nodded in agreement.

"Tell me what you need," Calza said.

Cyrus glanced at Lena before answering the Caretaker. "Um, nothing too fancy. Just something that will cause a non-suspicious death in an intended victim. Death by suicide would be preferable. Minimal side effects to the wielder if possible." He paused for a moment. "Please?" He finished quickly, his eyes wide as Calza leant closer to him.

"Very well," it said, finally withdrawing. "I may have something I am willing to part with. Stay here." It turned ready to head further into the vault before pausing for a moment to look at Lena. "My dear, please feel free to have a look around." With that, the naga slithered off between the shelves and disappeared from view.

Lena gasped in awe as she was finally able to take in the enormity of the Vault.

There were shelves upon shelves neatly stacked in parallel rows. The shelves were made of an indistinguishable material that had an almost blood red sheen. Lena noted that she could not see the back of the Vault as it seemed to go on forever.

"Holy crap," she said, stepping further into the room.

"This is the Vault, or one of them at least. This one in particular stores cursed objects which sometimes get handed out as part of deals, or dropped in various locations to create havoc," Cyrus said walking up to stand next to her.

"How do they get here?" she asked, still fixated on her surroundings.

"They're made by demons," he explained, "I'm not exactly sure how they are made, that's part of the design of the demon that makes them. Some make them from scratch, some have tools, or conduits, I believe, that help in making them. Not all cursed objects end up here. It depends on who made them or how they were made and how potent they are. Some objects start in general circulation top-side."

She walked among the shelves looking at each object in turn. "Do they affect demons?"

"Some can. Those are the really powerful ones and they are not kept in this vault. I think those are kept in the lower circles guarded by the Princes for their exclusive use. Nothing in here would affect us."

"And Calza decides which one to give in payment for a deal?" she asked, looking back at her friend near the entrance.

He nodded in confirmation. "The Caretaker assesses what we need and finds one with appropriate side effects that won't cause a breach of the terms of the deal on our end," he explained, placing his hands on his hips. "For example, we don't want an object that would cause the death of the person before the end of the seven years otherwise we wouldn't get the soul. They would be corrupted so they don't go to Heaven, but they don't come here either."

Lena wandered among the shelves close to the entrance to the Vault. The shelves towards the outer edge were carved out of the walls, like extensions of the Vault itself. She touched one of the shelves and it felt like the shelf breathed and moved under her fingers. Almost instantaneously, she could picture every object on the shelf within her mind. Books, jewellery, even a child's teddy bear were stored on that shelf. She could see the vibration of power that was both stored within and wound around each item. Out of surprise, she let out an involuntary gasp and recoiled her hand as fast as she had touched the shelf.

"They are fascinating, are they not?" Calza said, coming up behind her.

"They're beautiful," she whispered as she lightly touched a necklace laid with deference on a stand.

Calza turned to Cyrus and handed him a small box. "Here you are," he said pointedly, "this will cause paranoia in the intended victim. The wielder, however, will also suffer paranoia on a similar level to their victim. Whoever commits suicide first ends the paranoia of the other."

Cyrus pursed his lips in contemplation. "Not exactly what I would call minimal side effects."

"That," Calza said, "is Zagan's problem. He can come here personally if he wants something different. Be gone now."

"Fair enough," Cyrus said, spinning on his heel and almost racing to the door. "Oh," he paused looking back over his shoulder. "Lena, are you coming?"

"Um, you go. If Calza doesn't mind I'd like to look around a bit more," she said with a smile. Calza nodded in assent.

"Alright, see ya!" Cyrus said, promptly hurrying out the door, his eagerness to leave evident in his haste.

"Zagan is just going to send him back here you know," she said, turning back to the shelves, laughing slightly at the memory of her friend running scared.

"I know. I like Cyrus in general. However, he is fun to tease," Calza turned to Lena and moved next to her, watching her as she traced her fingers along the edge of the shelves. "The objects speak to you."

"Do they?" she asked, looking at the naga. "It's like I can see what makes them cursed, but I don't understand what they do."

"You may with time," it shrugged. "The Vault certainly likes you if you can so easily touch the shelves. They would otherwise cause you pain to stop you from potentially taking an object without my permission." The naga smiled at her and moved to straighten some objects on another shelf. "Have you found your design yet, my dear?"

Lena shook her head. "No, not yet. I've read and researched a lot of them now. But I don't know what I'm searching for. Morgan tells me that it will click, like a switch. Starting to think I won't find one."

"Perhaps, this will be your design," it said. "I would certainly welcome your company more often."

"Much like everything else down here, that would require me to figure out how it works," she said haughtily. "I can understand how things work, but I struggle to understand why. Why does Hell need to operate the way it does? Why do demons need designs? Is it just to stave off the boredom that comes with immortality, or is there an actual purpose to it all?"

"All very good questions to keep in mind as you continue your search," it commended her. "You will find it, my dear. It just takes time."

"I'm told the average is three weeks to both transform and figure your design out, four tops. Here I am almost five weeks later and I'm still where I started," Lena threw her hands in the air with exasperation. "I haven't transformed and my bindings grow at an almost daily rate. Oh, and to top it all off, the amount of unwanted attention from all of that is becoming exhausting!"

Calza sighed in sympathy. "I know it is hard to adjust to everything. I am a natural born demon so I do not have any understanding for what it must be like to be a boundling. But I have known enough in my time to appreciate the frustration the first few weeks can cause them. You will figure it out," it assured. "Just ignore everything and everyone else for now. Finding your place, and aiding your sire, should be the only matters of import to you at present."

"Zagan makes it very difficult to ignore him," she said angrily. "He has already tried to overtake my binding to Ambrose."

"Do you wish to bind to another?"

"No."

"Well, Zagan can be rather relentless, but he is not above the orders of Hell. Taking boundlings by force happens, but it is immensely frowned upon. Sacrificed souls are the right of the demon they are sacrificed to. The choice the boundling has made should be honoured. It is unwise for any demon to tear apart that bond," Calza said, retreating to a table in the corner where a few items had been placed. It picked up a couple of items and moved between the shelves, placing them here and there. "Your bindings, do they hurt when they grow?"

"Ah, I actually shouldn't have told you that," she sighed, turning to face it. "Any chance you could forget I said that?"

Calza smiled at her. "I promise I will not repeat it to another. It is not often I find a demon with an immediate appreciation for the objects here. Your secret is safe with me."

"Okay," she said slowly, wondering if she could, or should, trust a literal half-snake, but deciding she would, at least for now. "No, they don't hurt. They just... 'extend' for lack of a better term. I started drawing a line at the top and tracking how quickly they grow. Seems to be between one to two centimetres a day. Sometimes more."

"Either Ambrose really does not want to be able to break free of him yet, or you will be exceptionally powerful," Calza said, settling on its tail.

She'd been looking at the floor, but her head snapped up at its comment so fast she pulled a muscle in her neck. "What? Ow... why... why would you say that?" she asked, rubbing the nape of her neck.

"Say what?"

"About Ambrose."

"Hm? What about it?"

"I thought it was up to the bound demon whether they remain bound or not."

"It is," Calza said, nodding. "If you can figure out how to break from the binding, you can."

"But could he be preventing that?"

"It is possible. But if you say that your bindings are growing consistently, then it would seem unlikely. A spell to increase or strengthen bindings usually results in a quick and sudden growth of the markings."

"But possible?"

"Anything is possible, young one."

She fell silent for a moment contemplating Calza's words.

"Lena," it started. Her eyes shot up to look at it. "Most bound demons do not overcome their bindings until decades after of being with their sire. And even if Ambrose were strengthening the binding, that would only delay the inevitable so long. I would not worry about it yet if I were you."

"Right... of course."

"Focus on your training and finding your design. Figuring that out is the first step to overcoming your binding."

She nodded and turned to leave. "Goodbye, Calza."

"Goodbye, Lena. Come back soon."

"Will do," she said as she waved over her head and left the Vault.

Chapter Twenty-Four

Ambrose looked quizzically at the bracelet that lay at his feet, nudging it slightly with the toe of his boot. "What are you?" he asked to no one in particular, tilting his head to the side.

It had been just over a week since his date with Lena and the time since had been absolute bliss for him. He had gotten to the point where he almost forgot his role in the expansion of Hell's power. Specific summonings generally happened five to eight times a year, so when this one came round, he started to question if something in the universe was working against him in building his relationship with Lena. Her sacrifice included, three summonings in five weeks was highly unusual.

They had been relaxing in the sitting room, merely enjoying each other's presence. Ambrose had been lounging on the sofa, silently reading and running his hand through Lena's hair as she cuddled up next to him. He'd found out a few days before that she had gotten into making small origami figures in her spare time when she was alive.

"I didn't have a lot growing up in foster care. Origami meant I could make small things to play with and if they got left behind, I could just remake them," she'd told him as he watched her fingers deftly fold a tiny crane from a small scrap piece of paper he'd had lying around. The next day he had bought her a ream of paper suited to her needs.

As he read his book, every now and then he would glance towards her from the corner of his eye, captivated as she folded, unfolded and tucked the paper into various shapes and forms. The surface of the small table in front of them slowly disappeared as cranes, elephants, dragons and various flowers came into creation.

Watching her fingers work, thoughts of having her hands wander over his body had him hot and bothered far sooner than he cared to admit. Abandoning his book, Ambrose got to his feet and walked over to the drinks table he kept stocked in there.

"You okay?" Lena asked, letting her body fall into the space he had been occupying, looking up at him through her lashes.

"I'm fine," he responded with a smile, pouring himself a glass of brandy. "Do you want a drink?"

"Do we still have that ruby port?"

"Of course." Getting her drink he returned to the sofa, raising a brow at her as she stretched out across its expanse. "Comfy?"

"Yes, thanks," she smiled at him, a smile that still managed to take his breath away. She twisted on the seat, lifting herself up and into a seated position. Taking the glass from him, she put the paper in her hand to the side and pulled her legs up underneath her.

He sat beside her, resting his arm on the back of the sofa before sipping his drink. "Still uncomfortable with being called beautiful?" he teased.

Lena wrinkled her nose at him. "And if I say yes?"

"Then I'll just think of a different adjective," he said, running the back of his fingers over her cheek. "I could use gorgeous, stunning, magnificent. Even sexy."

She laughed before pushing herself closer to him and placing a soft kiss on his lips. "You think I'm sexy?" she whispered.

"I think you are beyond sexy," he said, placing his hand on the back of her neck and pulling her closer to him. Kissing her gently, the tastes of port and brandy mixed on their lips. Smiling, she pulled away and fixed her eyes on his. "What is it?" he chuckled seeing her gaze turn pensive.

"Can I ask you something?" she asked, resting her elbow on the back of the sofa and her head in her hand.

"You just did," he laughed as she poked him in the ribs. "Go on."

"I was talking with Calza the other day and—"

Suddenly very confused, he asked, "Who's Calza?"

"Oh, sorry," she said quickly, her eyes widening. "I bumped into Cyrus and he showed me the Vault. The one with cursed objects."

"I know the one," he nodded, wilfully ignoring the stab of jealousy in his gut at the mention of Cyrus.

"Calza is the Caretaker."

"It has a name?"

Lena's head dropped back as she stared at the ceiling and threw her hand up in defeat. "Seriously?"

Ambrose laughed at her reaction and took hold of her hand in his. "Sorry," he apologised. "Continue. You were talking with it?"

"Yeah, and it... he..." she paused an adorably confused expression forming on her features. "Does it have a gender?"

"Beats me," he shrugged, taking a further sip of his brandy. "As it's a natural born, I'd probably say no."

"I'll call it 'they' then. 'It' sounds more like a thing than a..."

"Thing? Hey!"

Lena hit him in the chest, an annoyed look only managing to maintain on her features for a second before she devolved into laughter with him. "Well," she said, her smile dropping slightly. "I may have let slip that my bindings have been growing to them."

"Lena..." Ambrose sighed, leaning forward to place his glass on the table.

"I know, I know," she said hurriedly, holding her hand in front of her defensively. "I'm really sorry. I didn't mean to, it just slipped out."

Leaning back, he looked at her. He wasn't really annoyed. He found it increasingly difficult to be upset with her over anything. "Was Cyrus there when you said that?"

She shook her head. "No. It was just me and Calza. They promised to keep it a secret."

Ambrose chuckled. "Probably because you're one of the only demons who's had a conversation with it." Pausing briefly, he acted as if he was contemplating what to do next, trying to ignore his building desire to kiss her again. "Okay," he sighed.

"You're not mad?" she asked, pushing herself closer to him.

"I'm not thrilled," he said, rubbing his thumb across the back of her hand "but it's done now. Don't tell anyone else about the growth of your bindings."

Lena's bindings glowed momentarily as the command took hold. "Yeah..." she sighed looking at her wrist, "that's fair."

"So, what did it, or *they*, say?"

She sighed, looking into her now empty port glass, twisting it between her fingers. "They mentioned that sires are able to increase a binding. Make the bindings grow to stop the boundlings from breaking from them, or delay it at least."

Ambrose looked intently at her, trying to gauge her emotions, suddenly very curious where this conversation was going. "Are you wondering if I am increasing your bonds?" he asked cautiously.

"No," she said, shaking her head slightly. "If I'm being honest, I did for a moment, just after Calza told me this, but..." she raised her gaze to look at him, "I've thought about it over the last few days and no. I don't believe you would do that."

Surprised at the feeling of relief that washed over him, he leant towards her, wishing to assure her further. "Even so, I promise I'm not," he said, placing a gentle kiss on her cheek. "If I needed to increase them to keep you around then I'm not doing a very good job as your lover," he whispered against her skin with a wicked smile.

"Ambrose!" Lena laughed, hitting the back of her hand against his chest, her eyes bright with humour.

"What?" he asked, raising a brow at her. "No one else is here to hear me." He laughed as she poked her tongue at him. "Was there a follow up question to the bindings thing?"

"Yes," she nodded. "I was actually going to ask if it was maybe a good idea. Could it stop, or prevent, other demons, one in particular, from trying to take me away from you?"

"Huh..." he sighed, resting his head back against the sofa. "I mean, it could," he said softly. He lifted his hand and took hold of a strand of her hair, twirling it around his fingers. "But I don't want to. Not that I don't want to make it harder for anyone to take you, but increasing bindings is a delicate process and it can go wrong. Not done right, it could break the bond instead. But, as you wouldn't be ready for it..." he trailed off, not even wanting to consider the possible outcome.

"Right," Lena said, nodding her head in understanding as she pressed her lips together. "Bad idea then."

"Not bad," he said, lifting her chin to look at him, "but I don't want to risk it."

"Agreed," she smiled before leaning into him and kissing him.

Slowly she snaked her hands to cup behind his neck, lifting up on her knees slightly. Eager to indulge her intentions, Ambrose caught hold of her waist, helping her adjust their position on the sofa as she placed one of her legs over his lap to straddle him. With a soft sigh, he pulled his head back slightly to look into her sparkling eyes.

"Lena," he whispered.

"Hm?" she responded, trailing soft kisses along his jaw.

"Thank you for telling me."

Lena stopped her affections and lifted her head to look at him, her expression softened with her surprise. Her slight smile, mixed with the desire in her eyes, made his heart sing with affection for her.

But all good moments have to end. He sighed heavily, his head dropping back with a loud thump against the wood of the sofa. "Unfortunately, my dove, I am being summoned."

Lena mimicked his despair with a sigh of her own, as she climbed off his lap. "Okay," she said, falling back against the sofa cushions. "Hurry back," she winked at him.

He got to his feet with a slight chuckle. "Oh, trust me. I will," he promised as the flames of Hell overtook his body, pulling him away to the summoning.

The deal had been straightforward, but there had been an energy in the air that had made him delay. Part of all deals was the clean up, so he had to remain longer than he wanted too anyway. It would not do to have the summoners arrested for murder and risk their life with corporal punishments or otherwise before the end of the seven-year agreement. Thinking the runes had something to do with it, he had already cleared them with the same ritual he used after Lena's sacrifice. The body had been collected by a reaper demon and Ambrose finished cleaning all evidence of struggle. But still the energy remained.

Focusing as best he could, despite his growing desire to get back to Lena as soon as possible, he had found the bracelet, lying beside the sacrificial pyre.

Slowly he bent down and picked it up, turning it over in his hand. It was coursing with power that trailed like small strings of flame interlacing with the metal and the charms. With seemingly great care the strings of power looped and folded over and over creating a fabric-like weave over the bracelet, tightening as close to the metal as it could before it faded out of perceivable vision. He could still feel it vibrating with power as it lay in his palm. The power had seemed familiar but it melded too quickly for him to figure out who it belonged to.

"Did it work?"

Ambrose turned on his heel just in time to see Lena flame into the room and promptly fall on her face. A small 'ow' came from her limp body.

"Lena?" he queried, bewildered and rushed over to her. "Are you okay?" He cast aside the bracelet and helped her sit up.

"I'm fine, just a little dizzy," she said, pushing against the floor. She tried to get to her feet, but her legs wouldn't support her. She settled to kneeling on the ground whilst he held her shoulders. "Did it work?"

"Did what work?" he asked, looking into her eyes. "The deal?"

"No," she said, shaking her head slightly. Her eyes were shining brightly, filled with excitement. "The bracelet?" Lena asked fervently.

"The bracelet?" Ambrose repeated as he looked over to where he had thrown it. He steadied Lena before getting up to retrieve it. "You made this?" he asked, returning to her and laying the bracelet in her outstretched hand.

"Yes," she said, clasping it tightly. "I wasn't sure it would work."

"What did you do?" he asked, kneeling before her. Lena was staring intently at the bracelet, turning it over and over to look at it at different angles.

"If I'm right, which I really hope I am, I've melded my power with some emotion from the sacrifice and stored it within this bracelet," she said proudly. She looked up at him absolutely beaming.

Ambrose felt overcome with affection for the woman before him, so much so it took everything in him not to claim her mouth with his then and there. But she looked so overjoyed at her achievement he didn't want to distract from her moment.

"You made a cursed object," he said adoringly.

"Yes!" Lena exclaimed. She pushed herself forward, flinging her arms around his neck. Caught by surprise but eager to hold her, he wrapped his arms around her waist pulling her closer to him.

"Ask me 'how'," she said softly resting her forehead on his.

"How, what?" he chuckled, puzzled, pulling back to look at her.

She rolled her eyes, but they gleamed with mischievous intent. "The bracelet," she said pointedly.

Ambrose laughed but complied with her request. "How?" he asked. Just when he thought her face couldn't light up any more, a new found pride washed over her features.

"I got bored waiting for you, so I went to the library. You know the crystallised book you have?" she asked, waiting for him to nod in acknowledgement before continuing. "I was studying it like I have before, trying to see if I could read anything from the pages. Suddenly, it was like I was looking down over the city. Like a window had been opened in my mind. I could see what people were feeling like smoke trails in the air. I found one that was so intense I was just drawn to it. I followed it here and I could see everything. Time moved differently and I saw the events of the sacrifice from before you arrived. I watched his death and saw his soul float above his body. He didn't move on, he just stayed there shouting at the other man, cursing him in every way possible. Some choice words that even I haven't heard used that way before," Lena chuckled slightly at the memory, her euphoria contagiously bringing out a humorous smile on his lips. "I could feel his anger and fear and hatred pouring through the book. I'm not sure why, it was just a random thought, but I sent some of my power into the book. It mixed with the man's emotions like they were made for each other. He'd bought the bracelet for his girlfriend and the protectiveness he had for it pulled the emotion and my power into it, almost like a magnet." Removing her arms from his shoulder, she sat back on her ankles and looked at the bracelet still in her hand. He could still feel its powerful vibration rippling through air around them. "It was like it wanted to be made. My power is just the glue between the object and the emotion."

Ambrose stared at her. "Lena," he started softly, "that's amazing. You are amazing." He lifted her chin to look at him. "I'm so proud of you."

She leant forward and kissed him again, with more care and warmth than he had ever felt in a kiss before. "Thank you," she said against his lips. "I did it, Ambrose. I found my design," she whispered with contentment.

"So, what does it do?" he asked, lifting her hand that still held the bracelet.

"I don't know," she said. "Not yet, anyway." She sighed softly. "And, I'm too tired to figure it out at the moment. Pouring my power through the book was exhausting. I barely had enough to get here. Still can't feel my legs. Doubt I'll be walking any time soon."

"Well then," Ambrose said, putting his arm under hers, lifting her up enough until he could hook his other arm under her knees. He picked her up as gently as possible, letting her head rest on his shoulder. "We take it home with us and you can study it when you're ready." He gathered the flames around them and in a blink, he was standing in their room next to the bed. He laid Lena down reverently, helping her take her shoes and jeans off.

"I know it's not meant to stay with me long, and it's not meant for the Vault," she yawned, letting herself sink into the bed's softness. "I can feel that I need to send it somewhere. Just need to figure out where and when."

"First, you need to sleep and rest." he said, pulling the covers over her. Lena placed the bracelet on the table next to her before sinking back into the pillows. Within moments she was asleep. He sat on the bed next to her holding her hand.

Lena had been so happy to discover her creation had worked. In that moment he had felt his chest bursting with pride for her. She had found her calling to aid in the growth of Hell. She still needed to figure out how it worked in the long run, but she had found it. He made a mental note to place protections around the crystallised book. It was hers now, and it seemed to play a pivotal role in her creation of the object. Without it, she would have nothing to continue her work. He told himself he should go now to protect it, but he couldn't bring himself to leave her just yet.

Watching her sleeping face, Ambrose knew he could not serve another day for Hell, if she was not by his side. He would destroy everything he had built before he would risk losing her. She had become the most precious thing to him now.

He loved her.

The thought struck him like a bolt of her lightning, slamming into his chest and taking what breath he had from him. Instinctively, he clutched her hand tightly, never wanting to let go. Bowing his head, he briefly touched his lips to the palm of her hand, vowing that she would never be taken from him, unless by her own choice.

"I love you, Lena," he whispered almost silently, testing out the words on his tongue. They felt natural. They felt right. They felt true. He meant them with every fibre of his being. She would be his undoing, and he welcomed it.

He tore away from her and forced himself to walk towards the library. Once there he used a length of black velvet to pick up the book and placed it inside an enchanted chest he had sitting on a lower shelf. He poured part of his own power over the chest creating a seal that could only be broken by his death. He would instruct Lena on how to do the same in the morning increasing the protection around the book. No one but her should touch it now.

By the time he had finished, his demonic form had receded. With reverence, he carried the box back to the bedroom and placed it on the table next to the bracelet. Looking at Lena's face again, he laid on the bed next to her and gathered her in his arms. He had no immediate need to sleep, but the need to hold her was overwhelming. Ambrose buried his face in her hair as she sighed in her sleep turning her body towards him and shifting closer.

In all his centuries as a demon, he had never felt so at peace.

CHAPTER TWENTY-FIVE

Now that Lena had found her design, she didn't need to go into the Repository as much. She still enjoyed going there, finishing up some last bits of training that Morgan had set up for her, but she spent more time now studying her book, testing the limits of its power. The day after making her first object, she had used the book to find out what to do with it, in the end selling it to a pawn shop. In that way, the bracelet ended up in general circulation on Earth to find whatever fate awaited it. From what she could tell, it would cause intense feelings of protection. It was not necessarily evil in its purpose; it would all depend on who came into possession of it.

She and Ambrose had stopped by the Vault that morning to drop off a new artefact for Calza to store. They had been ecstatic at learning of her design, intensely inspecting the artefact before rushing off to find its new home. Realising they were not going to be coming back any time soon, Lena let Ambrose lead her away and further down into the depths of Hell.

"So where exactly are we going?" she asked as they turned down yet another corridor.

"I told you," he smiled at her, "it's a surprise. But you're going to love it."

"If it's a surprise, how do you know I'm going to love it?"

"Because I know you."

Lena scoffed behind him, but smiled knowing he was right. "Putting aside the casual flirting from the last two years, you've only really known me for six weeks," she teased.

"And in that time, have you not told me more about you than anyone else?" Ambrose stopped walking and turned towards her. "By your own admission that's true."

"Curse you and your good memory," she sighed, her smile widening.

He checked the corridor to make sure no one else was present, before stepping towards her and cupping the back of her neck, angling her face up to his. His lips brushed against hers in an agonisingly slow kiss, drawing a soft moan from her throat after he pulled back. "I promise, you are going to love it."

"I'd love something else right now."

"Hm, what a lovely thought," he said against her lips. "But Marcus is waiting for us."

She groaned with frustration as Ambrose turned and started walking away again. Jogging slightly to catch up with him, she started to hear the sounds of cheering and shouting echoing through the corridor. They rounded a final corner as a flurry of black, grey and red rushed before them, whipping a gust of air over them.

"Bloody hell!" she cried, catching herself on the wall of the corridor. "Was that... were those hellhounds?" Her eyes wide with excitement, she looked up at Ambrose, as she made her way over to him by the junction in the corridor that had just been filled with movement.

"I told you, you'd love it," he laughed, placing his hand on her lower back and guiding her across the junction into the cavern overcrowded with jubilant demons. "Come on, Marcus should be over here."

With his hand firmly on her back, Lena turned her head taking in the sights around her. Demons all around her were conversing within their own groups, passing bits of paper or small objects between them. All completely oblivious to her, in stark contrast to how many that she recognised acted when seeing her in the corridors. Here she merely faded into the masses. It was fantastic.

"Hey, over here!" A familiar voice called out to them. Whipping her head round, she saw Marcus waving to them from beside a stone wall. Many other demons were clambering around him, hanging over the edge and pointing off to the side. "Lena, come here, I've found a foothold in the wall you can use to see over it."

As they neared the cambion, she realised what he meant. The wall was her height as a human. Most of the demons could easily see over it, but she wouldn't have a chance without assistance.

"Some days, I really can't wait until I transform," she sighed heavily, finding the dent in the wall that Marcus had been referring to and used it to lift herself up, resting her arms on the top. Ambrose and Marcus stood either side of her, pushing their shoulders into her back to help keep her in place.

"I wouldn't wish for it too quick," Marcus said. "The amount of attention you're getting, you'll have half of Hell trying to curry favour with you by the time you actually do."

She smiled as she heard Ambrose groan beside her. He hated the attention she was getting almost as much as she did. "Other demons may think that's a good thing. I hate the attention."

"It will pass in time," Marcus shrugged. "It's early days yet."

"Oh yeah? Name one demon off the top of your head that hadn't transformed by six weeks," she asked, looking at him over her shoulder.

"Eh," he laughed, "you got me there."

The thundering of paws hitting the stone floor grew louder as did the cheering of the crowd around her. Lena felt her excitement increasing with their enthusiasm, a wide smile forming on her face. Suddenly, she saw in greater detail the attraction that pulled the crowd's attention. Demons sat atop hellhounds, racing each other through the corridors of Hell. The beasts were fast, unbelievably fast, each snapping at the others, trying to force their opponents back or off the track. The riders threw powers at each other, trying to hit or knock them from their hounds. The cheers grew deafeningly loud as the hell hounds and their riders flew past the outcrop before her.

Again, she was blown back by the sheer force of the wind created by their hellish speed. She felt Ambrose's hand press firmly into her back, keeping her body from falling off the wall.

"So, what are they doing?" she shouted over the crowd, leaning towards Ambrose.

"Racing," he cried in answer.

"I got that," she said, rolling her eyes. "So, they race hellhounds, but like horses?"

"Yep," he nodded. "Demons can race their own hellhounds, if they have one, or one of the unbound ones."

"But they use powers?"

"The aim is to win," Marcus explained, leaning forward so that she could hear him. "But there's not many rules on how to achieve that.

Playing dirty is allowed and expected. We're demons after all. You only win if both you and your hellhound cross the finish line together. There are four laps in a race. First two laps, no powers allowed. It's a test of your hellhounds speed and strength. After that, all's fair. You get knocked off, you're out. Your hellhound can't run anymore, you're out. You can do whatever you want to try and knock your opponents off. The only thing you and your hellhound can't do is flame ahead. Flaming behind to catch out your opponents, fine. But you cannot gain distance."

"Is this a design?" she asked, craning over the wall as the sound of paws began to build again. "Do only certain demons' race?"

"Hell no! This is just for fun," Ambrose laughed, stepping further behind her, noting Marcus had moved slightly away, pushing himself closer to the wall to see the race. "Looks like this race is coming to an end."

The glow of the hellhounds' and demons' eyes could be seen before the rest of their bodies. Flashes of powers illuminated them briefly, before either colliding with an opponent or bounding harmlessly off the corridor wall. The leader of the group, a black skinned demon, was hunkered down close to the back of the pitch-black hellhound beneath him. A red fireball was thrown by one of the trailing demons aimed directly for the leader's back. In a blink, the leader flamed a fraction to the side of the track, the fireball missing him completely and extinguishing in the air. The crowd exploded with roars of encouragement as the hellhounds bounded past their location, the leader sitting back and raising his arms into the air in triumph.

"Woohoo!" Marcus cried, his hands shooting into the air. He turned away from them to take an indistinguishable object from the demon beside him who looked rather forlorn.

"The gambling is a big part of it too," Ambrose said into her ear, discreetly pulling Lena closer to him, his arm wrapped around her waist as Marcus was distracted by conversation with the demon next to him.

She allowed herself to lean back into him, fully aware that they had to be careful about public displays of affection, but hoped that the packed nature of the crowd would provide adequate cover for them. "What do demons gamble with?"

"Money, power, favours and allegiances," he explained, as he rubbed his hand over her stomach, pressing her against him. She could feel the hardness of his body pressed into her bottom. "Cursed objects and artefacts are also traded. Any demon can race as long as they can sit on a hellhound. Some demons are counted out on that, purely based on their size. Hellhounds are strong but even they have limits."

"Damn, they're quick," she said, looking on at the racers as they exchanged handshakes or death glares between themselves in equal quantity.

"Maybe when Zamira has had her pups, you'll race," he said, his warm breath sending shivers across the back of her neck.

Lena laughed at the idea. "Ha! No, thanks. I like to remain in one piece."

"Who says you wouldn't?" he chuckled. "Seeing what you can do in the pits, it would take a lot for another demon to knock you off."

"Howdy, Marcus!"

Both Lena and Ambrose turned their head towards their jubilant companion, trying to find the source of the voice that called to him. Ambrose groaned loudly into her ear as they spotted Cyrus walking towards them with a female demon. She laughed slightly, jabbing her elbow back into his ribs, even as he straightened and stepped to the side, helping her down from the wall. "Be nice," she whispered to him, ignoring the incredulous look he shot her way.

"Hey, Tegan!" Marcus cried, embracing the female. "Are you racing today?"

"Yup. I'm in the next one," she replied, her deep southern American accent washing over Lena like warm honey. Tegan was one of the smallest demons she had met since coming to Hell, being only half a foot or so taller than her. Her dark red skin was striking compared to Marcus' black and Cyrus' ashy tones. Black hair hung down to her waist, braided intricately around her horns, interwoven with gold rings and bronze beads. She turned her black eyes towards Lena and tilted her head to the side. "Who's this?"

"This is Lena," Marcus introduced them. "She's bound to Ambrose, who you've met previously. Lena, this is Tegan."

"Well, howdy, Lena," Tegan said with a warm smile.

"Howdy," she said, returning the greeting. Lena turned her eyes to Cyrus. "Hey, Cyrus."

"Hey, Lena," Cyrus said, stepping towards her, but halting as his eyes shot up to her sire who was standing behind her. "Ambrose."

"Cyrus," Ambrose responded curtly. Although Lena couldn't see her sire's face from behind her, she could feel the tension in his body rising.

"Marcus!" the cambion cried holding his hands up in mock greeting.

Lena and Tegan laughed, picking up on the need to break the awkward silence now forming between the impromptu group.

"Hey," Tegan exclaimed suddenly pointing towards Lena, "you're the boundling who knocked Archie on his arse."

"Ugh," she sighed, realising the normalcy of the moment was over. "Yeah, that's me," she said with an exasperated smile.

"You're wicked powerful, baby girl," Tegan said, folding her arms in front of her with an impressed look on her face.

"Um, thanks?" she chuckled, not really sure how to respond to the praise. Deciding that Tegan was at least someone to have fun with, Lena made a mental note to get to know her better. The demon seemed to be of a similar mind as the women stared at each other for a moment, their surroundings temporarily forgotten.

Suddenly, Tegan stepped forward and grabbed hold of her hand. "You gonna learn how to race? I heard you got a hellhound."

Laughing in response, Lena emphatically shook her head. "I don't think it's for me. I like to keep my feet solidly on the ground. Besides, Zamira's pregnant, so... couldn't even if I wanted to."

"You could always borrow an unbound one for now," Tegan said, tugging on Lena's hand pulling her along further into the crowd. "At least lemme show you mine. There's still some time before the next race."

"I don't feel like you're giving me a choice, so fine," she said humorously, checking over her shoulder to ensure that Ambrose was following them. He nodded reassuringly at her, as he, Marcus and Cyrus pushed their way through the crowd.

"Yay! Come on, baby girl!" Tegan cried with glee, turning as she walked, still holding Lena's hand tightly in her own. They finally made it to where the density of the crowd began to dissipate. A small archway had been carved into the wall which the men had to duck under to walk through. Beyond the arch were a number of separated pens in which hellhounds either lounged on beds of hay or stood awaiting their riders. Tegan made her way purposefully to a pen near the back of the room, a dark grey hellhound, with unusually sleek fur compared to its brethren, stood by the small gate, its red eyes watching carefully as they approached.

"Who is this?" Lena asked, amazed at the sheer enormity of the beast before her. It stretched out its neck as Tegan scratched behind its ear, pressing its snout against Lena's stomach.

"This 'ere is Gray. He's mine," Tegan announced proudly, running her hand down the length of his neck "He seems to like you."

"He's... huge," Lena said awestruck as the hellhound sniffed up her body before licking at her cheek.

"He should like you," Cyrus said, pulling Lena's attention over her shoulder and towards him. "He's Zamira's mate."

"What?" Lena and Tegan asked simultaneously.

A look of unease etched into his features as the women stared at him. "Ah, Gray is the father to Zamira's pups. They're a mated pair. He'll like you because you smell like Zamira. Likewise, Zamira will like Tegan as Gray imprinted with her." Seeing that the women weren't looking away from him, he pressed his lips together into a thin line. "There's not really any other way of explaining that," he said slowly.

The women looked at each other, then to Gray, who was still happily sniffing over Lena's body.

"I knew I liked you for a reason," Tegan burst out with a small laugh. "So, I gotta get ready for the race, but if you ever want a lesson in hellhound riding, hit me up, 'kay, baby girl?"

"Alright, thanks," she nodded with a smile. "Good luck!"

"Y'all watch, yeah?"

Lena looked at Ambrose, who nodded in confirmation. "Yeah, we will," she said, turning back to Tegan. "If we can find a spot with another foothold in the wall," she laughed.

"Marcus and I can hold you up if needed," Ambrose chuckled much to her annoyance as she pressed her lips together.

Cyrus hung back, looking over the other hellhounds as their racers came into the room to get ready for the race. Lena, Ambrose and Marcus forced their way back through the crowd, managing to regain their spot along the wall. Once she was securely in place with Ambrose leaning in against her, Marcus diverted off slightly, setting up his bets with neighbouring demons for the next race.

"Was I nice enough to your friend?" Ambrose asked teasingly, his face beside hers as he rested his hands either side of her body on the top of the wall.

"You said one word to him, Ambrose," she chuckled. "And his name at that. I wouldn't call that anything."

"I could have hit him," he said with a sly smile.

"Why would you want to do that?" she asked, raising her brow at him.

"For interrupting us earlier."

She laughed quietly, shaking her head in bemusement. "If that's all it takes for you to hit someone, it's a wonder Marcus isn't black and blue. He interrupted us on an almost daily basis five weeks ago." She could feel Ambrose's chest rumbling with soft laughter against her back.

The competitors for the next race lined up at the start line. Lena saw Tegan close to the edge. She looked tiny compared to the size of the demons next to her, regardless of the imposing profile of Gray beneath her. Six racers in total, jostling against each other as they waited for the starting mark. The crowd fell quiet as the countdown began. A pale demon was hunched on top of the wall, a little in front of the racers. He held up his hand and with a spark of golden lightning from his hand, the hellhounds bolted, their claws clashing loudly against the floor as they sped from their mark.

It was a split second before the racers rushed past their position, the rush of wind whipped at Lena's hair as she tried to follow them down the corridor. As they waited for the race to make its way round the lap, she leant back into Ambrose's solid frame, stealing a small moment of joy in the obscurity of the crowd.

"Thank you, Ambrose," she whispered to him. "This is amazing."

"You're welcome," he said softly, pressing a quick kiss to her cheek. "But, why do I feel like you're saying 'amazing' as if it's bittersweet."

Lena sighed heavily before responding. "It's my birthday."

"What?"

She smiled with amusement as she heard the surprise in his voice and felt his body stiffen behind her. "Today would have been my birthday," she clarified. "I would have turned twenty-five today."

"29th of March? That's your birthday?" His voice was barely a whisper beside her ear. Suddenly, she felt bad for springing it on him, not that she had expected him to know any way.

"Yes," she said softly, turning to look at him, worried by the blank expression on his face. "Don't worry. I know you didn't know. Figure, I don't really have birthdays anymore, anyway. I was just feeling a little melancholy. Besides, this was better than any present."

Ambrose looked at her, his expression indiscernible. The forced smile he formed made her feel uneasy even as he wrapped an arm around her waist in a quick embrace. "Right, yeah," he nodded. "Happy birthday."

Turning back to the race, she couldn't help but feel like she had upset him in some way. She tried to push it from her mind and focus on following Tegan, determined to enjoy the moment rather than fret over something she could be imagining. With a deep breath, she focused on the warmth of his body and the infectious energy of the crowd around her. She could sort through her uneasiness later.

CHAPTER TWENTY-SIX

"The 29th... she can't be..." Ambrose whispered to himself as he paced back and forth within his office.

It had been years since he thought about that deal. A deal that would force an unborn child on a path directly headed for Hell. It had bothered him endlessly for years after. Why those terms? What had possessed him to make a deal on those terms? He hated the idea of any innocent being subjected to the fate of Hell, much less a baby that would have no say in their own destiny. It was bad enough that innocence was needed to summon him specifically.

The intention had been to leave it at the mother and child being saved and the pregnancy being normal, as he had done for other deals of the same kind in the past. The summoning hadn't been specific so it didn't require intricate terms. That should have been it. He should have marked the soul and left. But that's not what happened.

Something had taken over him. It had taken a few days after for him to remember the experience. An icy hand had gripped his will, overriding it and forcing the abhorrent terms from him. It was like he had been compelled but with no way of fighting against it.

"Twenty-five. She's twenty-five so that would mean... born 1987... shit..." he ran his hands through his hair, trying to sort his thoughts into a coherent strand of reason.

It matched up too perfectly to be a coincidence, and Ambrose had been around too long to believe in coincidences anymore. Her power levels were extraordinary, but was that enough to say for certain she was that child?

"Thousands of children are born every day," he tried to reason with himself. "She wouldn't have been the only one born then."

The day the 29th of March 1987 had rolled around, he had paid special attention to the events. Nothing of historical significance had occurred, but astronomically, it had been of particular interest. A hybrid-solar eclipse had passed over the majority of South Africa. A rare event that occurs when a solar eclipse appears as annular or total at different points along its path through the sky. To both angels and demons, it symbolised the great split in morality, the merging and divergence of their purpose.

"Dammit!" he cursed, turning on his heel and barraging out of his office.

Lena was working in her altar room. Her spell work and rituals well exceeded his capabilities since finding her conduit so he had given her free reign of the room. He had questions for her, but he wasn't sure how she would react to them, or if he even wanted the answers. Turning to his room, he decided to have a shower, to try and clear his mind.

She'd told him on their date that she had been born two months early. Meaning, she had been born at seven months, just as the child was supposed to. But surely, there would have been other girls born under different circumstances. And, he had no way of knowing if the child was going to be a girl anyway. Ignoring gender, that doubled the chances that it was a different child subject to the deal. That Lena was not the one he had doomed to Hell.

But it would be all too perfect of a circle, if the child cursed by his deal, ended up in his care. Wouldn't it?

Roughly grabbing at the taps to turn the shower on, he ran it the hottest it would go. He felt immense guilt at the possibility that he was the reason why the woman he loved was a demon and he wanted to burn that feeling away. Stripping off, he practically jumped into the water, letting the heat radiate over his face, neck and shoulders.

"Please," he begged quietly into the water. "Please, don't let it be her."

"Want company?"

Ambrose turned his head sharply to see Lena leaning in the doorway, a seductive smile on her lips, her arms folded in front of her. Apparently, she already had designs on joining him regardless of his answer, having already taken off her trousers which now hung on the chair by the door. His body hardened instantly at the sight of her.

"If I ever say 'no' to that, you have my permission to electrocute me," he said as his eyes roamed her half naked body. Quickly, he adjusted the water temperature to a more reasonable heat.

With a smile, Lena pushed herself from the doorframe and deftly lifted her shirt over her head, throwing it to the floor. She pushed her panties off her hips and let them fall to her feet before gracefully stepping out of them.

"I'll hold you to that," she said, stepping into the shower and lifting onto her toes placed a gentle kiss on his lips. She looked up at him and he nearly moaned aloud seeing the glow of desire in her eyes, even as it mixed with apprehension. "Ambrose, did I upset you yesterday?"

His stomach dropped and his heart rammed into his ribcage. "No," he blurted, shaking his head fervently. "No, you didn't upset me." He cupped her face between his hands, running his thumbs over her cheeks. "I felt bad for not knowing it was your birthday," he lied, swallowing the guilt he felt for it. "But that's on me. I promise, I'm not upset with you. I want you, desperately." That, at least, was the truth.

She smiled at him, her expression relaxing. He was completely mesmerised by her as she turned to reach for the bottle of soap and poured some onto her hands. He placed a hand on her hip, simply wishing to touch her. Turning back to him, Lena lathered the soap before rubbing it over his chest and stomach, her fingers purposefully tracing every line. His breath caught in his throat at her touch as she pressed herself against him, continuing to rub his body with soap, first on one arm and then the other. After she had finished with the top of his body, she knelt before him and ran her hands over his hips and thighs. Her fingers traced around his cock, building his desire with small strokes as she washed every part of him.

A soft growl pulled from his chest as he looked down at the woman who had stolen his heart. Surely, she had to have been made by gods, not from a deal with Hell. This was a gesture that he would normally have done for her, but the look of contentment on her face gave him untold joy at being the recipient of her affections. He wanted to cry out, declaring his love for her, but a heavy pit of fear in his stomach made him hesitate. Instead, he tenderly brushed back a strand of her hair, leaving his hand to rest on her cheek as she continued her work.

After a moment, she rose to her feet and pressed her body against his, lacing her arms around his waist to rub his back. He rested one of his hands on her hips, pressing her abdomen against his cock. Taking hold of her chin to angle her face up, he pressed his lips to hers in a long, drawn out kiss that required no urgency. He had explored her body so many times already, but now he wanted to return the affections she had paid him. Keeping her close, he stepped back into the warm stream to let the soap run off his body.

"Ah, not my hair!" Lena cried against him, laughter in her voice. He smiled as she tried to pull away, straining her neck in the opposite direction. His grip kept her firmly against him so she couldn't get away, but he made sure not to pull her too far into the water. Once all the suds had washed away, he stepped them back out and grabbed the soap.

Much like she had done, he started with her stomach, tracing soft circles against her skin. He dropped rows of kisses on her shoulders as he moved his hands to cup her breasts only briefly brushing the pads of his thumbs over her peaked nipples. She sighed with pleasure as he raised his head to admire her beauty before moving his hands up and over her shoulders, tracing down her arms. With care he took hold of her hands and gently massaged each in turn, watching his hands work and revelling in the heat that was increasing between them. Her breath was quickening and from his peripheral vision he saw the sharp rise and fall of her chest.

"Your bindings are still growing," he said as he trailed his hands back up her arms and over her shoulders. The markings now converged at the back of her neck and branched down her spine stopping just past her shoulder blades.

"I don't want to talk about them right now," she sighed, gripping on to his upper arms.

Smiling, Ambrose moved his palms to her hips before dropping to his knees as she had done. He wanted to worship every part of her body. To show her how much he needed her. How much she meant to him. But the revelation of the love he had for her the other night, along with the possibility that he was the reason for her now being a demon, made him cautious. If she rejected him, or didn't fully return his affections, he knew that would be the end of him. He would never stand in her way if she wanted to leave, but he also knew he wouldn't survive such an event. He could feel she desired him, as much as he desired her, and he decided that was enough for now. He could live with desire and would keep his love secret, until he was sure she felt the same.

Rubbing the soap down each leg, he leant forward as Lena placed her hands on his shoulders to balance herself. He lifted one of her legs holding it against him and allowed her to rest her foot on his raised knee. He kept hold of her calf with one hand whilst with the other he rubbed soap along her inner thigh.

"Oh, Ambrose," she sighed breathlessly as her fingers pressed into his flesh, her nails just starting to dig in. He smiled with excitement as she said his name, letting his hands brush as close to her core as he could without putting soap where it didn't need to go. He could feel the heat coming from her as he roamed his hand up between her legs to squeeze her backside, the soft flesh supple under his touch. She whimpered above him and the pressure on his shoulders increased as she leant more of her weight onto him.

Ambrose looked up at the woman who now meant more to him than any power he had gained over the years and was taken aback at her radiant beauty. Her skin glowed with desire and her dove-grey eyes gleamed almost iridescently in the soft bathroom light. He was awestruck as he returned his hands to her hips. Placing her hands on either side of his face, she leant down to kiss him. Her tongue sliding into his mouth with no resistance as he met it with his own in a fevered swirling dance.

Breaking the kiss to his own dismay, he got to his feet and grabbed the handheld shower head, switching the water stream from the overhead. Testing the water first, he used it to continue his worship and rinsed the soap off her body, following the stream with his hand. At all times, Lena kept a hand on his body to keep herself upright.

Once all the soap had been washed away, he turned off the shower and pulled her against him. Lifting her in his arms, he placed his hands under her bottom supporting her against him, as she wrapped her arms around his neck. Claiming her mouth, he poured his desire and passion into their kiss. She moaned against his lips, as he stepped out of the shower, grabbing a towel to drape loosely over her back to keep her warm.

"I want you, Ambrose," Lena whispered as she pulled her head back slightly to look into his eyes. Her grey depths had darkened with her desire, firm resolve evident within. "I need you. Take me and show me again that I belong to you. Only you. Please."

In that moment, all speech had been stolen from him, so Ambrose merely responded with action. His arms contracted around her small frame pressing her firmly against his body. His cock twitched with eagerness to fulfil her request, pressing up against her bottom. Their mouths met again with a new urgency to claim the other.

Carefully, he walked back out to the bedroom and laid her down atop the towel. He stood to take a last look at the full spread of her naked body, endlessly thankful that she gave him the privilege of enjoying it, before he climbed onto the bed and nestled his hips between her thighs.

The head of his cock pressed gently against her slick opening, parting her ever so slightly, as he rested on his forearms so he could look down at her face. There was so much warmth and affection in her eyes that Ambrose wanted to stare into them forever.

"Are you ready, my dove?" he asked, brushing a strand of hair from her face.

Lena placed a hand on his cheek and ran her thumb across his lower lip. He sucked in her thumb, biting it gently as she gasped and smiled at him. "I need you in me. Now," she said, pulling his face towards hers for another kiss.

As their lips touched, he drove his hips forward, sheathing his length within her wet channel in a single movement. She exhaled sharply and her jaw dropped at his sudden presence within her. Her hands clung to his shoulders, her nails digging into his flesh. He didn't care as he watched her face in stunned rapture. Shutting her eyes, her chin lifted and her back arched pressing her chest against his.

Slowly, he withdrew, before again surging forward, quickening his pace with each thrust. He hooked his arms under Lena's thighs pulling them up into the air. Shifting onto his knees, he angled her body so that he could reach her innermost depth with the head of his cock. She flung her arms above her head, grabbing the pillow as she moaned softly into the air.

"Yes," Lena cried, "yes, Ambrose, like that."

Smiling at her affirmation, knowing he had found her pleasure point, he moved one hand to bring it between them, placing the flat of his thumb on her swollen clit. He circled his thumb around it as her hips bucked against him. She turned her head to the side, placing the pillow over her mouth, biting into it.

"No," he ordered, "don't muffle your moans. I want to hear them."

Letting the pillow drop and she turned her head to look at him, a wild expression on her face. Her moans rippled through the bedroom as he paid great attention to her sensitive bud.

"You are the most wonderful thing I have ever seen, Lena," he said as he felt her channel start to tighten. "I will never lose the desire to see you like this." He saw her toes start to curl and her fingers dig into the pillow either side of her head. Her skin glistened with sweat and her face was aglow with pleasure. "Come for me, my dove." Her eyes shut tight as she threw her head back with a cry that echoed through the room. "Good girl," Ambrose growled as her slick channel contracted around him and he watched her body convulse with the waves of pleasure that emanated from her core. He let the one knee he was still holding fall and moved his body to lay atop her again, never leaving her silky warmth.

Lena was panting still as she placed her hands on his neck, her eyes closed. Adoringly, he kissed each eyelid, then her cheeks, temples and mouth. Then with a wicked smile, he pulled out, paused and then slid back into her warmth. Her eyes flew open to look at him, as he picked a slower, steady pace, drawing out his and her pleasure.

"Ambrose," she said breathlessly, clutching at him.

He stopped her from speaking further as he crushed his mouth on hers. He grabbed her wrists and pinned them above her head with one hand in a swift, fluid motion. His other hand roamed her body, catching one of her nipples between his fingers and giving it a light but deliberate squeeze. She moaned into his mouth and her body shivered beneath him, her over sensitive channel still clenching against his hard cock.

"Now together," he said gruffly against her lips, as he thrust his hips against hers, his control crumbling.

"Yes," she cried, her body rocking in time with his rhythm.

"Wrap your legs around me," he ordered.

Lena obeyed willingly as her legs squeezed around his hips, locking her ankles behind his back. He could feel the tension rising within her again, as the walls of her pussy tightened around him. His own pleasure building, he wrapped his free arm under her waist pinning her body to his. Kissing her neck, he increased his speed, diving into her depth with renewed passion.

God, how he needed her. Everything in him needed her. She had become the breath in his lungs, the beat of his heart, the warmth in his blood. Damned be everything else if she was not with him. If she was not his. What did it matter how she came to him? She was here and he loved her. What else mattered? She couldn't be the one from the deal. It had to be someone else. It had to be. He couldn't risk losing her. Not when having her in his arms was the most exquisite and perfect thing to him. Fierce protectiveness washed over him as his arm contracted hungrily around her waist, as if to pull her body into his.

Pushing the fear of losing her from his mind, he focused on the feelings of Lena's pleasure coursing through his body. Pleasure she was feeling from him.

"Ambrose!" she screamed as her second climax racked her body.

Tightening his grip on her wrists and waist, he was undone. He groaned against her neck as his own climax sent waves of pleasure throughout his body as his hot release coated her walls.

They laid intertwined together unmoving whilst their breathing returned to normal. Eventually, Ambrose lifted his head, releasing her wrists. He stared at her flushed face before covering it with kisses. Lena giggled at his gesture as she raked her hands through his hair. Her joy infectious, he joined her in laughter, gathering her close in his arms.

"That was..." she started.

"Incredible," he finished for her.

"Although, I possibly need another shower now."

"I'll join you," he said with a sly grin.

"Ha!" she scoffed. "And risk getting stuck in a loop?"

Laughing, he placed a slow and tender kiss on her lips, before rolling off her and standing up next to the bed. With a warm smile, he held out his hand and helped her to her feet. He placed his other hand on the small of her back drawing her close to him. He kissed her again, deeply this time pulling a small moan from her throat. Looking her in the eye, he grinned wickedly. "It's worth the risk," he said before leading her back to the bathroom.

CHAPTER TWENTY-SEVEN

Early in the morning, Lena left the manor and made her way to the northern gate. She hadn't been to the lookout since her first day as a demon, and even then, she had been plagued with anxiety from the memories of what had happened to her back then. But lately, she found she needed to return. To face the memories and know they were no longer in control of her.

Even though her time with Ambrose was filled with heady passion, the last few days had felt different. He felt withdrawn, like he was distancing himself from her, and she couldn't figure out why. He'd been more focused on his work, spending more and more time in his office without her, stating he had been neglecting some work he needed to focus on now. Even Hell had its limits and couldn't magic money out of thin air. Deals that required the exchange of finances were reliant on the work that Ambrose and some other top-side demons did. Additionally, it was through this that Ambrose had built most of his alliances with other demons who in turn provided him with power and protections. So she knew that it was important that he focus on this for now.

But even their nights had been spent apart as he sought out random summonings, leaving her to pour over her book or simply pace around the manor. Something happened the day he found out about her birthday, and she didn't know how to fix it, or if it even could be fixed. Regardless of his assurances that nothing was wrong, she felt so lost within the manor, unable to settle back to how they were before.

Reaching the lookout, Lena looked around her, letting the memories of her capture flash through her mind. She could still feel the dread and fear build within her, but it no longer scared her or caused her heart to race uncontrollably. Like the last time, she found a relatively smooth rock she could turn over in the hand to help focus her mind, and sat with sigh on the bench. The weather was warming now, no signs of snow lingering on the ground and the small sounds of creatures returned to the forest at her back. It was almost inconceivable to her how much had changed in the last month and a half. How much she had changed. But here she was, in a place that she had once found peaceful, turned to a nightmare and now settled into a scene of tentative comfort. Seemed like as good a place as any to analyse a relationship that was becoming an integral part of her survival.

With the sound of running water rising from the stream, she sighed and let her head fall back to stare at the sky. Ambrose was still not telling her something, that much was now painfully clear to her. Three weeks ago, he had opened up to her about his life, but she knew she was still missing parts about his time as a demon. At their dinner she had learnt more, but had also been left with more questions. He had since told her some more things about his time with Zagan and what happened the first few years after he broke his bonds. He'd told her about how he met Marcus, how the cambion had saved his life from one of Zagan's attempts to destroy him. He hadn't trusted Marcus immediately, due to his prejudice against cambions, but as they were both dealers they couldn't avoid each other, and slowly, Ambrose's desire for a friend won him over. But anytime she tried to ask him about his more recent dealings as a demon, he seemed to close up. Whether he intended to or not, she wasn't sure and she didn't know how to push him further, without increasing the tension already growing between them.

Although, the explanation of seven years' time for deals had confirmed something she had already suspected. Her father had made a deal.

Thinking it through, she realised he had to have made a deal. There was no other explanation in her mind for her mother's miracle remission and her father's sudden death on the seventh anniversary of it. They had celebrated her remission like a sacred holiday, to the point that it overtook any other celebration. Her own birthday had been secondary to it despite it being almost five months after the event.

Taking into account Ambrose's odd behaviour since learning of her birthday, she had begun to wonder if he knew her father. If he was the demon who made the deal and he had somehow put the puzzle pieces together. The thought had hit her one night when she had been alone in the library. She'd tried to push it aside, calling herself ridiculous for even thinking it. She had no proof, no evidence of any kind to link him to her father, except a feeling. But that feeling grew stronger and stronger within her gut, heightened by his recent avoidance of her.

She rubbed her hands over her face, before reaching into her jumper pocket and pulling out an old, crumpled envelope. Gently, she extracted the letter within, unfolding it as she had done hundreds of times before. Taking a deep breath to steady herself, she began to read her father's letter.

My dearest daughter... My dearest Lena,

I hope that whenever you may be reading this, you still have some memories of me. I wish we could have had more time.

Time was the one thing I wanted. Time with your mother. But it is the price of that time that now cuts short my time with you. I know how that will sound confusing, and I wish I could explain it further to you, but unfortunately, I can't.

I am sorry, Lena. I'm sorry for everything you are going to go through in life. And even more so that I will not be there to help guide and support you through it. I have no idea what is in store for you, and I am afraid for you. I can only hope that what I have left for you and your mother can in some way help and protect you both when I am gone...

"Yeah, thanks dad," she scoffed, "that worked out real well." Looking over the town, she sighed heavily. It was undeniable to her now that he made a deal. He knew he was going to die and he knew when. But why did it seem like there were more terms than just saving her mother for his soul?

Pressing on, she read the remainder of the letter.

Although I can't explain everything, I want you to understand something. Everyone has a path before them. For some there are forks within that path that lets them change what fate has planned for them. I fear that for you, there are no forks. I did something, before you were born, that has set events in motion that will affect you in all the worst ways possible.

I understand you may not wish to follow the advice of a man you barely know, but please try to do something for me. Please do not regret any decision you make, regardless of where it might take you. Although the decision I made has led to me being taken from you far too soon into your life, I do not regret it. If I had not made it, I would never have met you. I would never have loved you. Like your name, you are a ray of light in my life that I could never regret, will never regret.

I hope and pray that we can meet again. In another lifetime perhaps. I love you, Lena. I hope that when you read this, you might still love me too.

Your loving father,
Matthew

Leaning forward, she rested her elbows on her knees, letting the letter hang loosely from her fingers, fluttering slightly in the soft breeze. Where the letter used to confuse her, it seemed obvious now. The deal had to have something to do with her. With her life. As if, it was responsible for everything she had lived through. All the abuse and neglect, culminating in where she was now. Did he know she would end up as a demon? Did he know how her mother would treat her after he died? Would it have mattered? He wanted more time with her mother, would he have cared if the aftermath affected a child he didn't even know at the time?

Was any of it real? Were any of the memories she held of her parents before her father's death real? Had they ever loved her, regardless of what the letter said? Her mother on many occasions would tell her how much she wished she had aborted her, blaming her for her father's death. Her mother had to have known then, about the deal, and despite the fact that Lena hadn't even been born yet, seemed to think that she was somehow responsible for her father's choices.

And if Ambrose had been the demon who made the deal, did he remember? Did he know it was her?

Suddenly, a shiver ran down her spine, causing her to straighten, carefully folding her father's letter and stuffing it back within its envelope. She took a deep breath and sat back against the bench, pushing the envelope into her jeans pocket. Looking back over the town, she strained her senses, letting the feeling of uneasiness wash over her so she could hold onto it and identify its purpose. The feeling was all too familiar to her now.

Someone was watching her.

Slowly and deliberately, she got to her feet, pausing briefly before turning on her heel and making her way back to the northern gate. Compared to the last time she had been followed up here, her senses were heightened now. She easily heard the footsteps on the stone path behind her, her heart beating rapidly even as she forced her feet to move at a steady pace.

Get back to the manor, the now eerily comforting voice said in the back of her mind. No kidding, she thought to herself as she passed through the gate and turned towards the manor. For a moment, Lena thought of going further into town, trying to lose her follower, but figured it probably wouldn't matter. At least in the manor, as long as Ambrose was there, she would be safe.

Pulling her key from her pocket, she unlocked the front door and dashed inside, closing the door behind her as she slumped against it, sighing with relief. No one but a demon could get in the manor once the door was closed. She started for the stairs, intending to go up to her altar room and stay there. The feeling of being followed had rattled her. She may not have anything to fear from mortals now, but she was still working through her mistrust of them.

The knock on the door might as well have knocked the breath from her as she froze, her foot on the first step. Turning back to stare at the front door, she went back and forth on whether or not she should open it. Pretending to not be home didn't seem like an option, as the person likely was the one that followed her here.

Lena jumped slightly as the knock came again. Taking a deep breath, she walked back to the door, checking to make sure her bindings were still covered. Unlocking the door, she pulled it open slightly, apprehension filling her chest as she kept her foot pressed against the back of the door. She peered out into the street.

"Hello," the man said with an odd smile. He was well dressed in a charcoal grey suit with black pinstripes. His white shirt underneath was unbuttoned at the collar. The tan felt coat fit perfectly around his broad shoulders. She estimated the man would have been around his late fifties.

Her body flushed cold as fear and ice spread through her veins. The man looked awfully familiar and she knew exactly where from. His dark hair and blue eyes. The high cheekbones and square jaw. He looked almost exactly like the man who slit her wrists all those weeks ago.

"Hello," she responded flatly, her eyes locked with his.

"Is this the residence of Mr Ambrose Sumner?" the man asked, taking a step forward.

Lena shut the door slightly, closing the gap between it and its frame, shielding herself behind it. "It is."

"May I come in?"

Slowly, she shook her head. "Mr Sumner doesn't allow for unexpected visitors."

The smile on the man's face spread. "I'm sure he will make an exception for me."

"Apologies, sir, but I cannot let you inside," she said. She made to close the door fully, but the man grabbed the handle, forcing it back against her.

"I'm afraid, Miss Hale, that I will have to insist," his smile was gone and his eyes filled with impatient anger.

Lena felt her stomach drop and swallowed. How did he know her name? She knew she could easily force the door shut despite the push back from the man, but the command to avoid exposure stopped her from acting on her impulse. Her bindings constricted around her arms and shoulders, aching slightly. Her hand on the back of the door was shaking as she struggled to control her breathing, her vision tunnelling to black.

Who in the hell does he think he is?

His face...

Breathe, don't panic. Not now.

I can't...

Breathe, Lena!

"Lena, who is it?"

Still holding the door, pushing back against the man as best she could without imposing her full strength upon him, she turned her head slightly in acknowledgement, keeping her eyes on the man. She had never been more thankful to hear Ambrose's voice. Finally, she sucked in a full breath of air.

"He hasn't given his name," she said flatly, emboldened by her sire's presence.

She felt his warmth come up behind her and relaxed as he placed his hand on her hip pulling her close to him and taking hold of the door with his other hand. He opened it, not allowing the man inside, but so that they could have full view of the other.

"Mr Sumner, I presume," the man sneered, placing his hands in his trouser pockets.

"And you are?" Ambrose replied with a curt nod.

"My name is James," the man responded. "James Carter. We need to talk."

Ambrose's fingers pressed into her hip, only slightly, but enough to bring her attention to it. She wanted to look at him, but forced herself to keep her head still.

"Well as you have already been told, I do not accommodate unexpected visitors. Perhaps, if a conversation is completely necessary, we could arrange a coffee?" Ambrose said with an obvious coldness to his voice.

James smiled almost cruelly. "I don't think this is a conversation you want to risk being overheard, Mr Sumner."

"Oh? Please, enlighten me."

"I know what you are, Mr Sumner," the man sighed. "And I know that Miss Hale here, should be dead."

Lena felt her breath catch in her throat. How could he possibly know?

Ambrose was silent for a while, seemingly sizing up the man. "If you know what I am," he said finally, "then being alone with me, should be the last thing you should want." His tone was warm, but the threat was unmistakable.

James nodded absently, but his smile was gone. "I have told others that I am here. If they do not receive a call from me within the next hour, they will call the police and lead them here with a wealth of evidence to make your life very difficult." His facial expression hardened as he looked up at Ambrose. "Of course, if you don't let me in, I will call the police to the same effect."

A soft chuckle broke from Ambrose's chest. "Very well, Mr Carter, come on in," he said, pushing the door open fully and pulling Lena back to stand to the side of the door.

James walked past them and gave a low whistle as he stepped into the entrance hall. "My, my, Mr Sumner, you have done well for yourself."

"I'll show you to the sitting room. We can talk there," Ambrose said, letting go of Lena as he shut the front door. He walked over to the door on the right and opened it for James to enter.

"Be a darling and get us some drinks, will you, miss," James said, taking a step towards Lena and lifting his hand to her cheek.

"Don't," Ambrose barked. James stilled in his movement and turned his face to Ambrose. "Don't touch her." The look on her sire's face was dark, unreadable and utterly dangerous. A look that would strike fear into any man, but Lena thrilled to see it. Regardless of the distance between them of late, he was still as protective of her as he always had been. "Putting aside that it is ten in the morning, you have threatened your way into my home, and I will not allow you to disturb my assistant more than you already have. There are drinks inside, if you are in such desperate need of one."

James looked at her from the corner of his eye. "Assistant, huh?" How desperately she wanted to punch the smug look off his face. She took a deep breath as he turned away from her and walked into the room, not bothering to look at Ambrose as he walked past.

"One moment, Mr Carter," Ambrose said before walking over to her with only a few long strides. "Lena, hide out upstairs. Please, I'm begging you, don't eavesdrop either physically or with your book." His hands were holding her upper arms although she didn't look at him, her eyes remained locked on the door to the sitting room.

"Is he..." she started, but found she couldn't bring herself to finish her question.

"Related to the men who killed you?" he sighed. "Yes. Please Lena, do as I say."

She nodded and finally looked him in the eye. They were filled with concern and worry. "Okay," she said softly. "What are you going to do?"

Ambrose looked at the floor and shook his head. "I don't know. Find out what he knows first off." He paused for a moment and she could almost see the wheels in his head turning. Lifting his head, he looked into her eyes. "Do not spy on us. Go to your altar room, prepare a finding spell with your book. Then wait until I come up to speak with you."

She felt her bindings accept the command. Without complaint, she allowed her feet to carry her up the stairs. She looked back briefly to see Ambrose heading into the sitting room. With a heavy sigh she turned to the right and headed to her altar room to complete her instruction. Whatever was going to happen, she had a feeling this would likely determine if they stayed in town or not.

CHAPTER TWENTY-EIGHT

"Well, then, Mr Carter, what can I do for you?" Ambrose said as he entered the sitting room. Finding himself in need of a drink now, he walked over to the side table and poured two glasses of whiskey. Noting that James had yet to answer him, he turned to face the man and held out the glass, almost like a peace offering. The sneer on James' face was somewhat unsettling, but nothing that Ambrose was not used to from his time as a demon.

"You can start by admitting you killed my sons," the man said cooly, taking the glass offered to him, inspecting the amber liquid as it swirled around the glass.

Keeping his face devoid of emotion or recognition, Ambrose sipped tentatively at his whiskey. "I'm sorry," he said with a polite nod. "I heard your sons were missing."

James looked at him with a steely gaze, the smile on his face never faltering. "They are not missing Mr Sumner, and you know it."

Meeting his gaze, Ambrose hardened his resolve, taking a purposeful step towards the man. "I'm afraid I don't," he said firmly.

"Funny," James chuckled. Ambrose appreciated that he didn't seem intimidated by him, as many a man had been want to do in the past. "You don't strike me as an ignorant man."

"How do I strike you, then?" he asked, tilting his head to the side.

"As a demon," James declared, raising his glass as if in toast of the revelation. "A demon who is very old and very good at surviving. You did a good job cleaning up the warehouse, Mr Sumner. Wouldn't have thought anything of it, except finding my sons' car in the sea at the end of the pier piqued my interest." Ambrose sighed. So, the car had been found. That had been left out of the papers. He had also been too wrapped up in Lena's training, and in Lena herself, to actively seek out any other information. He wondered how much time had passed from that night to when the car had been found. How long had they been in the sea? James continued; "Going through the paperwork in their apartments filled in the blanks. My sons disconnected all of the CCTV in the area, they were smart enough for that, at least. They didn't want any footage of them carrying that girl into the warehouse. But the GPS tracking on their car was still functioning for a little while after it went into the sea." Yet another advancement of technology that was going to make demons' jobs harder, Ambrose thought to himself. At least no video evidence existed of the night, cursing himself internally for not even considering that CCTV may have been on the dock. "For what it's worth," James said softly, genuine remorse in his voice, taking Ambrose by surprise. "I am truly sorry for the part my sons played in the death of Miss Hale."

Remorseful or not, Ambrose's anger flared at the mention of Lena's sacrifice. He may be happy that she shared in his life now, but the manner of her death still bothered him. "I'll pass it on," he said flatly. "I'm sure she'll be most grateful. What do you want, Mr Carter?"

James sighed, before placing his now empty whiskey glass on the coffee table. "My sons were stupid, even I will admit that," he said, placing his hands in his pockets. "Their ideas for the company would have seen it fold in a year. They're inability to think beyond the immediate gain no doubt factored into their deaths. But they were my sons. I want them back. Their sister wants them back." Ambrose watched cautiously as James turned to face him, his back straightening. "Make a deal with me. Bring my sons back and I will destroy everything I have collected about you and other demons. Hell, I'll even ensure no one else finds what I have."

"If you truly know about demons then you know deals are usually in exchange for a soul," Ambrose said calmly, setting his glass next to James'.

"You'll make an exception for me."

Ambrose chuckled at James' bravado. The man was made of stern stuff, that was for sure. A quality that he appreciated, regardless of the trouble this was going to cause him. "Even if I was inclined to make a deal with you, I can't bring your sons back."

"Then take me to a demon who can."

"That's not how it works," Ambrose said, shaking his head. "They summoned a demon. They condemned themselves. There is no bringing them back."

"You had better find a way," James said curtly, the smile on his face finally dropping as his expression turned dark and dangerous. "You have forty-eight hours to think it over. If at the end of that time, I do not have my sons, or at least a conversation with a demon who can help me, I will leak all of the information I have on you and demons." The men stared at each other for a while, simply sizing the other up. After a moment, James dropped his gaze and headed for the door. "Thanks for the drink, Mr Sumner," he said over his shoulder as he left the room.

Walking to the doorway, Ambrose watched as James' left the manor, before striding to the front door and locking it. With a deep breath, he squared his shoulders and turned towards the staircase looking up towards the altar room. He didn't know what to say to her. Bring back her killers? He doubted this would go down well. On top of his recent avoidance of her, he was certain this would be an uncomfortable conversation.

Taking a deep steadying breath, he climbed the stairs and went to the altar room. Entering the room, he looked around at the set up that Lena had created within. Normally, she liked working in the library with her book, but she had placed a tall ebony lectern in the centre of the room upon which her crystallised book sat proudly when needed. White ash and sage had been scattered around the lectern in a perfect circle, heightening any power within. His gaze rested on her dark auburn hair as she fiddled with two large poles with intricate runes carved into their surfaces. She must have heard him come in, her movements slowing momentarily before looking over her shoulder at him.

"The spell is ready," she said softly, finishing up with her placement of the poles. One was facing north, the other east.

"What are those?" he asked, walking further into the room, ensuring he kept out of the circle. Lena would work the spell with her book. Contaminating the circle with his power would only hinder her efforts.

"Enhancement totems," she explained, shifting the eastern one ever so slightly to the right. "Fused with cowslip and poke root. Usually used for finding treasure or lost objects. Should help."

"Good idea," he nodded approvingly. Leaning against the wall, he studied her as she fussed over the circle. God, he missed her. He didn't want to avoid her, but every time she was near, he was racked with a mix of desire and guilt, leaving him in a constant turmoil that was beginning to border on torture. He wanted to talk to her, to ask her about her father, to find out once and for all if she was the child of the deal. But she was smart. And if she suspected at all that her father may have made a deal, she would figure it out if he asked. And that would jeopardise their relationship. Although, he suspected his withdrawing from her was jeopardising it anyway. Swallowing his apprehension, he asked; "Are you okay to do this?"

"Don't have much of a choice, do I?" Lena shrugged, turning to look at him. "The spell requires a conduit and as you don't have one..."

"We can ask someone else," he said even though he knew there wasn't really anyone else to ask.

"No. That would mean involving someone else," she said, shaking her head. "You trust anyone else to know about this. Except maybe Marcus, but again... no conduit."

"Good point," he sighed, avoiding her gaze.

Lena huffed slightly before moving to the centre of the room to stand behind the lectern facing the north totem. "Here we go," she said softly, raising her hands to rest just above the pages of her book. Slow tendrils of electric plasma poured down from her hands and touched the crystals, spreading out and around them like red snakes on clear sand. The conduit glowed as it accepted her power and channelled it through the voids and realities it allowed her to access. "What did he want?" she asked as her mind's eye opened up to the visions the spell would show her.

Sighing heavily, Ambrose shifted against the wall, folding his arms over his chest. The white ash of the circle began to glow softly, swirling slightly in an invisible wind. The sage leaves stayed still for now. "He wants me to bring his sons back," he said, looking at her to see if there would be any reaction to the statement.

Her face was blank, her eyes shut as she focused on the spell. "Can you?" she asked, no emotion showing on her face or in her voice. Regardless, Ambrose felt the quick prang of fear flow through their bond at the thought of her killers returning.

"No," he said firmly, wishing to reassure her. "Their souls will have already been fed to the Pit. There is no bringing them back." Relief washed over her. Unfortunately, he knew it would be short lived. "He's given me forty-eight hours to figure it out though," he explained.

"So, we need to try and find what he has before then," she said, nodding absently. There was an air of determination in her voice that made him smile.

"Right," he confirmed. "What can you see?"

Lena sighed, shaking her head in annoyance. "I'm sorry, Ambrose," she said. "I'm struggling to bring anything into focus. The images just keep going in and out, fading like fog over water."

"Do you need more power?" he asked, pushing away from the wall. He couldn't enter the circle, but he could feed his power into it if needed, to help boost her connection.

"Power is not the problem," she said. "My... my mind is."

Yet another prang of guilt stabbed him in the gut. He knew she was aware of his pulling away from her. He had felt her sadness and confusion caused by it over the last few days. There was little doubt in his mind that was causing her issues now. "What are you thinking about?" he asked softly, hoping he could convey tender concern.

"It doesn't matter right now," she said, falling silent as her power worked the spell. Presently, she was only trying to find James, so although the spell was charging with her power, she was not utilising it to its full extent. As she had explained it to him, normally she would simply allow the book to show her what it wanted. She could guide it somewhat, but forcing it to show her what she wanted was more difficult. After a moment, Lena's body twitched like she had been poked by an invisible force. "I've found him," she breathed, her voice whisper quiet and far away. "He's still in town. He's getting into his car."

"Your book can manipulate time, right?" he asked, fascinated by her as she worked.

"In a way," she explained, her eyes remaining shut as she watched the scene in her mind unfold. "I can look back through past events. But the further I go back the more power it takes. The more it exhausts me. If it's more than twenty-four hours I won't be able to hold the connection for very long."

"Can you look back to what he was doing before he came here?"

"I mean, he was following me," she smirked. "Or do you mean before he came to town?"

Ambrose shook his head. Of course, she knew what he had meant, but she was always one to make light of a serious situation. A quality he found unbelievably endearing. "Yes, that," he chuckled. "Can you find him in the city, either earlier today or before? Sometime when he may have been looking over papers relating to us or to demons."

Flexing her fingers, Lena poured more of her power over the surface of the book. "Give me a moment," she said, rolling her shoulders slightly. Her eyes opened as she chanted silently activating the full extent of the spell.

The sage leaves burst into flames, their smell and charred remains mixing with the white ash which now snaked across the floor to swirl around her feet. Small sparks of lightning danced within the powder, lighting up the floor with a red aura, warm yet sinister. Two arcs of power shot from her book, connecting with the tops of the totems she had placed, electricity illuminating the carvings on them.

Raising his brow at the display, Ambrose was impressed by the control. The air in the room vibrated with power, making the hairs on his arms stand on end, static prickling at his neck. "I don't think I've watched you use your book yet. Is it always like this?" he asked intrigued.

"There's usually less lightning," she smiled. "Why?"

"Your eyes are white."

Without breaking the connection, her head tilted to the side, turning to look at him. Or at least, he thought she was looking at him. "What?"

"Your eyes," he said, nodding towards her. "They've turned completely white, like they've rolled into the back of your head. You didn't know?"

"You know, I've never watched myself do this," she said mockingly. He pressed his lips together in a chastised smile. *Touché...* he thought. "This is not helping with my focus," she sighed, shaking her head and turning to face the north totem again.

"Sorry," he laughed quietly to himself.

They fell silent as the spell whipped around the room, lightning and ash mixing within the air, working higher up Lena's body as she pushed her mind and the book further back through time. The stream of electricity to the totems increased in intensity, pulsing slightly as the spell struggled to keep connected to the caster. "I've got him," she said, her voice having become ethereal as if mixed with another. "And possibly something."

"Tell me what you see," he pressed her gently.

"His office," she said softly. "He's looking over a folder. Just one of those brown folios. Physical, not on his laptop. It's got your name on it... and mine. He's got my social service records, my birth certificate, my arrests... oh god, Ambrose–"

"Don't worry about it just yet," he said calmly, trying to help bring her mind back from panic. "Records on you don't mean much right now, no offence. Your life was recent. Focus on what he has on me and other demons."

"Okay, right, sorry..."

Watching her, he saw small beads of sweat break out on her forehead, her brow furrowing as if in pain. "You okay?" he asked, stepping as close to the circle as he dared.

"Yeah," she said, forcing out a slow breath. "I had to go back almost a week. The book is fighting me. It's difficult... maintaining the connection."

Letting her body relax, Lena took in a deep breath, before exhaling sharply, her power pulsing over her body in a sudden wave. The arcs to the totem crackled loudly, snapping and sizzling against the moisture in the air. The white ash and sage spun in a vortex around her and the book, glowing with red charge.

"Um," she said, closing her eyes briefly. "Something's off. Can you shift the north totem... just a centimetre to the left?"

Looking at the ground, he cautiously stepped around the outskirts of the room. Kneeling by the totem, he grabbed it by the base, sliding it ever so slightly to the left as instructed. "Done," he said, dropping his grasp and stepping away as quickly as possible. The vibrations of power emanating from the circle made his vision spin being that close. Lena's mind was protected, her conduit buffering the onslaught of power from the spell. Without it, the spell would overtake any mind that got too close, rending it into the void between realities.

The moment the totem shifted to the correct spot, the arcs of lightning subdued slightly, no longer crackling angrily but flowing smoothly like string through water. Lena sighed with relief, like the change in power eased a deep-rooted pain within her.

"Got it," she said, opening her eyes and staring with those white orbs blankly ahead of her. "Oh hell..." she whispered, her eyes widening. "He's got financial records, account details going back forty years. He's got pictures of you from the early 1900's." Her head jerked back slightly like she had seen something surprising. "You were on the Titanic?" she asked, her mouth agape with wonder.

"Yeah..." he chuckled. "A lot of demons were. Lots of souls to collect that day."

"Why on earth didn't you use pseudonyms?"

"I like Ambrose," he said with mock offence.

"Yeah, well, he's found information on your activities going back to the late 1700's so... maybe you make some aliases going forward yeah?" she said, shaking her head at him despite the soft laughter in her voice.

"Fair enough. What does he have on other demons?"

"I'm not sure. I'm struggling to clear it," Lena sighed. "I have a connection with you, so it's easier to focus on information about you. Pictures, documents... but I'm not sure what– Ah!"

As she cried out, the arcs connected to the totems snapped, rushing back to the centre of the circle, retreating to the book and up into Lena's hands. Her head flung back and her knees gave out as she fell to the floor, the ash and sage disappearing in flames.

"Lena!" Ambrose cried, rushing to her, his heart beating rapidly in his chest not caring about the circle anymore. But the spell was over, the connection lost. Reaching her, he pulled her into his arms, checking over her body as he did so.

"Sorry," she said quickly, grabbing onto his shirt as if to steady herself. "I'm sorry. I couldn't hold the connection any longer."

"It's alright," he said, taking hold of her face between his hands, looking worriedly into her eyes as their dove-grey colouring returned. "We know roughly what he has now. We know he's not bluffing."

"He's got more than one copy," she said softly, leaning her head forward until it rested on his chest. Closing his eyes, he wrapped his arms around her shoulders, holding her in place. Her pain had ripped through him, pushing all air from his lungs. He took a deep breath now, hungrily taking in her scent, relishing the feel of her against him. Sighing heavily, she pushed back slightly, much to his dismay, so she could look up into his face. "He's stashed them in various locations with different people with instructions on what to do with them. I just need to rest for a bit and then I can try again. Try to find them all."

"No," he said firmly, shaking his head. Seeing her in pain was too much. Not again. He wouldn't put her through that again. "You go rest, but don't try again. We'll figure something else out." Staring at her silently, he rubbed his thumbs over her cheeks, noting how she leant tenderly into his touch, her eyes gazing at him apprehensively. There was no other choice. They needed help. "I need to go to my council," he sighed with defeat. "Time to come clean."

"No," she cried, pushing up onto her knees and grabbing at his neck, panic in her voice. "We can sort this. On our own."

Even as his heart swelled with love for her at the concern she showed for him, guilt swirled in his gut negating any feelings of peace that he used to have when holding her. "No. Not something like this. There's too much at stake."

"Are you sure?" she asked cautiously, her beautiful, warm eyes earnestly searching his face.

"Yes," he said, helping her to her feet. "Stay here. In the manor. Don't leave until I get back."

"Okay," she sighed, hanging her head. "Ambrose?"

"Hm?"

"I... I'm scared."

Pulling her tightly against him, he took hold of her chin, lifting her face to his and placing a tender kiss to her lips. "Everything will be alright," he said as reassuringly as possible, resting his forehead against hers. "I promise. I'll see you soon, my dove." Stepping away from her, he gathered his flames and went to get Marcus before heading to the council. Something in him told him he had just lied to her. He had no idea if everything would be alright. He could only hope that she would be. If he lost her, it wouldn't matter if James leaked everything.

If he lost her, he lost everything.

CHAPTER TWENTY-NINE

The next day, Lena was in her altar room, pouring over her book trying to seek out some emotion powerful enough to create an object. So far, any time she had found something that might be of worth, her mind wandered to James and she would lose the trail.

Ambrose had gotten back from Hell early that morning after spending the entire night explaining the situation to his superiors and getting their advice. She had tried to ask him what had happened when he got back, but he had a financial investment meeting via a video conference he had to attend. Currently he was sitting in his office on his laptop speaking to the investment board about how best to manage one of the portfolios he oversaw for Hell. He had told her not to worry, that everything would be sorted soon, and that for now they should just continue as they had been. But she couldn't put aside the pit that formed in her stomach that something was wrong. Terribly wrong.

Taking a deep breath, she stretched out her neck trying to centre her thoughts. She looked back at her book and delved into the images it showed her, desperate to find something to distract her. Unsure of what she was looking for, she adjusted her view to a city on the other side of the world, a city currently in full swing of its nightlife, full of music and laughter. For a brief second, she thought of actually going there. A small jump through the Hell fires and she could join in the jubilance she now witnessed. She smiled ruefully to herself.

"Keep dreaming, Lena," she whispered aloud, shaking her head.

"You hate crowds."

But there was something that stood out to her. Not emotions of hate or fear she would usually follow, but one of joy and mischief. It intrigued her to the point of distraction. She couldn't see how she could turn it into an object, but if it meant she could forget yesterday, why not follow it for now.

Focusing on the trail, she allowed it to pull her in, diving through the roof of a house where a woman's laughter filled the room with brightness and warmth. The man she was with, dipped her over his arm as they waltzed around their room, his body radiating with love and contentment. She was entranced by their movements, graceful and free, as the woman twirled in his arms, her face sparkling with delight.

Wanting to hold on to their joy, she pulled the emotion within her, imagining her and Ambrose in their places. Suddenly, she wanted to be with him. To be in his arms. To put an end to this tension and distance between them. Financial meeting be damned.

Pulling away from her book, Lena let the emotion meld with her power, lightning crackling over her arms and down her spine, as it settled within her. She could transfer it later, but now she wanted to use it. Treading softly, she made her way to Ambrose's office.

She pushed the door to his office open, just enough for her to peek at him behind his desk. A small smile crept on her face to see how bored he looked, listening to the monotonous drawl of whoever was currently speaking. He was leant back in his chair, his elbow on the arm rest as he supported his chin on one hand. It never ceased to amaze her, how effortlessly handsome he was. She licked her lips before gathering her flames and transporting herself under his desk.

As she reappeared, she saw Ambrose shift his legs slightly, accommodating her presence. Looking up she locked eyes with him. He raised an eyebrow but gave no other indication that she was there. She pressed a finger to her lips causing him to cover his mouth with his fingers to hide his smile from the video call.

Silently as possible, she reached out and rubbed her hand over his trousers, feeling his cock harden under her touch. She knew Ambrose would make her pay in some way or another over this, but she wanted him so badly, she couldn't wait any longer. Deftly, she unbuttoned his trousers, her smile growing as his cock practically sprang from its confines. She trailed her fingers over his silky surface, marvelling at his size and eagerness.

Leaning forward, Lena flicked out her tongue, touching it to the sensitive skin just underneath the head, causing him to twitch. With a smile of satisfaction, she angled him towards her and slipped the head of his cock into her mouth. He was warm and hard against her tongue as she swirled it around the head, devouring his taste. Using her fingers to keep him positioned towards her and under the table, she quietly licked and sucked along his length, her body quivering with her own need. She was barely aware of the conversation that was happening over the call. Ambrose would occasionally ask a question, his cool exterior hiding any indication of what she was doing out of their field of view.

The thought that those he was talking to were completely unaware of her actions made her excitement grow. She smiled as she took him within her mouth again, sucking in as much of his length as she could. Warmth flowed from her core, coating her panties with slick desire. Ambrose let one of his arms drop from the arm rest, keeping the other up to cover his mouth, and rested his hand on the side of her face, twirling a strand of her hair between his fingers.

Encouraged by his action, Lena shifted on her knees slightly, angling her chin and sucked as much of him into her mouth as she could handle, the head of his cock hitting the back of her throat. Realising she wasn't gagging, assuming as a result of her no longer really needing to breathe, she pushed her head forward, relaxing her throat accepting his full length within her mouth. She felt him twitch within her throat and a soft growl pulled from his chest.

Pulling back, she looked up through her lashes at him. His eyes were glazed with his own desire, his chest rising and falling slowly and deliberately as he tried to control his outward appearance. He glanced down at her briefly and she knew he was close.

Sucking him back in, she bobbed her head, licking her tongue along his length, her hand massaging him under her mouth. She could feel his cock throb and swell as she focused on bringing him to his climax. Her pussy ached with longing, wanting desperately to replace her mouth, but she smiled devilishly against him as her plan started to come together. The video call wasn't finished yet. She had to make him come before it did.

Ambrose trailed his fingers along her jaw, enticing her to pull his full length into her mouth again. Stroking with both her fingers and her tongue, she felt his cock swell almost painfully stretching her lips around his girth. With a soft grunt, he exploded in her mouth, his hot, salty seed flooding her throat. She relished the bitter taste now coating the back of her tongue as she swallowed everything he had to give her.

Satisfied with her work, Lena licked the remnants of his climax off his still firm cock. She heard Ambrose cough slightly as he shifted his position. Looking up he was biting his bottom lip under his hand, his eyes barely focused on his screen, pupils blown wide with lust. With a proud grin on her face, she kissed the head of his cock and flamed out of his office, onto their bed.

Chuckling to herself, she touched her fingers to her lips, still tasting him on her tongue. She had no idea when his call would end, but she was ready to bolt as soon as she heard his office door open. The playful mood she had picked up on in her book was definitely going to get her into trouble with him, but she didn't care. That little escapade had been incredibly fun and she regretted none of it. Exactly what she needed considering recent events.

What she didn't expect was for him to flame in, standing at the foot of the bed a few minutes after she had left him, a wicked grin on his face. Biting her bottom lip, she winked at him and then flamed out to the top of the stairs.

"Lena!" Ambrose cried from their room, slamming the door open as she bolted downstairs. "Come back here, you little minx!"

Giggling as she ran towards the kitchen, she knew there was nowhere to go from there, but she could always flame out of a corner. Ambrose flamed in front of the door, his arms out ready to catch her. With a squeal she flamed behind him straight into the kitchen. She dived behind the island as he swung the door open stepping inside. Clamping her hand over her mouth, she heard his footfalls vibrate across the tiles.

"Come on out, Lena," he called, his voice dangerously calm. "You think you can just give me an admittedly, fucking amazing blowjob in the middle of a meeting and there not be consequences?"

Noiselessly laughing, she pressed her tongue to the back of her teeth, willing herself to remain silent. She saw his shadow fall across the cabinets opposite her, the feeling of being hunted by him causing her heart to race with excitement.

"I know you're there," he whispered. "I'll be nice, if you come out now. Your first day as a demon, I imagined bending you over these counters."

Her body shivered as his voice washed over her. "And if I don't?" she teased. From the corner of her eye, she saw his fingers curl around the countertop, just beside her head.

"You really want to find out?" he asked, amusement in his voice.

"Catch me if you can," she giggled as she flamed out, back into the hall, sprinting for the back room. Ambrose was close behind her, his fingers just brushing through her hair as she flamed to the top of the stairs, hearing him grunt as he caught himself against the wall. Her laugh echoed through the hall as she made for her old bedroom, ripping the door open and racing for the bathroom.

"Oh, you're in for it now, Lena," he called after her.

Looking behind her, she noted he hadn't made it to her door yet. She cried out suddenly as her body slammed into something solid. Ambrose had flamed in just in front of her, his arms now constricting around her, pinning her to his body. She gasped with delight as he placed his lips next to her ear and whispered, "After I'm done with you, you won't walk for a week."

She smiled, pressing her palms flat against his chest, but she didn't fight anymore. "Only a week?" she asked, pressing a kiss to his neck.

"Want to make it a month?" he growled as he turned on his feet, pulling her with him and throwing her onto the bed. He towered over her, kneeling beside her on the bed and placing a hand on her stomach. "You done running?" he asked, raising an eyebrow at her.

Breathing heavily at the sight of him, Lena caught her bottom lip between her teeth and nodded slowly, her eyes twinkling with mischief.

"You got caught up in your book, didn't you?" he queried, flattening his hand against her stomach, pressing her into the mattress.

"How can you tell?" she laughed breathlessly.

"Just a hunch," he whispered, grabbing her behind the neck and pulling her up towards him, crushing his mouth to hers. She moaned into his kiss, her hands grabbing either side of his shirt collar, desperate to feel him against her, to feel him use her. She was intrigued as to his game when he pulled away, leaving her panting, to stand at the side of the bed. "Get undressed," he ordered, putting his hands in his pockets. "Slowly."

She smiled at him as she laid back on the bed and began to lift her shirt over her head. Moving as slowly as she could, she tossed her shirt aside and moved her hands behind her to unhook her bra.

"Leave the bra," he said, his eyes dark with desire. "Your jeans."

Feeling her skin shiver, she moved her hands to the front of her jeans, unbuttoning them before pushing them down over her hips. She had to pull herself further onto the bed so she could lift her legs into the air to get the waistband over her ankles and feet, letting the jeans drop to the floor. All the while she kept her eyes locked on Ambrose's face. His gaze followed her hands as she trailed them back up her legs and over her stomach, before she hooked her fingers into the band of her panties and slowly pushed them down to join her jeans.

"Open your legs," he whispered hoarsely, licking his tongue over his lips.

Her core clenched at his command. Complying, she opened her legs, placing her feet either side of her hips, giving him full view of her womanhood. She was drenched with desire for him.

"Exquisite," he sighed, stepping forward. He reached out one hand and stroked along her inner thigh, causing her to drop her head back onto the mattress, the warmth from his hand burning into her flesh and sending waves of pleasure across her skin. His fingers made their way towards her centre, just barely brushing over the lips of her pussy, teasing her. "Stand up."

Pushing herself towards the edge of the bed, she got to her feet. She looked up at his face as she stood mere inches from him. Ambrose lifted his hand and ran his fingers along her collar bone, running traces of his power across her skin. Small shots of pleasure emanated from his touch, causing her to gasp as he trailed one finger down her chest to the front join of her bra. He hooked his finger in the join, sending power through it, lighting her bra on fire. The heat danced across her breasts, causing her nipples to peak as the last remains of the bra disappeared. Her breath caught in her throat as his eyes locked on her breasts, a satisfied grin on his face.

"Better," he whispered, capturing one nipple between his fingers and giving it a tug. Lena raised onto her toes, but stayed rooted to the spot, forcing her arms to stay by her sides. He trailed his other hand up over her arm, tracing along her bindings. "They've grown again," he said as his hand trailed up over her shoulder to where they met just behind her neck, continuing down her back until they began to touch the rising curve of her bottom. "At this rate, you'll be covered in them before you break."

"You keep making me wait, we'll see how fast I break from them," she teased, closing her eyes as she enjoyed the feel of his touch.

Ambrose smirked, stepping towards her and dropping his face close to hers, his warm breath washing over her. "Turn around and bend over," he growled before placing a brief kiss on her lips. "Arms over your head." He pulled his jacket off, tossing it on the end of the bed, and rolled up the sleeves of his shirt.

Lena thrilled at the sight and turned on her toes towards the bed. She leant forward, placing her hands on the mattress and letting them slide over the sheets until her cheek and chest rested on the bed, her arms extended above her. Ambrose used his foot to push her feet apart, providing him with full view and access to her dripping wet pussy. She cried out as his hand smacked across her rump, his fingers just barely touching her entrance. The pain from his hand sent a course of pleasure through her.

"Oh god!" she cried, arching her back and clutching at the sheets.

Ambrose braced a hand on the mattress, leaning down to whisper in her ear. "He's not here, my dove." He swung another smack against her arse as she gasped against it, her excitement growing. "You should have come out when I asked."

The sound of the smacks echoed throughout the room along with her cries as she silently begged for more. She felt Ambrose push off from the mattress and move behind her. He dropped to his knees and trailed his fingers up her inner thigh, sending shivers that rolled up from his touch to her spine. She sighed as he dropped soft kisses over where he had smacked her, lightly blowing against the now raw skin.

His breath moved over to her quivering core, now throbbing with longing for him. A low moan ripped from her throat as he dipped his tongue into her, his thumb rubbing over her clit.

"Hm, you taste divine, my dove," he growled against her, his tongue lapping up her juices. "Tell me, how did I taste?"

She moaned into the mattress, her mind barely holding onto a coherent thought. "You tasted wonderful," she panted, "salty and sweet at the same time." She felt him smile against her before covering her pussy with his mouth and sucking at her lips, his tongue moving inside her. She cried out into the room, all thought, but that of desire, vacating her mind. "Ambrose," she moaned, "I need you."

He pulled back, his thumb still focusing on her clit, his breath cooling against the wetness coating her skin. "I want to hear you beg," he said as he bit her bottom hard, the pain instantly mixing with her growing pleasure.

"Ah!" she cried, burying her face into the sheets. "Please," she begged. "Please Ambrose, I need you. I need you inside me. I need to feel you inside me. Please."

"Feel me where, my dove?" he teased. "Be specific."

"My pussy!" She was almost shouting, her need mounting uncontrollably. "I need to feel your cock inside my pussy. Please, I'm begging you."

Moaning with disappointment as his hand retracted from her completely, Ambrose chuckled at her reaction. "Patience, my dove," he said, running his hand over her lower back. She saw his shirt join his jacket at the end of the bed, and heard his trousers fall to the floor.

"Ambrose," she sighed, "please."

He positioned the head of his cock at her entrance and she shifted on her toes in anticipation. Lena gasped in surprise as he drove into her in one swift movement, burying himself to the hilt. Ambrose fell onto his hands, planting them either side of her hips, digging his fingers into her skin.

"Ah, Lena," he moaned, "you are so wet."

He began to pump his hips against hers, picking up his pace until their bodies collided together. Her legs were shaking, his grip on her hips being the only thing stopping her knees from buckling completely. Loud slaps emanated from where their bodies joined, pleasure building for them both.

"Rub your clit," he growled, pulling at her hips to bring them against his with more force.

She cried out into the room as his cock hit her innermost depth. Pushing against the mattress, she managed to move one of her hands down towards her clit, rubbing it in small frenzied circles with her fingers. Her channel clenched around his cock, pulling a groan from his throat.

"I'm so close," she panted against the mattress, her toes curling against the carpet.

Ambrose moaned as he reached out, grabbing a fistful of her hair and pulling her head up from the bed. The control of his grasp caused a wave of excitement to run down her spine, heightening the pleasure in her core. Maintaining his pace, he pushed her body into the mattress, using it as a brace as he slammed into her.

"Then come for me, my dove," he groaned through his teeth, angling her head to look into her eyes. Lena moaned as she fell into his hazel depths, her fingers still working her clit, her pleasure mounting under his gaze.

Her eyes rolled into the back of her head as her pussy clamped down on his cock, her climax sending shockwaves throughout her body. She practically screamed into the room, her body quaking against his. Ambrose groaned as his own climax followed suit and he pushed himself as deep within her as he could get. They shuddered together, before he almost fell atop her, catching on his elbows, his hand releasing from her hair. She kept her head up, pressing her forehead against his cheek as she tried to catch her breath.

He smiled, rubbing his fingers against her shoulder. "Don't think I'm done with you, my dove," he whispered, pressing a kiss to her neck. He lifted himself off her, pulling his cock out, before flipping her onto her back. Lena giggled as he did so, pulling herself further onto the bed as he followed her, grabbing her wrist when she had gotten far enough away from him. Lifting her arms to wrap around his shoulders, she welcomed him atop her, their lips meeting passionately. She smiled against him, eagerly looking forward to the day ahead.

CHAPTER THIRTY

Feelings of pure bliss and contentment radiated from Ambrose as he looked down at the face of the goddess who now rested peacefully, nestled in his arms.

He had received a thorough reprimand from his superiors to the point they questioned if he was best placed to remain as Lena's sire. They all agreed she is no ordinary boundling and discussions ensued as to whether she would be better off with a more powerful sire. Thankfully, Marcus had vouched for him, confirming his own involvement in her training, so they dismissed the idea of transferring her for now. Not that he thought she would go willingly, but he had been terrified at the fleeting possibility of losing her. Ambrose's only solace in that moment was that as she was not a dealer demon, she was not subject to the whims of his council. Her own council, for object creation, would need to be consulted before any action could be taken. However, seeing her appear under his desk earlier, told him all he needed to know. She needed him, as much as he needed her.

That said, he had been placed on warning that someone else would be directed to help in dealing with the situation with James Carter. He doubted they would allow Marcus to help, despite their assurances that they could handle it, and he feared the thought of someone else coming into his and Lena's lives. Too many already coveted her and her growing power. It was becoming all too easy to imagine someone taking her from him. If someone else took over her bindings, they would be parted at least until she broke from them, but so much could happen in that time. Would she come back to him?

Ambrose shook his head, pushing the thoughts from his mind. Lena was here now, in his arms, her head resting on his shoulder, her arm draped across his chest with her fingers lightly touching his jaw. He tightened his arms around her, pulling her closer to him. Perhaps it had been the terror he felt when faced with thought she would be taken from him, but the feelings of peace and joy she gave him had returned, untainted by guilt. She was with him, that was all that mattered.

Sighing, he kissed the top of her head and closed his eyes, hoping to simply forget the last day's events, at least for now. She had provided him with the perfect distraction earlier, but after he had exhausted her, he was left to the whims of his own mind. He would tell her everything when she woke, but for now, he was happy to just hold her.

"Ambrose!"

His eyes flew open, turmoil rekindling in his stomach as he heard Marcus' voice shout through the manor.

"Ambrose, where are you?" Marcus yelled, his voice sounding closer.

Lena's head lifted from his chest. "What's going on?" she yawned, rubbing her eyes.

"I'm not sure," Ambrose said, extracting himself from under her. He pulled on his trousers and started for the door when it flew open, Marcus looking panic stricken in the doorway.

"Oh, shit! Sorry!" Marcus said, turning his back to them as Lena pulled the covers over her naked body.

"This has become a startling habit of yours, Marcus," Ambrose snapped, practically jumping in front of the bed to shield Lena behind him. "What are you doing here?" He grabbed her clothes and tossed them to her. She pulled her clothes on under the covers, as he pulled his own shirt on, buttoning it over his stomach.

"Lena needs to get out of here, now," Marcus said, fear evident in his voice.

"What? Why?" she asked, pulling her shirt over her head. Ambrose cursed himself for burning her bra, seeing her nipples now poking through the thin fabric.

"Zagan's on his way here," Marcus said, turning back round to face the pair.

Ambrose looked at Lena, fear now spreading over her features and through their bond. "Shit," he spat, throwing power at the bed to remake the covers, hiding the evidence of their mornings love making. "Why?"

Marcus shook his head emphatically. "He's who the council is sending to help you with James. I tried to persuade them otherwise, but they wouldn't listen."

"Fucking bastards," Ambrose cursed, grabbing Lena's hand and pulling her after him as he pushed past Marcus.

"Where are you going?" Marcus cried, following close behind them.

Ambrose ran into Lena's altar room, quickly packing up her book into the chest along with some other items for her. "Lena, go grab some clothes from our room. Pack light, you can make anything you forget. Marcus, stay with her."

Lena and Marcus nodded and left the room, their footfalls racing down the hall.

"Shit," Ambrose cursed under his breath. He thought he could handle whoever they sent. It never occurred to him, they would send Zagan, especially considering their history and the headaches that had caused the council in the past. He grabbed some more random artefacts and spell craft items for her, stashing them in the chest. Picking it up, he made his way to his bedroom where he found Lena frantically pulling clothes out of the dresser, throwing them at Marcus who was stuffing them unceremoniously into a duffel bag.

"Are we really doing this?" Lena asked, lifting her head as Ambrose came into the room.

He nodded with a heavy sigh. "If Zagan is going to be here, yes. I won't risk you being around him."

Lena walked over to him, taking the chest and setting it on top of the dresser. She laid a hand on his chest, her dove-grey eyes searching his face. "I don't want to leave you."

Ambrose's heart felt like it was caught in a vice as he looked at her, worry etched into her beautiful face. He brushed the back of his fingers along her jaw and smiled softly. "Hopefully, it won't be for long. I'll come get you as soon as it's safe."

"Don't worry Lena," Marcus said with a warm, yet uncertain smile. "I'll keep you distracted until then." Both Ambrose and Lena raised an eyebrow at him, as his eyes widened in horror realising their interpretation of his statement. "No, no, no! That's not what I meant," he pleaded, holding his hands up defensively. Hanging his head, he turned back to the duffel bag to finish stuffing the clothes in it.

Lena chuckled but Ambrose simply shook his head at his friend.

"Marcus will keep you safe," he said, lifting her chin with his hand and pressed a soft kiss to her lips. "I'll check in when I can."

With a sigh, Lena dropped her head to his chest. He wrapped his arms around her, trying to burn the feeling of her body against his into his memory. He looked over at Marcus, who nodded sympathetically.

"We need to go, Lena," Marcus said softly, his gaze apologetic at breaking them apart.

Ambrose kissed the top of her head as she nodded into his chest. "Go on," he said, pushing her lightly towards the cambion.

"You stay safe too," she said softly before locking her eyes on the floor. Lena grabbed the chest and walked over to Marcus. He placed a hand on her arm, lifting the duffel bag over his shoulder. With a last look at Ambrose, he saw her eyes glistening with unformed tears. Who would have thought that after their morning together, they would be parted so soon. Marcus nodded one last time before gathering his flames and transporting him and Lena away.

Ambrose ran his hand over his face and through his hair with a heavy sigh, before turning on his heel and heading to his office to wait for Zagan. He didn't have to wait for long as his old sire appeared before him in human form, a dark blue suit draped effortlessly across his broad frame. His mother's Grecian features were prevalent in his appearance, a long slim jawline defined with a neatly kept beard. Long black hair swept back from his face with too much gel, causing it to shine under the lamplight. His eyes however, were that of his father's, the blueness of them shining bright as ice, striking against his dark tanned skin and reflecting the coldness within.

Without a word, Zagan sat in one of the chairs across from the desk. The men stared at each other, sizing the other up in the new environment. Ambrose felt his whole body tense at the sight of his old sire. Taking slow and deliberate breaths from behind his folded hands as he leant on his elbows, he tried to at least relax his shoulders. He couldn't afford to show how much this bothered him.

"You've made quite a mess, haven't you, Ambrose?" Zagan finally asked, an amused sneer on his face. Declining to answer, he leant back in his chair, hoping to convey he was no longer afraid of this demon. Chuckling, Zagan looked around the room, nodding appreciatively at the contents of the room. "So, where is Lena, then? Would have thought you'd be keeping her at your side constantly. I know I would be."

Ambrose's jaw clenched painfully at her name. "She doesn't need to be here for this."

"I can still smell her on you," Zagan sniffed, "so she's not been gone long." Ambrose's skin crawled at the comment. Putting aside her power and being bound to him, why was the cambion so focused on her. "Are you hiding her from me, Ambrose?" he smiled wickedly looking back at him.

"I'm keeping her safe, if that's what you mean," he answered curtly.

"Well, probably best she's not here right now, anyway," Zagan said, shifting in the seat slightly. "You possibly don't want her overhearing us. If I'm going to help clean up your mess, I need to know everything."

Ambrose scoffed loudly. "You only need to know what is relevant and that is that I killed his sons and now he wants to expose us. Nothing else matters."

"Of course, it matters, Ambrose," Zagan tutted, shaking his head. "Why did you kill them? And not the story of them trying to capture you. I know that is a lie, regardless of if the council believes it or not."

His stomach churning, Ambrose considered how much would be safe to disclose to his former sire now. His bond to Lena was strong, strengthened more so by their relationship with each other, so it would be difficult for anyone to take her from him without her consent. But Zagan was incredibly powerful, even among cambions. He could take her with minimal effort. What leverage could he gain now from knowing more about their history that he already had?

With a heavy sigh, Ambrose concluded there was little he could do in the situation. He had to be truthful, at least, to an extent. "I knew Lena before she was sacrificed to me."

"Ah," Zagan smiled knowingly, a sinister gleam in his eyes. "And you fancied her. So, revenge?"

Swallowing the bile rising his throat, Ambrose simply shrugged. "Sure, why not."

"Ambrose..." Zagan started, a soft warning in his voice, his eyes trying to pull more from him than he was willing to provide.

"You honestly think that after everything you put me through, I'm going to just tell you everything about me?" Ambrose asked, keeping his tone even and calm.

"You will if you want my help."

"I don't want your help. I never wanted your help," he spat coldly. "The council sent you to help. I would rather jump into the Pit than accept *your* help." Getting to his feet, Ambrose walked around the desk to his liquor tray, pouring himself a shot of whiskey. Feeling the familiar stress-induced twitch in his eye that Zagan was so adept at creating in him, he poured another glass and placed it loudly on the desk in front of him. He'd always found the cambion more tolerable when they were drinking, so might as well facilitate that now.

With a bemused smile, the cambion took the glass and sniffed at the amber liquid. "You liked her, didn't you?" he asked, taking a sip.

"Don't be absurd, she was mortal."

"I can still tell when you're lying," Zagan chuckled, finishing his glass in a single swing and turning it around in his hands. "You wanted her, so you killed those that took your chance to bed her away from you. And then bound her to you so you could live out your fantasies on a daily basis."

Finishing his own glass, Ambrose tried to ignore the racing of his heart as rage built within him. "Must you always be so vulgar?"

"What?" Zagan sneered, leaning forward, rapt interest in his eyes. "Honestly, I'm rather impressed that you finally succumbed to your demonic nature. Were your dreams of making a little cambion child with her dashed?"

"I would sooner die than have a cambion," Ambrose snapped. "You being such a stellar example of one."

"So, what was it, then? What drew you to her?"

"Enough, Zagan," he hissed, his patience with the topic spent.

The cambion raised a brow, his smile unfailing. "Could it have to do with the deal you made with her father?"

Staring at his old sire, Ambrose's blood ran cold, icy fear gripping his chest making it difficult to breathe. How did he know? How was he sure that Lena was the child from that deal? Ambrose wasn't even sure, having convinced himself there had to have been hundreds, if not thousands, of children born on the same day at seven months. "What?" he breathed almost silently.

"Don't play dumb with me, Ambrose," Zagan said softly, leaning closer. "I know about that deal you made. A deal sealing the fate of an unborn child to Hell. And I know it's her."

No, it wasn't possible. It couldn't be her. Zagan had to be wrong. Ambrose had thought of looking through both the council's and his records, but fear at the truth driving her away, stopped him. "How do you know? I'm not even sure about it."

"I have my ways," Zagan shrugged, leaning back in his chair. "Cyrus knows almost everything about her from when they were kids. I don't even need to compel him to talk about her. His affection for her is almost as nauseating as yours." He paused for a moment, placing the whiskey glass back on the desk, looking at it as if he was contemplating its design. "You have no idea what she is," he said softly. Something seemed off, like he was saddened by some knowledge he couldn't share.

"And you do?" Ambrose questioned, raising a brow trying to figure out what game his old sire was playing.

"Better than most," his voice seemed distant as he spoke, his gaze still fixed on the glass. "You will hold her down, preventing her from becoming the greatest power Hell has ever known. You are dead weight dragging her down, and if it wasn't for the fact that killing you now would kill her, I would wipe you from the face of this Earth." Raising his gaze, Ambrose saw genuine hatred in his eyes. There was the Zagan he knew so well.

"Well, aren't I fortunate that she's bound to me then," Ambrose smiled, keeping his eyes locked with the cambion.

"For now."

"Don't try it, Zagan," he cautioned, raising a finger pointedly. "Stealing boundlings is low, even for a cambion like you."

"I won't need to steal her," Zagan retorted dangerously. "Once she realises that you are holding her back, she'll seek me out. Once she learns about the deal you made with her father, she won't be able to get away from you fast enough."

"I wouldn't hold your breath," Ambrose said under his. "Or, you know, do." Standing up he placed his hands in his pockets, staring down at his old sire. "As much as I would love to continue this conversation, perhaps we should resolve the issue of the man seeking to expose all of demon-kind first?"

"Fine, but we are not finished," the cambion smiled, getting to his feet. "Not by a long shot."

Ambrose rolled his eyes. "Can't wait," he sighed sarcastically.

Gathering their flames, they transported themselves to the office of James Carter. The man in question sat behind his desk, his back to the window behind him that looked out and over the city below. White walls reflected the sun off every surface, giving the room an unnatural illuminance. Two black leather chairs sat in front of the desk, their metal legs gleaming in the light.

Seemingly unfazed by their sudden appearance or by the flames that slowly extinguished around them, James looked up from his laptop through his lashes.

"I wasn't expecting two of you," James said curtly, leaning back in his chair, folding his arms across his chest.

Zagan sneered at the man, walking closer to the desk. Ambrose kept in step with him, knowing it was best to show a united front with his old sire in this regard alone. "Situations like this, we do not go alone," Zagan said, nodding in greeting.

"And if I hadn't been alone?" James asked, raising a brow. The cambion merely smiled in response, a cold cruel thing that seemed suited to his features. Finding a new form of respect for the mortal, Ambrose smiled softly as James merely stared at the demon, unflinching at the silent threat. He didn't even want to attempt to guess at the images that ran through Zagan's mind right now. The cambion relished other's pain, and even more so when he caused it. "So, who are you?"

"Zagan. I am Ambrose's superior."

"Only in your dreams," Ambrose scoffed. United fronts only went so far.

"Can you bring my sons back?" James asked, leaning forward and shutting his laptop, coming to rest on his elbows over his desk.

"No," Zagan shook his head. "Regardless of the result, they summoned a demon, marking their souls for Hell. They cannot be brought back."

Ambrose rolled his eyes, stepping closer to stand directly next to Zagan. "Why would you want them back anyway?" he asked, staring at James. "The deal they wanted would have had you deposed from your own company."

Zagan nodded in agreement, raising one brow at the mortal. "It's a good question, Mr Carter."

James smirked and shook his head. "You two obviously don't have children. At least this will be amusing, if nothing else. Sit then."

With a glance at each other, the demons moved to sit in the chairs. Lowering himself with a sigh, Ambrose tried to fortify himself. Wherever this conversation was about to go, he knew the resulting conversations with his old sire would be less comfortable.

CHAPTER THIRTY-ONE

"Dammit!"

Marcus jumped in surprise as he looked up at Lena, her body covered with her lightning as she paced across the floor, her book lying forgotten on the table.

"Lena?"

"Sorry," she said quickly, taking a few deep breaths, regaining control of her powers. "I'm sorry, Marcus. I'm just... frustrated."

Marcus chuckled, igniting her annoyance as she stared daggers at him. "It's only been three days, Lena," he laughed, shaking his head at her.

"Not like that!" she cried, walking over to him and sitting on the chair opposite him. "I can't focus on my book. I haven't made an object in over a week now and I'm going insane."

"I see," Marcus sighed, leaning back in his chair. "I understand that making deals is one of the easier designs to have in that it's something that happens at the whim of others, so I'm sorry, I can't help you."

"I get these headaches that I can't shift when I feel like something needs to be made. They linger until I make something or find where something I've already made needs to go," she said, dropping her head back to look at the ceiling. Marcus didn't live on Earth, but rather had chambers within Hell. They were nice compared to what she had been expecting. Various rugs were strewn across the stone floor, giving the room a warm and cosy feel. The walls were carved out of the standard black and red stone that covered all corridors and caverns in Hell, but he had hung warm grey drapes with silver threading around the walls, breaking up the monotonous colour. A bed sat against one of the walls, dark wooden panels surrounding it providing it with some privacy from the rest of the room. A large round table sat in the middle of the room with a few mismatched chairs around it. She and Marcus sat in the only armchairs in the room, placed in front of an unlit fireplace carved into the wall. "Marcus, can I ask you something?"

"Of course."

Raising her head, she looked at the cambion, as he lifted his head from the book he was reading. She still wondered how he could be comfortable sitting back in a relatively small armchair compared to his demonic size. Especially, she wondered, how he managed to accommodate his wings over the arms of the chair.

"I have this feeling that Ambrose isn't telling me something," she started, shifting in the chair to sit more upright. "Moreover, I have this feeling of dread that something bad is coming and it scares me. I am also well aware that there are demons conspiring to take me from Ambrose."

Marcus closed his book and put it on the small coffee table between them. He leant forward, resting his elbows on his knees. "Lena, we're not going to let that happen."

"It may not be something you can stop," she stated firmly. "Realistically speaking, I'm going to be bound for another fifty, sixty years? I've only been a demon for seven weeks and we're already hiding me from Zagan. And he is not the only one asking me to change my bond. How long do you think we can keep this up? You can't watch me forever."

Marcus dropped his gaze to the floor. "You may be right. But Ambrose and I will do everything we can to try and prevent it," he said softly.

"I know that if I end up bound to someone else, I will suffer," Lena continued. "I can survive that. I have suffered my whole life until I met Ambrose, so I know... I know I can survive whatever Hell throws at me. I've survived everything else it threw at me in life."

Confusion spread on his face as he looked back up to her. "Lena?"

Sighing heavily, she looked at her hands, twisting them in her lap. "My father made a deal, Marcus. And I'm pretty sure it's the reason I'm in Hell in the first place."

"How do you know?"

"It just makes sense," she shrugged. "My mother was sick and one day she wasn't and he died exactly seven years after. But it doesn't matter, now." She shook her head before continuing. "If someone does take me, if someone does overcome my binding to Ambrose, can you promise me something?"

"I know what you're going to ask. I'll always look after him, Lena."

She swallowed, raising her eyes to look at him. "I'm afraid, Marcus," she whispered. "I have others who will look out for me. Archie, Calza... even Morgan to an extent. But Ambrose only has you. He's told me that he is protected because of how he manages Hell's finances, skimming some into personal accounts for demons living top-side, demons that want that arrangement to continue. But... I'm afraid he'll stop doing that if he's worried about me. He'll need you to keep him grounded. I can survive as long as I know he is safe."

Silence fell between them as they simply stared at each other, allowing the weight of her request settle over them. Quietly, Marcus reached over and took hold of her hand, holding it gently between his own.

"I promise, Lena. I'll take care of him," he vowed to her.

Smiling softly, Lena squeezed his hand in thanks. "Thank you." As she finished those words, sharp pain stabbed behind her eyes. Slamming her palms into her eyes, she leant over in the chair, resting her elbows on her knees. "Ah, my head," she sighed in annoyance. "I'm going to try again to make something. I need to go to the Vault later. Do you want to go with me?" Her voice was directed at the floor as she waited for the white lights in her vision to fade.

Marcus shook his head, leaning back in his chair. "I have something else I need to tend to," he said ruefully. "We know Zagan is otherwise occupied at the moment, so you go. Hurry back here though, okay?"

"Okay," she nodded, before pushing to her feet and returning to the table and her book. Marcus left shortly after.

After almost an hour pouring over her book, she managed to craft two objects, her mind finally peaceful after Marcus' promise. Thankfully, one she needed to take to the Vault, giving some truth to what she had told him earlier. The other, she tucked safely in her chest, noting to give it to him later with strict instructions as to its use. She left Marcus' chambers, heading to the Vault.

Later, Lena flamed into her old apartment. It hadn't been sold or rented yet, which, whilst unfortunate for her old landlord, she was grateful for. Most of her old furniture was still there, but there were no covers on the bed or pillows on the couch anymore. Gingerly, she sat down on the couch, placing the books she had brought with her on the coffee table. She folded her hands between her legs and sighed as she looked around the studio. It no longer felt as comforting to be there as it once had, but she didn't need it to be. Not tonight.

After leaving the Vault, she had returned briefly to her altar room in the manor. After ensuring no one was home, she grabbed a small bag and filled it with black candles and dried herbs. Pulling them out now, she arranged them purposefully on the table. The candles were placed at equidistant points and with the herbs she made three overlapping circles within the candles.

"Eight apple seeds to symbolise the free will and seven sins of man," she whispered to herself as she worked. "Anise to stimulate psychic ability. And wormwood to remove anger and summon the soul. Placed in three interlocking circles to symbolise Heaven, Earth... and Hell." Sitting back on the couch she surveyed her work, adjusting it slightly until she was happy with the placement. "Please let this work," she prayed, crossing her fingers briefly.

Lena twitched her fingers sparking the candles alight with a small burst of her lightning. The flames were black offering little light to push back the darkness within the apartment. They crackled in the silence as the ash and sage within them met with the flame.

Taking a deep breath, she sat upright and pulled a small knife from the bag. She began to chant under her breath, holding her left hand over the circle and plunged the knife into the centre of her palm. Her powers tried to heal her almost instantly, but she rotated the knife slowly forcing the wound to remain open and allowing her blood to drip from her hand, falling to the table.

The air around her stirred, catching at her hair as she continued to chant. Shadows fell across the wall, disturbing the curtains and rattling the fixtures as they went. The candles flickered, growing and shrinking as the spell worked its power within the room. Melted wax ran down the body of the candles, snaking out across the table to mix with the herbs and her blood. The inside of the circles began to glow.

She shut her eyes, focusing on her chant and its purpose. If it truly worked, no one outside would notice any of this. If it didn't... well, she just hoped no one was outside at 2am.

"Hello?"

The small voice was ethereal as it spoke. Far away, yet so close. Lena didn't dare open her eyes. She had to finish the chant or everything would fall apart. If she lost focus now, she wouldn't be able to repeat the spell until the next new moon.

"Hello," the voice said again. "I can see you. Did you call me?"

Falling silent, she slowly opened her eyes, looking at the soul that now stood in front of her. She got to her feet, simply staring at the woman she had summoned. The soul's body looked solid but had a haze to it when it moved.

"Hi mum," she said softly.

"Mum?" the soul laughed. "There must be a mistake. You can't be my daughter."

She pressed her lips together. "Yeah... I know this will seem weird, but I am your daughter. I'm Lena."

"No, no, no, no..." the soul said, shaking her head. "My daughter is ten years old."

"Sorry to break it to you mum, but that's just when you died. Astonishingly, I continued to grow. You do know you're dead right?" Lena said suddenly unsure if she was going to have to break that to her mother.

"Of course, I know I'm dead," the soul snapped. "I was just speaking with the reaper and... ah..." the soul fell silent for a moment, holding its hand out like trying to grasp onto an errant thought. "I don't remember."

"You chose Purgatory, didn't you?"

"Yes..."

"Which is why you still think I'm ten. Time doesn't mean anything in Purgatory."

The soul looked at her sceptically. "How do I know you're my daughter?"

Lena placed her hands on her hips, pursing her lips in annoyance. "The last thing you said to me, was you wished you'd aborted me, immediately after I'd knocked over your liquor glass. Then you back handed me across the face and threw me outside."

The soul stared for a moment. "Yep, you're my daughter."

"Geez, thanks Grace," Lena said, rolling her eyes.

"So, what do you want? I'm guessing I'm not back permanently," Grace said looking around the room. "What is this dump anyway?"

Lena sighed and rubbed her hands over her eyes. Maybe this was a mistake. "This was my apartment. It's the only empty place I could go to. Mum, we don't have much time, I need to ask you something."

Grace looked at her daughter, her face blank. "Well, ask then," she said impatiently.

"The only good thing about this situation is that the spell forces you to tell the truth. Something, you were not keen on doing in life."

"I seem to remember you being full of lies too, child. Don't take the moral high ground with me."

"I only lied to avoid getting hit by you!"

"I only hit you when you deserved it."

"Must you always be so stubborn?" she snapped, throwing her hands in the air.

"Must you always be so defiant?" Grace retorted. "I am your mother after all."

"Mothers don't hit their children and blame them for their father's death."

"And yet, here we are."

Lena tilted her chin, staring down at her mother. "I need to ask you about dad." She could have sworn Grace's eyes lit up at the mention of Matthew. "Did you know? That he made a deal with a demon to save you?"

Grace's head dropped and she stared at the floor. "Yes," she whispered. "He told me. He told me a few days before he died. When he gave me the letter he wrote for you. He told me about you as well."

"About me?"

"Hm," Grace nodded. "The deal came with the stipulation that your life was set on a straight line to Hell. Destined to become a great force for evil. He wanted me to help you avoid that."

Lena's mouth ran dry, her gaze dropping to the floor. "Is that why... why you... never loved me?"

Grace sighed. "I loved you."

Her head snapped towards her mother in surprise. "What?"

"I loved you," Grace repeated looking at her, sadness filling her eyes. "I wanted you so badly, I was willing to risk not receiving treatment for my cancer until after you were born. Your father, he couldn't accept that. We fought endlessly about what to do. He wanted to abort, have me go through treatment, then try to have another child later." Grace took a small step towards Lena. "I had no idea he would go to the lengths he did. The doctors and I honestly thought it was a miracle, but deep down

I knew something was wrong. Then when you were born you were so beautiful, so perfect, I didn't care. You were two months early, you know?"

Lena looked at her mother surprised by the sentiment in her voice. "I know," she said softly.

"You were so small. So tiny. But you were strong. The doctors were so worried, but you surprised all of them. You became my new miracle. I thought, what could possibly be so bad if it resulted in you?"

She drew breath rapidly, barely able to comprehend what her mother was saying. This whole time, her mother had wanted her, not her father.

"We were so happy those first few years," Grace continued. "I loved everything about you, and even your father did in his own way. But after he told me about the deal, I... I didn't see my little girl anymore. I saw a monster."

Tears stung in her eyes as Lena looked away, feeling sick to her stomach.

"And it looks like I was right," Grace sighed.

"What does that mean?" she snapped.

"Summoning souls? I may be dead, but I'm not stupid, girl. I know witchcraft when I see it."

"It's not witchcraft," she said, turning on her heel and storming across the room. "That would imply a witch cast it, and witches can't pull souls from Purgatory."

"And you know about witches?"

"Honestly, I thought you would know, as you were one."

"Must you try to turn everything into a joke?" Grace said, pinching the bridge of her nose.

"I wonder who I got that unhealthy coping mechanism from?" Lena sneered, staring daggers at the mother.

"So, what are you then?" the soul chuckled. "Because you are certainly not human."

Lena chewed the inside of her cheek, hesitant to answer. "I... I'm a demon," she sighed finally.

"Then it was all true. You have become a force for evil," her mother said, malice in her voice.

"Oh, get off your high horse, mother. You weren't a virtue of good," Lena said, placing her hands on her hips. "I get to choose what I am now. I may be a demon, but that was my choice, and no one, not even Lucifer himself, has any say in how I live as one."

Grace raised an eyebrow in disbelief. "Sure sweetheart," she sneered callously. "How did you become a demon then?"

"Much like how you got your miracle remission," Lena smirked, "A man made a deal with a demon."

Her mother laughed, a genuine laugh that would have brought tears to her eyes if it had been possible. "Ha! Who would have thought we would have that in common?"

"Yeah, go figure," she said unimpressed. "Did dad tell you which demon he made the deal with?"

"He did mention a name, but I don't really remember it. Something flowery. It was weird for a demon," Grace said, continuing as she looked at the ceiling. "You really need to dust in here."

"I don't live here anymore, mum," Lena sighed. "Was it 'Ambrose'?"

"That's it!" Grace snapped her fingers. "Ambrose. Not what I would call a demon."

Lena chewed the inside of her cheek at her mother's confirmation. "I hate you." She hadn't meant to make that declaration to her mother. It had simply slipped out in the moment. But she didn't regret saying it.

"I know," the soul said softly. "I wanted you to hate me."

Lena shook her head at her mother. "Why?" she asked exasperatedly.

"Because it made it easier to not love you."

"Then why, when social services took me away, did you go through the program to get me back?" Lena asked, walking towards her mother. "You were free of me. Free to drink and gamble your way into oblivion without giving me false hope that my mother maybe wanted me!"

Grace started at her daughter. "I was going to kill us both."

She stopped in her tracks, murderous rage washing over her. "I was ten years old," she said through gritted teeth.

"Yes, and that's why I didn't kill you," the soul said flatly. "I had everything ready. But despite everything you had done, and everything I had done, I couldn't do it. Despite all of that... I still saw my tiny perfect baby. And I still loved you."

Silence fell over them as the women simply stared at each other, comprehending the words that hung over them. Finally, Grace sighed looking away from her daughter to the candles that were almost burnt out. "I think our time is almost up."

Lena looked at the table, seeing her mother was correct.

"Last question then," she said quickly, struggling to hold back tears. "Why didn't he tell me?"

"Your father?" Grace asked before simply shrugging in response. "He didn't want to influence what would happen to you, I suppose. He thought if you didn't know, then you could at least try to have a normal life."

"So, his only mistake was telling you," she spat.

"Seems so," Grace said under her breath. "Goodbye, Lena. It was... interesting."

"Bite me," Lena said, swiping her hand over the table and breaking the spell. Her mother disappeared instantly.

With a heavy sigh, she leaned back into the couch and closed her eyes. Pulling her legs up on the couch, Lena curled her body into the cushions. Her world had been turned upside down with one conversation. How desperately she wished she could go back and forget everything, but wishes rarely meant anything other than denial and fear of reality. And she was not one to run from reality. Not anymore.

CHAPTER THIRTY-TWO

They had spent the last few days going back and forth with James Carter, trying to reach some amicable agreement that would see him hand over whatever information he possessed. The discussions seemed to be going nowhere as they were only able to have one to two hours with James before he had to attend to his mortal obligations. Under council orders, Zagan had essentially moved in with Ambrose to keep an eye on him until matters were settled. Due to this, he had not been able to see Lena, which bothered him to no end.

Hiding in his office, Ambrose desperately tried to ignore the fact that Zagan was lounging somewhere in his home. More than likely his library or availing himself of Ambrose's liquor. He hated having his old sire around. He hated even more not having Lena there.

The phone on his desk rang, causing him to jump slightly. It was rare for him to receive a call at the manor.

"Hello?" he said, picking up the phone.

"Hey you."

"Lena," he sighed with relief, her voice sounding through the phone like a sweet melody. Silently he gave thanks that the phone in his office was the only one in the house, removing any possibility of Zagan listening in on another line. "I see you remember the phone number for here."

"Yeah," she chuckled. "Not that I ever imagined I'd be calling it." There was a slight pause where he just listened to the soft sounds coming through the receiver. He could hear cars and distant conversation. Wherever she was, she was somewhere busy. "I miss you," she said after a moment.

Closing his eyes and smiling, Ambrose leant his head back until it came to rest on his chair. "I miss you too," he said, hoping to convey his desire for her through his voice alone.

"Dammit, this is so stupid!" she cried suddenly, frustration in her words. "Calling when I could easily be there in a second."

Running his hand through his hair, he shared in her annoyance. "I know this is not ideal, Lena," he said softly, gripping the receiver tightly. "But I don't want you here whilst Zagan is still around."

"I know..." she sighed. "Is he staying in my room?"

"Do you really want me to answer that?" he teased.

"I suppose not..."

He chuckled at her defeated tone. "He hasn't been staying anywhere. Not really. He doesn't sleep often so no need for a bed. My liquor stores are running dangerously low, however." Hearing her laugh through the phone line was bittersweet. Imagining her smile made him want to find her. To plant as many kisses as he could on her soft-pink lips. Shifting uncomfortably in his seat, he tried to divert his mind to other matters. "Where are you calling from anyway?"

"Do you really want me to answer that?" she said mockingly, returning his earlier comment.

"Lena..." he sighed, despite the smile forming on his lips.

"Don't worry," she laughed quietly. "I'm at a payphone in the city. Marcus is with me. We're testing out an object I made yesterday. I just needed to hear your voice."

"Okay," he nodded, thankful she wasn't alone. "How are you getting on at his?"

Her sigh was like a punch through the phone. He could both feel and understand her desire to come home. "His apartment is nice enough, I guess. A little too close to Zagan's for my liking. I know Zagan's not there at the moment, but it gives me the creeps."

"Are any of the other cambions bothering you?" he asked, leaning forward and resting on his elbows, fiddling with an origami flower Lena had made him a while ago.

"Some, but Marcus keeps them at bay mostly." She went quiet for a bit as a few emergency sirens rushed past her location. "Something tells me Zagan's warned a lot of the others off. They're not being as pushy as they used to be."

"Not sure if I should be happy about that," he said wryly.

"I'd be cautiously optimistic. Or cynically optimistic maybe."

He chuckled, smiling as she joined in his laughter. "I *will* be happy when you're back in my arms."

"Me too," she whispered. "Ambrose?"

"Hm?"

"Can I ask you something?"

Something in her voice caused him concern. Straightening in his chair slightly, he listened intently down the line, hearing the slight rush of her breath over the microphone. "Of course."

"Ah..." she started, but fell quiet. He kept silent, waiting for her to speak. "Actually, you know what, no, never mind."

Confused, he furrowed his brow. "Lena?" he gently prompted.

"No, it's fine," she responded firmly. "I'd rather wait to ask you in person."

"Are you sure?"

"Yes. I should go anyway. Probably going to run out of minutes soon," she chuckled.

He didn't want the call to end. He could listen to her voice all day. "What are you doing today?"

"Um... actually," she hesitated, pulling further confusion from him. "I'm going to hang out with Cyrus."

Sighing heavily, he shut his eyes again. "Lena, please don't shout at me, but I don't think now is a good time for you to see him."

"I'm not going to shout at you," she said emphatically. "I say I'm going to hang out with him, really, I'm just going to be hanging out at the den, and only for a few hours. Zamira is so close to giving birth. I want to be with her as much as possible. Especially if I can't be with you right now. I need the distraction. If it helps, Marcus will be with me," she assured him.

"It does," he said softly. "Alright. But if anything feels off, even in the slightest sense, I mean anything, you leave," he ordered, hoping that she would understand. "Even if it means leaving Marcus behind, you get yourself somewhere safe, okay?"

"You know, I'm truly impressed that a command works over the phone..."

At least she didn't sound angry. "I'm sorry," he apologised

regardless. "I'm not trying to control you here."

"I know, it's fine. I understand. I won't tell Marcus you told me to leave him behind, though. He might take offence at that."

"I'll leave you to judge that," he chuckled. "Zagan and I are going back to see James this afternoon. We're meeting at his home without distractions, so fingers crossed we can finally get this all sorted. I'm hoping I can be home tonight, but it will likely be tomorrow. I'll come get you as soon as Zagan's gone."

"Be safe, okay?"

"Always. You too."

"See you soon?" It was a question more than a statement. She wanted reassurance.

He wanted to say so much more to her. *I love you*, he thought, wishing he had the strength to say it aloud. Instead, he sniffed slightly, trying to ignore the churning in his gut. "See you soon, my dove."

His hand lingering on the receiver after putting it down, Ambrose sighed heavily. He missed her so much. He missed her scent, her warmth, the feeling of calm he had when she was around. How desperately he wanted her there, now, to fall into her arms and forget everything that was happening. But, at the same time, the guilt in his stomach that had taken up permanent residence after Zagan's confirmation that she was the child of his deal, made him anxious at the thought of seeing her again. He had to tell her, to explain, but he doubted she would understand. And that would mean losing her. Or at least, risk losing her. For good. And if she didn't understand and pulled away, would she go to another demon? Would she go to Zagan? She would have her choice of other demons willing to become her sire. Would she leave him once she learnt he was the reason she was a demon? It was becoming all too easy to believe she would.

After a couple of hours of failing to distract himself with his work, he finally gave up and, pushing to his feet, left his office in search of Zagan. It was almost time for them to go see James anyway. Finding him in the library, Ambrose sat down at the table, silently studying his old sire who had a few different books laid out in front of him.

"So, how's Lena?" Zagan asked, not looking up from his reading.

"Please tell me you weren't eavesdropping?" he sighed heavily. "That's juvenile, even for you."

"I don't need to eavesdrop," the cambion sneered, peering across the table through his lashes. "Your demeanour is different, so I can only assume you've been speaking with her."

Rolling his eyes, Ambrose shook his head. No matter how much he tried, Zagan was still able to read him so easily. He had to find some way of overcoming that. "She's fine."

"I understand why she wasn't here a few days ago, but why has she not come back? You are hiding her from me, aren't you?" Zagan smiled as he leant back in the chair, folding his arms across his chest.

"She doesn't want to be around someone she finds repulsive," he smirked, tilting his head in annoyance.

"Oh, so she doesn't live here at all then?" Zagan scoffed. Ambrose scowled at him. "Oh, come on, Ambrose, you made that too easy for me."

Keeping his face blank, he swallowed the bile rising in the back of his throat. "Should we not be getting on to see James?" he asked, taking a steadying breath.

The cambion nodded, looking back towards the books on the table. "We will soon. I'm just waiting for Cyrus to bring me an artefact."

"What artefact?"

"Once we have the information that James has on demons, I plan to wipe his memory. Regardless of whatever agreement we might reach with him." Zagan leant forward and crossed his arms on the table. "I thought about just killing him, or making a straight-out deal, but both would bring too much unwanted attention."

"Do you really trust that he's going to hand over the evidence he has?" Ambrose asked, raising a speculative brow.

"Not at all," his old sire shook his head. "That's what you are going to be doing whilst Cyrus and I are talking with him this afternoon." Looking up, Zagan gave Ambrose a pointed look. "You did that finding spell with Lena. Do it again. Find all the copies and get them. Call me when you have everything."

"You don't command me anymore, Zagan," he growled, leaning forward, keeping his gaze locked with the cambion.

"In this respect I do," Zagan said firmly, raising a finger and pointing it at his face. "Our council is still open to the idea of forcing Lena to bind to another. So, I suggest you do exactly as I say or you may find yourself permanently separated from your little *dove*."

His stomach dropped and his blood ran cold. How in the hell did

Zagan know that endearment? He had never said it around anyone except Marcus and there was no way Marcus would tell Zagan that. He also couldn't believe that Lena would have told anyone. He knew she liked hearing him call her that. Surely, she would have kept it to herself. Unless... would she have told Cyrus?

Suddenly, flames appeared in front of the library door as Cyrus and Lena stepped through together, board smiles on their faces. Looking at them shocked, Ambrose tried to regain control of his thoughts. He was so happy to see Lena again, but hated that it was marred by the jealousy he felt of seeing her next to Cyrus.

"What are you two doing here?" Zagan snapped, seemingly annoyed by their intrusion.

"We have an idea to sort the James situation," Cyrus said, stepping closer to the table.

"Excuse me?"

"Well, Lena had the idea," Cyrus answered, gesturing to her. "But I think you should hear it out."

"When have I ever cared for what you think?"

Ambrose had to struggle against his laughter as he felt Lena bristle at Zagan's casual dismissal of the boundling. She was evidently very protective of Cyrus and although that bothered him slightly, he didn't really blame her for it. Looking at her, he saw her chewing the inside of her cheek as she held her anger in check.

"I know you don't care what I think," Cyrus said, folding his arms across his chest. "But I do know you care about what she thinks."

"What's the idea then, beautiful?" Zagan said with a wicked smile, turning his gaze to her.

"I don't answer to you," she snapped at him, placing her hands on her hips.

Ambrose chuckled at the frustrated scowl she created on Zagan's face. "What's the idea, Lena?" he asked, looking warmly at her.

She sighed softly as she looked at him. How he'd missed the sight of her eyes. "So, I completed another finding ritual and, with Marcus' help, managed to pinpoint all of the locations of the physical copies of information James has. By the way, Zagan, since you spoke with him, he's found some choice stuff on you too." Zagan huffed, leaning back in his chair, an amused and slightly proud look on his face. "But he also has a singular digital copy, stored on his laptop. Well, I made this."

Biting her bottom lip, Lena held up an intricate Celtic knot pendant.

Ambrose could feel her pride bloom within his own chest. "And what does that do?" he asked, noting the power radiating from it.

"It will completely wipe his laptop," Lena said with a smile, placing the pendant gently down on the table. "I made it from two artefacts I'd already created. My very first object, which Marcus hunted down for me, being the bracelet that causes an overwhelming feeling of protectiveness to the point of obsession, and a book that sucks souls that are looking to disappear into it. I removed the curses from them and poured them into the pendant, which Calza kindly provided. The pendant is like a magnet and can be used to draw the truth from someone. All three together will extract all the information from his laptop and store it within the pendant."

"You sound awfully confident," Zagan sneered, his gaze still locked on her.

Ambrose's brow furrowed as he saw Lena and Cyrus exchange a glance. She was practically jubilant looking at him. What was it between them and why did it feel like more than just sibling love?

"We've already tested it," she said, bouncing slightly on her feet as she answered. "We picked up a mobile and downloaded various bits of information onto it."

"In less than a minute of the pendant lying on it, everything was gone, with no recoverability," Cyrus continued for her, sharing in her enthusiasm, even as Zagan glared at him.

"All of it was in the pendant. I could then extract it with my book and make it simply vanish into the ether," Lena said, picking up the pendant and looking at it proudly. "All you need to do is get close enough to the laptop, place the pendant on it and the curse will do the rest."

"The pendant will also remove James' memory. Lena has shown me how to use it to draw out specific memories, so we won't leave him as a useless lump of flesh," Cyrus finished explaining.

Zagan sighed, making a show of contemplating the usefulness of the pendant. Ambrose knew that even he would have to admit, it was an elegant solution. Of course, James would know it was them, but what could he do? Other than to recompile the evidence again. But if they wiped his memory as well, then the situation would be solved completely. "You said you have the locations of all the physical information," the cambion said, looking at the top of the table.

"Yes," Lena said slowly.

"Ambrose, you will get those," Zagan said, getting to his feet. "I will go see James. Cyrus will come with me with the pend—"

"Hey, it's my pendant," she snapped indignantly, clutching the pendant close to her chest.

He gave her an amused smile. "You want to come with me, beautiful?"

Pressing his lips together to contain both his annoyance at the question and his laughter as Lena's expression turned to one of abject horror, Ambrose kept his eyes locked on his boundling. "Here you go, Cyrus," she said quickly, holding the pendant out for him, before she sighed in defeat. "Doesn't matter anyway. Unfortunately, I can't be of any further assistance to any of you."

"What's happened?" Ambrose asked, standing and walking over to her, concern filling him.

"I've been summoned by my council," she said, annoyance ringing clear in her voice. "Direct orders from Mammon."

"Mammon?" Zagan asked, drawing her gaze to him. "Prince of Hell, Mammon?"

"Apparently," she said dryly. "So, not something I can ignore."

"How intriguing," he sighed, putting his hands in his pocket. Ambrose eyed him sceptically, knowing this would only serve to heighten the cambion's desire to claim her. "Well, we've still got some time before we are due to see James. You go to your council and Ambrose, Cyrus and I will sort out the finer details."

Lena gave him a dubious look, before turning to Ambrose. "Can I talk to you privately?"

"Of course," he said, placing his hand on her back and leading her out into the hall.

"Here are the locations for all the physical folders," she said, turning to him once the library door was shut behind them. She was holding out a piece of paper.

With a soft smile, he took the paper and looked at the details written on it. He shouldn't have any difficulty getting in and out of all of them. "You said you wanted to ask me something in person. What is it?"

"Ah..." she sighed. "Now is not really the time. I really do have to go. The headache caused by the council is becoming unbearable." She grimaced as if to drive home her point. "Ambrose... Cyrus has been trying to tell me something all day, but his bindings are preventing him. I have a bad feeling about all of this and it is centred on Zagan." Glancing at the library door, she ensured it was completely shut before stepping forward and laying her palms on his chest. Wanting more, but not wishing to risk anything, Ambrose simply placed his hands over hers, giving her hands a longing squeeze. "*Please*, be careful."

"I will be," he assured her, "I promise."

"I'll go back to Marcus after I've seen the council. Call me as soon as you get back."

Dropping her hands, she took a few steps back and gathered her flames as she disappeared. Rubbing his cheek, Ambrose felt plagued by the knowledge she wanted to ask him something. Did she know about her father? How could she? But then how did Zagan know about his name for her? Zagan knew about her father, so it didn't seem like a stretch that Cyrus would know as well. Had Cyrus and Lena talked more than he realised?

Bracing himself, he walked back into the library, the conversation between Zagan and Cyrus halting immediately as he returned.

"Don't stop on my account," Ambrose said coldly, returning to his seat. "Do not lose that pendant," he said pointedly towards the boundling. "Lena will need it back."

"Now Ambrose, that's not very nice to Lena's childhood friend," Zagan smiled at him, leaning back in the chair.

"I'll be nicer when he's broken from you."

"Will you?" Zagan sneered. "Breaking from me would remove the last thing that makes Lena reserved around him. She and Cyrus knew each other long before you came along, promising to be together when they got older. Isn't that right Cyrus?" Looking at the boundling, he nodded slowly, his bindings glowing faintly. What did that mean? "Have you ever thought that maybe you are just convenient until Cyrus can be truly free to be with her?"

Forcing a deep intake of breath to steady himself, Ambrose tried to keep his rising anger under control. "She is free to be with whoever she wishes," he said softly. "I'm not stopping her."

"Aren't you? You keep telling her to stay away from him. From me," Zagan leant forward again, smiling cruelly at him. "Is that not stopping her? Has there been nothing to give you pause? To give you doubt? Has she fought to be with you as fiercely as she's fought to be allowed to see Cyrus?"

Shaking his head, he tried to ignore his old sire's words. "It's been a long time since I fell for one of your mind games, Zagan."

"Think about this then," the cambion said as he and Cyrus got to their feet. "If she wasn't bound to you, if the risk of her death was taken away, and she had to choose to save you or Cyrus, who do you think she would choose? The demon she was sacrificed to, the demon who has lied to her and is the cause for her being in Hell? Or the adopted brother with whom she made a joint promise, to always look out for the other? I know who I'd choose." Staring at the sire and boundling, Ambrose noted that Cyrus could, or would, not meet his gaze. "Get the physical folders. Then meet me at our council." With that, the pair disappeared in their own flames, leaving Ambrose to his thoughts.

CHAPTER THIRTY-THREE

The council had asked her questions about her process of creating objects, pushing her to explain the function of all objects she had made since finding her design. They had all been vocally impressed by what she had achieved in her time. Despite having been summoned by Mammon, the Prince had been absent, leaving her instructions with the council. They had warned Lena that Ambrose's council were considering forcing her to bind to another. As a countermeasure to this, they explained the Princes of Hell were devising a test that would show she could not be forced into anything. She wondered if they saw the irony in that, but didn't question them on it.

After her meeting with the council, she rested in one of Marcus' armchairs thinking over her conversation with Ambrose that morning and the tension between him and Zagan. Marcus busied himself at the table, making sure he could control the object she had made for him the day before. She had lit the fireplace and stared into the flames as she recalled every other conversation she'd had with Ambrose, analysing them, trying to figure out if he knew that she had been cursed by one of his deals. She had been so nervous to see him earlier, but her eagerness to share her creation of the pendant had tempered that slightly. She wasn't sure how she would react to seeing him again though. Now she found herself questioning her feelings for him, wondering if they were simply the result of the deal. She knew she missed him, desperately, but was that even just a byproduct? Here in Hell, she had nothing to remind herself of him.

"I need to go back to the manor," she said suddenly, getting up from the armchair.

"Hm?" Marcus queried, raising his head to look at her. "Why?"

Sighing heavily, she walked over to him, placing her palms on the table. "I'm suffocating down here. I need to go top-side and for more than just a ten-minute visit. I need a break from Hell."

Marcus chuckled but nodded his head. "Fair enough. Do you want me to come with you?"

"Actually, I'd prefer to go by myself," she said calmly. As much as she liked Marcus, she needed a break from him too. "There shouldn't be anyone there so I should be okay for a little bit."

"Alright," the cambion smiled. "I'll come check in on you in a couple of hours, okay?"

Lena nodded her understanding. "Thanks. I'll see you soon."

She left his chambers making her way to a nearby junction which she knew would be quiet this time of day. Once there she quickly flamed out of Hell, transporting herself to the manor's entrance hall.

The manor still had the same feel to her. Secure and safe, regardless of what she had learnt about Ambrose. She had no idea how she would react seeing him again. Did she even care that he was the demon her father summoned? Did it honestly matter? If it hadn't been him, would another demon have made the same deal? And if it had been another, would she have ended up bound to them? Would she even know Ambrose? Her mind raced with her questions. Questions she had been asking since she spoke to her mother.

Rubbing her arms in front of her chest, she turned and walked up to Ambrose's room. The sight of the bed flooded her mind with memories of their time together, their nights together. Crawling onto the bed, she grabbed his pillow and hugged it to her body, breathing in his scent of sage and cedar that still clung to it. Her body instantly reacted to the smell, craving him and his touch. Surely a deal couldn't control how she felt about someone. Surely, that was only something she could control.

Closing her eyes, she remembered the night she chose to bind to him. That night, regardless of her death, she'd known that things were different. That she was different. The choice hadn't scared her. It had seemed like an inevitability, but for the first time in her life, or her death, she'd felt like she really could have made whatever choice she wanted.

Choosing Ambrose was what she wanted. But she hadn't felt controlled by it, or like she was drawn to one choice over the other. Her life may have been controlled, destined on a set course, but was the same true of her death? The voice she had been hearing since becoming a demon, was that her, or someone else still pulling the strings? Annoyingly, that voice had now been silent since the conversation with Grace as if it too didn't know what to make of the situation.

Feeling like she would never get her answers, she rolled onto her back and stared at the canopy above.

"Hello?"

Sitting bolt upright, Lena stared at the bedroom door. There shouldn't be anyone here, she thought. Not yet anyway. She still had time before Marcus was going to check on her. So, who was calling out?

"Hello? Lena? Ambrose? Are you guys back? I'm really sorry about dropping in like this."

"Cyrus?" she said softly, dropping her legs off the side of the mattress. She got to her feet and walked to the door. Opening it she called out louder. "Cyrus?"

"Lena?"

Walking to the top of the stairs, she looked down and saw her friend standing in the middle of the hall, in human form, looking exactly how she had remembered him from all those years ago. His dark brown eyes looked up at her, a warm smile lighting them up brilliantly. He'd been in human form earlier, but with Ambrose and Zagan around, she hadn't had a chance to fully appreciate it.

"Hey," he said smiling up at her, his one dimple clearly showing on his cheek.

"When did you get back? Is everything sorted?" she asked as she finally noticed her hellhound, Zamira standing at the bottom of the stairs. "Hey girl," she said walking down the stairs, scratching the side of Zamira's neck.

"Ah, yeah. Zagan and I sorted James a few hours ago. Ambrose got everything. He also has your pendant for when he gets back. They had to go straight to their council after so they might still be a while. But everything should be fine now," Cyrus said reassuringly. He nodded to her hellhound and lifted a basket in his hands. "Zamira had her pups just after I got back. She's eager to show you them."

"Zamira! Hey! Did you have your pups finally?" she laughed, wrapping her arms around Zamira's front haunches. The hellhound licked at her check, nudging her closer to the basket. "Alright, alright," she said, pushing back against her. "I'm looking, hold on."

Cyrus placed the basket on the ground, untucking a blanket he had placed over the pups. There were five in total. Small tiny bundles of black and grey fur, curled together in sleeping bliss, little mewling sounds escaping them as Lena brushed her fingers along their backs.

"Oh, they're beautiful Zamira," she sighed, picking up one of the pups in her arms. Zamira nuzzled her nose into Lena's hands, licking her pup as it suckled on her thumb. "Well done, girl." Scratching behind Zamira's ear, Lena got to her feet, still holding the pup.

"How you doing, little mouse?" Cyrus asked, standing up, putting his hands in his trouser pockets.

"I'm fine," she lied, pressing the pup to her cheek. "All the better for seeing these little guys." Cradling the pup against her chest, she leant into her hellhound. "So, do Zamira and the pups stay here now? Ambrose and I set up a den a few weeks back."

Cyrus shook his head. "Not yet. Soon though. They just need some time first for the pack to adjust to the change. Zamira is an alpha female. She'll pick her replacement in a few days, then she and her pups are all yours. The pups will move back to the pack when they are around a year old."

"A year with six hellhounds. This is going to be fun," she smiled ruefully. Sighing, she looked up at Cyrus. As a human he was only slightly taller than her. "It's good to see you again. This you."

"Thanks, little mouse."

"Any chance, I could get a hug?"

Chuckling, Cyrus stepped around the basket and held out his arms, wrapping them around her as she pressed her free hand to his back, holding the pup to the side of the embrace. Closing her eyes, she sought comfort from his warmth. He was the last tie she had to her life before becoming a demon. A life that had led her to this moment. A life she didn't regret, so maybe, she shouldn't question her life now with Ambrose.

Revealing in the faint peace washing over her, she didn't notice her sire flame in beside them.

"What is he doing here?"

Lena pulled back from the embrace and looked towards the front entrance to see Ambrose standing there. He was home and despite her previous reservations, she smiled with joy to see him again. She bounced on her feet and ran over to him with the pup still clutched to her. "Welcome home," she said with a laugh, forgetting about Cyrus and lifting onto her toes to kiss him on the cheek.

As she rested back on her heels, she took in the expression on his face. It was dark with his brows drawn together and a scowl on his lips. Something was wrong and Lena felt a hollow pit forming in her stomach. His eyes were fixed on Cyrus, who now stood awkwardly in the middle of the hall. Tension filled the room as the men stared at each other, until something snapped and Cyrus dropped his gaze to the floor.

"Cyrus came to show me Zamira's pups," Lena said, trying to ease the mood and held up the pup she was holding. The pup licked at the air, stretching its neck towards her sire.

Ambrose looked at the pup briefly then stormed away from her. He headed towards Cyrus and made to walk past him. He paused briefly next to the boundling, then without turning his head, Lena heard him growl; "Get out," before he continued on and up the stairs.

Lena and Cyrus stood in shocked silence, with only the whimpering of the pups filling the void. They both flinched as the sound of Ambrose's office door slamming broke through the heavy tension. Zamira walked tentatively up to Lena, nudging her snout into the hand holding the pup.

"It's okay, girl," she whispered softly, scratching under Zamira's chin.

"I should go," Cyrus said timidly.

"That might be best," Lena agreed as she walked over to him to place the pup back in the hamper with its brothers and sisters. "I'm sorry, Cyrus."

"Don't apologise," he smiled at her with apprehension in his eyes. "You've got enough to deal with, you don't need to worry about me." He bent down and picked up the hamper, holding it carefully in front of him. "Good luck."

"Thanks," she said dryly, stepping back slightly as Zamira and Cyrus disappeared in a flurry of flames. Nervously, she looked up the stairs and briefly thought of hiding in the library for a while. "Buck up, Lena," she said to herself before ascending the stairs. She made her way to stand in front of the door to Ambrose's office.

She knocked tentatively, but she was met only with silence. Testing the handle, she noted that it was not locked. Taking a deep breath, she pushed open the door and stepped inside.

Ambrose had his back to her, as he stood in front of the fireplace looking at the flames. She couldn't see his face, but if the one she had been met with earlier was anything to go by, that was possibly a good thing.

Lena coughed trying to get his attention, but he didn't move or acknowledge her in any way.

"Ambrose, are you okay?" she asked, her voice barely louder than a whisper.

There was a pause in which she thought it might be best she simply leave and wait for him to come to her. She sighed and started to turn to the door when suddenly he spoke. "How long was Cyrus here?" he asked, his tone cold.

"What?" she said more out of surprise than not having heard him.

"You heard me."

She bristled at his callousness. She had never been the recipient of it from him before. Surely, this was not just because Cyrus has been here. Firming her resolve, she took a moment before answering. "Only a few minutes. Does it matter?"

"That's all?"

"Yes. Ambrose–"

"Why here?" he interrupted and Lena felt her annoyance grow.

"Excuse me?" she snapped.

"Why here?" Ambrose repeated, finally turning to look at her. His face was unreadable and despite her annoyance, she felt uneasy, but she refused to look away from him. "You weren't even supposed to be here. Why weren't you with Marcus?"

"I... I wanted to come home. And, I thought you were okay with Cyrus now." She shrugged to try and convey that it wasn't as big of a deal as he seemed to be making of it.

"Not with him being in my home when I'm not here. Need I remind you, *again*, that he is bound to Zagan. After you said you had a bad feeling earlier. Lena, how could you be so reckless?" he asked, stepping away from the fireplace and closing the distance between them.

"Reckless? It's not like I invited him explicitly."

"Then your relationship with him is such that he feels entitled to my home?"

Now she was angry. "*Your* home? I thought this was *our* home now."

"You know what I mean!" he snapped.

"Do I?" she retorted, her voice rising. "Because I'm struggling to figure out what the problem is."

"How does Zagan know I call you 'dove'?" he asked as he turned away from her, moving to his desk to sit behind it.

Her body ran cold, trepidation washing over her. "What?"

Leaning back in his chair, Ambrose's eyes darkened dangerously as he stared at her, folding his hands in front of him. "He used it against me earlier. Just before you turned up with Cyrus."

"I don't know," she said, shaking her head. "I haven't told anyone. Why would I?"

"You tell me."

"I don't know, Ambrose!" she cried, throwing her hands up in the air. "He's been here for days, maybe he overheard you on the phone or something. But he didn't learn it from me." Pinching the bridge of her nose, she sighed heavily, squeezing her eyes shut. "Did it honestly look like I was trying to hide something when you got home?"

"You pulled away from Cyrus awfully quick."

What is with this mood of his? Lena thought to herself as she stepped forward and placed her palms flat on the top of his desk, locking her eyes with his. "Because I was excited to see you! Don't try and spin this into something it's not."

"You, yourself, said you love him," he said calmly, even as his face flinched with malice.

"As a friend, as a brother. Nothing more!" She was almost shouting now. She knew she needed to calm down but his cold demeanour was infuriating. She wanted to slap him, to see if it was still possible for emotion to register on his arrogant features.

"And yet at every turn, you have argued to keep that friendship, completely ignoring my concerns."

"You fucking arsehole!" she cursed, pushing off from the desk and turning away from him. She walked to the middle of the room, taking a deep breath, desperately trying to keep calm. "You know that's not true. I told you..." she sighed heavily before continuing, turning back to him and placing her hands on her hips. "I told you; you were the only one I needed. You told me to keep being his friend."

"*Were?*" he asked haughtily.

Lena held up her finger at him and pressed her lips together, stopping herself from snapping at him. "I am not taking that bait," she said, deliberately taking her time with each word. "The only reason I am having this conversation is because I still need you."

"You only needed me once you learnt you would die if I did."

Her stomach dropped and her body flushed with anger at his casual dismissal. "You want to go there? You think I'm not being honest about Cyrus? You think I'm keeping secrets from you? Fine, let's go there," she snapped, crossing her arms in front of her chest. "I know it was you who made a deal with my father."

The look on his face was priceless for the situation. Shock registered across his features, his eyes widening behind his hands. "What?" he asked softly.

"Matthew Hale," she said coldly. "Remember him? Summoned you to save his wife because she wouldn't accept cancer treatments whilst pregnant and wouldn't agree to an abortion." Ambrose remained silent as she stared pointedly at him. "Not ringing any bells? Need more? That child, *their* child, destined to end up in Hell as a powerful force for evil. Remember now?" she asked, studying his face. His breathing was rapid and shallow as he merely stared at her. She could see that he was struggling to comprehend what she was saying, panic creeping into his eyes. "Don't know what to say to that? Cat got your fucking tongue?" she shouted wanting him to react in some way, his inaction fuelling her frustration with him. "Did I ever have a choice when it came to you? Or was it all some sick game to see how much shit could be thrown at one person? How much would it take before they broke? Or were you just looking to create the perfect fuck buddy for yourself?"

"Lena..." he whispered finally.

The sound of his voice only served to fan the flame within her. She'd opened a door she didn't know how to close. "Shut up!" she screamed at him, lightning crackling over her arms. "I don't want to hear what lame arse excuse you have for setting my life on the freak show roller-coaster that it was! You don't get to lecture me about keeping secrets."

Ambrose shook his head, leaning forward onto his elbows, his brow furrowed with frustration. "I told you that I was not intentionally keeping anything from you. I didn't know he was your father."

"Would you even have told me if you did?" she asked through gritted teeth. "How the hell would I know? I can't compel you to tell the truth." He flinched at her comment, dropping his gaze to the top of his desk. "Is that it?" she asked, taking another step towards him. Her body flushed with anger, her chest heaving as she tried to control her breathing. "Do you need to compel me to know once and for all that there is nothing between Cyrus and I? To finally trust me completely? Or are you too scared to find out that right now I trust him more than you."

"Then why don't you just climb into bed with him!" Ambrose shouted, rocketing to his feet and slamming his palms down on the desk. Lena jumped back in fear and took a few steps away from him. His face was one of pure rage as he shouted, but instantly turned to one of shock as he realised what he had said.

Pain hit her squarely in the chest as her heart broke with his outburst. She could see that he regretted his words, but the damage was done.

She shut her eyes tightly for a moment as she drew in her breath. Looking back at him, she spoke calmly and clearly, ready to be done. "I have no idea where that came from but it is a massive fucking leap, even for you. So, I am going to leave, before either of us say anything else as utterly ridiculous as that."

She turned on her heel and started for the office door.

"Lena!" Ambrose yelled after her. "Don't walk away from me! Come back here!"

Her bindings glowed and she cried out as pain shot through her arms. Her body responded to the command despite her mind screaming in defiance. Turning, she walked back to Ambrose, thunder in her eyes. Shock was plastered across his face, but her blood boiled with rage and she no longer cared about his feelings. She stopped a few steps from him, her nails digging into her palms, breaking the skin and causing warm droplets of blood to fall to the floor.

"Lena... I- I'm sorry," he stammered.

"Let. Me. Go," she said forcefully, her jaw clenching painfully.

"Lena..." he started. He fell silent and dropped his gaze. "You may go."

The pain subsided and the bindings dimmed to black. She spun on her heel and almost ran out the door desperate to get away from him. Once in the hallway, she looked towards the right, to Ambrose's room, and with a choking sob, she turned left and ran to her old room. She slammed the door behind her and threw herself onto the bed, the ache in her heart pulling painful cries from her chest. Tears flowed freely as she clutched a pillow to her face.

CHAPTER THIRTY-FOUR

After Lena had left his office, Ambrose fell back into his chair and let his face drop into his hands. Coming home to see her and Cyrus embracing had pulled everything Zagan had said to the forefront of his mind. The doubt caused by them screaming in his ears. Jealousy and anger had swept through him like fire and he hadn't been able to hold it back. He had wanted to lash out, to lash out at Cyrus, to permanently remove him from Lena's life. It had taken what little remained of his self-control to simply walk past the boundling knowing that action would truly have driven Lena away from him. But then, he'd done that without Cyrus' help.

"What have I done?" he whispered as guilt washed over him.

"What *did* you do?"

He startled at the question and looked up as Marcus walked into his office. Despite being a friend, he grew angry at the question.

"Stay out of it Marcus."

"Oh, I don't plan on getting involved," the cambion said, an amused smile on his lips as he moved to stand in front of the desk. "I'd only come here to collect Lena, but as she has just burst from here seemingly close to tears, I thought you may want to talk. I thought you and her were getting along."

Ambrose sighed heavily looking at the ground. "We were. I screwed up."

"How?"

"I broke a promise."

"To Lena?"

"No, to Lucifer. Of course, to Lena," he snapped glaring at his friend.

"Sorry," Marcus said hurriedly, holding up his hands. "I mean, you are a demon, despite how nice of a demon you are, which is not necessarily a compliment. Demons break promises almost hourly."

"Not this promise. Not to Lena."

"I'm sure you two will sort it out. It's not like you accused her of cheating on you with Zagan, right?"

He stayed silent.

"You didn't," Marcus said in disbelief.

"Not with Zagan... Cyrus."

"So, Zagan adjacent."

Ambrose stared at the cambion coldly, but the point was valid and well made.

With a heavy sigh, Marcus folded his arms across his chest. "Give her a few days to cool off. She'll come around. Do you want me to ask the Caretaker to speak with her?"

"I do not need all of Hell meddling in my affairs, Marcus."

"Fair enough. Don't give up on her, Ambrose. She's bound to you after all. And as long as she doesn't choose to defect to another demon, she will be around here for a while."

"Thanks for the pep-talk," he said, leaning his head back against his chair.

"Well consider this then, if you're bent on wallowing in self-pity," Marcus said sharply. "Lena has yet to transform and she has been a demon for almost two months now. Add to that she's evidently powerful enough to warrant a hellhound imprinting on her which is rare enough as it is considering their numbers. Finally, her bindings continue to grow daily, and I don't see you casting spells to increase them, so they are growing at the same rate as her own power. Based on that alone, you do not want to be on her bad side when she does finally transform," he said, stepping forward and laying a folder on the desk. "So as your friend, I suggest you find a way to fix this."

Ambrose looked along his nose at his friend as uneasiness washed over him at the warning. Marcus wasn't wrong. Lena's power was growing daily and he could feel it through their bond. He was fully aware that her power had surpassed his own and many others in Hell, even if she and the other demons had not yet fully realised it. It had not concerned him before. He had wanted her to become a demon, he was not about to hold her back from reaching her full potential.

"Maybe you should warn the Caretaker as Lena will no doubt go to confide with it," he said wearily staring at the ceiling. Marcus merely nodded in acknowledgement. Ambrose sighed heavily as he pulled his head forward and looked at the folder on his desk. "Investment reports?"

"Yeah," the cambion said, looking at the folder with disdain. "I didn't know you were going to be back, so I was going to leave them on your desk. But as you are here... I can't get my head around them, so I was hoping you might have a look at them. A dealer in America just took out a large portion of the investment so we may need to rework some of the portfolio to try and make up for that."

"Back to work then," Ambrose said, leaning forward to grab the folder.

"Give her some time," Marcus said, placing a hand on his shoulder. "Then grovel. Grovel like your life depends on it. Because it just might."

The next day, Ambrose and Lena were heading to the training pits. She hadn't spoken one word to him since their fight, and he was too afraid to push. He's spent the night pacing both his office and room, finding himself standing outside her door more times than he cared to count, feeling her pain coursing through his chest. This part of the bond he cursed. Feeling her joy and pleasure was one thing, but feeling her sorrow, knowing it was a direct result of his actions was agonising. He desperately wanted to speak with her, to make her understand that he had hoped she hadn't been the one born of his deal, that he regretted ever being a part of it. He wanted to tell her how much he loved her, but knew that right now, she would push him away. So, he kept his mouth shut as they walked through the corridor.

Today Lena was to be tested. Eight weeks a demon and she had still not transformed. Word had gotten to the Princes of Hell about her. Their emissaries had been sent to call for her to show the full extent of her power. They had devised something that would push her limits, but no further details had been provided to either of them.

Trying to find the courage to say something, Ambrose reasoned that at least her anger would likely serve her well today.

"Lena?" he asked tentatively as they rounded the final corner.

"What?" she snapped.

He swallowed the guilt that rose within his throat, knowing she was completely justified in her treatment of him. "I just..." he started, unsure of how to continue. "I'm sorry, Lena. I know it doesn't mean much right now. But I am. I wish I could take everything back." They reached the entrance to the pits, freezing in their tracks as they took in the scene before them. Hundreds of demons had turned up to watch the test. Winged demons clung to the ceiling and walls, whilst others had put together makeshift bleachers around the centre pit so all could see. "I know you're angry," he said quietly as they walked forward. "You have every right to be, and you should use that to your advantage. But you also need to keep calm. If the Princes have devised this test, it will be brutal, and I can't do anything to help."

"I don't need your help," Lena spat at him.

He bristled at her remark, but simply clamped his mouth shut.

Archie approached them, a solemn look on his face, his wings hanging lower behind him than usual. "Ambrose, Lena," he greeted them with a curt nod. "I need to speak with Lena before the test begins."

Ambrose nodded and turned to her, his chest tightening as she refused to look at him. "Good luck," he said softly before making his way over to Marcus, who had secured a place for him close to the edge of the pit. He spied Zagan and Cyrus on the opposite side of the pit from him, his stomach churning at the sight of them. Clenching his jaw, he sat beside his friend, anxiety overwhelming him.

"Hey," Marcus said softly. "She okay?"

Ambrose shrugged. "She's barely said two words to me."

Looking over to where Archie and Lena still stood, he watched as they huddled together in a hushed exchange. The expression on her face was unreadable, but he didn't need to read it in order to know she was pissed.

"Are they arguing?" Marcus asked, leaning over to him.

It did look like they were. Lena was holding a finger up to Archie's face, her mouth moving rapidly even as he shook his head at her, trying to talk over her. At one point, Archie raised his wings to shield them from onlookers, the whisperings in the pits growing louder as all turned to look at them.

"Maybe I should have been more worried about Archie," Ambrose said ruefully, immediately hating himself for the thought.

Marcus patted him on the back. "There are many you should have been more worried about than Cyrus," he said. "But Lena doesn't care about any of them. Trust me."

Ambrose looked sideways at his friend, about to ask for clarification as a heavy silence fell over the cavern. Whatever conversation was going on between Lena and Archie, it was over, as they now strode towards the crowd. Lena jumped down into the pit, landing deftly on her feet before walking into the centre. Archie dropped in beside her, but moved to stand off to the side. Three demons, unknown to Ambrose, flamed in around her in an equidistant triangle.

The demons were large. Although Ambrose didn't know their names, he knew they were from the inner circles of the Princes. More than likely from Satan's, the Prince of Wrath, who kept the greatest of warrior demons close to him. Condemned souls who excelled through the lower pits, unbound and forced to learn on their own. All looked relatively similar in demonic appearance, their bodies distinctly defined by carved out muscles; scars and tattoos covering their dark red skin. Two had large black horns atop their heads, twisting in different directions. The one in front of Lena had four, two of which twisted and curled under his ears back towards his jaw, with large bat-like wings protruding from his back. Their eyes were all bottomless pools of black.

"Are you fucking kidding me?" Lena shouted, turning on her heel and glaring at Archie, who looked at the ground, seemingly unable to meet her gaze. Ambrose looked between them, trying to figure out what was going on.

"She knows that demon," he whispered to Marcus. "The one with the wings."

"What? How?"

"I don't know. But I can feel her recognition of him. If she was angry before, she's pissed now..."

"That doesn't bode well," Marcus sighed, rubbing his temple.

Lena closed her eyes and took a deliberate breath before turning back to the winged demon. "Hey TJ," she said, malice dripping from her voice.

Ambrose's back straightened. *Fuck*, he thought.

"What?" Marcus asked, noticing his friend's reaction.

"He's her ex," he answered, fighting desperately to keep his panic in check.

"Oh hell..."

"Hey Lena," TJ nodded to her. "Long time."

"Not long enough," she sighed, pinching the bridge of her nose. "Shall we get this over with?" she asked, clenching her fists and sparking her lightning over her arms. She was wearing a broad shoulder vest top which clearly displayed the bindings on her arms, but concealed where they now covered her shoulders and back. Ambrose could only hope that the fabric would stand up to the trail of today.

"Fine with us," TJ said, black flames igniting over his fists. The other two demons channelled their own powers of blue and red fire. Unbound demons rarely manifested anything but fire, their auras being their only distinguishing features. At least it would be easy to tell who was throwing which fireball.

"Hold on," Archie barked. No one moved, but their powers continued to light up the pit. "Before you begin, be aware, there are no rules except to stay within the pit. A barrier has been cast over the pit, bodies can move through it, but your powers cannot. If you are thrown out of the pit, you're out. Feel free to try and kill each other... if you can." He sighed as he stepped towards the demons. "Killing is not the object however. At least, not for the three of you. Your object is to force Lena out of the pit. The Princes would prefer you don't kill her, take that how you will. Lena's object is to stay in. You have an hour." With a flap of his wings, Archie left the pit, landing by the edge where he and Lena had originally entered. "Begin," he shouted.

The word had barely left his lips before the three demons threw fireballs at Lena. The fires met with a blinding explosion, gasps coursing through the onlookers. As the cloud of smoke cleared, the scorched earth was revealed. But nothing else.

TJ stepped forward, looking at the spot where she had been, fanning his wings to further clear the smoke. Ambrose held his breath, watching intently as the other demons looked at each other.

"Where did she go?" one asked, turning to look around the pit. As he did so, Lena flamed in behind him, her body in the air, her arm already swinging. Her fist connected with his jaw, lightning exploding across his face, sending his body slamming into the ground with a concussive thump. Before his body had hit the ground, she flamed away, reappearing behind the other demon opposite, hitting him squarely in the back and rocketing him towards the other. Twisting on her feet, she sent a powerful arc of lightning from her body to collide with the two demons, creating a crater around their bodies that crackled with electricity, holding them within.

TJ lunged at her, his wings beating behind him to increase his speed. Turning her head to look at him, Lena disappeared in flames as his fingers curled around the empty space that had, just before, been her neck. He turned on the spot, increasing his fire to fully cover his body like a suit of armour, his eyes darting around the pit, looking for her.

"Come out, Lena," he called, stepping towards his comrades as they scrambled to their feet, shaking off the effects of her lightning. "You're supposed to stay in the pit. Hiding within the fires of Hell hardly seems fair and kind of defeats the purpose, don't you think?"

"I'm not fighting you, TJ. Not yet anyway," Lena's voice echoed through the pit although her body was absent.

"How'd she learn to do that?" Marcus asked, his eyes wide.

"Oh, it's something she figured out with her book," Ambrose answered, a small smile of pride on his lips. "It's freaking cool!"

"She is full of surprises," the cambion agreed.

"Still bitter about our last fight?" TJ jeered. "I promise, I'll let you get a hit in this time."

"You won't bait me, TJ," she answered, her voice ethereal and calm. "I'm over what you did to me. First, I'm going to take out your companions. After all, you're the real test, aren't you? They're just dead weight." He chuckled at her comment as the two demons looked at each other worriedly.

Lena appeared on her knees behind them and slammed her palms into the floor. Two arcs of lightning shot up from between the two demons' feet, overtaking their bodies and catapulting them into air. With a cry from each of them, they were thrown from the pit, her lightning fanning out underneath the protective dome-barrier.

TJ spun on his heel as Lena brushed her hands up from the floor and in front of her, electrical waves pouring from her fingers, rushing towards him. With a powerful beat of his wings, he lifted into the air, the waves harmlessly travelling beneath him. Twisting in the air, he rocketed himself towards her, pulling back as she disappeared again.

"Coward!" he roared, spinning in the air.

"I'll admit," she said, reappearing on the other side of the pit, the fires of Hell still coursing over her body. "That was probably a bit cheeky of me. But then, I'm two down in less than ten minutes. Next, I'm going to make sure you can't fly."

"Oh?" TJ sneered at her, raising himself further above the ground, his fire flicking away from his body like black tongues lapping at the air. "And how do you plan to do that?"

Lena tilted her head and smiled, her lightning mixing with the fires. "Like this."

Immediately transporting herself onto TJ's back, she grabbed at the base of his wings, coursing electricity through them, paralysing his muscles. Screaming, TJ plummeted to the floor, clawing for her. Ambrose clenched his jaw in pain, as TJ's claws found their mark, slicing down Lena's arms as she desperately held on. Her tactic to paralyse his wings was a good one, but it put her in a vulnerable position.

As they landed, she rolled to the side, putting a good distance between her and the winged demon, her arms covered in lightning as her powers fought to heal her as quickly as possible. TJ scrambled to his feet, trying to lift his wings, bellowing at her as he realised they were now useless to him.

"Now it's fair," she spat at him. Gathering her lightning in her fists, she ran towards him, ducking easily under his arm as he swung at her, connecting her fists with his ribs. They sparred with each other, their feet moving across the floor in graceful motions. Powers in their fists, they jabbed hoping to connect and hurt the other. Lena had her size as an advantage. Much like with Archie, untransformed she was small enough to dodge the attacks. But TJ had strength. His blows were hard and fast, and when they landed, she would curl away from the pain.

Their anger and hatred for each other had turned the fight into a cage match, hits and kicks swinging through the air trying to land a decent blow. In a flash of red and black, their fists connected, the shockwave emanating from the clash sending both of them back along the floor. Ambrose could feel Lena's rising frustration as she came to stop near the outer wall, resting on one knee. TJ was in much the same position, his wings still lying limply across his back.

"She needs to keep calm," Ambrose said under his breath. "He'll get the advantage if she loses focus."

"What is it between them?" Marcus asked quietly.

"He taught her to fight. But their separation was messy. He put her in the hospital for a week," he explained.

His friend coughed slightly. "Well, this should be foreboding for what might happen if you don't fix things with her."

"Thanks for the reminder," he snarled.

"That's what I'm here for."

Breathing heavily, Lena stared at TJ, lightning now covering her entire body, crackling with sinister ferocity. Without a word between them, they took the opportunity of space to throw their powers at each other. Arcs of lightning crossed with fireballs within the space, hitting the floor and walls as they each dodged out of the way or flamed to a different location. TJ tried to surprise Lena by appearing behind her, but her heightened senses had her disappear before he had fully materialised.

The crowd had begun cheering for their favourites, Lena's name forming the loudest chant within the room. Ambrose saw some demons exchange bets with each other much to his disgust. He looked at Marcus silently, who discreetly held up his hands. "I'm not stupid enough to bet on this. Although, if I was, I would bet on Lena," he said, avoiding Ambrose's gaze.

The exchanges in the pit were intensifying, more and more power being poured into their attacks. The protective dome was constantly reacting, keeping the power contained from hitting the crowd. Bits of rock were flying throughout the pit, spraying down on the two demons within.

Narrowly avoiding a black fireball, Lena lunged to the side, tripping over a large rock fragment, landing on her hands and knees. Her stamina was fading as she struggled to get back to her feet. Ambrose could feel the dull aches that radiated from her sides and shoulders where TJ had managed to hit her during their fist fight. TJ noted and took advantage of her current state, sending two fireballs at her in quick succession. The gasp from the crowd was deafening as Lena was thrown at full force into the side of the pit, sinking to the ground in a curled-up heap.

Ambrose and Marcus launched to their feet, as did many other demons around them. Panicked, Ambrose's gaze sought out Zagan, fear pooling in his belly as he saw the sinister grin on his old sire's face. As the dust settled, hushed whispers echoed through the cavern. Lena's shirt had been burned. The bindings that spanned down her spine, now branching over her hips, were fully exposed for all to see.

CHAPTER THIRTY-FIVE

"Shit," Marcus swore under his breath, his gaze locked on Lena.

Ambrose couldn't tear his eyes away from Zagan, who also stared unapologetically at her, his grin increasing as his eyes travelled along her bindings. Glancing slightly to the side, he saw Cyrus, a pained expression on the boundling's face as he looked at Ambrose shaking his head slowly.

"What do we do?" he asked, his heart racing.

"We can't do anything," Marcus sighed in defeat. "The test is not over."

Back in the pit, TJ stalked over to Lena's body, his wings flinching behind him as he started to regain the use of them. She lay unmoving, her back turned towards him. Slowly, he placed his foot against her hip, rolling her onto her back. Her eyes were closed, a large gash across her forehead, lightning sparking from it, healing her as she lay there.

"Now, this seems familiar," he sneered as he crouched down beside her and hit the back of his hand across her cheek. Lena's head flopped to the other side at the impact, but no further response came from her. "Still pathetic." Grabbing her arm, TJ made to lift her from the floor and throw her over his shoulder.

As soon as his hand touched her skin, his body stilled, rooted to the spot. The crowd fell silent, watching intently as the two demons in the pit seemed frozen in place. Ambrose drew in a sharp breath as Lena opened her eyes. They had turned pure black, endless pools mimicking TJ's that now opened wide with pain and fear.

Slowly, Lena curled her wrist, digging her nails into his skin, lightning arcing from her back and pulsing against the ground as it lifted her to her feet. Her body began to glow red as small sparks of electricity danced across her skin, electricity that now coursed through TJ seizing his every muscle. Lifting her foot, she slammed it down into his knee, forcing it to bend backwards at an unnatural angle. His mouth hung open in a silent scream, as she squeezed his forearm holding him in place, the sound of his knee snapping ringing through the cavern.

"How's this for pathetic?" she said through gritted teeth. Holding up one finger, sparks emanated from its tip. Purposefully, she touched her finger to his opposite bicep. The muscles beneath her finger spasmed uncontrollably, constricting around his bones until they broke, his arm twisting against his side. Sliding her finger down his arm, the muscles contorted his flesh until she reached his hand. "Hit me now, TJ," she said softly as she focused her lightning and exploded his hand from the inside, leaving a bloody stump where it had been.

Retracting her hand from his intact arm, TJ's screams ripped through the cavern as he clawed at the ground, pulling himself away from her, his damaged arm dragging beside him.

Some demons cheered as it appeared the test was over. TJ was beaten. Even if he had the ability to heal himself, it would not be before Lena could throw him from the pit. But Ambrose knew she wasn't done. He could feel her desire to hurt TJ overwhelming his own rationality.

"She's going to destroy him," he said, his breathing turning rapid and shallow as her state overtook him.

"No rules," Marcus said. "She's free to kill him if she wants."

A demon behind Ambrose leant forward to whisper to him. "You hit the jackpot in boundlings, mate."

His jaw clenched as he considered turning and punching the demon. Taking a deep breath, he forced himself to remain still, focusing on Lena.

Stalking her prey, Lena closed the distance between her and TJ, placing her foot on the part of his back between his wings, preventing his escape from her. Leaning down, she grabbed the base of his wings and pulled. With her foot anchoring him, TJ screamed as she ripped his wings from his back, throwing them unceremoniously to the sides of the pits. Audible gasps of shock and awe echoed through the crowd at her show of brute strength. Ambrose swallowed hard, fear of his boundling washing over him, realising he was genuinely screwed if he didn't fix things with her. Raising her head to the ceiling, Lena looked around the crowd before her gaze rested on Zagan.

"What is she doing?" Marcus whispered.

"No idea," Ambrose said warily. "But she's angry."

Holding her hands up beside her, palms upwards, lightning danced across her body, vertical arcs springing up to clash with the protective dome. The crowd silenced, some leaning back from the blasts with disconcerted murmurings. Zagan however, leant forward, his face rapt with excited interest. Lena's lightning overtook her in a single arc focusing on the centre of the barrier above her, TJ lying forgotten as he stared at her, terror on his face. The murmurings grew louder as the protective barrier flickered, fighting to contain her power. With a singular cry, Lena blasted her power out, filling the pit completely, ripping TJ's body apart as it spread. A loud crack echoed through the cavern as the barrier failed, a shockwave pushing out knocking all those in close proximity to the ground.

"Ambrose!" Archie shouted, catching himself with his wings even as the blast sent him sliding along the ground. "Stop her!"

Scrambling to his feet, Ambrose ran to the side of the pit. The widespread lightning had dissipated, but the solitary arc still coursed towards the ceiling. Winged demons that had clung to the walls, dropped from their perch, fleeing the raw power.

"Lena!" he yelled, hoping to all that is and was, that she could hear him. "Stop!" he commanded

The lightning cracked, the arc faltering, as Lena screamed within it, her bindings glowing, constricting around her body. Her head flung back as she fell to her knees, a ripple of power exploding from her as she hit the floor, cracking the ground and sending rubble into the air.

Taking to the air, Archie rushed towards her, even as Ambrose jumped down into the pit. The trainer reached her first, wrapping his arms around her as she slumped forward.

"Lena!" Ambrose cried running towards them. Something was wrong. He could feel it. The look on Archie's face hit him squarely in the chest as he raced towards them. He halted in his tracks as Archie pulled his wings around him and Lena and flamed out of the pit with her. "Lena!" he screamed, falling to his knees as Marcus landed beside him.

They were gone.

"Come on," Marcus cried, grabbing him under the arms trying to pull him to his feet. "We need to leave, now!" Gathering the flames around them, Marcus took them back to the manor. Ambrose pushed him away, falling to the office floor. "Ambrose?"

"Shut up!" he shouted, shutting his eyes and trying to focus on Lena, trying to find her.

"Ambrose, stop!" Marcus pushed against his shoulder. "Archie is not going to hurt her or take her."

"Are you blind?" he cried, getting to his feet. "He has taken her!" Panic racked his body and mind. All he knew was he had to find her. Nothing else mattered.

"What exactly do you think you're going to do, huh? She obliterated her ex and destroyed in a matter of seconds a barrier that would take us days to break through. She's pissed at you. Can you even imagine what she would do to you right now?"

Flames appeared beside them as the demonic trainer stepped through, a solemn look on his face.

"You bastard!" Ambrose shouted, lunging forward and grabbing Archie by the neck. "Where is she?"

The demon easily removed his hands, punching him in the chest and forcing him back towards Marcus. "She's fine," he said calmly, raising his wings behind him. "She's safe, for now."

"What the hell are you doing?" Marcus asked, placing a hand on Ambrose's chest, keeping him back.

"Lena asked me to do this," Archie replied.

Ambrose clenched his jaw. "Bullshit!"

"Believe it or don't. Doesn't matter. I'm only here to tell you, not to look for her. She doesn't want to see you right now."

"She's my boundling," he said through gritted teeth. "You can't keep her from me."

"Yes, I can," Archie sighed. "I'm sorry, Ambrose. The test served its purpose. TJ was sent to push her mind as well as her body. Her transformation is just below the surface, fighting to get out, but she is keeping it locked away which is incredible in and of itself. Lena's power commands a level of respect that even I will not fight against. She's asked me to keep you away, but to let you know that she's fine. She just needs time to calm down."

"You know there are those that will try to take her. I need to be with her, to keep her safe."

"Those wishing to take her are far more powerful than you. They won't find her with me, I promise you that," Archie said earnestly. "I know this is hard to accept, Ambrose, but you must. Your council doubted your ability to train her, but now they doubt your ability to protect her. Do not make the mistake of proving them right."

Ambrose swallowed his rage, clenching his fists but making no further comment.

"When she is ready to return to you, I will bring her back," Archie said, disappearing in flames.

Everything had gone so wrong, so quickly and all he could do was watch. Feeling utterly lost and empty, he walked over to one of his armchairs, falling into it as his body reverted to human form. Marcus followed suit, resting on his elbows to look at him. Nothing was said, as they both sunk into their own thoughts.

Lena spent a few days staying with Archie, either hiding in his chambers, or hopping around creation seeking solitude, considering what her next move should be. Other than him, her only real company had been Zamira, who had become incredibly protective of her. She'd managed to convince Archie to let her take Zamira for a walk through the corridors of Hell, giving the hellhound a break from her pups. Although she sought to avoid anyone else at the time, she noted that the few demons she did come across, would stare at her quietly, or scurry away, the scents of their fear and awe mixing with the undertones of sulphur. Archie had tried to convince her to go back to Ambrose, but anytime she tried, she would chicken out, fearing his reaction might be the same. She had scared everyone with her power, and whilst that had its benefits in some respects, she hated feeling like something was wrong with her.

She needed to speak with someone who didn't look at her like a monster. Who didn't know she was a demon or of the powers she possessed. Someone, she hoped, who could help her sort through her fight with Ambrose. After arguing yet again with Archie about her safety, she had simply left him, going top-side and back to town. Flaming into her old apartment again, she showered, scrubbing the smells of Hell from her body, before making her way to Cafe Marie.

"Lena!" Marie ran up to her, throwing her arms around Lena's shoulders. Lena gratefully accepted the embrace. "Oh, it's so lovely to see you again, my dear. The usual?"

She shook her head slightly. "No, not today. I was hoping I could talk to you."

The older woman's face lit up at the suggestion. "Of course! Come, come, sit."

Marie gently guided her to a table by the window. "Oh, Marie, please don't. It's awkward enough getting pastries in the morning from you," she said despite Marie practically pushing her into the chair.

"Don't be silly," the matron said, waving her hand dismissively. "You sit, I'll be right back." The woman hurried off behind the counter, leaning into the display to grab a couple of pastries. She had whispered to Sarah who started on some coffees.

Moments later, Lena was staring gratefully at the apricot and mango tart and latte placed in front of her. Marie took the seat opposite and sipped on her own black coffee.

"What did you want to talk about, Lena?" Marie said with a warm smile.

"It's difficult to know where to start," she said, overcome with sadness. She dropped her gaze and stared into her coffee.

"I'm assuming this has to do with Mr. Sumner," Marie asked.

"Huh? Oh, right, Ambrose... yes," Lena stammered. She so rarely heard Ambrose's surname she often forgot it.

"Has something happened?"

"Kind of. Nothing terrible, I guess. I just..." she sighed heavily before taking a sip of her latte. "We had a fight a few days ago. I found out that he knew my father. That he knew something about my past, that I didn't know, and he didn't tell me."

Marie tilted her head as she stared at Lena for a moment. "He knew your father. How old is Mr. Sumner exactly?"

Shit.

"Ah, he's a few years older than me. I say he knew my father, it was more like his father knew my father, but Ambrose knew him in passing," Lena said quickly, holding her breath.

"I see," the older woman said with a knowing smile. "You've told me bits about your past before you came here. Does it matter that Mr. Sumner knows something about it?"

"This matters. I don't remember much about my father. I needed to know this."

"I'm assuming you won't tell me what it is."

Lena shook her head sadly, her bindings constricting beneath her shirt. "I'm sorry. It's not something I can tell anyone."

"Fair enough," Marie said softly. "So, is it something that he intentionally kept from you?"

"I'm not sure. He says he didn't," she said, using her fork to push a piece of the tart around on the plate.

"Did he know you were your father's daughter?"

"I don't know. From his reaction, I'd say no. He looked horrified when I told him I knew, but that could have just been because he was caught out."

"Assuming he didn't know who you were, do you think he would have kept this from you if he had known?"

"I don't know," she sighed, starting to feel like a broken record.

"You've been together for what, two months?" Marie asked, pausing only long enough for Lena to nod her head. "Do you think if he knew, he would have told you eventually or kept it from you indefinitely?"

"I don't know!" she exclaimed, throwing her hands in the air. "I just don't know, and that is annoying me more than anything!"

"You don't know a lot of anything about this situation, do you?" the matron teased.

Lena scrunched her nose at her in defiance of the statement, but she was right. Marie reached over the table and took hold of her hand, giving it a comforting squeeze.

"Well," the older woman said with a smile, "I'll tell you something I know. Ambrose loves you."

She stared at her old boss in surprise before she laughed nervously. "No, he doesn't. As you said, we've only been together two months."

Marie shook her head slowly. "Oh, Lena. He loves you. He may not have said so and you may not have noticed, but he does. You never saw the way he would watch you when you were working. Or the way he looked at you that day you hid in the kitchen. You didn't see how he looked back at you the day he finally asked you out for dinner." Lena sat speechless, her eyes locked on her old matron as she continued. "You remember when those out-of-town boys that harassed you and Sarah non-stop came through a few months ago?" Lena nodded. "You didn't see how, after I made you two hide in the kitchen and bought Michael out front, Ambrose told them to leave. But he told them to leave you alone. Not Sarah. It was implied, but he was focused on you. He loves you, Lena. I have no doubt in that."

She was silent. Marie noticed so much that she had been completely oblivious to.

"I also know this," the older woman continued, "that regardless of what you may say, you love him. I see how happy you are around him. The chemistry between the two of you. It is like you were made for each other, something that most people don't get to experience in their lifetimes. And getting angry at him for not telling you something, something that he may or may not have known related to you, and that he may or may not have chosen to disclose to you once he did know, without giving him the chance to explain, is throwing away one of the best things to happen to you."

Tears had formed in Lena's eyes, threatening to overflow. A couple escaped as Marie finished and she brushed them away hurriedly with the back of her hand.

"He accused me of wanting to be with someone else."

"Ah well, that is another matter," Marie said leaning forward. "But something that can be easily solved with a proper conversation, especially if that conversation ends with an 'I love you'. Finish your coffee and cake," she said, getting to her feet and placing a motherly hand on Lena's shoulder. "Think about what I said. Then go and talk to him."

She nodded silently as her old matron walked away. She stared out the window looking at the square and the fountain she was so fond of, reminiscing on the feeling of that morning when Ambrose asked her out for dinner. Visualising the blanket of snow that had covered the square. Marie was right. Lena knew she was right, despite her having tried to deny it for so long.

She loved Ambrose.

And, if she truly loved him, then it shouldn't matter what brought them together. He made her happy, he made her feel wanted, he made her feel safe. And if he truly loved her as well, as Marie suspected, then surely, they could work all of this out. The overwhelming need to speak with him took over her, as she shovelled the last of the tart into her mouth and got to her feet. She pulled some money out of her pocket and almost threw it down on the table.

"Lena! Don't you dare pay," Marie called out as Lena raced over to her.

She wrapped her arms around the older woman who had become

like a mother to her in a tight hug and kissed her on the cheek in thanks. "Too late," she laughed before turning on her heel and practically running out the door. "Thank you!" she cried over her shoulder with a wave.

Once outside, she broke into a full run racing towards the manor. She pulled her key from her pocket and nearly dropped it in her excitement as she fumbled with the lock.

"Ambrose!" she called out once she was in the hall, slamming the front door behind her. She wasn't expecting an answer straight away. She wasn't even sure if he would be home, and if he was, where he would be. "Ambrose?" she repeated as she ducked her head within the library before turning and heading up the stairs to his office. He wasn't there either, nor was he in any of the bedrooms or her altar room. Almost in desperation, she even checked the kitchen. "Well, that's annoying," she sighed, placing her hands on her hips.

Lena closed her eyes and took a deep breath. The mental binding between her and Ambrose had diminished significantly due to the turmoil over the last few days, but she hoped she might be able to feel his general location. Unfortunately, she felt nothing in that moment, but instead felt the pull of a cursed object. She exhaled sharply letting her head drop back in exasperation, before finally admitting defeat and heading back to the library to collect her conduit which Marcus had brought back for her the morning of her test.

Retrieving the chest, she decided to set up in the library rather than move to her altar room so she could hear if Ambrose came back through the front door. She wouldn't hear anything from the altar room, not that she would hear if he flamed in upstairs from the library. But she decided she would simply wait until he did come home. It was preferable to her flaming all over creation looking for him.

She pulled out her crystallised book along with the pendant. Hopefully, now she'd cleared it of the information James had, she could find the resting place it needed rather than just creating something new. Pulling her legs under her, she looked into the book and slowly traced her fingers over the surface, beginning her process.

Engrossed in her work, she didn't hear the door to the library open.

"Hello, beautiful."

CHAPTER THIRTY-SIX

Three days.

She had been gone three days and he was going out of his mind, insane with worry. Marcus had desperately been trying to keep him focused on work, but he felt like he couldn't even read the figures on the pages in front of him. Lena had been spied in one of the corridors of Hell with Zamira, but Marcus had forced him to stay in the manor, going to look for her himself instead. Whisperings had spread like wildfire through the ranks and Ambrose had somehow become most wanted.

Hordes of demons wanted Lena now. They wanted her favour or to somehow persuade her to bind to them over him. But all were too afraid to approach her directly. Ambrose now proved to be the perfect bargaining chip, his reaction to her disappearance fuelling rumours that they were more than just boundling and sire. Getting to him meant being able to control her. It was too much of a risk for him to go to Hell now.

He needed to see her. To explain everything. He wanted to tell her about the deal and what had happened. How those terms about her life had come about. He wanted to tell her; he loved her.

"Fuck!" he shouted into the room, throwing his power into the fireplace, cracks appearing in the stone base, as he fell to his knees and clutched at his temples. "Lena..."

How had it all gone so wrong? What did he miss? Were there any signs that he should have seen? He knew that listening to Zagan had been a catalyst and he wanted to rip his own heart out for ever entertaining his venomous words. But had there been something else? Why had she run to Archie for help? To get away from him?

Sitting back on his knees, he raised his head to look at the ceiling, feeling the pull of a summoning wash over him. Closing his eyes and groaning with self-loathing, he couldn't fight the call as he pushed to his feet.

"Ambrose!"

His eyes widened even as the flames overtook his body. Lena? Was she back? He scrambled to his feet, a small seed of hope at her return mixed with despair as he was unable to stop the summoning. With a defeated sigh, he transformed as he was transported to an abandoned church. At least, knowing she was back at the manor, he would have a chance to speak with her once he managed to return. Looking around the room, his stomach dropped as his gaze came to rest on two familiar faces.

Cyrus stood in demonic form towards the far corner, his eyes turned to the floor, his bindings glowing. Closer towards Ambrose, a young girl lay on the floor as the man who killed her stood over her now lifeless body, summoning symbols painted on the floor around her.

"James..." he said under his breath, looking at the middle-age man. "What are you doing?" he asked, glancing between the two men.

"Well, I'm here to do to you, what you did to my sons," James said with a cruel smile on his lips. "He," he said pointing to Cyrus behind him, "is here to make sure you don't leave before I do."

"Cyrus?" he queried, staring at him.

"I'm sorry, Ambrose," the boundling said softly, still staring at the floor. "I don't have a choice." His bindings glowed brighter momentarily, lending truth to his words.

Turning back to James, he tilted his head to the side. "What makes you think you could kill me?" As he spoke, he radiated his power up his arms, the red tendrils wrapping around his wrists like snakes.

James simply smiled as his body started to convulse and deform, his clothes ripping as the muscles beneath his skin bulged and shifted. The sound of his bones cracking echoed through the church as his limbs elongated, reshaping his form into something grotesque and monstrous. A guttural growl escaped his throat as his hands turned into fearsome claws, capable of rending flesh with ease. Sharp fangs protruded from his mouth which resembled more of a red slit across his stretched face. Amber eyes burned with an insatiable hunger.

"James," Ambrose whispered, "what have you done?" He failed to comprehend what would have driven James to accept this fate. He had become a monster of Hell, a lesser thing, bound to serve and obey whichever demon turned him. An attack dog. Not something he would have ever expected someone like James to agree to. What lies must Zagan have told him to incite this drastic action?

A feral roar erupted from James' throat, resonating through the church walls, shaking the ground beneath him, as he lunged forward, arms outstretched, aimed directly for Ambrose.

Anticipating the movement, he rolled to the side, deftly landing on his feet with incredible agility. He may not have power like Zagan or Lena, but he had survived many a round within the pits and learnt how to read his opponents. James turned on his foot which now resembled that of a wolf, long talons spiking from his toes, unleashing a barrage of punches and swipes at him. Easily evading each strike with a blend of agility and precision, he stepped back between the rotten pews, ducking and throwing small spikes of his power up into the contorted flesh over James' ribs and stomach.

The spell the mortal was under provided a certain amount of invulnerability to his current form, causing Ambrose's attacks to merely bounce off his skin without damage. Realising he would need to get closer for a physical attack, Ambrose flamed to the other side of the church, giving himself some distance to assess his situation.

Glancing towards Cyrus, he noted the boundling's fists were clenched as he struggled with whatever command Zagan had given him. Something was very wrong. As their eyes met, Ambrose saw deep regret and sorrow within them, the demon's jaw pulsing with invisible effort. What was going on?

"Cyrus!" he shouted, flaming to another corner as James neared his position. "If I die, so does Lena. She is still bound to me."

The bindings glowed and constricted around Cyrus' arms as he opened his mouth trying to speak. His mouth clamping shut as he flinched against the pain, his eyes still locked with Ambrose's. Evidently, he has been told not to get involved. At least, not yet.

Looking back at James and fuelled by anger, Ambrose tried to find a weakness in his movements as the monster bounded towards him. Sidestepping the current assault, he seized the beast's arm, twisting it as he turned his body, flowing his power over the pale skin to tighten his grasp until an audible crack echoed through the church. The monster's cry of pain filled the air as he collapsed to the ground, momentarily incapacitated.

Recognising the opportune moment, he flowed power through his leg as he swung it up through the air and brought it crashing down on the back of James' head, slamming him into the ground. Flaming a reasonable distance away, Ambrose stood quietly, watching as the monster's body convulsed, the spell over him healing the damage. Killing this kind of creature was not an easy task, something that required preparation and planning, neither of which Ambrose had. But the spell only worked for a limited time. His only chance was to outlast it.

As James staggered to his feet, his arm repairing under crackles of black lightning, Ambrose's eyes widened with horror. Pain ripped through his chest, causing him to cry out and fall to his knees.

Lena!

She was hurt. She was hurting. Something or someone was hurting her. His vision faded in and out as he struggled to regain his breath, gasping and staggering back, trying to get to his feet as James closed in on him. Panic rising in his throat, he was unable to avoid the attack as the hell beast struck him squarely in the chest, sending him hurtling backwards into the wall.

Watching as the monster now stalked towards him, Ambrose's body was frozen as both his and Lena's pain mixed within him. A wicked grin spread on James' features as he lifted his clawed hand, a quiet aura of confidence emanating from him.

Not like this, not now, he begged silently. He had to get to Lena. He had to help her. He couldn't die here.

Sucking in a deep breath, Ambrose bellowed at James, releasing a shockwave of power from his body, using his and Lena's pain to push it out with incredible force. The power would do nothing to the beast, but it would give him space with which to find his next move.

But it didn't matter. The church went quiet except for the choked gurgles coming from the monster's throat, a large hole punched through its chest.

Lena startled and turned her head to stare at the man in the doorway.

"Zagan?" she said slowly. "What are you doing here?"

"I came to see you," he said walking towards her.

"Ambrose isn't here," she said. She cursed herself internally for admitting she was alone. Her confidence in her powers had grown significantly over the last few days, but something about Zagan truly scared her. To the point where she had trouble maintaining a straight thought around him.

"Oh, I know," he continued to get closer.

Her anxiety skyrocketed at his nonchalant statement. Standing up from the table, Lena quickly wrapped up her book and placed it in the chest, sealing it shut along with the pendant. "So, you shouldn't be here," she turned on her heel to walk further into the library, carrying her chest as a visual excuse for why she was retreating from him.

"I don't think Ambrose will mind." Something in his voice made her blood run cold. She put down her chest on a nearby table and turned to look at him. He was closer than she thought, stopped only two or three strides from her.

"What does that mean?" she asked hesitantly.

"It means, he won't be coming back from the summoning. I set up a little surprise for him," he said. "James is waiting for him."

Lena's stomach dropped and her vision darkened. "So what? James is human," she said, trying to hide her fear.

Without warning, Zagan flung out his arm and grabbed her by the throat. She didn't even have time to scream as she clutched at his wrist. Her eyes widened with fear as he pulled her towards him, his other hand roughly pulling her hair back so she was forced to look up at him. "Not anymore," he said coldly, malice in his eyes. "He was so desperate to make Ambrose pay for killing his sons. He has enough power to deal with your precious sire now."

"Ha! If James kills Ambrose, I die too. You still lose Zagan," she spat, pulling on what little bravado she could muster.

He shook his head slowly. "Cyrus is there to make sure that doesn't happen. At least, not until after you belong to me."

"No..." She could barely get enough air to make any sound as his fingers tightened around her throat.

The sneer that grew on his face was something of pure evil and despite her time within Hell, she was terrified by it. "Now, beautiful, you will be mine." He started to gather flames around them and in a moment of sheer panic, she slammed her palms onto his face and sent a wave of lightning from her arms into him.

The flames instantly disappeared as he cried out and let go of her, clutching at his face. Unfortunately, she hadn't been able to sleep since she left with Marcus over a week ago. She was exhausted from her test and her attempts to reconnect with the power she had unlocked during it since. Adding the constant flood of anxiety she had been living with recently, she knew she wouldn't be able to fight for long, but she would rather die than go quietly.

Lena darted past him heading for the door. She tried to gather her own flames to get back to Archie, but Zagan slammed his body into her. Crashing into one of the pillars with a sickening thud, pain washed over her body as she tried to get her feet back underneath her. Letting instinct take over, she flung her arm behind her, red lightning springing from her fingers aimed for Zagan's chest. He dived out of the way at the last moment and the lightning ripped apart a bookshelf instead. Flaming bits of paper flew everywhere, as she took the opportunity to run out of the library. Slamming the doors behind her, she used her power to melt the handles sealing him inside. It wouldn't hold him for long, but it might buy her a brief moment to gain some distance from him. She turned on her heel and raced to the stairs.

She thought of trying to get to Ambrose, but she had no idea where he had been summoned to. Unsure if Archie or Marcus would even be at their places, her mind raced trying to think of where she could go. With Zagan so close and assuming he was prepared for the possibility of her just leaving, he might be able to track wherever she flamed to. She felt utterly alone, hesitant to stay and fight but equally terrified to leave, potentially putting anyone else in harm's way.

Suddenly, her vision blurred and her knees collapsed beneath her as images of her sacrifice flooded her mind. She cried out with pure panic burying her face in her hands trying to push away the memories. She thought she was over them, so why did they plague her now? Why now, when she needed her mind clear, more than ever...

She heard the library doors open with a deafening crack as the metal split. She was fairly sure one door fell off its hinges completely. Looking over her shoulder she saw Zagan stalking towards her, the expression on his face darkened with anger. She desperately tried to get to her feet reaching for the railing.

“Zamira!” she shouted as she fell on the stairs.

There was a wave of heat as her hellhound appeared at the top of the stairs. The influx of power Lena had grasped during her test had fed Zamira’s size and strength, her now leviathan-like form lowering onto her haunches, growling at Zagan who had paused to assess his position. Zamira launched herself over Lena’s head and collided with the cambion forcing him back towards the library doors.

Gathering her flames, she transported near to the top of the stairs. It was as far as she could manage for the moment. If she could just get to Ambrose’s office, she could at least try to force him back to the house. Depending on the summoning, it might not work, but she had to try. She heard the cambion cry out as Zamira bit into his arm. After a final glance towards them, seeing that Zagan was transforming, Lena pushed herself to her feet and ran down the hallway as fast as she could. There was a loud thud behind her and she knew either demon or beast had been thrown aside. Everything in her hoped it was the former. She didn’t have time to find out as she ripped open the door to Ambrose’s office.

Falling over her own feet, she lunged for the desk trying to grab the summoning crystal that Ambrose had made a few weeks ago, cursing that she had left it behind when she left with Marcus. He had tied it to his power, creating a link that would activate upon smashing it, hopefully calling him home if she needed him. Just before she could reach it, she felt flames behind her and a hand grabbed her by the back of her neck, throwing her against the wall, knocking over a pedestal and smashing the vase on it. She slumped to the floor as the winged demon stood over her. Her head was spinning and her body felt numb as he picked her up like a rag doll and flung her over his shoulder.

“Fighting only excites me beautiful,” Zagan said cruelly. “Your hellhound is no match for a demon like me, you know. It’s time to come with me.”

Flames encompassed them and the world went dark. She knew they were in Hell as the smell of ash and sulphur pervaded her senses. He dropped her unceremoniously on a stone slab. She cried out at the jolt of pain that rocked through her spine.

“Now,” he sneered as he flipped her onto her stomach, “let’s do something about those bindings, shall we?” He ripped open her shirt to expose her back. The markings had completely overtaken her back, with small offshoots now snaking towards her chest. Towards the hollow of her back they splayed out like fingers across her waist and hips converging over her abdomen. "They've grown even more. You really are an enigma aren't you, beautiful?"

He placed one hand on the nape of her neck and the other on her lower back. Her skin crawled under his touch, desperately wanting to recoil from him. She tried to roll away but the strength in his arms held her firmly against the stone.

"It's time for you to submit to your fate, Lena. You will be mine and I will shape you into the weapon I know you can be. We will be a force to be reckoned with. Lucifer himself will fear us." His voice invaded her ears ruining any and all efforts of hers to try and dispel her fear and calm her mind. Images of her sacrifice still plagued her thoughts and she knew she would be lost to them if she couldn't overcome the helplessness, they made her feel. She tried to breathe but her racing heart forced the last of her air to leave her lungs.

Pain ripped through her spine as she felt Zagan's power pour over her. He was trying to remove her bindings to Ambrose and replace them with his own, like he had in the Repository. Sucking in a sharp breath, Lena screamed against the pain, tears pooling on the stone beneath her. Her fists beat on the cold stone trying to force her body up despite his grip on her.

Use this...

It was like the voice made a map within her body pulling Lena's awareness to something inside her. It was the last remnants of the cursed emotions of pain and anger she had been tracking, swirling deep within her gut. Emotion that she hadn't finished binding because of Zagan's interruption.

She knew this would be her last chance to save herself. This would likely sap her of all remaining energy so she couldn't waste it. Squeezing her eyes shut as tightly as possible, she drew the pain from Zagan's work deeper into her body. She mixed it with the cursed emotion and her own power. Letting out a deep breath, she pushed the pain, emotion and power out like an explosion, channelling it up towards Zagan's hands. Red lightning flashed from her body, illuminating the cavern and hitting him squarely in the chest, sending him flying into the ceiling. He crashed into a stalactite causing it to plummet to the floor with a loud crack that echoed off the walls. He landed on top of the splintered rock, unmoving.

As the pain subsided, Lena rolled off the stone slab and fell onto the floor with a thud. She tried to pull her feet under her but her limbs wouldn't respond. Her vision blurred until slowly everything went dark.

CHAPTER THIRTY-SEVEN

Shock was prevalent on the monster's contorted face as Ambrose stared in horror. Cyrus' hand protruded from its chest, holding a still beating heart between his fingers. As the heart stilled, James' body reverted from its monstrous transformation, hanging limply around the boundling's arm.

"What–?" he asked, his mind desperately trying to figure out what was going on despite the pain that now ripped through him.

"James served his purpose," Cyrus said, tossing the man's body to the side and discarding the binding stone that had allowed him to end the spell prematurely. "Zagan doesn't want you dead. I was told to make sure you stayed here long enough for him to get to Lena and to prevent James from killing you, not that James knew that," he sighed, shaking the blood of his arm. "By the look on your face, Zagan's succeeded in overcoming her bindings, or is close to it. I'm sorry, Ambrose."

"Fuck you!" he ground out through gritted teeth as he clutched at his chest, trying to breathe through the pain coursing through him.

"I know you won't believe me, but I am sorry," the boundling said walking away from him. "I've tried to talk him out of this. I can't stand the idea of Lena being bound to him. You of all people know what he is like."

He tried to get to his feet, but barely made it two steps before falling back to his knees. "I should rip your throat out," he spat as he watched Cyrus begin to gather flames around him.

"Kill me and you'll never see her again," Cyrus sighed, turning to face him, flames licking over his feet. "Zagan likes games as you know, so he's giving you a chance to stop him. They are in a ritual cavern near the racing pits, hidden in the walls behind the holding den. With no races on, it's unlikely anyone would interfere." Taking a deep breath, he gave Ambrose a pitying look. "For what it's worth, I hope you can get to her before he claims her completely. Good luck."

With that, Cyrus disappeared.

"Dammit!" Ambrose shouted as he flamed back to his office. The damage was immediately noticeable, broken shards of porcelain scattered across the floor. Some drops of Lena's blood were on the wall near the door, her scent filling the air, mixed with Zagan's. Looking to his desk, he saw the summoning crystal, knocked over, but intact. She had been trying to reach it.

"Ambrose!"

His head snapping to the door, he pushed himself forward, ripping it open and stumbling through.

"Marcus!" he shouted as he saw his friend reach the top of the stairs. "She's gone! Zagan has her!"

Marcus caught him, lifting him to his feet as her pain continued to pulse through him. Groaning with effort, Ambrose clung onto his friend, finally turning his head to look down the stairs. The door to his library lay splintered across the floor mixing with small traces of blood.

"Zamira?" he whispered as he saw the hellhound slumped against the wall. She lifted her head at her name, whimpering as she did so. Flaming to her side, he ran his hand over her neck, Marcus rushing over to them. "Oh Zamira..." he sighed, finding the wound in her side. It should have been healing, channelling Lena's power. But nothing was happening.

"If she can't heal, Lena must be unconscious or..." Marcus trailed off, unable to bring himself to finish the sentence.

"She's not dead," Ambrose snapped. The pain in him was easing, but he knew she was alive. And for now, she was still bound to him. Zamira yelped under his touch as he traced his fingers over her wound, running his power through them to heal her as much as he could. "Shh, girl. It's okay. We'll find your mistress, don't worry," he said even as he doubted the words himself. "Go to your den, be with your pups."

Flames taking over her, Zamira disappeared, leaving him and Marcus kneeling in the hall.

"We need to go now. Cyrus told me where they are," Ambrose said, pushing to his feet.

"Probably should have taken Zamira with us," Marcus sighed, rising next to him.

"She's not fully healed. She needs Lena for that."

They travelled to a junction cavern near the racing pits. Before they had fully materialised, Ambrose transported them straight to the holding den.

"Cyrus said there is a ritual cavern hidden in the walls here," he said, running his hand over the cavern wall.

"Ambrose, we need help. Together we may stand a chance against Zagan, but if he claims Lena... we're screwed," Marcus said chewing the inside of his cheek. "She'll wipe us out."

"We don't have time," he sighed, closing his eyes trying to concentrate on Lena. The last thing he needed to do was flame into solid rock. Where was she?

With a sudden gasp, pain ripped through him again, his fists slamming into the wall as he tried to keep focus. The pain was not as intense as before. She was fading. He was losing her.

"Ambrose! What is it?" Marcus cried, grabbing his friend by the shoulders, holding him up.

"I can feel her pain," he managed through gritted teeth. "Zagan almost has her."

Clasping Ambrose's face between his hands, Marcus stared into his eyes. "Focus, Ambrose, where is she?"

Pulling the pain into him, he fought to hold on, reaching out through what remained of the bond to find her. "There!" he cried, flaming him and Marcus behind the wall.

"No!" Lena's scream ripped through the cavern as he and Marcus appeared. She was lying atop a carved-out altar, Zagan standing above her, pinning her into the stone, his black lightning coursing over her body.

"Lena!" Ambrose yelled, immediately throwing a wave of power towards Zagan in time with Marcus. Red strands and black smoke collided with the cambion's chest, forcing him away from the table. He caught himself in the air, his wings spread out as he landed on his feet only a few strides from the altar.

"Zagan, what have you done?" Marcus whispered, his gaze locked on Lena's body. Ambrose too, looked towards her, his chest tightening with grief as he realised, he could no longer feel anything from her.

Lena lay motionless atop the altar, her shirt torn at the back, revealing the results of Zagan's work. Her bindings, still stark black against her creamy white skin, now spiralled around her body in an angular pattern, wrapping around her arms, shoulders, back and waist. Even her neck sported the pattern like a black collar, binding her to her new sire.

"Nice of you to join us," Zagan sneered, rising to his feet, a triumphant look on his face. "She's mine now," he said, smiling cruelly at Ambrose.

"I'll kill you!" he shouted, making to lunge at him. Marcus caught him, holding him back. Shocked at his friend's actions, he struggled to free himself. He had to get to Lena.

Zagan chuckled at the display. "At least Marcus has some sense. You won't touch me, Ambrose," he said walking towards the altar. "Kill me, you kill her." With a grin, he ran his hand along Lena's spine, causing her to startle and flinch away from him, rolling off the altar and landing on her side with a cry. Opening her eyes, she looked at Ambrose, horrified realisation of what had happened washing over her beautiful face.

"You fucking bastard!" Ambrose spat at his old sire, desperately clinging onto Marcus' wrist, trying to hold onto some semblance of rational thought.

"Lena, come here," Zagan commanded, stepping to the side of the altar looking down at her on the floor.

Her bindings glowed brightly as she struggled to fight against his will. "Ah!" she cried as her body forced her onto her feet, turned and walked over to him.

"It's less painful if you don't fight," he smiled at her, placing a finger under her chin to lift her gaze to his.

"Screw you!" she ground out through gritted teeth.

Zagan leant closer to her, his smile widening. "Oh, trust me, you will."

"Dammit, Zagan!" Ambrose cried, shrugging Marcus' hold off him. "Don't you dare touch her!"

"Pipe down, Ambrose," Zagan snapped, turning his head towards him. "She doesn't belong to you anymore. Lena, why don't you show Ambrose who you belong to now. Kiss me," he compelled her.

Knowing she had no choice but to obey, Ambrose's heart broke for her as her bindings glowed forcing Lena to raise onto her toes and press a kiss to Zagan's lips. Her eyes were tightly shut, pain etched into her features, her hands balled into fists against his chest, trying to push away, yet unable to act on such desires. A pained groan pulled from her as her bindings faded to black, her knees buckling beneath her. She landed with a sickening thud against the ground, hunched forward, panting from exertion.

"So accommodating, beautiful," Zagan said, tangling his hand through her hair, yanking her head up sharply to look at him. "Tell me, Ambrose, did she kneel for you?"

"You're a fucking pig," he growled. He felt sick, watching the woman he loved, forced to kiss the demon he despised more than anything.

"And you're pathetic," the cambion snapped at him. "Bound to me for almost a century and look how weak you turned out. You are such an embarrassment."

Anger boiled within him, as he took a step towards the cambion. "Is that why you're doing this? Because I embarrass you?"

Smiling cruelly, Zagan turned his head back to Lena. "Stand up." Grunting with the effort, she got to her feet and craned her neck to look at him. "Tell me, has Ambrose told you about Margaret?"

"He has," she answered coldly, her body shaking with quiet rage.

"Has he told you how she died? I don't want a yes or no. Tell me what he told you."

"She killed herself by jumping into the Infernal Pit."

"She didn't jump," he whispered to her, his voice sinisterly calm. "Ambrose pushed her in."

"That's a lie, Zagan!" Ambrose shouted, his power whipping out from his hands, twisting aimlessly through the air. "And you know it!"

Zagan rounded on him, his expression thunderous. "It's not a lie!" he shouted, matching Ambrose's volume. "Margaret was a powerful demon. My crowning glory. She would never have thrown it all away," he said, emphasising his point with a wave of his hand. "You just couldn't stand the fact that she wanted me more than you."

"You're delusional," he spat at his old sire. "You compelled her to want you! She couldn't stand you!"

"Now," the cambion sneered, raising a finger to point at him, "that is a lie. You took her from me, so now, I'll take what you hold most dear." He turned back to Lena and took hold of her jaw between his fingers.

"I don't believe you," she said firmly, raising her chin from his hand.

"I don't care what you believe," Zagan said through gritted teeth, closing the distance between his face and hers. "He's not the wonderful demon you seem to think he is. What would you think if you found out he made a deal with your father? A deal that is the sole reason you ended up in Hell. What would you think of your precious Ambrose then?"

Ambrose clenched his fists in anger, the heavy pit of guilt in his stomach returning, threatening to drown him. He knew she had come home just before he was summoned away, but they hadn't had a chance to talk. He hadn't had a chance to make her understand. "Shut up, Zagan!" he yelled.

Lena stared silently at Zagan, her gaze softening to one of apathetic exhaustion. "I already know," she said softly, "and I don't care. My father was an idiot."

Chuckling cruelly, Zagan straightened and folded his arms in front of him. "This should be interesting," he sighed, raising his hand for her to continue. "Please, elaborate."

"My father thought he knew better than everyone, even his own family. He knew the terms of the deal and he still agreed. He was so caught up in his own needs, he happily threw his own child to the fucking wolves." Ambrose could almost see the malice that dripped from her voice as she spoke about her father. "He made his choice." Lena took a deep steadying breath before continuing, her eyes locked with Zagan's. "He wrote me a letter before he died, a vague non apology of a dying man desperately trying to clear his conscience. But at least he told me one thing, that no matter what I did, I had no control over my life. My whole life someone, or something, else has been pulling the strings. My father did that to me. I never had a choice until I died. I knew in the moment of my reawakening that suddenly my choices mattered." Her eyes darted towards Ambrose for less than a second, but in that moment, he saw a glint of fire in them he hadn't seen before. "I chose Ambrose and I will always choose Ambrose. For the rest of my existence, no matter what you do to me, I will choose him. I love him!"

Ambrose caught his breath and stared intensely at Lena, a sharp arrow of joy piercing his heart at her declaration. He knew he loved her. Until now, he only hoped that she might feel the same. Now they just had to survive Zagan.

"Then you are as idiotic as your father," the cambion spat, his anger clearly plastered across his face. "Look at him. Look at Ambrose," he commanded. As she turned to look at him, Zagan walked behind her and leant down to whisper in her ear, his voice still loud enough to reach Ambrose and Marcus. "Kill him."

Lena's bindings glowed brightly as her face contorted in pain. "No!" she screamed, fighting against the command, even as her lightning focused in her arm and shot towards him in a powerful arc.

"Ambrose!" Marcus cried, flying towards his friend, gathering his flames as he flew. He slammed into Ambrose, transporting them away just as the static of Lena's lightning made the hairs on their arms stand on end, immediately flaming away again as they passed through the junction.

Finding himself back in his office, Ambrose rounded on his friend. "What are you doing?" he shouted, pushing Marcus away from him. "I need to get back to her!"

Marcus grabbed his arm, trying to force something on his wrist. "You can't!" he cried. "She will kill you!"

He swung at Marcus, his fist connecting with his friend's jaw. "I can't leave her with him!"

Marcus staggered back slightly, before beating his wings and crashing into him, forcing him against the wall. "You have to," he said through gritted teeth, pushing his forearm against Ambrose's throat. "Running after them will just get you killed. You need to be smart about this."

"I promised her, Marcus," he pleaded, desperately clawing at his friend's arm. "I promised I would keep her safe!"

"Dammit, Ambrose!"

Pulling back, Marcus punched him in the face, black smoke increasing the power behind his hit. Darkness enveloped him as he passed out under the blow.

Waking up in his bed, he stared momentarily at the canopy above. Panic overtaking him, he sat bolt upright as the events of what had just happened resurfaced to the forefront of his mind.

"Lena!" he cried out, gasping for breath as he looked around his room.

Marcus was sitting in one of the chairs by the fireplace, reverted to human form. Anger building within his chest, Ambrose got to his feet, balling his fists. Stopping in his tracks he looked at his hands, realising that he too was in human form. Flexing his fingers, he tried to summon his powers, but they refused to listen. A thick strap of leather was wrapped around his wrist, the symbols and patterns on it glowed as he tried to transform his body or access his powers.

"It won't work," Marcus said from his seat, looking up at him, sadness and pain in his eyes. Ambrose started for him as the cambion held up his hand defensively. "Before you hit me, I made Lena a promise too." Confused, he kept a wary eye on his friend as he walked to the opposite chair and sat down. Marcus sighed, looking at the floor. He looked tired and broken, surprising Ambrose. "I promised I would keep you safe," he continued. "She knows she has other friends who will try to help her, try to protect her from whatever Zagan has planned for her..." he trailed off, shaking his head slightly, his eyes shut evidently pained by what he had to say. Looking up at him, Marcus pointed to the leather cuff. "She made that cuff when she was staying with me. Only I can take it off. It suppresses everything demonic in you. It was intended for her. She knew someone taking her was an inevitability. Lena thought the best way to avoid that was to take herself out of the equation by locking away all that makes her desirable. But then with the test, she didn't have a chance to use it." Leaning back in the chair, Marcus swallowed, tears in his eyes as he spoke. "She said she can survive whatever may come, but she can't survive losing you. And to be honest, neither can I."

Ambrose hung his head, running his hand over his face. He understood that Marcus was just looking out for him, in the way that Lena had asked him to. He couldn't be angry at him for that. Looking at the ceiling, fear and despair started to mix within his stomach creating an internal turmoil he knew would remain until Lena broke from her bindings. "He'll destroy her," he whispered, firmly believing that to be true.

"No, he won't," Marcus said emphatically, shaking his head. "She's too valuable to him. She's too valuable to Hell. Think of how many demons have been vying for her favour since she arrived. They recognise how powerful she is becoming. There would be a civil war if he did anything to her. Taking her from you like this is bad enough. It's not going to go down well. But she needs you to stay alive, Ambrose. If she's going to survive Zagan, you need to be strong for her."

Closing his eyes, he knew Marcus was right. He'd long since lost the ability to protect Lena physically. Her power way exceeded his own. If anything, she had become his shield, keeping him safe by the mere fact that killing him would have killed her. Now he was exposed, only protected by the alliances he had built. But how long would they last now that she was gone, now that he had no desire to continue the work that maintained those alliances.

His world had been ripped from him in an instant and he had no idea how to get her back. He wanted to curse everything that led to him making that deal. He wanted to regret it, but that would mean regretting meeting Lena. It would mean regretting loving her, and he couldn't bring himself to do that. Somehow, he needed to find the strength to carry on without her, hoping that they might one day find their way back to each other.

"I love her, Marcus," he sighed, closing his eyes as despair overtook his mind.

Marcus looked at him sympathetically. "I know," he said simply. "I'm sorry, Ambrose."

CHAPTER THIRTY-EIGHT

Walking through the corridors of Hell, Lena stared daggers at Zagan's back, as he paraded her for all to see. She didn't even have the capacity to care anymore as she walked only in her bra and jeans, the remnants of her shirt left on the floor in the altar room. No one spoke as they came across small groups of demons, their eyes wide in shock as they took in her new bindings. She could smell their fear, but noted that it was not primarily directed at her anymore.

She was pissed. Pain radiated through her body as she tried to fight against Zagan's control. She had accepted the inevitability that someone was going to overtake her bindings from Ambrose. The more she had thought about the aftermath of her test, the more likely it had become. But why did it have to be Zagan? Of course, she knew why, but of all demons, why *him*... She, in some way, had hoped it would be someone else.

Rounding a corner, they came to a large residential cavern. It was an open expanse with spiralling walkways jutting out from the walls, interconnecting various doorways behind which large rooms or apartments demons claimed as their own could be found. Marcus' chambers could be found within this cavern, as most cambions gravitated to this area of Hell. Archie lived in another cavern, but all looked relatively the same.

Not really looking where they were going, Lena simply followed

Zagan until he led them through a doorway into his apartment. It was sparsely decorated; the walls bare except for the furniture pushed against them. The main room housed a large table in the middle with a small kitchen like area carved into a recess in one of the walls. Simple wooden chairs were spread around the table, books and scrolls scattered across its surface. There were two other doors near to the back of the room leading deeper into the apartment. Flaming torches were dotted around the walls, illuminating the contents of the room.

"Oh shit, you did it."

Her legs no longer forcing her forward, Lena turned her head to see Cyrus walking out of one of the doors, his eyes wide, locking with hers.

"You doubted that I would?" Zagan sneered, walking over to the table and sorting through some of the scrolls.

"I hoped you wouldn't," Cyrus sighed, looking at Zagan who now glared at him in anger. "What?" he said with a shrug. "You compel me to always tell you the truth."

"Show Lena to her room," the cambion commanded, gathering some of the scrolls in his hands. "And make sure she stays there until I get back. Be a good girl and stay put," he said stalking over to her.

"Fuck you," Lena spat at him.

With a cruel sneer, he lifted her chin and pressed a kiss to her lips. She wanted to be sick, bile rising in the back of her throat as her bindings stopped her from punching him. "All in good time, beautiful," he whispered against her lips, his scent making her nauseous. "I have other matters to attend to now." Straightening, he stepped around her and opened the door to the cavern.

"Where are you going?" she asked, keeping her back to him.

"Don't fret," he said coldly. "Your sweetheart is not on my agenda."

The door slammed behind her, making her jump at the sound. Spinning on her heel, she flung her lightning at the door, watching as it spread out over the surface. She was too tired to put any force behind the attack, but it served to vent a small portion of her frustration. With a scream she turned back into the room, her breath catching as she saw Cyrus looking at her, a pained expression on his face.

"I'm so sorry, Lena," he sighed, taking a step towards her before hesitating. "Follow me," he nodded to the door behind him. With a shuddering breath, she shut her eyes and forced her feet to carry her over to him. "I truly am sorry, Lena," he said as she walked past him and through the door. "I'm sure you don't want to see me right now, but—"

"It's fine," she interrupted, her voice sounding hollow and far away to her ears. "I know you have to stay. But I'd rather not talk right now."

"Fair enough."

The door led to a small hallway from which three other doors branched off. Cyrus pointed to the right door. "That's my room, the one at the end is mainly for storage, but... Zagan has prepared it for Zamira when she's ready." Lena flinched with sadness at her hellhound's name, hoping Cyrus didn't notice. "This one is yours." Opening the door on the left, he ushered her inside.

The room was small, containing only a bed and a desk with a chair. The bed, if it could be called that, was just a mattress atop rock in an alcove carved into the wall, but she walked over to it, sitting on the edge and looking around the room. Cyrus made his way to the desk, turning the chair out to face her and sat down.

"Whose room was this?" she asked.

"It hasn't been anyone's in a while. Summoning Zagan requires a double sacrifice, so he keeps two rooms in case he has two boundlings," he explained. "The girl that was killed with me didn't accept the offer to bind to him. He's not summoned often and no one has accepted since me."

Silence fell over them as Lena stared at the floor, painfully aware that Cyrus was studying her. Despairing at her situation but grateful that he was with her, a deep sorrow gripped her heart, digging in with icy fingers that pulled a sudden and painful sob from her chest. Dropping her face into her hands, she leant forward, crying loudly into the room, her shoulders heaving as sobs racked her body. She barely heard Cyrus get to his feet and sit next to her on the bed. She didn't have the strength to fight him as he pulled her into his arms, holding her head to his shoulder, simply allowing her to cry against him.

Everything was so wrong. On the same day she had realised her love for Ambrose, she had declared it to Zagan in anger. She had been ripped from the one she loved in the worst way imaginable, leaving her to desperately wish she could wind back time to any moment before today. Any time that would allow her a chance to fix things with Ambrose properly. Allow her to make sure they would never be parted.

Leaning into Cyrus' warmth and comfort, Lena took a steadying breath, trying to stem the flow of her tears. He rubbed her back, the same way he had when they were kids. Blood or no, he was her brother, and she needed him to survive whatever was coming next.

She sniffed, raising her head from Cyrus' shoulder, looking into his eyes, missing the warmth of their human dark brown colouring. "I think he killed Zamira," she said sadly, feeling the sting of tears threatening to spill again.

"As soon as he's back, I'll go find her," Cyrus promised, cupping her cheek in his hand and wiping away the last few stray tears. He kissed her forehead comfortingly and held her tightly against him.

"Thank you," she sighed, lowering her head and wrapping her arms around his waist, holding him as they had many a time hiding in their rooms from irate foster parents.

Thankfully, Zagan left her somewhat alone for the next two days. Now that he had gained her as an asset, he had to shore up his control over her, warning off other demons that had also coveted her. For the moment, he kept her locked away in his apartment, leaving her with Cyrus. Zagan's general absence had allowed her to reflect on her situation, working in the room that was to become Zamira's den, endlessly thankful that her hellhound was alive and recovering in the main den. Cyrus had found her there, still wounded but alive and nursing her pups. He had managed to get Zamira to the apartment just long enough for Lena to heal her completely.

The morning of the third day, she was fighting off a migraine caused by the need to make a cursed object. Having been interrupted in the creation of the last one, her body was crying out, needing to do something other than just sit in her room.

Sighing heavily, she knew she was going to have to ask Zagan for a favour, dreading to think what he might ask for in return. Running her hands through her hair, she left her room and made her way to the main area. Somewhat surprisingly, she found Zagan sitting at the table, his wings held up behind him as he leant forward, pouring over a book. He looked up as she came into the room, before returning his gaze to the book in front of him. Considering how hell bent he had been in claiming her, she almost felt insulted at his current apathy towards her.

"I need my book," she said flatly, placing her hands on her hips.

Zagan sighed, leaning back in his chair to look at her. "What?"

"My book," she repeated, stepping closer to the table. "My conduit to making cursed objects. I need it."

"You can't make them without it?" he asked exasperated, folding his arms across his chest.

"No, and I'm going insane." Close enough now to the table, she placed her palms on its surface, leaning towards him, hoping her disgust for him was visible in her eyes. "Unlike you and Cyrus who's designs kind of just happen, mine is like an itch in my brain that I can't scratch."

Pinching the bridge of his nose, Zagan let out a long, slow breath. "And your book would be where?"

Lena smirked, pleased that he seemed to be aware of what she was about to say next. "At Ambrose's manor."

"Of course, it is," he sighed, giving her a dubious look. He pushed the chair away and got to his feet. "I'll send Cyrus to get it," he said walking around the table towards her.

"He can't," she said, shaking her head, pushing back from the table as he got closer. "No one can touch it but me. The chest I keep it in is protected. Can't risk someone destroying my conduit, can I?"

Zagan took hold of her neck. What was with him and holding her by the neck? "Do not lie to me, Lena."

"I'm not lying," she spat through gritted teeth, holding onto his wrist. "I swear, if you put your hand on my throat again—" She managed to push his hand away, only for his other hand to grab her by the hair, forcing her face up and pinning her body against his.

"You'll do what?" he sneered at her. "Hm? You are bound to me now. Accept it."

Pushing against his chest, she felt her body flush with anger. "Never."

Replacing his hand on her throat, he leant down, closing the distance between their faces. His breath washed over her face, making her want to gag. "The sooner you accept it, the sooner I'll take my hand from your throat," he whispered, tightening his hold on her neck and hair. "You do not speak to Ambrose, and you will do exactly as I say. I will kill him if you step out of line."

Her bindings glowed at the command as Zagan gathered his flames and transported them to a junction and then the entrance hall of the manor. Once there, he roughly let go of her, pushing her back slightly, before turning to face the stairway.

"Ambrose," he called loudly, placing his hands on his hips. Lena stood by his side, crossing her arms in front of her, rolling her eyes. She could have just gotten her chest; he didn't need to tease Ambrose with her presence. But selfishly, she also wanted to see him.

Looking up at the top of the stairs, she saw Ambrose and Marcus exiting his office. Seeing her former sire again, her heart started to race. Everything in her wanted to run to him, to fall into his arms, but remembering Zagan's threat she forced herself to remain still.

"Lena!" Ambrose cried, rushing down the stairs, Marcus close behind him.

"I wouldn't," Zagan said coldly, placing his hand on the back of her neck, pulling her closer to him and causing Ambrose to stop in his tracks.

Again, with the neck... her inner voice sighed.

She could see Ambrose's chest heaving beneath his shirt. He was barely containing his anger and she couldn't blame him. Hers generally only remained in check because of the commands Zagan had put into effect. "What do you want?" he asked through gritted teeth.

"Lena needs her book," Zagan sighed in annoyance. "Where is it?"

Ambrose looked over to Lena, studying her, making sure she was ok. Her bindings stopped her from speaking, but she gave him a small nod of assurance. "Where you left it when you stole her from me," he said looking back at Zagan. "It's in the library."

Eliciting a small cry from her, Zagan shoved her towards the library doors. The one he had torn from the hinges still laid on the ground. "Go get it."

"Screw you," she spat over her shoulder, stepping over the splintered wood.

The look on Zagan's face was glorious to her. His frustration was her joy. "I told you to be quiet," he retorted, his voice dangerously quiet.

"You commanded me not to speak to Ambrose," she sneered, turning in the doorway to look at him. "You never said anything about speaking to you."

"I did tell you to do exactly as I say," he pointed a single finger at her, directing her into the library. "Go get your damn book."

"I'll kill you for this, Zagan," Ambrose said, putting his hands in his trouser pockets, Marcus stood defensively at his side.

Zagan chuckled at the bravado. "Kill me, and you kill her."

"I can wait for her to break from you."

"Can you?"

Lena picked up the box housing her book, trying to ignore the tightness in her chest at the exchange from the hall. It felt heavier than before, realising that Ambrose likely filled it with other things in case she came back for it. She smiled softly, hoisting it against her stomach as she returned to stand next to Zagan.

"Can I get some of my things from upstairs?" she asked, putting the chest on the floor. "Being stuck in the same clothing for the last three days is less than appealing."

"You can make new clothes," Zagan turned to her, noting she'd set down her chest with an annoyed sigh.

"It's not just my clothes," she said lifting her chin, "there are other things I would like to have. If I'm stuck with you, I might as well have some creature comforts."

A dubious scowl on his lips, he lifted his hand holding up two fingers. "Two minutes."

"Seriously?" Lena scoffed, raising a brow. "After the stunt you pulled whispering into Ambrose's ear about Cyrus and me, I've been living across two rooms. It will take me more than two minutes to get everything I want."

"If I give you three minutes, will you stop whining at me?" he practically shouted at her, his eyes wide with barely contained frustration.

"You think this is whining?" she snapped, placing her hands on her hips. She desperately wanted to say something else inflammatory, but thought better of it. "Give me four, and I'll think about it."

Letting out a slow and deliberate breath, Zagan pinched the bridge of his nose. "Fine." Raising a finger to point at her face, he commanded her; "Do not write any notes. I will get you to tell me if you did. Back in four minutes or I kill him. Go!"

"Trouble in paradise?"

Lena smiled as her plan finally came into action. Archie and Pasha flamed into the hallway, remaining in demonic form, standing just in front and either side of Ambrose. It was Pasha who made the comment, an amused smile on her lips as she looked at Lena and nodded in greeting.

"What are you doing here?" Zagan spat, lightning charging over his fingers.

"Fulfilling our promises to her," Archie said, nodding towards Lena. "Protecting Ambrose."

Zagan's jaw was clenching, the small muscle just under his ear pulsing furiously. He turned to Lena, grabbing her by the arm and pulling her roughly towards him. "Explain," he hissed.

She smiled confidently, drinking in his frustration, relishing that she had managed to surprise him. "I knew someone was going to take me. Really it was just a matter of time," she explained. "One of the first things Archie said to me was to get used to taking orders from demons more powerful than me. Well, I think it's safe to say, since the test, I am more powerful than most demons," she chuckled. "And most demons know it too. So, I started making my own alliances, setting up protections for Ambrose should I be taken from him. Oh," she said, ripping her arm from Zagan's grasp, and walking towards the staircase, "they've also promised to kill you, if necessary, regardless of if I'm still bound to you."

Archie and Pasha took the opportunity to close the gap in front of her former sire, forming a wall with their bodies, their own powers channelling through their hands. She could see the shocked look on Ambrose's face, staring at her as she walked past him, mixed with pride and love in his eyes. Winking at him, she started to climb the stairs.

Zagan looked at them haughtily, his face visibly giving away his uncertainty at the situation. "They wouldn't risk killing you," he said finally.

"Look, I can explain, or I can get my things?" Lena said as she reached the halfway point of the stairs, looking over her shoulder at him. "Can't do both in four minutes."

"You have three minutes left."

Rolling her eyes, she ran up the last few steps, rushing to her altar room to grab a bag. Keeping the doors open as she went, she could still hear the conversation from the hall.

"I could just tell her to kill you all now," Zagan said, impatience and annoyance prevalent in his voice.

"There are things we can do to you that won't kill you, Zagan," Pasha threatened. "Including removing your ability to compel her."

She heard Ambrose laugh, closing her eyes hoping to permanently burn the sound into her memory. "I'm surprised you haven't tried to kill me before today, now that you've got what you wanted."

"Your pain is what I want," Zagan spat. "Keeping you alive means I get to witness it every time you see her with me. Times nearly up, Lena." Sighing in defeat, she grabbed the last of her things from Ambrose's room, ducking finally into his office and grabbing the summoning crystal, stuffing it between some of her clothes. Folding a small piece of paper, she left behind an origami heart in its place. Not technically a note, so hopefully she could get away with it. Racing back to the hallway, she bounded down the stairs, dropping the bag on top of her chest. "Come here, stay still and quiet."

Groaning internally, she walked over to Zagan and stood in front of him. He grabbed her under the chin and captured her mouth with his, forcing his tongue past her lips. Now she did gag, as the kiss ended and she pushed away, stepping to the side and leaning over her things.

"You're out of line, Zagan."

"Shut up, Marcus," Zagan snapped at him. "You are a disgrace to cambions. I will be more than happy to wipe your stain out. See you around, Ambrose."

"Lena!"

Feeling Zagan grab her behind the neck, his flames overtook them, Ambrose's voice shouting her name still ringing in her ears.

"You're a fucking bastard!" she screamed at him as his apartment came into view, her bindings stopping her from throwing as much lightning her body could harness in his direction.

"Go make your objects," Zagan snarled, returning to his seat at the table and pulling the book towards him.

"Oh, bite me," she spat, grabbing her bag and chest, lifting them in her arms.

He looked up at her, a brow raised. "Only if you say please," he mocked, a cruel smile on his lips. "Go," he ordered, returning to his reading.

Storming out of the room, Lena slammed the doors as she went, her anger boiling within her. Once in her room, she dropped her bag on the bed and placed the chest on the desk. Closing her eyes, she took some solace in knowing the arrangements she had set in place were working. Ambrose was safe, for now. Now she had to save herself.

Chapter Thirty-Nine

Seeing Lena again had been torturous, but Ambrose welcomed the pain it had brought. At least she looked healthy, the fire in her eyes ever present. He had no idea if Zagan had done anything to her as yet, but it seemed, at least for now, that she was holding her own against the cambion. Finding the heart she left for him in place of the summoning crystal had filled his with hope that at least one day, everything would be okay again. He would get her back. One day.

Archie and Pasha had spent some time with him after Lena and Zagan had left to explain the arrangements she had made for his protection. She had amassed a number of demons who were willing to follow her orders, on the basis that she would make bespoke objects to their needs, objects that housed a sliver of her power, and were bound to Ambrose's life. If he died, the objects would cease working. Even demons that he'd had nothing to do with previously had pledged to her. Titus, another dealing demon, and his boundlings became Ambrose's personal bodyguards when visiting Hell. Lena had cast alerting spells around his home so that a pool of almost thirty demons would be notified if Zagan or anyone affiliated with him came to the manor. Even she would sound the alarm, accounting for any possibility of Zagan sending her to kill him. She had thought of everything, and Ambrose couldn't love her more for it.

Calza had contacted him that morning through one of Titus' boundlings, to let him know that Lena would be visiting the Vault today.

Apparently, she had been very busy with making objects since collecting her book and refused to let Zagan or Cyrus deposit them for her. Unable to resist the possibility of seeing her again, Ambrose now hid deep within the Vault, near Calza's nest, hoping that the naga could think of some reason why Lena would need to venture this far on her own.

Looking at the shelves, he heard footsteps approaching and turned to see her standing in the walkway, her eyes wide. Those beautiful dove-grey eyes locked with his. His heart skipped at the sight of her, the same way it had when she appeared in the hall a few days ago.

"What are you doing here?" she whispered in a hushed tone, panic in her voice, her body unmoving. "You can't be here."

Surprised at her reaction, Ambrose took a step towards her. "I had to see you."

"No," she cried quietly, stepping back. "Stay back."

"Lena?" he half pleaded, searching her face, his stomach tightening as he saw fear in her eyes.

Pressing her lips together she shook her head. "I'm sorry, Ambrose. He'll pick up your scent," she said, her voice shaking.

"Then run with me. Now," he said, holding out his hand for her.

"I can't."

"Why not?"

She looked at him desperately, her eyes brimming with tears. "He'll kill Cyrus if I don't go back with him."

Ambrose hung his head, realising that Zagan did indeed have full control over her. As long as he had Cyrus to use as leverage, Lena wouldn't risk his life for her own. Sighing heavily, he closed his eyes, afraid to ask his next question. "Has he..."

"No," she said quickly, shaking her head. "He wants me to submit to him willingly. But he's fucking persistent."

He could be grateful for that at least. Looking at her, he wanted nothing more than to pull her into his arms. "Marcus and I—"

"Don't," she interrupted, drawing in a sharp and sudden breath. "Don't tell me anything. I can't keep it secret from him anymore."

"Lena!"

She turned her head sharply as Zagan's voice as he called for her. Lifting her chin, Ambrose could practically see the waves of anger rising from her body.

"Oh, give me a fucking break!" she shouted into the Vault. Turning back to him, she gave him a sorrowful look. "I'm sorry, Ambrose. I'm so sorry," she whispered as she started to head back. She stopped briefly, before cursing under her breath and spinning on her heel, racing towards him. He caught her in his arms as their lips collided in a hard, desperate kiss. He wanted to melt into the kiss, to become an inseparable part of her, as his arms gripped hungrily at her back.

"Lena! Come here now!" Zagan bellowed.

She winced as her bindings glowed, forcing her to obey. "I'm coming!" she called over her shoulder, pushing away from him. "I'm sorry. Bye."

Tugging slightly as her fingers left his hand, Ambrose whispered hurriedly, "Lena, I love you." He had to say it to her. At least once.

Even as she walked away, she looked back over her shoulder and sighed, smiling softly. "I love you, too."

Pressing his fingers to his lips, he savoured her scent and taste, taking a moment for them to leave. The pain in his chest as she walked away made him wish he hadn't come. He missed her terribly and feared for her, but seeing her if only for a moment, made it so much worse.

He thanked Calza for their help, before transporting home. Appearing in his office, he started to see two huge demons standing either side of his desk.

"Who the hel–" he started before their auras, embodiments of darkness and malevolence, announced their identities to him. Eyes wide, Ambrose quickly bowed his head. "Apologies, my Princes."

The two Princes of Hell smiled at his reaction, nodding their heads in return.

"Please, Ambrose, we have come uninvited into your home. There is no need for formalities," Asmodeus said, walking over to him and placing his clawed hand almost comfortingly on his back. The Prince of Lust stood well above his sister, the Prince of Greed. His dark mottled and leathery skin, resembling something akin to cracked obsidian, reflecting little to no light from the lamps. Defined muscles rippled beneath his skin, lending an aura of unearthly strength and power. Unlike most demons, his eyes glowed icy blue, radiating an intense and unholy intelligence. Above them, sharp, jagged horns protruded from his forehead, twisting and curving with a sinister elegance. Living up to his title, even Ambrose would admit Asmodeus was incredibly attractive.

Contrary, his sister, Mammon boasted a twisted fusion of terrifying features, evoking a sense of primal fear. Her limbs, elongated and disproportionate, still had a stunning elegance to them as she stood behind one of the chairs, exuding a supernatural flexibility, granting both agility and a predatory grace. She sported no horns, but her hair was braided in a single, thick line over the top of her head, hanging over her back before ending past her knees. Large, half feathered wings raised proudly behind her back, the bat-like tips ending in wicked barbed talons, capable of delivering deadly strikes. Her eyes were fiery orbs of molten gold, glaring out from deep sunken sockets. She smiled at Ambrose, her fangs gleaming with an eerie luminescence, ready to rend and tear her victims apart. "We are not here as Princes, but as friends. Sit down, we need to talk," her voice dripped like honey from her forked tongue.

"About what?" Ambrose asked, moving to sit behind his desk, his eyes darting back and forth between the Princes.

"Lena," Mammon replied, eying up one of the chairs on the other side of the desk, seemingly trying to figure out how she might sit in one.

"Don't even try, sister," Asmodeus chuckled, simply leaning on the back of the chair. "Unfortunately, we are afraid you will not exactly like what we have to say."

"What do you mean?" he asked, dread rising in him. What could possibly be happening that the Princes are getting involved?

Still studying the chair, Mammon didn't make any movement before answering him. "Although we would have preferred that Lena have remained in your care," she sighed, raising her head finally to look at him, abandoning her assessment of the chair. "We are going to ask that you and Marcus cease your planning to take her away from Zagan."

"What? Why?" he cried, jumping to his feet.

"Please, do not misjudge us here, Ambrose," Asmodeus said, holding up his hands, whilst still leaning on his forearms. "We are well aware of the relationship that you and Lena have developed. I, of all demons, am very aware of your desire for each other and I encourage those feelings to continue."

Confusion washed over Ambrose as he stared at the Prince of Lust. Why wish the relationship to continue, yet ask him to stop pursuing her return to him?

"She is where she needs to be right now," Mammon assured him, stepping round the chair and walking towards him. "Her powers are still developing. Under you they flourished, your patience and guidance allowing her to expand her knowledge and understanding of the power within her."

"But," Asmodeus continued, "under Zagan, she will be forced to build her strength and will. It is our belief this will help her fulfil her destiny and become who we hope for her to be."

Breathing heavily, Ambrose tried to comprehend what they were saying. "Who you hope her to be?"

Asmodeus nodded. "The Princes orchestrated her birth. Finding a child that met our criteria took a long time, but we can already see that our patience has been well rewarded with the power we have witnessed from her thus far."

"Orchestrated?" he queried. "It was you... who took over my will in the deal with her father."

"Yes," Mammon answered him. "Lucifer took control momentarily to provide the appropriate terms. We needed a child born of a deal that would be seven months gestation at the time of the hybrid solar eclipse."

"You would think that with the ever-growing population of humanity there would have been more fitting that description," Asmodeus sighed, "but it still took us almost two millennia to find her. Only two others have been born under those terms, and both failed us. One of them was Zagan."

He shut his eyes at the cambion's name. That explained why he was so interested in the deal Ambrose made with her father. Why he had been so desperate to claim her. He knew what she meant to Hell, to the Princes. "So, what does that mean?" he asked. "What is she?"

The Princes glanced at each other, hesitating to answer. Asmodeus nodded slowly as Mammon looked back at him. "She is power," she explained. "We can't explain more than that, I'm sorry. There is still a chance she won't become what we hope, in which case, we will need to restart our search."

"Which is why, as unfortunate as it is, we need her to stay with Zagan," Asmodeus said, sadness in his voice. "If she had remained with you, we would not have gotten involved directly. The Princes have discussed this at length and the majority of us believe she is best placed where she is right now."

"The majority," Ambrose noted, "but not all?"

Mammon chuckled and shook her head, her braid swaying gently behind her. "No, not all. Abaddon and Satan believe she should be returned to you."

"As do I," Asmodeus said, raising a hand.

"Yes, but you want anything that builds the most lust, dear brother,"

Mammon smirked at him.

Asmodeus nodded and pressed his lips together in amusement. "That is true," he confirmed. "And there is no lust between Lena and Zagan. Well, at least not from her."

Ambrose smiled at the Prince of Lust. The confirmation was unnecessary, but he would admit it was nice to hear. "So, only a slight majority then," he mused, folding his arms in front of his chest.

"Lucifer was the deciding vote," Asmodeus shrugged.

"Ambrose," Mammon called, pulling his attention to her. "We understand it will be hard to let her go. We are not asking for you to avoid her, or to even abandon your love for her. In fact, she will need it more than ever. We are just asking that you do not attempt to rebind her to you. Or to convince someone else to take over her binding."

"Just for now," Asmodeus said, standing up and placing his hands on his hips. "We are keeping an eye on Lena and her development, and we will intervene if Zagan does anything that threatens our plans for her."

"So please, leave it be," the Prince of Greed pleaded. "Should circumstances change, and we decide to intervene, we will contact you again."

Sighing and closing his eyes, Ambrose let their plea settle over him, the pit of fear in his stomach now mixing with defeat. Who was he to defy the will of the Princes?

"Alright," he said, nodding his head and looking at them again. "I will follow your orders. As with all things, my Princes," he said with a bow.

Nodding her acknowledgement, Mammon disappeared in her flames. Asmodeus remained briefly; his eyes locked on Ambrose. "For what it is worth," he said, walking closer to the desk, "I sincerely hope that you and Lena find a way back to each other. I have not felt a love like yours among demons in a long time."

Ambrose stared at him, wondering what he meant by that. "I don't care how I came to love her," he said softly, "but is it not just a side effect of the deal?"

Smiling warmly, the Prince shook his head. "We used you to make the deal, everything else was merely chance. Or fate," he said with a shrug. "The deal attuned your souls to the other, which is why you felt drawn to her when she was alive. Her importance is what continues to draw demons to her now. But we have no control over your hearts. The feelings you have for each other are completely your own. There is a certain poetry, however, in her being sacrificed to you." His flames began to lick over his body as Asmodeus nodded his goodbyes. "Might even write about it one day." And with that Ambrose was alone.

Sitting back in his chair, he reverted to human form, leaning his head back against the soft leather. With a heavy sigh, he stared at the ceiling. His mind was racing from what the Princes had said to him. He wasn't sure he would be able to give up the idea of rebinding Lena to him, but he knew he had to try. If the Princes said they were watching her, ensuring her survival, then that had to be better than anything he could think up. But he didn't want to think anymore. Not now.

Getting to his feet, he grabbed a bottle of whiskey and a glass from the side table before returning to his desk. He poured the sharp, golden liquid into the glass and downed it in one swing, relishing in the sharp burn of the liquor coursing through his chest. It wasn't long before the bottle was empty and he let his head fall onto his desk with a thud. He groaned into the wood as he repeatedly banged his head against it. "I'm fucking screwed..." he groaned pushing himself to his feet to grab another bottle of whiskey. Forgetting the glass, he drank straight from the bottle. It took a lot for a demon to feel drunk, but quick succession of full bottles of whiskey might just do the trick, or so he hoped.

"Do I want to ask?"

Slowly placing the bottle on the desk surface, Ambrose smiled wryly as Cyrus appeared before him. "This is far too many visitors for one day. What the hell are you doing here?" he sighed.

Raising a brow, Cyrus folded his arms in front of his chest. "I'm here for Lena," he said softly. "Ah, and here come your guard dogs." As if on cue, Titus and one of his boundlings flamed in behind Ambrose's desk, either side of him. Ambrose had to admit their timing was impeccable. "Lena really did do a good job in setting up protections for you, didn't she?"

Titus chuckled menacingly. "She's asked we be lenient on you, but call me a guard dog again and I'll thrash you."

Smiling at the confirmation that Lena truly had thought of everything, Ambrose held up his hand to the demon. "Titus, please," he said, keeping his eyes locked on Cyrus. "Is she okay?"

"As well as she can be," the boundling answered, an underlying anger in his voice. Curious as to what that meant, Ambrose pushed himself to his feet, feeling a little too small in human form between three demons. "I don't have a lot of time, Ambrose. I told Zagan I was going to the den, and if I don't want him to realise that I came here, I will still need time to go there." Sighing, Cyrus dropped his arms and placed his hands on his hips "He's got her, and me, on a tight leash. He only lets one of us out of his apartment at a time. If we don't get back within an hour, the other is commanded to kill themselves."

Pinching the bridge of his nose, Ambrose exhaled loudly. It was the perfect control. Two adopted siblings, seeking only to protect the other, forced to return to their captor or risk the life of the other. An hour didn't leave either with a lot of time to do anything outside of the apartment, essentially binding them to it as well.

"He's not going to do anything to her. He doesn't want to just take her," the boundling continued.

"How noble of him," Titus sneered from his corner.

Cyrus glared at him, turning back to Ambrose to explain further. "He wants to hurt you, in the worst way possible."

"Lena said, he wants her to submit willingly." Ambrose placed his hands in his pockets.

"About that," Cyrus sighed, a rueful look on his face. "I came to warn you. You cannot go near her again. He was furious after the stunt you pulled in the Vault. You were an idiot to try and see her."

"Who cares if he gets pissed off?" he snapped as the effects of the liquor started to get the better of him.

The expression on Cyrus' face was murderous, as he stalked towards the desk, prompting Titus and his boundling to step forward, catching him by the shoulders. "You should care!" he shouted, venom dripping from his voice. "You, of all people, know what he's like to his boundlings. He beat the crap out of her for it when they got back! If it wasn't for the fact that she heals about as fast as he hits, she'd be dead!" Ambrose's stomach dropped sharply, as his breathing became laboured. He wanted to be sick thinking of her, his Lena, his beautiful, brave Lena, being beaten by Zagan. Why had he been so selfish, so stupid, to go see her... but Cyrus wasn't done screaming at him. "And for fuck's sake, I care! I love her as if she really was my sister. You think I want to see her bleeding out on the floor? Let go of me!" he yelled, shoving Titus and his boundling back. He raised a single finger to point at Ambrose. "You do anything that puts her in that position again and *I'll* kill you." Taking a deep breath, Cyrus turned away and walked back to the other side of the room. "He's told her to kill you on sight. So, if I were you, I'd stay away."

"Why should I believe you?" Ambrose asked, still trying to shake the images of her hurt from his mind. "Zagan could have just told you to tell me that. How do I know it's true?"

"You don't," the boundling shrugged, turning back to face him. "But do you really want to risk leaving her with the knowledge that she killed you?" he asked, raising a brow. "Goodbye, Ambrose."

In a flurry of flames, Cyrus disappeared. Titus stayed for a moment to make sure he wasn't coming back before he too left. Returning to the whiskey bottle, Ambrose finished it in a single swig, letting the bottle slip from his hand and smash over the floor. He had been the cause for her pain, again. If it wasn't for the visit from the Princes, he was certain he would have thrown himself into the Infernal Pit simply to erase the images now in his mind.

CHAPTER FORTY

She was tired. So incredibly tired.

Lena's body was screaming for rest, but Zagan seemed to have a plan in forcing her transformation out by depriving her of sleep and her sanity, compelling her to remain awake no matter what. Even simply relaxing on her bed for too long was enough to cause her bindings to activate the command. Additionally, the exhaustion was wreaking havoc on her powers. In the last week, two of her objects had exploded in her face before she could complete the binding. The other day she'd accidentally killed a demon in the training pits when her lightning got out of control.

Combine the sleep deprivation with the beatings Zagan doled out on an almost daily basis and her mind was beginning to shut down.

Three weeks. She had been bound to Zagan for just over three weeks, and this was so much worse than she had imagined. She had suffered in the past, but this was relentless. At least she got to sleep in her life and escape temporarily. Now she got an hour every second day to leave the apartment, and when she was there, Zagan was there, harassing and pushing her, torturing her. It would take but the smallest infraction on her part for his fist to connect with the side of her face, her commands preventing her from hitting back. He would command her to remain still as he sliced into her, over and over, carving runes into her skin that looped her power through her body continuously, trying to pull the near transformation she experienced during the test from her again. Her only solace was that he could feel the pain he inflicted on her, wilfully ignoring the fact that he seemed to enjoy it. Cyrus tried to step in twice, resulting in his own beatings, after which Lena begged him not too. She knew it was hard for him to see her like that, but she also knew Zagan wouldn't kill her. He might kill Cyrus.

She was meant to be going to the training pits this morning, however, the half hour sparring sessions were becoming intolerable. Not enough time to adequately vent her frustrations, yet simultaneously too long under the gaze of what she could only call her 'fans' now.

Trying to find some mental relief, Lena let her mind fall silent simply allowing her feet to carry her through the corridors, unable to care anymore for the demons around her. Realisation dawning on her, she found herself standing by the edge of the Infernal Pit. Zagan had brought her here soon after binding her to him, threatening to throw her in if she continued to defy him, telling her again about Ambrose throwing Margaret into it. She still didn't believe him, and considering his current treatment of her, the idea seemed even more ludicrous. Now she wondered how Margaret had managed almost a century of this. How strong she must have been.

Staring into the Pit, she briefly entertained the thought of jumping in. At least she'd get some rest. And yet, whilst she would get peace, others would suffer. Cyrus would die, commanded to kill himself if she didn't return in an hour. Zamira would die without her power now to sustain her. The pups... Ambrose... Ambrose would survive, but would he want to, if she was gone. She hadn't seen him since the Vault. She had done so much to ensure his survival, knowing she needed him to, so that she could hold on to some strand of hope of getting back to him. A hope that would allow her to survive. Killing herself now, would destroy everything she had worked so hard for.

"Lena! Stop!"

Startling at the shout, she half turned away from the Pit. "Ambrose? What are you–?" Catching herself, she quickly turned away, fixing her vision on a distant point along the wall. "Stay back!" she cried. "How did you find me?"

"Pasha saw you heading this way. She got me." His breathing was laboured. Evidently, he had raced to reach her. "Lena, please, I'm begging you, don't jump. *Please*. Come away from the ledge."

Lena shook her head, but did take a step back. "You shouldn't be here. Zagan told me—"

"I know," he said with a sharp exhale. "I know about his command. So just don't look at me."

Chuckling with derision, she threw her hands in the air. "Ha! You say that like it's easy."

She could feel him getting closer, his warmth and scent washing over her senses. "I know it's not," he said, brushing his fingers over her shoulders sending shivers down her spine. How she missed his touch. "Close your eyes," he whispered.

Unable to resist him, she did as he said, nodding to confirm she had done so. She felt his hands tighten on her shoulders, turning her body towards his, her back to the Pit, before they travelled up to cup her face. Her lips parted in anticipation, sighing with desire as she felt his breath near her face, his lips brushing over hers. The tenderness of his lips was unbelievably sweet, as she reached up and trailed her fingers along his jaw, wanting to pull him closer, to drink him in.

"Lena," Ambrose said against her lips, his voice meeting her ears like a soft melody. "I know you're hurting. I know you're pissed and angry and just want to end everything to get some peace. I know this is probably the hardest thing you have had to endure. I know that because it is all of those things for me as well. But I can't imagine a future without you. I want to be able to hold you in forty, fifty or sixty years, when you've finally broken from your bindings, knowing that even after everything we went through, the tough days, the painfully sad, even the impossibly hard days, that our love never died. In that moment, we'll finally be able to say that we made it. Together, for eternity."

Tears stung behind her eyes, a soft sob catching in her throat. "Ambrose..." she sighed, squeezing her eyes shut, desperately wanting to look at him.

"Do you know why I call you 'dove'?" he asked, gently nuzzling his nose along her jaw.

She shook her head in answer, her body instantly responding to his affections. "I thought it had to do with my eyes."

His breath by her ear, she sighed pressing her cheek against his, not daring to increase their contact despite wanting to drown in his scent. "Not just because of your eyes," he whispered, kissing the skin below her ear, pulling a soft moan from her throat. He smiled against her. "I call you that because you are my peace, my calm, my joy. When I am with you, when I hold you, nothing else matters. You are everything to me."

A single tear of joy escaped her eye as he claimed her mouth again and she fell into his tender kiss, never wanting it to end. She tried to hold him in place, even as he pulled away, chuckling at her reaction. "You have to go back," he whispered against her lips.

She shook her head violently. "I don't want to."

"You have to," he said, rubbing his thumbs over her cheeks. "Cyrus told me about the one-hour command."

With a heavy sigh, she pulled back slightly, still holding his arms to steady herself. "You have to leave first," she breathed softly. "I can't go if I can't open my eyes."

"You won't jump?"

"No," she promised. "I wasn't going to anyway."

"I love you so much, Lena," he said, pressing another gentle kiss to her lips.

Holding onto his wrists, she leaned into him, into his strength. "I love you, too."

"See you soon, my dove."

Standing still, she listened to his footsteps as he walked away. Once she was sure he was gone, she slowly opened her eyes, looking around the cavern in sorrow. His absence left a huge hole in her chest, but that was not something she could dwell on now. Unsure of how much time had passed, she bolted, her heart racing as she made her way back to Zagan's apartment. With her exhaustion, travelling through the fires of Hell had become exceedingly difficult for her, her aim putting her halfway into a wall the other day.

Demons quickly jumped out of her way as she ran, unsure of what to make of her desperation. Finally, she burst through the apartment door, jumping slightly as it slammed against the wall behind it. "I'm back," she panted, seeing Cyrus sitting at the table.

Cyrus looked up at her with an amused yet relieved smile. "Cutting it close, Lena."

"Sorry," she breathed heavily. "I'm sorry." Taking a moment to catch her breath she looked around the room. "Where is he?"

"He's out looking for you. We heard that Ambrose was in Hell so he went to find you." Cyrus got to his feet and walked over to her, wrinkling his nose as he got closer. "Please tell me you haven't been with him." When she didn't answer, he ran his hand through his hair in annoyance. "Fuck, Lena."

"If I go shower quickly, hopefully he won't pick up on it," she said, making her way to her room. "After all, he thinks I went to the training pits so..."

"Well hurry up," Cyrus sighed, pushing her along.

Dashing into her room, she jumped into her shower, scrubbing furiously with a pumice stone. She hated washing away Ambrose's scent, but if she wanted to avoid an immediate beating, she had no choice. Dried and dressed, she quickly visited Zamira's den and gave her and her pups a tight hug, hoping their scents would cover anything left.

"How do I smell now?" she asked, returning to Cyrus.

"Better," he said, nodding approvingly. "Zamira makes for a good cover up. So, if you didn't go to the pits, where did you go? Not to the manor. His scent wasn't strong enough for that."

Raising her brow at him, she smiled dubiously. "Do you really want me to tell you?"

"Probably not."

They both sat at the table, waiting for the return of their sire. They didn't have to wait long as he burst through the door, much in the same way Lena had done moments before.

"Where the fuck have you been?" he shouted, rounding on her and pulling her up from the chair roughly. "And don't say the pits, because I know you weren't fucking there." His hand was in her hair, pulling her head back so she was forced to look into his eyes. His other hand, clamped painfully around her arm. Cyrus jumped to his feet but made no move to intervene, his bindings glowing as he struggled against his own commands.

"Why don't you just compel me to tell you?" she spat, pushing her palms against his chest, wanting to put as much distance between their bodies as possible. "You do every other day."

Zagan sneered at her. "I'm giving you one chance to make me believe you or I will."

Her anger flaring, she beat her fists against his chest, pulling her body down and out of his grip, scrambling a few feet away from him. "I'm tired, Zagan!" she cried, turning on her heel to face him, stepping back as he stalked towards her. "You haven't let me sleep since you took over my bindings and I hadn't slept for over a week before that. Five weeks! I haven't slept in five weeks! I'm fucking exhausted! I went somewhere quiet so I could at least rest. My powers are all over the place because I can't even do that!"

"You wouldn't need sleep if you would just transform," he snapped, his voice full of malice like he was blaming her for not yet transforming.

"Trust me, if I could bring that about sooner I would," she said, a slight panic rising as she felt the edge of the kitchenette at her back, preventing her from retreating further. "Anything to give me some form of advantage over you."

Zagan neared her, keeping his hands by his side, towering over her as she leant back over the stove. "As long as you're bound," he whispered, his face nearing hers, "I will always have the advantage."

"Screw you," she hissed, using the last of her bravado.

"You offering?" he asked, a sinister smile on his lips as he took hold of her chin, pulling her closer to him.

"You're fucking disgusting, you know that?"

With an exasperated sigh, Zagan pushed her away, walking back over to the table. "What is it going to take to get you to submit?" he said, swiping over the surface, sending books and scrolls flying through the air.

"Let me fucking sleep!" she shouted, pushing away from the stove.

Turning back to her, she saw thunder in his eyes. "I'm willing to let you sleep, if you submit."

"I will never submit to you!" she yelled, her hands balling into fists by her side. Being near Ambrose again had stoked a fire in her, one she had been keeping in check for the last few days. Now she wanted to let it out. "I will fight you for the rest of my time bound to you. If you ever touch me, as soon as I break, I will kill y—"

His hand shot out and grabbed her by the throat cutting off her words. She clutched at his wrist, gasping for air. "I am getting tired of your insolence," he snapped, his talons digging painfully into her neck.

Fuck you! the voice in her mind screamed, further fanning the flames in her stomach. "And I am *tired!*" she screamed.

As she screamed, the fire within her exploded, lightning sparking from every pore of her body. Her bindings tried to contain her, constricting with white hot pain around her limbs. Exhaustion overwhelming her, her mind went blank allowing her raw, uncontrolled power to take over. A shockwave of lightning burst from her core, pulsing out and through the room, sending Zagan and Cyrus crashing to the ground. The table in the middle of the room cracked and splintered, the books and scrolls burning on impact.

Her lightning subsiding, Lena tried to look around the room, even as her vision spun and the ground rushed up to meet her. Crying out softly, she collapsed to the floor, her world going dark as she passed out.

When she woke, she found herself in her bed, staring at the top of the alcove. Remembering what had happened, she sat bolt upright in the bed, turning her head towards the door, her breath catching in her throat as she saw Zagan leaning against it. He had not come into her room before, leaving most of their interactions to either the main room or out within Hell. Now this small final sanctuary she had was gone.

"What are you doing here?" she asked, trying to swallow the fear building within her chest.

He was silent, his bright orange eyes burning into her. His face was expressionless, but she could feel the rage radiating from his body. She was scared, and everything in her told her she should be. He had always been menacing but now he was downright terrifying. Forget fighting, she wanted to flee. When he finally spoke, his voice was deathly quiet, a silent anger behind his words. "You got your sleep, now lie back and stay still. Do not use your powers."

Her body obeyed, despite her mind protesting, an unsettled feeling wreaking havoc within her gut.

No, no, no, don't you dare!

"Wh- what are you doing?" she asked, her voice breaking.

Panic fully set in as Zagan placed his palms on the mattress either side of her head, lifting his knee and wedging it between her legs. "I'm done waiting for you to submit," he said leaning down towards her, his face mere inches from hers. "I will make you if I have to."

"Zagan, please, don't do this," she begged, her eyes wide, horrified by what was happening. Why now? She'd been trying to prepare herself for this, telling herself he wouldn't leave her alone forever, but now that he was above her, she was totally unprepared. Her mind wasn't working, frozen with fear.

"Quiet," he snapped, his fingers curling around her throat. Her mouth clamped shut at the command, even as she whimpered beneath him. "I do not want to hear another sound from you. You will learn your place as Margaret did. Now kiss me."

Her mind screamed in protest as he crushed his lips to hers, her mouth forced to obey him. As his tongue explored her mouth, she shut her eyes, trying to shut down, to shut everything out. She didn't want to feel or see or taste him. She prayed for the rock beneath her mattress to crack open and swallow her whole. She wanted to disappear. How bitterly she regretted not jumping into the Pit regardless of everyone else.

The ripping of her shirt startled her, forcing her to be aware of what was happening. Zagan had leant back on his knees, opening the front of her shirt, baring her body to him. She still had her bra giving her some cover, but she knew that wouldn't last long. Feeling his eyes on her skin, she wanted to be sick, her body shivering, not from desire, but utter terror.

He trailed his fingers over her stomach, the tightness in her chest increasing painfully as he did so. Unable to fight, he hooked his fingers in the seam of her jeans and ripped them down her legs, pulling her panties along with them. Death would be preferable to this, she thought, as he held her knees apart, staring at the point between her thighs. The growl he gave at the sight of her was feral, only serving to heighten her fear.

"I've never taken a boundling who hadn't transformed yet," he growled, laying back atop her, pushing his hips against hers, the fabric of his trousers still separating them. She could feel how hard he was beneath them, her body desperate to escape yet unable to act on it. "I wonder how tight you'll feel." He caught her mouth with his again, using his hand to angle her chin up to account for the size difference between them.

As quickly as he had kissed her, he pulled back standing off the bed and began stripping himself of his clothes. Lena stared at the top of the alcove, shock washing over her as she spied an imp looking over the edge, its black eyes locking with hers before it scurried up the wall and over to her desk, a small poof of flame indicating it had left. Glancing quickly to Zagan, she realised he hadn't seen the imp, too focused on looking at her. What was going on?

Fully undressed now, Zagan climbed back onto the bed, lowering his body over hers. She could feel him pressed between her legs, not yet entering her, but enough that she felt completely violated. His mouth was on her neck, biting and sucking painfully, his hand stroking down the side of her body. "I'm not going to make this quick, beautiful," he whispered into her ear, her mind rebelling against his hold of her. "I plan to enjoy your body in every way possible. You won't even remember Ambrose's name when I'm finished with you."

His hand slipped between their bodies, two of his fingers sliding into her suddenly. There was no gentleness to his touch and she felt a sharp pain run from her core through her stomach. His talons dug into and ripped through her flesh as he entered her. The command to keep quiet preventing her from crying out, she squeezed her eyes shut. If she must be subjected to such treatment, she was not going to witness it visually.

Zagan began to move his fingers, not caring for any pain caused by his talons as he did so. His other hand and mouth travelled everywhere over her body. She was going to need a bucket full of pumice stones after this to get rid of every bit of skin he touched. Desperately, she tried to think of something, anything else, reciting demonic lore in her mind, trying to shut out the sensation.

A slight warmth washed over her side, but she refused to acknowledge it. Nothing in her mind could ever associate warmth with what was being done to her now. As soon as the warmth disappeared, there was a loud crashing sound, the air forced from her body as a great weight suddenly collapsed on her. Gasping, her eyes flew open, locking with Morgan's red glow, her wings spread out behind her filling the small room.

Zagan was still on top of her, his head pressed against the wall, his body slumped motionless. Morgan grabbed Zagan's shoulders and pulled him from Lena, throwing him onto the ground with a loud thud. Quickly, she turned back around and grabbed the blanket at the foot of the bed, wrapping it gently around Lena's body.

"Lena?" Morgan said, cupping her face in her hands. "Are you okay?"

We are now, her inner voice replied even though she couldn't.

"You can't speak, can you?"

She merely blinked at Morgan, hoping she could convey her gratitude with her eyes alone. Her body remaining limp from her command, Morgan lifted her into her arms and, stepping over Zagan's body, left the room. Lena knew he wasn't dead, but she wished he was. She wished she was.

"Cyrus," Morgan called as they entered the main room. Lena could see him from the corner of her eye as he jumped up from the table and rushed over to them. "Take her," she said, transferring her into his arms. Lena welcomed the warmth of Cyrus' arms under her as he pulled her tightly into his embrace. She could see his face now, saddened to see such worry and fear etched onto his features. "Go to Archie. Zagan won't be knocked out for long so hurry. I'll stay here as long as I can to delay him."

Cyrus' chest was shuddering as he breathed, "Did he...?"

"No, not completely," Morgan said, shaking her head. "But if I'd been any later... Don't think on that. You need to run with her, now."

"But how did you know?"

"There is more at work here than you know, Cyrus. Now please, listen to me and go."

Turning away slightly, Cyrus paused before looking back at the Keeper. "Thank you, Morgan. Thank you."

The huge demon smiled and touched her fingers to Lena's cheek. "She's worth the trouble this is going to cause. Now go."

Looking down at her, Cyrus nodded in agreement, his flames encompassing their bodies as they left Zagan's apartment behind.

CHAPTER FORTY-ONE

"Archie! Help, please!" Cyrus cried as they reappeared in his chambers.

As Lena still couldn't turn her head, she strained to look out from the corners of her eyes. She could make out Archie's frame in the corner of the room as he stared at them bewildered.

"Cyrus? Lena? What are you... What's happened?" he rushed over to them, his face coming into her field of view as he searched her face.

"Zagan was going to rape her," Cyrus said hurriedly, his chest heaving against her body. She could feel the panic in him. "He was so angry. I don't know what happened, he just told me to stay out of her room. Morgan came out holding her. We had to run, Archie. We had to!"

"Morgan?" Archie queried looking at Cyrus. Quickly, he placed his hand on Cyrus' back, gently guiding him into the room. "Come on, lay her on the bed. I'll find some clothes. Why isn't she moving?"

Holding her firmly against him, Cyrus rushed over to the bed, gently placing her atop the mattress. She didn't want him to let go. If only she could move her arms and hold on to him. He seemed to be of the same mind, as he knelt by the bed, taking hold of her hand within his. "I'm pretty sure he compelled her not to. I also think she can't speak right now."

"Okay. It will take some time for those commands to wear off," Archie said, coming back with some clothes. Lena chuckled internally noting they were the clothes she had left there just before Zagan took her. He handed them to Cyrus before turning his back. As gently as possible, Cyrus dressed her, keeping the blanket over her as best he could until she was fully dressed. Feeling better now that she was not exposed for all to see, she took some deep breaths, trying to slow down her heart. Panic still felt necessary, but she needed to clear her head. Archie turned back to them and sat on the other side of the bed from Cyrus, taking her face in his hands. "Lena, look at me. Blink once for no and twice for yes. Are you hurt?"

Of course she was hurt, but regardless of the command to not use her powers, her instinctual healing ability had not been affected. All physical wounds were gone, but she ached internally, disgust at what had happened to her sending prangs of pain through her stomach. But she blinked once as there was nothing Archie could do about that.

Cyrus breathed out in relief at her answer. "Zagan will wake up soon," he said, holding her hand tightly between his. "He won't be far behind us."

"Would he have any reason to think you came here?" Archie asked, looking at him.

"I don't think so..." he shrugged. "Morgan told us to come here."

"I'm curious as to why Morgan has gotten involved. She usually stays out of things like this," Archie said, turning back to Lena. Sighing heavily, he pressed his lips together. "Well, he'll figure it out soon enough through your bond anyway. Stay here for now. I'm not going anywhere. If anyone, I mean *anyone*, flames in or knocks, you take her and run. Don't wait to find out who it is. Try not to go anywhere obvious or predictable, and if you do, do not stay there long. I can hold Zagan back for a while. Do not let him get hold of her again," he emphasised, looking pointedly at Cyrus.

The boundling sighed and pressed his lips to her hand. "I never wanted him to have her in the first place," he said sadly.

"Cyrus," Archie said sympathetically, "you are as susceptible to his commands as she is. You have to stay together at all times. Do not let the other get under his control again." Slowly, Archie turned on the bed slowly and held his hand up over Lena's chest. Small licks of blue flames sprang from his hand reaching out to her body before snaking over her skin. "Why didn't you take her to Ambrose?" he asked, not looking up from his work.

"She's been commanded to kill him on sight," Cyrus explained, squeezing her hand tightly.

"Right. Good point," Archie nodded. His flames continued to travel over her body and Lena breathed with relief as the warmth eased some of the pain caused by her bindings. "Let's see what we can do about getting some of her movement back. I'm sorry Lena. I'm not strong enough to overcome Zagan's bindings, but I can try to ease his commands. Especially whilst he's knocked out."

He worked silently for a while. Lena closed her eyes briefly, but remembered the feel of Zagan atop her, so quickly reopened them, focusing on Cyrus' face instead to distract her. He wasn't looking at her, his eyes staring off into some distant point only he could see. Her hand was still firmly grasped within his, pressed against his lips, holding onto it like it was a lifeline.

"I never wanted Zagan to get hold of her," Cyrus repeated suddenly, his voice barely louder than a whisper. Archie looked up at him, but continued to run power through her body. She could just about twitch her fingers and toes now. "I tried to talk him out of it. He would just tell me to shut up. I made a promise to her when we were kids that I would keep her safe. That I would come back for her. I've failed in every way possible." Dropping his head so her hand was against his horns, Lena was sure he was holding back tears. Her own eyes stung with emotion. "She's my little sister, Archie. I love her."

Archie pulled back his hand, smiling softly as he stopped the flow of his flames. "I think you are not alone in that sentiment, Cyrus."

Lifting his head, Cyrus looked in her eyes, just as her own tears escaped down her face. Inhaling sharply, he pulled her into his arms, pressing her cheek against his shoulder, as he held her tightly against him. "I'm so sorry, Lena. I'm so sorry."

After Zagan's callous touch, Cyrus felt so safe and secure, the same way he had felt when he saved her from their foster father. She used to think her time in foster care was hell, now a small part of her would give anything to go back to it. To forget everything that had happened. The other part, the larger part, wouldn't change anything. Well, except maybe Zagan... But she would never give up Ambrose. Not for anything. Regardless of how Cyrus felt, he had not failed her. He was with her now, when it mattered most, and as soon as she got her voice and body back, she would let him know that.

She heard the igniting of flames before she felt the heat. Cyrus' grip tightened as his own flames coursed over them, even as Archie shouted, "Run!"

Unsure of where they had landed, Lena accepted it might be better she didn't know. She shut her eyes, as Cyrus lowered her body to the floor, resting her back against a wall. Being carried, without being able to adjust her body at all, was starting to make her feel dizzy. The hardness of the rock beneath her was steadying, as she opened her eyes and realised they were in a hellhound alcove.

"We can't stay here for long, but I need to think about where to go," Cyrus said, crouching back on his feet, looking into her eyes. "All the dens look more or less the same so we should be okay for a bit. He'll go to mine first, but I doubt he'd think of this one for a bit. I don't get along with the Keeper here, generally. Oh hey, Gray..."

Tegan's hellhound, Gray, approached them cautiously, sniffing as he came closer. Ignoring Cyrus, he padded over to Lena, nuzzling against her cheek, soft huffs of breath teasing at her hair. Slowly, she managed to lift her hand, her fingers shakily scratching beneath his muzzle. Her arm ached with the movement, but at least the command was easing, so she welcomed the pain. With a gentle push against her cheek, Gray huffed and turned away, moving to sit in the entrance of the alcove, filling it with his size.

Cyrus chuckled slightly, before moving to sit next to her, taking hold of her arm and massaging it gently, helping to ease the pain. "Gray will want to protect you as much as Zamira does as her mate. Not quite sure why he's here and not with Tegan, but I don't really care right now. As long as we don't look at him, Zagan shouldn't figure out where we are too quickly."

Swallowing, Lena tried to test out her voice. After a false start, she managed to croak out a soft sound. "C-Cyrus..."

"Hey," he smiled, nudging her with his shoulder, "there's that wonderful voice of yours."

"Th- thank you," she stuttered. "Thank you, for... for being my brother."

With a contented sigh, Cyrus leant over her and kissed the top of her head, wrapping one arm around her shoulders. "Thank you for being my sister."

"We should go top-side," she said, her voice still shaky. "Somewhere crowded where no one can use powers."

Cyrus shook his head. "No," he said softly. "It's not a bad idea as such, but it would mean we can't flame out. Zagan gets near enough for us to hear him and we're screwed."

"Right... yeah," she sighed. "This is crazy, Cyrus. We can't run forever. Zagan is powerful enough that even if we wanted to bind to someone else, there's only a handful that could manage it."

"You want to go back?" he teased.

She poked her tongue at him, scrunching her face, thankful she could move it again. "Of course not. I just want to lay this all out. This is feeling oddly reminiscent of when we were twelve and sixteen hiding in our rooms. What's our next move, other than running? Hide? Where?"

"I don't know," he sighed. "I don't know where to go from here."

"I really miss my powers right now," she groaned. "Hopefully they come back soon."

"We could go find Ambrose," Cyrus chuckled. "They'd come back real fast then."

She elbowed him in the ribs. "Not funny."

"A little funny."

Falling silent, Lena tried to think of where to go next, as she tested her ability to move her body. "Help me up, I think I can just about bend my knees now."

Making sure to keep his hand on her, Cyrus got to his feet and lifted her up. Testing her strength, she managed to support herself, taking a few steps within the alcove. Hovering her hand over Cyrus' so they could leave together in a second, she held herself up as her limbs finally began to obey her own mind again.

Everything in Ambrose hurt as he had walked away from Lena. He hung back in the corridor, watching from a little outcrop, making sure she couldn't see him, but so he could ensure she didn't return to the edge of the pit. Sighing with relief when she ran off down the opposite corridor, he gathered his flames and headed home. In his rush to get to her, he didn't have anyone with him, having lost Pasha on route and too many of Zagan's allies were looking for him. Retreating to his office as quickly as possible was his best protection. He hated hiding, but he accepted that his safety was one of the things still giving Lena hope of surviving Zagan, so he swallowed his pride.

If only he could swallow the fear of what Zagan was going to do to her if he realised, they had been together.

Sitting back in his chair, he stared at the ceiling. Giving up on his plans to find someone he trusted to overcome Zagan's bindings had been one of the hardest things he had to do. It felt like he was giving up on her. But he was in no position to refuse the will of the Princes of Hell. Regardless, it killed him inside slightly to do so. He hadn't told Marcus about their visit. Something felt like he needed to keep it to himself for now. Instead, he just told Marcus that they needed to take some time for things to settle, give Zagan a false sense that they had given up. Lying to his friend felt almost as bad.

With a heavy sigh, he tried to busy himself with his work. He had let things fall slack for a while and although he had the protections Lena set up for him, his own alliances had become a little strained in his despair. He needed to repair them or risk having one of them turn on him. Lena's alarm system was rather encompassing, but only she understood the full extent of who would alert it. Whether his own allies would trigger it if they turned on him was unknown.

After a couple of hours, he had managed to shore up at least three of his alliances, sending them slightly more than he would normally from his own finances to make up for his recent distractions. He was just in the process of calling another when Marcus burst through his door, an overly excited look on his face.

"You won't believe what is going on down there!" he burst out, running up to Ambrose's desk.

Raising his brow dubiously, he leant back in his chair and folded his arms over his chest. "Are you really going to make me guess?"

"Hell no," Marcus said, practically bouncing on the spot. "Lena and Cyrus are on the run."

"What?" he cried, jumping to his feet with such force that his chair toppled behind him, crashing against the wall.

The cambion nodded enthusiastically. "They ran a few hours ago. It's chaos!" he said as Ambrose walked around the desk to him. "No one knows if they are even still in Hell, but everyone is looking for them. Well, I mean, Zagan and his buddies are looking for them. Some others are looking as well, but everyone else is just trying to delay Zagan, holding him back from finding them."

Still trying to comprehend what Marcus had said, he stared at his friend, an apprehensive joy building in his chest. "What happened? Why now?"

"Ah..." Marcus hesitated, his face falling slightly. "You don't want me to answer that."

The joy was gone, replaced by sudden, indescribable rage. Zagan had touched her. No way she had submitted willingly. With a loud cry, he swiped across his desk, his lamp, laptop and paperwork flying across the room. "I'm going to kill him," he shouted, beating his fist down on his desk, causing it to crack under the force. "Screw the Princes!"

Marcus tilted his head at the comment. "The Princes? What?"

"Mammon and Asmodeus came here a few weeks ago," Ambrose said, pushing away from his desk and running his hand through his hair. "They told me they were protecting her. They told me to stop trying to find a way to get her back and I did and now they've let him... Ah!" Power burst from his hands, the red strands shooting across the room and hitting one of his armchairs, the fabric bursting on impact.

"Ambrose, the Princes did protect her," Marcus said, drawing his friend's attention back to him. "Morgan saved her. Before Zagan could go too far. Morgan only intervenes outside of the Repository if ordered to by Belphegor. That's what has gotten everyone so riled up down there."

Studying his friend, Ambrose struggled to understand, his mind racing, his primal need to find Lena and protect her keeping his mind from functioning properly. He needed to calm down, to think rationally. Taking a deep, steadying breath he looked at his fireplace. "I'm going now," he said through gritted teeth, beginning his transformation into his demonic form.

Marcus shook his head slowly. "We don't know if Lena's command to kill you is still in effect, Ambrose. You should stay here."

"You think I'm just going to sit here after you told me that?" he scoffed, turning back to the cambion.

Admitting defeat with a shrug, Marcus transformed and walked over to his friend. "Fair enough. But I think we should try to avoid her at least."

"Fine. I'm going after Zagan anyway."

"That's a worse plan."

Smiling at his friend, Ambrose could see the glint of fire in his eyes, despite his vocal objections. "You'll need that cuff to stop me."

Marcus chuckled, placing his hands on his hips. "And if I could find where you hid it, I would."

"Come on," he said, holding out his hand. "Let's go help our girl."

Returning his smile, Marcus reached out and clasped his arm. "Now that I can support."

Flaming into Hell, Ambrose could tell the moment they arrived that everything was different. There was a tension in the air that was almost oppressive, but also full of excited energy. Demons were rushing around them, racing off to wherever they were destined. Some stopped and stared at him, hushed whispers breaking out around them. Keeping his power close to the surface, he looked around them, ready to react in an instant.

"Ambrose, Marcus!"

Turning on his heel, he saw Pasha running up to them.

"About time you got here," she said, pulling up just in front of them. "They were spotted in one of the hellhound dens a few minutes ago. Gray attacked the one who found them. One of Zagan's allies."

"Gray? Why was he in a den?" Marcus asked.

"It was just a coincidence. Lucky coincidence. Tegan was renovating his den, but why am I wasting time explaining that?" she shook her head, berating herself. "They're with Xavier at the moment. He—"

"Pasha," Ambrose interrupted her. He'd never heard her speak so fast. "Where is Zagan?"

"Oh no," she said, staring at him. "Don't go there, Ambrose. He's pissed. You wouldn't stand a chance right now. Archie and Damon are tracking him. Titus and his boundlings are trying to delay his allies, but..." she trailed off. "This is going to turn into civil war. With Morgan getting involved... Do you not want to find Lena anyway?" Pasha asked, confusion on her face.

"He can't," Marcus answered quickly. "Last we heard, Zagan commanded her to kill him on sight. Can't risk it."

"Great..." she sighed. "Well, come on. You can't stay here. I've already spied two demons that will run straight to Zagan. We need to protect you as much as her."

Nodding in agreement, Ambrose and Marcus followed Pasha through the corridors as she led them towards the nurseries. Looking over her shoulder, she explained further what had been happening as they walked.

"Word got round very quickly that Morgan got involved, knocking Zagan out so Lena and Cyrus could get away. Knowing she only acts on the word of the Princes, it has caused quite a stir," she said, turning down another corridor. Ambrose recognised she was taking a long, non-direct route, making it harder for anyone to track where they were going. "They went to Archie first. Lena was commanded not to move or speak so she's still regaining control of her body. Her powers are also unavailable right now, but Xavier is working on that. When they went to Xavier, she could just start to walk on her own again. She and Cyrus are staying close though, making sure they stay in physical contact should they need to flee. Can't even say for sure if they are still with Xavier." Entering the nurseries, Pasha took them to a small room off to the side. Her office. "We can take a moment in here," she said, ushering them inside. "Zagan and his men started scouring Hell, looking for them. Damien and his boundlings went to the Repository, the Vault, even setting up lookouts in the pits. The group Lena set up for you, have been taking them out systematically but we've lost track of Damien for now."

"How long can we really expect them to run?" Marcus asked.

Pasha shrugged. "I don't know. But there are so many that want to help her. So many that don't want Zagan to get her back."

"Cyrus needs to be protected as well," Ambrose said, hardly believing he was saying those words. "If he gets Cyrus, Lena will go back. She won't risk her brother."

"We know," Pasha nodded. "We will."

"Where's Lena's conduit?" he asked, folding his arms across his chest.

"In her room," she answered. "We've already tried to get it. Nessa is still knocked out from trying. No one can touch the chest it's in."

"I can," he said with a deep breath. "There are things in it she might need. I'll go get it."

Pasha scoffed. "You realise Zagan's likely told her to empty it. It might not have anything inside."

"We need to check," he said, turning to Marcus. "I never thought I'd go back there."

"Which room do you think she's in?" Marcus asked, looking at him.

"Most likely Margaret's," he sighed. "Pasha, can you try to find her? Tell her I'm here at least?"

Pasha nodded, a soft look on her face. "Of course."

He and Marcus flamed away, travelling directly to Zagan's apartment, powers at the ready in their hands.

CHAPTER FORTY-TWO

After they had been found in the den, Cyrus, on Lena's suggestion, took them to Xavier's archive. She'd hoped it would have been empty, but had been pleasantly surprised to find Xavier there. He had quickly informed Pasha of their location with the intention that she could misdirect Zagan's lackeys. Unaware of what had been going on, Xavier filled them in as best he could.

"Pasha has been organising the group you put together as best she can. They would prefer to listen to you, but understand the circumstances are less than ideal," he explained, running some of his power over her back, trying to ease her commands as Archie had done. "In less than an hour, she's found enough demons that won't actively fight, but are happy to act as watchers, looking out for Zagan's movements and alerting her as soon as they see or hear anything. Archie took quite a hit when Zagan found you with him, but he's tracking Zagan personally."

"Is he okay?" Lena asked, keeping Cyrus' hand firmly between hers as he knelt in front of her.

"Archie is fine," Xavier assured her. "There are a few healers in our group. Try that."

Lifting one hand, Lena tried to summon her lightning. Small sparks danced across her fingers, tingling against her skin. Focusing, the sparks grew pooling in a plasma ball, building and turning over in her palm. Pouring a little more power into it, she was able to draw her lightning over her arm, sparking up to her shoulder, before she extinguished it. "Much better," she sighed, feeling her power again coursing through her body. "Thank you."

"Don't mention it." Xavier walked to her side and sat down next to the pair. "Zagan is familiar with my archive, so you can't stay here long. The plan is to keep you moving for the next few days, until things can settle a little."

"Settle?" Lena scoffed. "This will never settle, Xavier," she sighed, shaking her head. "Zagan will never stop hunting us, and until I transform, I still need to sleep and eat, even down here."

"Food is easy enough. Sleep, however," Cyrus said, tilting his head. "The only option for now would be for me to carry you round whilst you sleep, and I doubt that would be comfortable."

"How much sleep did I get before... you know," she asked.

"About five hours."

"So, I should be fine for a week or so," she nodded, pressing her lips together. "I know somewhere we can go. But," she groaned, "we need to get something first."

"Where from?" Xavier asked, looking curiously at her.

Bracing herself for their reaction, she smiled at them. "From... Zagan's apartment."

"No," Cyrus and Xavier said simultaneously.

Rolling her eyes, she looked back and forth between the men. "I know it's an insane idea, but I left something there, and I can't risk Zagan finding it."

"Lena, it's more than insane," Cyrus said, tugging on her hand. "If anyone is there, anyone at all..." he shook his head. "We might as well just walk up to Zagan and say we surrender."

Xavier placed his hand on her back. "What is it?"

"It's a summoning crystal. Ambrose made it so I could call him to me if he'd been summoned away," she explained looking at the floor. "I should never have taken it with me, but it was all I had to still connect myself to him."

Cyrus sighed and dropped his head onto their joined hands.

"Is it in your chest?" Xavier asked.

"Yes, but Zagan made me give him access to it. So, it's not safe in there anyway," she whispered, guilt building in her gut.

"Does he know about it?"

She shook her head. "Not explicitly, but he could figure it out."

"Alright," Xavier said, getting to his feet. "We'll go get it. But we go to the Vault after, stash it there. The Caretaker can look after it, hide it among the other objects."

Lena nodded, rubbing her thumb in apology along Cyrus' forehead. He huffed his annoyance, but looked up at her, nothing but concern in his eyes. "Stay close," he said, standing and pulling her to her feet.

All three jumped as the door to the archive slammed open, crashing loudly against the wall behind it. Cyrus' flames were already flaring around him and Lena as Zagan stepped through, his face dark with rage.

"Don't flame," he commanded, his voice deathly calm.

Cyrus' flames extinguished immediately, both his and Lena's bindings glowing in the dim light. Xavier twisted on his heel and grabbed their hands, disappearing in his own flames, the sound of Zagan's roar of frustration fading as they fled.

"He can't command me," Xavier said, quickly pushing them down a corridor. They ran as fast as they could, Cyrus quickly picking Lena up and straddling her across his back, cursing under his breath as he did so. "The cambion residences are just down the next left."

Lena shut her eyes, simply feeling the movement of Cyrus against her, focusing on her power, making sure she could still access it, despite being cut off from the flames of Hell. It was there. The plasma ball of raw energy, filling and sparking within her chest. She could still fight if needed. As they rounded the last corner, she felt Cyrus pull up quickly, her eyes flying open as she saw what was ahead of them.

Within the cavern she saw Titus trading fire with Damien and two of his boundlings. Similar in power manifestations and their hoarding of boundlings, it seemed like they were evenly matched. But for what he lacked in size compared to most demons, Damien made up for it in strength, the muscles under his sienna-burnt red skin rippling as he flung fireballs with abandon towards Titus. Oppositely, Titus was fast, diving effortlessly out of the way. Uniquely he was able to create explosions of power a few feet away from his body, using this now to offset the footing of the boundlings assisting Damien.

Spotting them, Damien snarled as he turned his fire towards them, a fireball landing between Cyrus and Xavier, separating them.

"Shit," Cyrus cursed, landing deftly on his feet, trying to find Xavier.

"Put me down," Lena cried, scrambling down his back onto her feet. Clapping her hands together, she sparked her lightning over her arms. On throwing her hands out, a wide fan of electricity spread throughout the cavern, moving rapidly through the air. Damien and his boundlings quickly disappeared to avoid the wave; Titus dropping to the floor as it passed over him harmlessly. Dissipating the force, Lena ran up to Titus, clasping his hand in hers.

"Good to see you, sparky," Titus said, brushing off his stomach. She smiled at the nickname.

"Sparky?" Cyrus chuckled coming up behind her.

"Yeah, I kind of, *accidentally*, blasted one of Titus' boundlings across the Repository once," she smirked. "Name kinda stuck."

"Good times," Titus chuckled, patting her on the back.

"Simpler times," she commiserated. "Zagan found us. Cyrus and I can't flame anywhere now."

"Right, so where do you need to go?" he asked.

"We were heading for Zagan's apartment," Xavier answered, walking up to them.

"Bad plan," Titus shook his head. "He's alarmed the area. I heard Ambrose was around here so I came to find him. Damien got to me first."

"I have to try," Lena pleaded, grabbing him by the arm.

"Damien will be back soon, and likely with Zagan," he said firmly. "You need to keep moving. Go to the Vault, regroup there and then track back if you really ne—"

They were interrupted in their conversation as Damien and three boundlings flamed back into the cavern, surrounding them. Unable to react appropriately, Titus grabbed Lena as Xavier caught hold of Cyrus, flaming to one of the cavern's entrances, outside of Damien's circle, but still within firing range. A ball of fire hit Lena in the back as she and Titus landed, ripping her from his grasp and sending her hurtling across the floor, pain radiating through her body.

"Lena!" Cyrus screamed for her, scrambling away from Xavier trying to reach her. Xavier and Titus threw their powers towards the four demons, trying to give them cover.

Her body was already healing as she pushed herself up onto her feet. Her shirt was burnt but at least it was still intact for the most part. Covering her body with lightning she quickly retaliated, sending bolts of electricity directly at Damien. Nearing her, Cyrus joined in her efforts, sending his own fireballs to mix with her lightning as it flew through the air.

"You two need to get out of here!" Titus shouted over his shoulder. "We'll hold them back!"

One of the boundlings flamed out suddenly, immediately reappearing behind Lena. Feeling his presence, she dropped to the floor, ducking underneath his arms as he reached for her. Twisting round, she gathered her lightning in her palms and touched them to his stomach, shocking him and sending him staggering over his own feet. Looking towards Cyrus she tried to reach for him, but felt the boundling wrap his arms around her shoulders, his flames just starting to lick at their feet.

"Zamira!" she shouted, calling her hellhound, who appeared beside them, immediately snapping at the demon's arms and ripping him away from her with a hellish snarl. Jumping forward, she caught Cyrus' hand as he lifted her onto his back again, bolting out of the cavern. Looking over her shoulder, she saw Zamira running close behind them, Titus and Xavier forming a wall with their bodies in front of the corridor entrance. Turning back to the direction they were heading, Lena directed Cyrus to turn down various corridors, heading towards the Vault, doubling back here and there to confuse anyone tracking their scents. A group of demons tried to stop them at one point but quickly retreated as Zamira rushed them, coursing lightning over her fur chasing them down one of the hallways. Lena tried to call her back, but Zamira was locked on to her prey.

"She draws too much attention anyway," Cyrus panted, heading down another corridor.

"Sure, like we don't enough on our own," Lena scoffed, holding tightly onto his shoulders as he ran. A chill ran down her spine as the voice in her head screamed at her. *He's here!* Turning her head, she strained her hearing, picking up on the flapping of wings closing in on them. They were near a junction so at least her current plan wouldn't cut them off from an escape. "Put me down!" she cried.

"Are you crazy?" Cyrus snapped at her.

"Possibly," she huffed, "but all the same, put me down. Now!" Slowing slightly, he lowered her, looking at her with a confused expression. "Keep going," she said, pushing him forward.

Turning back the way they came, Lena gathered as much lightning as she could muster over her body, arcs shooting from her and hitting the corridor walls, creating small blasts against the rock. Cyrus nodded and turned on his heel heading for the cavern. With a cry, she unleashed her energy, pouring her anger and fear into the blast, sending it rippling through the corridor, tearing at the rock and causing a cave-in. Staggering slightly from the aftermath, she spun on the spot and raced after Cyrus. Hopefully, the cave-in carried far enough to trap whoever was behind them.

"No, you need to leave now!"

She heard Cyrus shouting in front of her, pushing her legs to move faster to catch up with him.

"Run!" he yelled as she rounded the curve into the cavern, her eyes locking with Ambrose.

"It's him!"

Immediately diving out of the way, Ambrose felt the warmth of the fireball as it passed over his head, thrown by one of the demons in the room. Sending out a burst of his own power, his tendrils hit the demon squarely in the chest, slamming him against the wall. The demon's body slumped to the floor. Marcus overcame the other demon that stood behind them by the door, knocking him out quickly. Boundlings left behind by Damien, evidently waiting to see if anyone would come back here.

"That felt a little too easy," Marcus said surveying the room.

"They're new boundlings, so unprepared. Likely only placed here so they could run and alert Damien. But let's assume other alarm systems have been activated," Ambrose said, striding towards his old quarters. "Zagan more than likely had Lena do the same here as she did at the manor." Dashing into the two rooms, Lena was indeed in Margaret's old room. He found her chest on the desk and carefully opened it. The book and everything else was still in there, including his summoning crystal. Sighing with relief, he picked it up and looked around. It had been centuries since he'd been here, and nothing had changed, except for the room now smelling of Lena's citrus scent. He avoided looking at the bed not wanting to risk conjuring images of her and Zagan upon it. Leaving the room, he ducked his head inside his old room, noting it now belonged to Cyrus. The third room, he could tell, had become Zamira's den, but neither she nor her pups were there presently. Hopefully, they'd returned to the main den for now whilst their mistress was absent. Sighing, he returned to Marcus. "Let's go."

"Where to?"

"The Vault. We need to pick up the cuff."

Marcus stared at him wide eyed. "That's where you hid it?"

Smiling at his friend, he held out his hand for him, transporting them directly to Calza's nest. The Vault was quiet but he knew the naga would have felt them arrive. Putting down Lena's chest, he walked off through the shelfs to retrieve the cuff. Heading back, he tossed it in the air to Marcus, who caught it with a laugh. "Hiding it in obscurity. I knew you would focus on searching the manor."

"That and I dislike coming here," Marcus shook his head. "What's the plan with the cuff then?"

"Get it on Zagan, if we can. I'd say get it to Lena, but..." he trailed off for a moment before shaking his head to clear his thoughts. "Zagan would just compel her without powers. I suppose it's possible the cuff doesn't stop his ability to compel her in which case he could still control her but he'd have a harder time of getting to her." He sighed heavily. "I'm not sure what to do next, Marcus. But I need to help in some way."

Marcus nodded. "Let's take this back to mine," he said, nodding to the chest. "I've got somewhere we can put it. Then let's help the others by taking out as many of Zagan's allies as we can. Thin the number of demons looking for her. That should give her some breathing room."

"Ambrose? Is that you?"

"Hey Calza," he called, turning as the Caretaker slithered towards them.

"Oh, it is good to see you," Calza cried, clapping their hands together. "Have you seen Lena? Is she safe?"

He shook his head slowly. "I don't know, sorry. Pasha said she is with Xavier at the moment. But I haven't seen her. Not yet."

"Zagan came by a few moments ago looking for her here," Calza said sadly, resting on their tail.

"Are you okay?"

Calza nodded. "Yes, I am fine. They cannot do anything to me here. The Vault protects me as much as the objects. You have the cuff?"

"Yes," Ambrose confirmed. "Thank you for keeping it safe. I'll let you know if I hear anything important."

"Thank you," they smiled and bowed their head. "I wish I could do more to help her, but I cannot leave the Vault."

"I know. Lena may still come here, and she will need you if she does. Good luck."

"You too, Ambrose."

Ambrose and Marcus disappeared in flames, taking Lena's chest with them. They stashed the chest in a secret compartment Marcus had built into one of the walls. As they were preparing to leave, they heard a loud commotion from the residence cavern outside.

"What the hell is that?" the cambion asked heading to the door.

"Careful," Ambrose cautioned as they opened it slightly.

Both jumped, ducking reactively, as waves of power rushed past the doorway. Flames, tendrils and lightning alike, clashed and lit up the cavern, a battle taking place below the walkway.

"Damien," Ambrose hissed, spying the demon below them as he pushed past his friend and into the cavern.

"Wait up!" Marcus called, following close behind him.

Below them, Damien and two of his boundlings traded blows with Titus, Xavier, Cyrus and... Lena! She threw bolts of lightning across the expanse of the cavern, ducking quickly out of the way as a demon flamed in next to her. Crouching down, she twisted and placed her hands flat on his stomach, sending a pulse of electricity through his body and forcing him back a few paces. Staggering, he quickly recovered and lunged at her, catching her around the shoulders, as Cyrus desperately tried to reach her.

Marcus quickly grabbed his shoulder, pulling him back slightly from the walkway.

"You need to stay out of her line of sight," he said quickly.

"Not a problem," Ambrose said, nodding towards her. He couldn't hear anything from below, but suddenly Zamira appeared beside her mistress, striking out immediately at the demon grappling with Lena. Taking the opportunity, she reached out for Cyrus who deftly lifted her onto his back, turning and running off down a corridor, Zamira close behind them. Titus and Xavier fought desperately to keep Damien and his boundlings focused on them, giving Lena and Cyrus time to escape. "Shall we?"

Smiling, Marcus lifted his wings behind him. "Absolutely." Launching into the air, he swooped down heading straight for one of the boundlings, his smoke trailing behind him. Ambrose jumped from the walkway, landing with a solid thud on the floor below, rolling to the side as Damien sent a charged fireball in his direction.

"Ambrose, look out!" Xavier called, throwing his smoke as a solid, dense ball to hit the boundling that was trying to come up behind him. The ball exploded against the boundling, forcing him back, giving Ambrose enough time to push towards Damien, his power swirling around his arms like snakes.

He and Damien met with a cry, grabbing each other by the shoulders, trying to knock the other off their footing. They had sparred many times in the pits, and so far, were even on wins and losses. Damien had greater strength, but his form got sloppy the more frustrated he got. All Ambrose had to do was piss him off, which shouldn't be too hard.

"How's Zagan's favourite lackey?" he quipped, pushing back and swinging a right hook, his power forming just before his hand, trying to connect with Damien's jaw.

Damien stepped back, leaning away from the punch as it missed him, a scowl on his face. "How's Zagan's weakest boundling?" he retorted, jabbing up for Ambrose's ribs. Sidestepping, Ambrose managed to land a couple of punches against Damien's shoulder as his swing caused him to over balance slightly.

Marcus had easily overpowered the boundling, he and Titus working to tie him up. Xavier took out the other boundling, leaving only Damien to be dealt with.

"I'm going after Lena," Xavier called, turning on his heel and rushing down the corridor she and Cyrus had taken, his wings beating furiously to boost his speed to catch up with them.

"Zagan's on his way," Damien spat, twisting on his heel, throwing fireballs one after the other at Ambrose, Marcus and Titus. The trio flamed in and out, sending waves of their own power focused on Damien. "They won't get far. I'm not the only demon helping him get her back. Give it up, Ambrose. She's not yours anymore!"

Anger flaring, Ambrose flamed in directly behind Damien, placing his hand swiftly on the back of his neck and punched out with his power. Staggering forward, Damien tried to swing back behind him with his claws and power, but met empty space as Ambrose flamed out of reach. Marcus threw a ball of smoke towards Damien, hitting him in the chest, knocking him back just as he regained his footing. Titus flamed to Damien's side, his fire in his hands, creating an explosion of flames as he clapped his hands together next to Damien's head. Collapsing to the side, Damien rolled across the floor, unmoving as he came to a stop. Titus ran over to him, checking to see if he was still conscious.

"Knocked out," he confirmed, raising up to look at Ambrose. "Lena has only just gotten her powers back but they're stuck to physical travel. They had a run in with Zagan and he commanded them not to flame. The plan is to take her to the Vault next. You should hurry."

A sinister laugh echoed through the cavern. "Thanks for the tip, Titus."

Looking up, Ambrose saw Zagan fly above them, dashing through an opening near the top of the cavern. "Shit," he cursed.

"I'm sorry," Titus said hurriedly, his eyes wide.

"Don't worry," Marcus shook his head. "We can still head him off. There are a few caverns between here and the Vault. Come on."

Pressing his lips together, Ambrose knew what was coming next. Taking hold of Marcus' hand, he gritted his teeth as the cambion lifted them both up into the air, heading down the same opening Zagan had taken, following his scent. Ambrose hated flying, preferring to keep his feet on the ground as much as possible. Regardless of their being demons, he found flying unnatural. But it had its uses. Marcus couldn't carry him for long though, eventually resting in a corridor to continue on foot. They lost Zagan's scent so had to guess how far he might have gotten in front of them.

"Do you think they reached the Vault by now?" Marcus asked, jogging beside him.

"Only if they went direct," Ambrose answered. "Lena knows to make a convoluted trail, doubling back and changing direction."

Marcus chuckled. "Just like we taught her. Go that way then. Hopefully, with how much time has passed, we should hit a cavern just after Lena and Cyrus and just before Zagan. Assuming they took this direction."

"Here's hoping," Ambrose said, changing direction to the corridor Marcus directed them to. It was only a few moments before they came across the cavern. It was empty for now, as they hung back in the entrance, listening carefully for any movement. There was a loud crash from the corridor on the opposite side of the cavern as it lit up with a red aura.

"Crap," Marcus sighed. "Looks like we got ahead of Lena."

Eyes wide, Ambrose couldn't speak as he saw Cyrus running up into the cavern. The boundling stopped in his tracks, his eyes locking with Ambrose's for a moment, shocked realisation overtaking his features.

"No, you need to leave, now!" Cyrus shouted, turning on his heel, his eyes darting to Lena as she pulled up behind him. He turned back to Ambrose and screamed across the cavern. "Run!"

Marcus grabbed hold of Ambrose's arm. "We need to go," he whispered harshly.

But it was too late as Lena turned to face the cavern, her eyes coming to rest on Ambrose. His breath caught in his throat as he saw immediate panic in her eyes. He couldn't move even as she lifted her hand and a bolt of lightning shot towards him.

CHAPTER FORTY-THREE

"Ambrose! No!" Lena screamed as she saw her lightning connect with his chest, sending him flying across the room and slamming into the wall. Her bindings burned with white-hot pain as she fought, desperately trying to control her limbs. "Marcus! Please," she pleaded, "get him out of here!" Cyrus grabbed her wrists, trying to pull them behind her back. In her mind, she wanted him to succeed, but the command overrode her will as she pushed out a shockwave, throwing him to the ground. "I'm sorry!"

A dense ball of smoke enveloped her, forcing her to her knees. She gratefully allowed it to overwhelm her. With Ambrose out of her sight, the command receded allowing her to breathe. She could hear shouting and the scrambling of feet around her, even as the smoke blocked off her remaining senses. Silently, she thanked fate for giving Ambrose a friend like Marcus. Someone who could shut her off from everything.

She was tired of running. Again, she asked herself how long could she and Cyrus reasonably run, anyway? All it would take was one hint of Zagan's voice in their ears and they were doomed. He'd come so close already. If he managed it again, he would have complete control over them, and she doubted he would allow anything like this to happen again. She didn't want to run for the rest of her time as a bound demon. No matter how powerful she got, Zagan could bring her down with a word.

Panic rising, she felt a hand clamp around the back of her neck, pulling her up and out of the smoke. She had become all too familiar with that hand being round her neck in the last few weeks.

"No!" she cried as Zagan pulled her body against his, clamping his arm around her waist.

"Be still," he commanded. Pain ripped through her body even as it fell limp in his arms.

"Let go of her, Zagan!"

Lena felt a small wave of relief at hearing Ambrose's voice behind her. She willed her head to remain against Zagan's chest, not daring to look at him. The command to kill him activated on sight, and she wasn't about to accommodate it any further.

Zagan's laugh echoed through the cavern, his arm tightening around her painfully. "Like you could make me," he sneered. "Give it up, Ambrose. She's mine."

"Like hell I am," she whispered, bile rising in her throat.

"Quiet," he snarled at her. Her mouth clamped shut as her bindings glowed. Everything in her screamed in rebellion.

"You have overstepped, Zagan," Marcus' voice carried with authority through the cavern. "You cannot control her forever."

Zagan's talons pierced the skin on her arm. She winced, but couldn't cry out or move away from the pain. "I don't need to control her forever," he said calmly. "Just long enough to get what I want." He looked down at Lena's face which she hoped adequately conveyed her utter contempt and disgust for him. His smile was terrifying as he set her down on her feet. "Be a dear, beautiful, look at Ambrose. Don't kill him, not yet. You may speak."

Her heart dropped as she heard Marcus shout at Ambrose to run. She saw Cyrus from the corner of her eye, his bindings glowing as he threw fireball after fireball at Marcus, forcing him away from Ambrose's side. Screaming internally, she turned on the spot, her eyes searching for her demon. She found him, his face contorted in pain as he fixed his own gaze on her.

"Run," she whispered, her breath catching in her throat with a pained sob. "Please run."

"I'm not going anywhere," Ambrose said, his eyes burning with a passion she had not seen before. "Not without you. I'm done hiding."

Her heart hurt more than it had ever before, breaking with both joy and sorrow at the sight of him. She would give anything to fall into his arms, to forget the world around them. But she couldn't, and it killed her inside. "Please, Ambrose," she begged, tears streaming down her face, "please, just run. I can survive Zagan. I can't lose you."

"Enough," her sire barked, coming up behind her. He bent down and whispered in her ear. "Kill him."

"No," her voice didn't feel like her own as red sparks ignited over her skin. Her gaze was locked on Ambrose as her bindings constricted like barbed wire around her arms, throat and waist. They burned unbearably as her head snapped back and a blood-curdling scream ripped from her throat. A shockwave emanated from every inch of her body, pulsing out and colliding with the men around her. Zagan flew back towards the wall, catching himself mid-air and landing with his hands shielding his face. Cyrus crashed loudly against a pillar, the force knocking him out. Marcus and Ambrose as the furthest away, fell to the floor as the shockwave started to dissipate.

Lena fell to her knees, clutching at her throat and shoulders, trying to scratch at the pain that coursed beneath her skin. The voice whispered in her mind. *Let me out... let me help...* Where it used to terrify her, with her desire to save Ambrose overwhelming her rational thought, now she welcomed it.

The transformation hit her like a train. Her body felt like it was on fire as her screams echoed through the cavern. Staring at her hands, she watched as her skin shifted to a bright blood red, her nails turning black and thick like talons with sharp cutting points. Deep red horns burst from the crown of her head flaring out and up like a towering crown interlaced with her hair. Hair that now, falling in front of her face, smouldered like burning strands of lava. She clawed at her back, opening her skin with her new talons even as her power fought to heal her at the same time. Sharp barbed points at the end of four black feathered wings pierced through her skin, bursting into the air as lightning crackled from their tips, arcing towards the ground and ceiling. The pain in her chest forced her upper body up and back so her face looked at the ceiling, her mouth open in a now silent scream, fangs ripping through her gums and settling either side of her human canines. Her limbs lengthen as her power enveloped her body like a suit of armour, creating thick, black straps of leather to bind around her torso, a strip of heavy fabric forming on her hips and over her legs.

Panting, her body relaxed as the pain subsided. Still on her knees, she managed to lift her head, poignantly aware of the weight of the horns that now adorned her crown. She looked at her hands, turning them over, taking in the sight of their now monster-like appearance.

"Finally."

Zagan's voice sounded far away as she attempted to get to her feet. But she no longer had feet. Now smooth hooves were in their place and she recognised the new found strength in her legs, the muscles under her skin rippling still with transformation energy. Placing one hoof flat on the ground, she pushed up to stand, her wings stretching behind her, helping her adjust her balance on the singular points.

"Oh my god," Marcus whispered as he propped himself up on his elbows.

Lena was acutely aware of the eyes on her. Raising her head, she looked around the room. Ambrose and Marcus were staring at her, mouths agape, as they lay on the ground. Zagan had a proud, vicious smile on his face.

She saw Cyrus lying motionless on the ground and in an instant, she was by his side, the flames disappearing as fast as they came. Kneeling down she checked over him, touching her fingers to his face. He was alive, just stunned. He groaned under her touch, his eyes fluttering open, widening as he took in the sight of her. "Lena?" he whispered. She nodded in answer.

"Leave him," Zagan snapped. Although the transformation seemed to have wiped her previous commands, her bindings were still intact as her hand dropped from Cyrus' face and she stood up and over him. She looked at Zagan, her mind racing as she tried to figure out the new sense of power she felt within. "Come here."

Slowly, her hooves moved as they carried her over to him, her skirts swirling around her legs. Her new height meant she no longer had to crane her neck to look into his eyes. He was still taller than her, but now only by a few inches. The smile on his face was sickening, and she wanted nothing more than to remove it.

"Look at me," Zagan commanded. She complied, seeing herself in his eyes. Against their red-orange gleam she could see that her own had turned black, glowing like endless voids. He lifted his hand and took hold of her chin, turning her face to the side and back as he inspected her. "Very nice," he said, grinning at her.

From the corner of her eye, she saw Ambrose and Marcus get to their feet. Marcus rushed over to Cyrus, helping to pull the boundling up from the ground and away from her and Zagan. Once she saw they were clear of any fallout she focused back on Zagan.

Time to play, the voice inside whispered.

Yes, she thought, yes, it is.

With a new found speed, she swiped with her arm, her talons ripping through Zagan's throat with ease. She heard Cyrus gasp behind her as their sire staggered back from her, his hands over his now haemorrhaging throat, black lightning sparking from his fingers as he tried to heal himself.

"You can't compel me if you can't speak," Lena snarled, her voice deeper and louder than before.

Spreading out her wings, she beat against the air, pushing herself forward and crashing into his body as he stared at her horrified. Her fist connected with his jaw, red lightning coursing up her arm to increase the force behind it. He was sent sprawling to the side, but didn't manage to go anywhere before she grabbed the edge of his wing, pulling him back towards her sharply just to sink her other fist into his stomach. Lightning exploded with the hit, sending him flying into the wall with a loud crash. His body slumped down to the floor as she started to stalk over to him, watching as his mouth opened and closed as he tried to speak.

"Lena, wait!" Marcus shouted. "You kill him, and you and Cyrus die. You're still bound to him."

With a sigh, she stopped in her tracks, mere inches from Zagan, savouring the taste of his fear in the air.

Let's do something about that, shall we?

Bending down, she wrenched his hands from his throat, ignoring his desperate attempts to push her away. "Stop moving," she ordered. "Or are you that eager to die?" Zagan stopped fighting her, and she placed her hand over the gash, coursing her energy through her fingers, healing his throat. "Make one sound, just one, and I will slice it again," she threatened, her voice deathly quiet.

With his blood no longer trying to escape his body, Zagan scowled at her as she helped him to his feet. To his credit, he kept his mouth tightly shut even as his heavy breathing did nothing to hide his rage. Lena kept her gaze on him, watching carefully as he began to flame away from her. Grabbing his arm, she moved with him, appearing before him wherever he landed. In tandem, they transported behind Ambrose, who spun on his heel even as they disappeared again. Zagan tried to push her hand from him as they travelled through the fires of Hell.

Her eyes never leaving his face, Lena saw glimpses of different corridors, the training pits and even the Repository from the corner of her eyes. He was trying to get distance between them. Enough that he would be able to make some kind of command out of the reach of her talons. Silently, they struggled against each other. Every time he would get her hand off his arm, she would lash out, ensuring some part of her still had a hold of him. She would not let him escape her.

"What's the matter, Zagan?" she sneered. "All this time, you've been trying to get close to me. Now you can't wait to get away." The expression on his face said it all. His frustration was like a drug to her now. But she'd grown tired of the cat and mouse game. "Enough," she snapped, pulling back and colliding her fist with his throat, paralysing his vocal cords and sending his body rolling across the ground. They'd ended up in the training pits, as the cavern filled with gasps of the various demons within. She looked around her, staring at each demon in turn, noting with satisfaction that most seemed to back away at the sight of her.

"He's here!" Archie barked, rushing over to them, Pasha and another demon Lena didn't know close behind him. His eyes locked with hers as he stopped in his tracks, Pasha colliding into him, surprise etched on both their faces. "Lena?"

She smiled at him, returning her gaze to Zagan. "Hello, Archie. I'm glad to see you are alright. I know you have been tracking Zagan, but I'm afraid I have to insist you don't interfere," she said walking over to her prey, who was now scrambling to his feet, his face thunderous.

"Don't have to tell me twice," the demonic trainer said. Turning back to the other demons he shouted, "Unless you feel like getting in *her* way, I'd take cover."

Lena held her hands either side of her body, pulling lightning across her body, sending vertical arcs lazily across the floor towards Zagan. Demons scrambled across the room, either making their way towards the exits or into the pits to watch the events unfolding before them with twisted fascination.

"Archie?" she said softly. He looked over his shoulder at her. "Would you find Ambrose for me? He's with Marcus and Cyrus in one of the lower caverns." Glancing at Zagan, Archie nodded and disappeared in flames. "Now," Lena said, stepping towards her sire, "where were we?"

With a strangled snarl, Zagan sent his own bolt of black lightning towards her. Flapping her wings, she easily dodged out of the way. He bellowed in anger, spreading his own wings charging at her, swinging his massive fists. She noted that her speed vastly outranked his own as she darted aside, her lightning crackling behind her. His body met with the remnants of her power as it rippled across his skin, threatening to send him to the ground.

She took to the air, hearing him roar behind her, confident that he would chase her. She heard his wings beating furiously as he leapt into the air, trying to gain on her. He swung a massive clawed hand at her legs hoping to catch her. Twisting her body, she effortlessly veered to the side, dropping underneath him as his wings whipped a gust of wind through her hair.

Now she was behind him.

Letting out a fierce cry, she launched a flurry of attacks, darting and weaving around Zagan's much slower, yet powerful strikes. Keeping her lightning in her fists, she jabbed at his back, waist and stomach. Her wings blurred as she spun and kicked, connecting a hoof with his chest sending him to the ground with a loud, deafening thud. Dust formed a thick cloud around his body as she landed gracefully a few feet from him, her wings flaring out behind her.

"Lena!"

She turned at her name, her breath quickening to see Ambrose's face as he sprinted through the entrance of the pits. Marcus, Cyrus and Archie followed close behind him.

"Stay back!" she shouted, her wings beating out with her command. Ambrose stopped in his tracks, but kept his eyes locked with hers. She was glad he was there, that she could see he was safe and well, despite the seared skin in the middle of his chest. She would fix that later, as soon as she fixed her problem with Zagan.

Sensing movement behind her, she stepped back just in time to see the cambion charging at her again, his wings buffering the air. Holding up her arms, they caught each other, hands on their upper arms, both pressing against the other in the hopes of gaining ground. Digging her hooves into the floor, Lena pushed against him, her lightning crackling across his skin, as his own black power coursed over hers. Simultaneously electrocuting each other was not going to work, their own powers counteracting the other. She knew that she was outmatched in terms of strength, her body still reeling from the effects of the transformation. Her only advantage had been speed.

Pushing as much power as she could muster through her arms, she managed to gain some space between them. She leapt into the air and soared above him, her wings flapping fiercely to gain altitude. Fighting on the ground was one thing, but feeling the currents of air beneath her was exhilarating. She had been made for this.

She turned in the air to see Zagan desperately trying to reach her, black lightning arcing from his body towards her. Baring her fangs, she sent a jolt of her own lightning towards him. The energies collided, causing her to drop in the air slightly as the clash affected the currents underwing. Black and red glowed together, forming a ball of building power, shockwaves and strands of arcing plasma emanating from its core. Small rocks loosened from the ceiling of the cavern, as plumes of dust rained down on the crowds beneath them.

"Lena!" Archie shouted from the ground. She could barely hear him over the blood rushing in her ears. "I'm not trying to interfere, but you need to end this! The cavern cannot handle much more!"

Not letting up, she glanced around her to assess the situation. Archie was right. Every now and then a powerful arc of power would break from the building force between her and Zagan, grounding to a wall or the floor, leaving behind a charred crater. Additionally, she calculated that Zagan's vocal cords would likely be working again soon and unless she could get close enough to shock them again, she was running out of time.

With a furious cry, she forced as much power as she dared forward, then leant back, dropping down beneath the ball of power to fly underneath Zagan. She could only hope that he was still looking to where she had been and wouldn't notice her current movements. Finding a rising current, she beat her wings quickly, adjusting her body to soar up behind him. Coiling her leg, she twisted in the air and landed a devastating kick to the back of Zagan's head, again sending him crashing to the ground below.

The force broke, a powerful shockwave ripping through the cavern, knocking over all things in its wake. Lena, herself, was thrown out of the air, her body slamming into the wall with a grunt, before falling to the floor. Her entire body ached from the impact, protesting against her as she rolled herself onto her hands and knees, trying to stand. Ambrose was helping Marcus up from the floor, his eyes frantically searching for her as the dust in the air started to settle.

Turning her head, she saw that Zagan had already made it to his feet. One of his wings was torn, bleeding profusely. He glared up at her, his eyes burning with rage. She groaned as she strained every muscle to push herself from the floor, using her wings as added support. Dread washed over her, as she recognised she was not ready for another encounter with him. Regardless of the sharpness of her mind, her body was shutting down. The transformation had been brutal. She needed to rest.

"You're hurt," Zagan rasped, scowling at her, his chest heaving as he regained his breath.

Lena looked down for a moment to see the shard of rock protruding from her hip. *Fuck.* Unable to take any action, she heard him spread his wings, despite the tear and rush at her. His arm collided with her neck, forcing her back against the wall with a sharp cry.

"Give it up, beautiful," Zagan sneered at her, a cruel smile on his lips. Her bindings glowed, but they didn't hurt. "You belong to me."

Her eyes darted to the cavern entrance, Ambrose's face pulling her focus. His anguish was unmistakable, mirroring her own as Zagan's arm pressed in on her neck.

Enough of this, the voice whispered internally.

A soft smile formed as she pulled her eyes away from Ambrose and stared at Zagan. His brow furrowed in confusion.

"No," she whispered. "I don't."

CHAPTER FORTY-FOUR

"What do we do?" Cyrus said, holding his side and standing next to Ambrose.

"Nothing," Marcus replied. "Look at them. Look at *her*. They're titans. They'll rip the rest of us to shreds."

Ambrose knew he was right, but his mind raced as he watched Lena and Zagan trade attacks above his head, trying to think of some way to help.

"Well, they better end this soon," Archie sighed. "They'll bring this place to the ground if they don't."

"We need to do something," Cyrus cried. "If Lena kills him, she will die as well. No matter how strong she is."

"So will you," Ambrose said flatly.

Cyrus shot him an annoyed look. "I don't care about myself. You think I cared about myself when I ran with her?"

"That's not what he meant, Cyrus," Marcus sighed, patting the boundling on the back. "But the threat on your life might be more persuasive to her than her own."

"Lena!" Archie shouted, causing Ambrose to flinch at the suddenness of it. "I'm not trying to interfere, but you need to end this! The cavern cannot handle much more!"

Ambrose turned his head, finally looking away from the battling demons to stare at the trainer. "Interfere?"

Archie shrugged in response, keeping his own gaze locked on Lena. "She told me not to interfere. This is me, not interfering."

"Brace yourselves!" Marcus cried as the shockwave hit.

Ambrose covered his face, as his body slammed into the floor, dust showering over him and the others. His only thought was to find Lena. Scrambling to his feet, he found Marcus and helped pull his friend up from the ground. Desperately, his gaze searched the cavern, trying to find any form of movement within the dust cloud.

"You're hurt."

He heard Zagan's voice and could just make out his frame. Following his gaze, he saw Lena, his stomach dropping as he saw the rock shard that was buried into her hip. Within a blink, Zagan had her pinned against the wall, his arm on her throat.

"Oh shit," Marcus whispered.

Ambrose lunged towards Zagan, fighting against Marcus and Archie as they tried to hold him back.

"Don't be stupid, Ambrose," Archie said. "They'll kill you."

"Let go of me!" he shouted, shaking their hands off him, although he heeded the warning, taking only a few steps forward. He felt helpless, cursing that he did not possess even a fraction of the power that had been displayed moments ago. If it meant Lena would survive this and be free of Zagan, he would gladly lay down his life, here and now.

Lena looked at him, her eyes locking with his. Eyes that now resembled endless pools of darkness, drawing him into their depths. His chest constricted painfully, pushing all air from his lungs. Every fibre of his being prayed to the powers of Hell to save her.

The smile that formed on her face was like a beacon to him in the darkest of nights as she turned back to Zagan and whispered to him. Ambrose couldn't hear what she said, but the light that emanated from her bindings was blinding. He was forced to look away, shielding his eyes, fear coursing through his body.

"What's happening?" Cyrus cried.

"What makes you think any of us know?" Archie barked at him.

"You are witnessing history in the making," a low, silky voice replied.

As the light receded, Ambrose raised his eyes to see Mammon standing before him. Her face was lit up with joy, her golden eyes looking past all of them towards Lena and Zagan. Taking a deep breath, he followed her gaze to see Zagan flying across the room, red lightning rippling across his body, continuing to pulse over his skin as he crashed into the ground.

Lena stood proud and tall, her hooves clipping loudly against the stone floor. Without pausing, she pulled the shard from her hip as she neared his body and threw it down like a knife, the point piercing one of his wings, pinning it and him to the floor. Her body crackled with energy and Ambrose saw, clearly, what the result of the light had been.

"Her bindings," he whispered to no one in particular, "they're gone."

And he was right. Her blood red skin was flawless, unmarked by any bonds.

"How?" Marcus asked, turning to Mammon. "How is this possible?"

The Prince of Greed smiled and nodded towards the other end of the cavern. Adjusting their gaze they saw Asmodeus walking alongside a large human-looking demon with long, tousled blonde hair and sharp features. Tattered, black feathered wings trailed on the ground behind him as he and Asmodeus walked towards Lena.

"Is that... Lucifer?" Cyrus asked, his voice barely more than a whisper.

"It is," Mammon responded, coming up to stand beside the boundling. "She is everything we hoped she would be. Lucifer has come to welcome our new sister."

Ambrose's eyes shot to her. "Sister?"

Mammon nodded, smiling warmly at him. "We have been awaiting her arrival for a long time."

"Cyrus," Lena called, as she stamped her hoof into the middle of Zagan's back, preventing further movement, as he struggled uselessly beneath her. "Come here."

Glancing at Ambrose nervously, Cyrus swallowed with fear. Ambrose nodded at him reassuringly. "Go," he urged.

"Don't you dare, Cyrus!" Zagan shouted, his voice broken.

Lena bent down, grabbing the cambion by his horns and slammed his head into the ground. "Shut up," she barked. Standing back up, she turned her face to Cyrus, her features devoid of emotion, and held out her hand for him. "Come here."

Cyrus took a deep breath and, after a slight push from Mammon, slowly walked towards his sister. Ambrose could have sworn Cyrus bowed his head as he approached Lena, noting that she now stood a few inches taller than him.

"Not so little now, little mouse," he said softly.

Lena smiled warmly at him. "Cyrus, I do not wish to kill Zagan whilst you are still bound to him. But I am going to kill him. Here and now."

"I understand," he replied. "It's okay. I'm ready."

"Take my hand, Cyrus," she said, flexing her fingers in invitation. Raising his hand for her, Lena took hold of his wrist, encircling her fingers around him. "Do you wish to bind to me?"

Marcus drew in a sharp breath, but Ambrose smiled. Even now, she continued to surprise him. The sudden thought of having to accommodate Cyrus into their lives did give him pause, but then if she was sister to the Princes of Hell, they were going to have to accommodate a lot more than just Cyrus.

"Yes," Cyrus whispered without hesitation, his grip tightening on her wrist.

Lena's smile grew, her power beginning to spark where their hands joined, before suddenly it stopped. "Ah, hang on," she said, holding up her finger and dropping Cyrus' hand. Ambrose raised a brow in curiosity as she removed her hoof from Zagan's back and reached down to flip him over, returning her hoof to his chest. "I want you to watch this," she spat at him. Pausing briefly, she pulled the shard from his wing and swiftly stabbed it through his shoulder, his cry of pain echoing off the walls. Returning her gaze to Cyrus, she took hold of his wrist again. "Sorry, can you repeat that?"

Ambrose chuckled at her actions and shook his head. She was always one to ruin a serious moment. Archie had to turn away to hide his laughter, whilst Marcus slapped his hand over his face in despair.

Cyrus dropped his head, closing his eyes and pressing his lips together. "Lena," he sighed, looking back up at her, "I wish to bind to you."

The lightning reignited over their hands as Lena coursed her power through Cyrus' body. His spiral-like bindings glowed and shifted. There was no pain as his bond transferred to his new sire. Eventually the light and power subsided revealing his new bindings. Thin, jagged lines snaked up his arms, refracting like her lightning across his skin. They travelled further than before, stopping as the last points of the lines just touched the curve of his neck. Letting go of her hand, Cyrus held his arms in front of him, turning them over to inspect his new bindings.

"Thank you," he said looking up at his sister and sire with adoration. "Thank you."

Lena nodded, before indicating for him to retreat. He hurried back over to them. Marcus caught him in an embrace, patting him on the back and kissing him on the cheek. "Welcome to the family, kid," the cambion said with a slight chuckle. Cyrus smiled, but kept his head down, seemingly overcome with emotion.

Ambrose returned his gaze to Lena, his breath catching in his throat as their eyes met. She smiled at him, affection and love brightening her features. Her demonic form was as breathtaking as her human one.

"You bitch," Zagan coughed, his hands gripping at her hock. It was unclear if he was simply holding it or trying to push it away from him. "I'll kill you for this."

"I'd like to see you try," Lucifer called out, coming closer to the pair. His voice was soft and velvety, but travelled with ease across the cavern.

Lena's head snapped towards him. "Your voice," she whispered in shock. "I know your voice."

Lucifer smiled at her. "Welcome home, sister."

She pushed away from Zagan, causing him to grunt with pain, and she walked slowly towards him. "Sister?" she queried.

"Yes," he nodded.

"I don't understand," she said, stopping before him.

"You are a new Prince of Hell," Lucifer explained. "I have been waiting an age for you, my dear sister."

"You've been the voice in my head this whole time?"

"Yes and no," he said. "It is my voice, but it was not me. All demonic power in some form or another extends from me, so you hear my voice, but it is your own strength that guided you. I am so glad you found your way home," Lucifer clasped Lena's hands between his and kissed her knuckles with reverence. Asmodeus smiled at her and bowed his head.

Mammon came up beside Ambrose and bent down to whisper to him. "Come on," she said, placing her hand against his back, "Lucifer wishes to thank you for bringing our sister to us." Glancing at her briefly, Ambrose allowed himself to be led towards the Princes.

As he neared them, Lena turned her head to look at him, confusion etched into her features.

"Ah, your Consort," Lucifer said with a cheerful smile, looking at Ambrose.

"My what?" she asked, raising her brows, swiftly looking back to Lucifer.

"Her what?" Ambrose mirrored, as Mammon chuckled silently beside him.

The Prince of Pride blinked, looking between them. "Have I misunderstood? Do you not wish to be together?"

"No... I mean, yes... I mean," Lena stammered, looking panicked at Ambrose, before turning back to Lucifer. "What?"

"Asmodeus was under the impression you would take Ambrose as your Consort. Almost all the Princes have one," he said, undertones of confusion behind his words.

"Okay, maybe we need to clarify the term here," she said. "And sorry to sound like a broken record, but... what?"

"You are a Prince of Hell," Lucifer explained nodding to Lena, "he is your lover," nodding to Ambrose, "hence he is your Consort. Unless you wish to choose another for that role?"

"No!" Ambrose and Lena cried simultaneously.

The Prince smiled knowingly. "Details can all be discussed later. For now, returning to the matter at hand, what do you wish to do with him, sister?"

Lena and Ambrose turned to look at Zagan. Marcus and Archie were standing over him. Archie placed his foot where Lena's had been, keeping him pinned to the floor. It didn't look like Zagan was up to protesting, however, his body lying limp against the group, a scowl on his face. Cyrus stood behind them, his face a picture of shock.

"I will not allow him to live," Lena said firmly, turning back to Lucifer. "He has gone unchecked for too long, abusing his power, even for a demon."

Lucifer nodded in agreement. "You may mete out whatever action you deem fit."

She paused for a moment, contemplating her decision. Slowly, she reached out for Ambrose's hand, interlacing her fingers with his. He smiled softly as he took a step closer to her.

"Throw him into the Infernal Pit," she said finally, staring into his eyes. "He can serve Hell with his dying breath."

Forgetting the company around them, Ambrose pulled Lena towards him, placing his free hand on the side of her face and crushed his lips to hers. She smiled against him and wrapped her arms around his waist, pulling her body against his. For the last few weeks, he had hoped beyond hope that he would be able to feel her against him again, without fear of retribution. Now, she was here, in his arms, and he couldn't be happier.

"Ahem," Mammon coughed, awkwardly looking at the floor. Lucifer and Asmodeus stared shamelessly at the couple.

Ambrose wasn't sure how Lena managed to blush with skin as red as hers, but it was enticingly endearing. She stepped to his side so she could wrap her hands around his arm, keeping close to him, but so that she could face her new siblings again.

Lucifer smiled at her. "Mammon, please see to our sister's command."

She nodded, moving away from them, heading towards Zagan. The Prince of Greed called a few names, those belonging to them appearing in a flurry of flames beside their mistress, ready and willing to follow her orders. Marcus and Archie stepped back, as Mammon's demons grabbed Zagan's limp body under his arms, lifting him between them.

"Ah," Lena started, turning towards them, "not that I wish to imply any form of mistrust or doubt, but... Cyrus, go with them and report back to me when Zagan is dead, please." Cyrus' bindings glowed softly and he nodded in understanding, stepping towards the demons. "I hope there are no objections to that?" she asked looking back at Lucifer.

The Prince shook his head and smiled. "None at all," he assured her. "We are demons after all."

Mammon extended her hand for Cyrus, disappearing with him, Zagan and her demons.

"Now, to other matters," Lucifer said, drawing their attention back to him.

"Perhaps," Asmodeus interrupted, "we should leave such discussions to a more private setting, brother."

Ambrose looked around them, noting the number of demons watching them intently. None spoke, aware of the momentous nature of the scene in front of them. More demons were still arriving as word spread throughout Hell that three, well *four*, Princes had gathered openly. Even more so that Lucifer had ventured up from his domain. He spied Xavier in a corner, furiously writing down in a small book, looking up occasionally, Pasha beside him, shaking her head in despair. He smiled fondly at the sight of them.

"Of course, but first, Lena," Lucifer said, stepping towards her, "the other Princes and I helped to bring about your birth, but it is your choice to take up the mantle as the eighth Prince of Hell. It is my sincere hope that you will, but regardless, it is up to you. Will you become our sister? Will you become a Prince of Hell?"

Turning his head, Ambrose looked at Lena's face, trying to figure out what she was thinking. The loss of the bond between them had been a stark shock when Zagan overtook her bindings, but now more than ever he mourned its absence. He would now have to rely on his own intuition to know what she was feeling. She turned to look at him and he saw a range of emotions in her eyes; love, joy and excitement. He may no longer have their bond, but he welcomed the chance to learn her anew.

"What do you want to do, my dove?" he asked, placing one of his hands over hers on his arm.

Her smile was mesmerising, the soft curve of her lips brightening her face. "Could be fun," she whispered to him. "As long as we're together."

Returning her smile, he nodded his head slightly. "For eternity," he promised.

"So?" Lucifer prompted, bringing her attention back to him.

"Yes, to all questions," Lena answered, squeezing her fingers around Ambrose's arm, excitement in her voice. Lucifer held out his hand for her.

At that moment, Cyrus returned with Mammon, appearing beside his new sire. Lena looked at him, his eyes wide as he stared at Lucifer, realising where exactly he had returned to. "Sorry," he said hurriedly, glancing towards Lena.

"It's alright," Lucifer laughed. "Fulfil your sire's command."

Lena reached out and placed her hand on Cyrus' arm, searching his face. He nodded his confirmation, looking uncomfortably between the Princes. She smiled, telling him to stand with Marcus. Relief washing over his face, Cyrus quickly retreated.

With a final glance at Ambrose, Lena stepped away from him and placed her hand in Lucifer's. He guided her to the centre of the room, holding her hand high between them.

"Behold, your new Prince," Lucifer announced, looking around the room, his voice loud and clear. "Her domain will be Earth as the powers of Hell extend their hold to secure our position in our continuing war with Heaven. Revere and honour her."

A cheer erupted from the crowd as Ambrose's chest swelled with pride, watching her face light up at the adoration. All demons would know her now and all would fear her. Since she became a demon, he had done everything he could to keep her safe. Now, she was the safest she had ever been, and he could see her with fresh eyes, no longer needing to fear for her safety. In many ways, she had saved him, finally removing the one person he had truly feared and brought him a peace and warmth he had long thought he would never find. He silently vowed to spend the rest of eternity finding new ways to show her how much he appreciated her. How much he loved her.

"Behold her Consort," Lucifer continued, turning and gesturing to Ambrose. His eyes widened in shock as Mammon and Asmodeus pushed him forwards. "He will be her voice and hand wherever she may choose to extend them. Give to him the same respect as the other Consorts of the Princes."

Ambrose locked his eyes on Lena, walking towards her, trying to ignore the multitudes of eyes now on him. She was smiling at him sympathetically, taking his hand in hers and mouthing an apology.

"Sister," Lucifer said quietly, drawing her attention yet again to him. "In time you will form your own council. An inner circle of those you trust. But we must discuss your position now. Other than Ambrose, is there anyone else, here and now that you would like to be privy to such matters?"

Lena looked behind her and nodded. "Marcus and Cyrus," she said looking at them. "And Archie, if he is willing."

Lucifer smiled and beckoned them over. The three men all looked between them, exchanging confused expressions. "Do you wish for them to be part of your council, or merely witnesses?" Lucifer asked as the men approached.

"As part of my council," she confirmed with a firm nod.

"Very well," Lucifer nodded. "Asmodeus, Mammon, please escort Lena's council to the lower ring. We will meet you there."

Asmodeus approached Marcus and Cyrus, touching their shoulders and disappearing with them. Archie left with Mammon.

"Lena, the lower ring, being my domain, is only accessible to Princes, and those they transport with them. You should know the way there as a birthright," Lucifer explained. She nodded in confirmation. "The others and I will explain to your council what is going on. Take a moment to reunite with your Consort. I am well aware how trying the last few weeks have been for you both. Meet us there when you are ready." With that, Lucifer left in a flurry of white fire.

Grabbing his hand, Lena pulled Ambrose's arm against her body and gathered her flames around them. Smiling at her, he noted she had brought them back to the manor. To their room.

"Here," she said breathlessly, placing her palm on his chest. "Let me fix that." Her power felt warm against his skin, healing the burn she had put there.

"Take a breath, my dove," he sighed softly, cupping her cheek tenderly in his hand. "Your first transformation back to human can hurt as much as becoming a demon."

"Do you prefer me human?" she asked mockingly, even as her expression winced in pain, her demonic features receding into her body. A small cry escaped her lips, her gaze dropping to the floor as she grasped the top of his arms, her nails digging into his flesh. "Damn, you weren't kidding."

Ambrose transformed with her, holding her steady before him. "I don't care what you look like, my dove. I love you."

Lena looked up at him, stepping forward into his embrace. Wrapping them around her, his arms contracted hungrily behind her back, hers snaking around his neck. He claimed her mouth with his, delving his tongue to meet with hers, eager to taste her again. Holding her firmly, he lifted her against him and carried her to the bed, laying her gently beneath him.

"Ambrose," she breathed into their kiss. "I love you. I've missed you so much."

He smiled mischievously, brushing the back of his fingers along her jaw. "And I you," he sighed, "my Prince."

She burst out laughing and hit him in the chest. "Never again," she cried. "You never get to call me that, again."

Ambrose leant down and kissed her passionately. "I prefer 'dove', anyway," he whispered, staring into the very eyes that inspired his favourite endearment. "Lena," he started, trailing off, unsure of how to continue.

"I know," she responded, cupping his face between her hands.

"I'm sorry, Lena," he said, shaking his head. "I'm sorry I wasn't able to protect you."

"Hush," she whispered, placing her fingers gently against his lips. "I'm here now, that's all that matters. And I am never leaving you again." She kissed him softly, her kiss filled with love and affection. He melted into her touch. "I love you," she sighed.

"I love you," he returned, deepening the kiss, revelling in the warmth of her body beneath him. She was here and she loved him. His heart wanted to burst from his chest for the love he held for the woman that now owned it. Within her arms, he felt whole again.

CHAPTER FORTY-FIVE

Lying in the bed, Lena nuzzled her cheek against Ambrose's chest, listening intently to the beating of his heart and the breath in his lungs. Running her fingers over the back of his hand, she looked over her arm, inspecting the lack of bindings.

"I almost miss them," she said softly, smiling when her head bounced as he chuckled at her comment. "Maybe I'll get tattoos."

"Of which ones? Mine or Zagan's?" he teased.

"The insult, sir!" she cried, slapping him on the chest and propping up on her elbow to look at him. His smile was beautiful, pulling her towards him to place a warm kiss on his lips. Biting his bottom lip, she looked into his hazel eyes and smirked. "Zagan's, of course," she mocked.

Ambrose's eyes widened and with a cry he flipped her onto her back, tickling her sides.

"Ah, stop!" she laughed, trying to pull away from him, even as every nerve ending in her body fired with happiness.

"Apologise!" he demanded, laughter filling his own voice.

"Okay!" she yielded, "I'm sorry!"

As their laughter subsided, he remained leaning over her, looking into each other's eyes. He sighed, tracing the back of his fingers along her jaw, his gaze softening.

"What's wrong?" she asked, reaching up to touch his cheek.

"Nothing," he whispered. "Nothing is wrong. It's just, everything is going to change now."

She smiled at him and nodded. "Yes, it is," she confirmed. "Does that bother you?"

Ambrose leant down and pressed a kiss to her forehead. "Yes and no," he responded honestly. "Yes, because I want you all to myself, and no, as long as I get to remain by your side."

"What makes you think, after everything, I would let you leave?" she asked. "You are my Consort after all."

He pulled a face, but smiled at her. "I suppose, I'll have to get used to being called that, won't I?" he mused. "As you will have to get used to being called Prince."

Lena sighed, looking away from him. "Yeah... three months ago, I would have laughed at anyone who said demons were real. Now I'm a Prince of Hell. Might still laugh at anyone who calls me that in all honesty."

"The more I think about it, the less surprising it is."

Her eyes shot back to his in shock, his expression serious. "Why?" she asked.

"The way your bindings grew, the Princes coming out of their long absence, the way you had demons flocking to your aid when you were escaping Zagan. How long your transformation took... How could you not be?" he explained. "Everyone knew your importance well before today, even if we couldn't quite explain what it was. I could feel it whilst you were alive, because of the deal I made with your father. But Marcus picked up on it the first time he met you."

"Ambrose," she said softly, cupping his face between her hands, emotion overcoming her. "I love you."

He smiled and kissed her, a soft, gentle kiss, filled with love and reverence. "I love you, too, my dove," he whispered against her lips. "I love you more than anything in this world."

They held each other for a moment, before Lena sighed and pushed his head back gently with her touch.

"As much as I never want to leave this bed," she said sadly, "I think we have extended the moment that Lucifer allowed us to capacity. I highly doubt that Marcus and Archie are feeling particularly comfortable alone with the other Princes. I *know* Cyrus is uncomfortable. His anxiety is overwhelming."

Ambrose smiled with badly veiled amusement. She assumed at the thought of her now experiencing what it had been like to be him to an extent. On a similar thought, she was curious as to how Cyrus' emotions would likely impact their future moments together.

"Hm, we should probably rescue them from such a fate," he sighed as he pressed a firm kiss to her lips, before pushing off to stand beside the bed, holding out his hand for her. "My Prince," he said with a smile.

"What did I tell you about that?" she chuckled, but she took hold of his hand and allowed him to pull her to her feet.

"If you get to call me Consort, I get to call you Prince," Ambrose replied, dropping a kiss to the top of her head.

Looking up at him dubiously, Lena knew she would never be able to deny this man. "Fair enough," she sighed, moving away to retrieve her clothes from the floor. A sudden thought crossed her mind as she pulled on her jeans and a new, unburnt, shirt. "We're going to need to move," she stated.

"Yes, I figured we might," Ambrose responded, buttoning his shirt. "Demons will be coming to you for counsel now. We can't risk them coming here."

"Cyrus will need to move in, as well." She looked up as she heard Ambrose sigh heavily. "I'm sorry, I didn't have time to think of anything else," she said quickly.

"It's fine," he smiled at her. "I'm glad you saved him. Truly, I am. I was just lamenting the ability to take you in any room of the house."

She chuckled heartily. "It's not like he will be around all the time."

"True," he nodded, slipping his shoes back on.

Lena left her boots to the side, looking appreciatively at her feet. "I'm going to have to get used to losing my toes every time we go to Hell."

"The wings make up for it," he laughed, walking over to her.

Smiling, she stood next to him, wrapping her arms around his waist. "Well, shall we get this over with?"

Ambrose nodded, draping his arm over her shoulder. "The sooner I can get you alone again, the better." As she laughed with desire, he kissed her deeply, passion building once again within her core. "Lead on, my Prince," he whispered against her lips, his voice full with sincere adoration.

Staring into his eyes, Lena gathered her flames around them and pulled Ambrose with her to Hell's lowest ring, their bodies transforming as they moved through the fires. There was little pain for her this time, even as her wings ripped through her back, beating out at the empty space behind her as they appeared before the other Princes.

"Ah, sister," Lucifer said, a warm yet mildly terrifying smile on his lips as he walked over to them. Lena returned his smile, giving Ambrose's hand a reassuring squeeze as he shifted next to her. "Come, come. Let me introduce you to our other siblings."

Glancing at Ambrose, she walked forward, pulling him along with her as they joined the rest of her council and the other Princes. All seven had gathered to meet her, along with key members of their own councils. Archie was calmly chatting with Morgan and a demon that Lena knew to be Amicus, the last demon before her to take more than four weeks to transform. Marcus and Cyrus kept close together, simply listening and observing the gathering around them. Lena smiled at them, catching the small pangs of uncertainty emanating from... *her*... boundling.

Working around the room, she was introduced to the four Princes she had yet to meet. She decided fairly quickly that she liked Abaddon and Satan, but she would need more time to determine how she felt about Belphegor and Beelzebub. Overall, her new siblings were very welcoming and eager to meet her, but if she had learnt anything during her time in life and in death, it was to treat everyone with healthy caution.

"So, you were the one that sent TJ to test me?" she said as Satan wrapped her in a warm embrace.

"Apologies, sister," Satan said with a meek smile, his deep red eyes gleaming brightly even in the dim light. Everything about the Prince of Wrath was red, from his eyes to his skin to the scales and horns that covered almost every inch of his body. "You have to admit though, he was a good test. Or at least, you enjoyed tearing him apart."

"I admit nothing," she laughed, winking at him.

Lucifer led them all to a room in which a large round table sat, nine chairs at equal distances around it, reminding her of the legend of King Arthur. Watching the other Princes and their councils, Lena took a seat next to Abaddon, the one to her left remaining empty. Ambrose and her other men stood behind her. Feeling incredibly uncomfortable in the chair, Lena tried to find some way that her wings could rest either side of the seat, the back pressing against them almost painfully.

"If you sit a little forward, like just on the edge of the seat, it makes it easier," Abaddon whispered to her, demonstrating on her own chair, her pitch-black wings, raised ever so slightly behind her.

"Thanks," Lena whispered back with a small smile. She could hear

Archie and Marcus chuckling at her struggle.

"Welcome, my siblings," Lucifer said from his seat opposite her. "We haven't had cause to gather like this in a long time. And now, we come here to welcome our new sister."

Shifting in her seat, Lena dropped her gaze as all the Princes turned to look at her. *How awkward...* She smiled hearing the voice, happy to find it was still with her.

"Lena," Lucifer said, drawing her gaze back to him. "All Princes have a domain. The lower ring is mine. The six other Princes oversee different levels of the upper rings. Your domain will be Earth, among humans. I cannot leave Hell, and the others cannot leave for very long. But you can. You are the only one of us with a human form. And because of this, it is you that will fill the seat to your left."

Looking at the empty seat, Lena took a deep breath. "A ninth Prince?"

"Yes," Lucifer confirmed. "Seven sins made seven Princes and the seven rings of Hell. Earth and Heaven are the seats of the Thrones of God. For centuries it has remained this way, balanced and tempered with Heaven and Hell working quietly against the other. But time moves on and we progress towards the Apocalypse."

"So that's a thing?" she asked, looking around the room, folding her arms over her chest. "We are actually working towards an apocalypse."

"*The* Apocalypse, and yes."

"So, you need nine Princes. The seven of you for down here. Me for Earth, and the ninth for Heaven."

"Yes."

Staring blankly ahead, Lena let the information settle over her. "Huh..." she huffed slightly. "'The'? Not 'a'? So, there's only the one?"

"There have been some in the past. Test runs, if you will," Satan answered her. "For example, the bubonic plague."

"But that wasn't a fight between demons and angels," she said, her confusion mounting. "Or at least, that's not what I learnt."

"Illness among humans," Belphegor explained, his voice sinfully indulgent causing shivers to ripple across her skin, "is a side-effect of the fight between angels and demons."

"The powers we emit are incredibly toxic to mortal life," Mammon continued, her golden gaze locked on Lena. "Humans are not aware when we battle, but they feel the fallout all the same."

"Right," Lena said, breathing out heavily. "So how am I supposed to find the ninth Prince? I'm guessing they're on Earth. But you said it took a long time to find me. How long do we have?"

"Unfortunately, not as long as it took us to find you," Lucifer said slowly. "You have less than a century."

"How long did it take you to find me?" she asked cautiously.

"Two millennia."

Lena burst out in a singular laugh of surprise. "Excuse me? It took seven of you two millennia, and I have less than a century? I haven't even been a Prince for three hours yet."

Cyrus' amusement at her statement filled her chest. Damn, that was going to be distracting. How had Ambrose managed it? The number of times she would have flooded him with her desire for him. Pressing her lips together she turned her head slowly to glare at her boundling. He dropped his gaze to the floor, breathing out slowly, shifting uncomfortably under her stare.

"Lena," Lucifer called, her eyes snapping back to him. "You will have the full resources of Hell to find them. Where we had to keep our search for you among us only, you may include anyone you deem worthy of knowing into the search. Finding you, was merely the first step towards the Apocalypse. And the biggest one at that. You being on Earth, your power and your conduit will all be key factors in finding the ninth Prince."

"Unfortunately," Asmodeus said softly, "we don't know where to start or where to direct you in your search. But we will help where we can."

"The first thing we can do to help," Lucifer continued, "is to provide you with our collective knowledge. Everything we have learnt since our creation. If you still wish to take up the mantle of the eight Prince, place your right hand flat on the table."

The seven Princes around her did as Lucifer instructed, watching her to see if she would do the same. Glancing over her shoulder she looked at the men she had chosen to form her council, gauging their reaction to the conversation. Ambrose and Marcus smiled at her and nodded. They would stand with her no matter what, she knew that. Cyrus had no choice but to follow her for now, but she was certain he would stay with her, with or without his bindings. Looking at Archie, she wondered how he would feel about this. She trusted him and she knew he would follow her orders, but did he trust her? Their eyes locked and she saw a deep reverence and respect within his fire-like eyes. He nodded slowly, confirming his commitment to her.

Turning back to her siblings, Lena took a deep breath and slowly placed her hand flat on the table. Lucifer smiled as white fire sprang from his fingers and travelled over the surface of the table, running along invisible lines connecting him to each Prince in turn. Watching intently, the flames snaked towards her fingers before gently licking over her skin. Gasping at the sensation, she closed her eyes as waves of memories, images and information coursed through her mind, settling in among her own thoughts. Creation and destruction mixed together in perfect union. As suddenly as the knowledge took over, it released her.

"Bloody hell," she breathed, leaning forward slightly, keeping her hand firmly on the table to steady herself. "And I thought the non-exposure command was intense." Her men, along with the rest of the room, chuckled at her comment. She shook her head as if attempting to rattle her thoughts into place.

"By the way," Abaddon said with a warm smile, "that command, obviously, no longer applies to you."

"Good to know," she said, blinking hard to clear her vision.

"You will need time to sort through everything," Asmodeus explained. "We do not need to rush into further explanations today."

"Our brother is right," Lucifer agreed. "You have been through enough for today. We'll come back here in a few days once you have had time to settle into your new role."

"Great," Lena sighed, her mind still racing with the new information given to her, as she and the other Princes got to their feet. Well, she got to her hooves...

Smiling, she walked around her chair to Ambrose, pulling him close to her, leaning into his warmth and strength. Asmodeus and Mammon walked up to them.

"Come with us," Asmodeus beckoned them. "It's time to form your council."

Lena looked at him confused, as did the men around her, exchanging glances between them.

"Is that not already done?" Marcus asked softly.

Mammon smiled at him and shook her head. "A Prince's council is bonded to them, in a way. We will show Lena how to extend her power to all of you."

"So, we are to become boundlings again?" Archie joked, chuckling slightly,

"I want to say no," Asmodeus started, scratching his cheek with a singular claw. "But, I guess, it could be seen that way. Lena cannot command you in the way she can Cyrus whilst he bears her bindings, nor is your life bound to hers. But she will be able to find you wherever you are and call you to her when needed."

"You will also share in her power. Significantly increasing your own," Mammon explained as she led them into an antechamber.

"Would have been nice to know how to do that before Zagan took me," Lena scoffed to no one in particular. Ambrose tightened his arm around her shoulders, pressing her closer to him. She knew he would still be feeling some remnants of pain lingering from their separation caused by the cambion. Her own pain from it still clung stubbornly in her chest. It would take some time for that pain to heal fully. She wished she could wipe it away for both of them, but hopefully, they would become stronger for it.

Very aware they were being watched, Lena looked up to see Asmodeus simply staring at them, a wide smile on his lips. She tilted her head at him, raising a brow in silent question.

"I'm so happy to see you two reunited," the Prince of Lust said after a moment, placing his hands over his heart in warm affection. "Battling through Hell to save the other despite so many obstacles standing in your way. Finally, for your love to reunite in such a way that brings about Lena's true birth."

Ambrose laughed and shook his head. "Another thing for you to write about someday?"

"What?" Lena asked at the odd exchange, looking up at her Consort.

"I'll explain later," he said, dropping a light kiss to her lips.

"Ah!" Asmodeus cried, clapping his hands together. "There is that intoxicating spark!"

"Now it's just creepy," Lena sighed awkwardly, dropping her hold of Ambrose's waist and stepping away from him. He caught her hand, interlacing his fingers with hers, pulling her back towards him with a sympathetic smile.

Mammon hit the back of her brother's head, shaking hers in disgust at him. "You just can't help yourself, can you?"

"Ow," the Prince of Lust leered at his sister.

"Lena, please stand in the centre of the room," Mammon said, pushing her brother towards the wall. "Ambrose, Mar— I'm not saying all of your names," she sighed, placing her hands on her hips. "If you are willing to be part of her council, please stand around her."

Smiling with amusement, Lena moved into her position as instructed. Ambrose stood in front of her, warmth and love in his eyes. Even in demon form, she could look at him forever.

Asmodeus and Mammon instructed her carefully as she extended branches of her lightning to envelop each of the men around her. She could feel her power mixing with theirs, settling within them like a seed ready to grow as and when needed. Suddenly, she was very aware of them. Of them standing around her. Closing her eyes, she focused on each of them in turn, centring on their strength, attuning to the vibrations of their own power. It was like they were beacons in her mind, each one unique and personal to them. Turning her head slightly, she felt Cyrus looking at his arms, as his bindings glowed and shifted across his skin, lengthening down his spine as her power flowed within him. Breathing out slowly, she opened her eyes as her lightning receded into her, the forming of her council complete.

No words needed to be spoken as she and the men stood silently, each simply adjusting to the connection now between them all. She had found her family. A place where she belonged. Where she was needed and wanted. Protected and loved. Safe. And it was all thanks to the demon who stood in front of her now. Smiling at him, Lena stepped forward into Ambrose's outstretched arms, pouring as much love and devotion for him as she could into their kiss.

EPILOGUE

One Month Later...

Lena and Ambrose walked side-by-side through the courtyard of their new home. Together with Cyrus and Marcus, they had bought a large plot of land in the desert, enjoying the warmth and near constant sun. Using a number of different spells, she and Marcus had constructed the large u-shaped building, its two storeys surrounding the courtyard filled with granite paving, cacti and desert shrub arrangements lining the walls and railings by the outside lounging area. A thick limestone wall enclosed the courtyard providing them with ample privacy even if someone should stumble upon them. It also allowed for demons to flame in to meet with Lena without fear of exposure.

Archie had lived with them for a fortnight before, with Lena's agreement, returning to Hell to be her ears and eyes there as needed, although he visited often. Cyrus had to remain close, and she had insisted on Marcus moving in, finding his presence and guidance invaluable. Ambrose, of course, went wherever she did.

Now as they walked across the yard, Ambrose narrowed his eyes at the man who had essentially strolled through their gate without a care. Marcus and Cyrus stood off to the side, the latter leaning against a supporting pillar of the vine canopy, his arms folded over his chest.

"Who are you?" Lena asked sternly, stopping a few strides from the man. Ambrose stood to her side, placing his hands in his pockets. "Get out of my home."

"I would think twice before throwing me out, Lena," the man said calmly. He had proud features, his jaw starkly defined in the desert sun. Dark black hair hung down to his shoulders, his deeply tanned olive skin giving him a Mediterranean look. Narrowed brown eyes gleamed with a light Ambrose was unfamiliar with.

"Who are you?" she repeated, placing her hands on her hips. "You are not a demon."

The man smiled, a smile that didn't quite reach his eyes. "I'm an angel. Raphael."

Raising her brows, Lena clicked her tongue sharply. "An arch-angel," she said, turning her head slightly as Zamira stalked out of the doorway behind Cyrus. The hellhound laid down beside the boundling, her eyes focused on her mistress.

Raphael glanced at the beast. If he was concerned, he did a good job of hiding it. "Good to see you know me," he said softly, turning his eyes back to her.

"I attended Sunday school," she shrugged. "Once." Marcus snorted loudly from his position at her comment, coughing slightly to cover it up. "Where are your wings, angel?"

"Where are your horns, demon?" Raphael retorted, folding his arms.

Smiling slowly, Lena stepped closer to him. "I'll show you mine, if you show me yours?" Simultaneously, she and Raphael transformed. Hers was certainly more drastic than his, her wings ripping through her flesh as it darkened to its blood red tones. Raphael grew in size as a bright light radiated from his back, his white feathered wings appearing from thin air. Ambrose noted with a slight satisfaction that she towered above the angel, forcing him to look up at her to continue their conversation. "What are you doing here?" she asked.

"I come as a friendly emissary."

"Friendly?" she laughed with a sinister smile. "I doubt that. Get out."

"You need to hear what I have to say, Lena," he said, raising his wings proudly behind him.

"That's 'Prince' to you," Ambrose said, stepping closer to her side. Marcus and Cyrus pushed off from their position, moving to stand next to him. A united front of her council behind her.

"I recognise no crown on her head," Raphael spat maliciously.

"Yet, here you are, as an emissary," Marcus said softly, an air of warning in his voice.

Raphael sneered at him. “I am here under the authority of God.”

“I recognise no God,” Lena lifted her chin proudly. “I give reverence only to that which I can see.”

“To accept God is to see him.”

“To see is to believe,” she retorted. “Say what you have to, *messenger*, then leave.”

Raphael folded his arms across his chest, his gaze travelling up and down Lena’s body, sizing her up. Ambrose bristled at the brazenness of it but kept his possessiveness in check. He knew Lena’s affections were for him alone. An angel was no threat. “I am guardian to God’s Third Heaven on Earth,” Raphael said after a moment. “I will not allow demons such as yourself to endanger that.”

“I thought you were here under the authority of God. That sounds like a personal problem,” Lena smiled, a soft laughter in her voice.

“Your kind belongs in Hell.”

“And your kind belongs in Heaven, yet here we stand,” she said waving her hands around her to emphasise her point. “If angels may have a foothold on Earth, then so shall demons. We must maintain balance after all.”

“It is for that reason alone, I cannot force you to leave the surface,” Raphael sneered, taking a step towards her, his wings rising as if to gain some height on her. “But I caution you, step out of line and I will bring the full heavenly force down upon you and your brethren.”

“We’re a few decades off from the Apocalypse, Raphael.”

“I’d be willing to accelerate the timeline.”

“You and I both know, that’s not up to you.”

“Just give me a reason.”

“Careful, angel,” Lena cautioned with a snarl, baring her teeth at him, her own wings rising menacingly behind her, soft spikes of lightning dancing across her skin. “Be mindful that you stand alone before me and my council.”

Picking up on their cue, Ambrose, Marcus and Cyrus transformed behind her, their demonic features forming on their bodies. They kept their power beneath the surface, ready to use if needed, but not on display. Zamira raised from her position, ambling across the yard to stand next to Cyrus, her snout glowing with lightning as she huffed in annoyance. Ambrose smiled as he noted a slight panic form in Raphael’s dark eyes.

Shifting on the spot, the angel tried to regain his composure. "Lena is an odd name for a demon, don't you think?" Raphael mused, smiling even as he swallowed his fear. "'Ray of light'."

"Lucifer means 'light-bearer', does it not?" Lena responded, raising her hand delicately to watch her lightning arc and fold over her palm. "Perhaps Hell is not as evil as you angels preach."

"We shall see," Raphael trailed off. He turned on his heel, making his way towards the gate. *How dare he turn his back on a Prince of Hell*, Ambrose thought to himself. As if sensing his annoyance, Raphael looked back over his shoulder, placing his hand on the gate. "The Apocalypse will decide whose cause is more righteous. See you around, Lena."

"Can't wait," she sighed impatiently as Raphael pushed the gate open and disappeared in a beacon of bright white light. She didn't move, simply staring at the gate as it swung shut, the latch clicking softly. "That was... interesting," she said, her voice barely louder than a whisper.

Cyrus chuckled, bringing her attention to him with a haughty glare. "You're bricking it," he said, a wide smile on his face, lifting his hand and scratching under Zamira's snout as she yawned loudly. The hellhound shook out her body before turning and heading into her den, her pups eagerly awaiting the return of their mother.

With a gentle laughter, she joined in his amusement. "Oh, very much so!" she laughed, turning to face them.

"You handled that brilliantly, Lena," Marcus said as he allowed his demonic form to recede. The rest of them followed suit, generally preferring to be in human form when alone.

"It doesn't feel brilliant," she sighed, rubbing the back of her fingers under her chin as she stared at the ground in contemplation. "I think, unfortunately, that will not be the last time we see him."

"Agreed," Marcus nodded. "What do you want to do?"

"I'm not sure yet. But I don't want to be surprised by him again," she shook her head and walked over to Ambrose. Smiling at her, he eagerly took her into his arms, wrapping them around her shoulders and placed a chaste kiss on the top of her head. She frequently sought the comfort of his embrace now when she needed to think things through and he was more than happy to accommodate her in this regard. "I need to go to the Repository. See if I can find a way of creating some form of warning system for angels. I don't want anyone to know about this encounter yet."

"Lena, you have a boundling now," Cyrus said, placing his hands in his pockets. "Let me go."

"He's right," Ambrose agreed, looking down into her soft grey eyes. "Boundlings can come and go through the Repository without raising questions. If you don't want anyone to know, he should go."

Her eyes glazed for a moment as her mind wandered, absorbing the advice. "Alright," she nodded. "But don't tell anyone about this. Not yet. Not even Morgan."

"Do we not trust Morgan?" Marcus asked, tilting his head to the side, mild surprise in his eyes.

"We do, but..." Lena trailed off, her hand absently running up and down Ambrose's back. "She's part of Belphegor's inner circle. Not mine. I'm still not sure what to make of him. I need to think about this more before I bring it to the attention of my siblings."

"Fair enough."

"Do you want to compel me to keep it secret?" Cyrus asked, raising a brow in sibling jest.

"No, I'm not Zagan. I trust you," Lena smiled at him.

Ambrose chuckled, placing his hand on her cheek and raising her gaze to him. "Thank goodness for that," he sighed adoringly, lowering his head and pressing a warm kiss against her lips.

"Alright, you two," Cyrus laughed, rolling his eyes at them and shaking his head. "I'll be back soon."

"I'll go with you," Marcus said hurriedly, quickly moving to stand beside the boundling, smiling at him.

Suddenly, Lena drew in a sharp breath and stiffened against him. "Lena?" Ambrose asked, looking at her. Her eyes were bright with some untold emotion, her lips pressed together like she was trying to hold back a delicious secret. Her gaze snapped to Cyrus as her fingers dug into Ambrose's back. Utterly confused, he looked back and forth between the sire and boundling.

Cyrus stared at her, abject horror on his face. "Oh no, Lena..."

"What? Nothing! What?" she said hurriedly, her breathing rapid as she pressed herself closer to Ambrose as if to steady herself. "I didn't say anything."

"You don't have to, I can see it all over your face," Cyrus snapped at her, holding up a finger as if to chastise her.

Biting her lip, she buried her face into Ambrose's chest as he and

Marcus simply stared at each other in total confusion at the odd exchange.

"I don't know what you're talking about," she said, her voice muffled by his shirt.

"Lena, I swear," the boundling said firmly, his expression hardening as he drew in a deep breath, eyes locked on his sire despite her avoidance of his gaze. "Keep that to yourself."

"Just go already," she pleaded.

Shrugging at his friend, Marcus placed a gentle hand on Cyrus' shoulder and they disappeared in flames.

"You two are going to be a nightmare..." Ambrose chuckled, shaking his head. Running his hand through her hair, he smiled adoringly at her as she breathed out slowly, her face still pressed against his chest. "What was that about?"

She shook her head even as she answered him. "Cyrus has a crush on Marcus."

Definitely not what he expected her to say. "What?"

Finally lifting her head, Lena looked up at him, an amused smile on her lips. "You do know he's gay, right?"

Ambrose looked at her, shaking his head in disbelief. "You think I would have been so worried about him if I had?"

"Sorry, it never occurred to me to tell you."

Chuckling good-naturedly, he tightened his embrace, resting his head atop hers. "Cyrus and Marcus, huh?" he mused, looking off into some distant point, a soft smile tugging at his lips. "I think they'd make a cute couple."

"You say that like Marcus is gay too."

"Not sure you can really label Marcus. He's never said anything directly, but cambions don't really care for gender."

"Hey, look at me," Lena said, taking firm hold of his chin and angling his face down to lock eyes with him. "We do not get involved, okay? If they get together, they do so on their terms. It's going to be bad enough feeling Cyrus' attraction for Marcus. I don't want to start feeling... that..."

"Ha!" Ambrose burst out with laughter, taking her adorable face between his hands. Lowering his face to hers, he caught her lips with a deep and passionate kiss, delving his tongue into the warmth of her mouth, smiling as he pulled a soft moan from her throat. "Have I told you recently how much I love you?" he sighed against her, watching intently as her eyes darkened to a midnight storm, desire taking over her body.

"Yes, but I love hearing it," she whispered, raising on her toes to capture his mouth, snaking her arms around his neck, pulling herself closer to him. Needing no further encouragement, Ambrose lifted her into his arms, placing his hands firmly under her thighs as her legs wrapped around his waist.

Her kiss was addictive, her scent intoxicating, as he carried her across the yard and into the house. They still had a startling habit of getting carried away when they were alone together. Lena made him insatiable. He couldn't get enough of her and he hoped he never would. For so long he had thought he would never be worthy of the kind of love she gave him. A love she gave him freely and without expectation. A love that made his heart swell with joy and peace beyond imagining.

"I love you," he moaned into her mouth as he laid her beneath him on the bed.

"Ambrose," she sighed, grasping his face tenderly between her hands. "I love you."

A soft gleam shone within her eyes, giving him pause. Kissing the tip of her nose, he brushed the back of his fingers along her jaw. "What's wrong, my dove?"

"I'm not sure," she replied softly, rubbing her thumbs over his cheeks. "I think we're going to be in for a wild ride."

Smiling softly at her, he leant down and rested his forehead against hers. "We'll be okay," he reassured her. "As long as we're together."

Loving warmth washed over his body as Lena pulled his mouth to hers, whispering against his lips. "For eternity."

AFTERWORD

Dear Reader,

Thank you for reading Demon's Choice. I really hope you enjoyed reading it as much as I enjoyed writing it.

Demon's Choice started out with a fleeting thought of "*how would a demon react if their lover/girlfriend was sacrificed to them in a summoning*". This thought lit a spark, which became a flame and grew into a fire until I knew I had to write it. Initially, I thought I would write a few segments just to get the idea out of my head with no real intention of publishing it.

But the idea didn't leave. Instead, Lena and Ambrose lived in my head for months. They became my passion and although I have been writing for years, they were the first couple I have actually wanted to share with others. They continue to live in my head even now, still helping me build the world in which they reside.

I do hope they have captured your heart as much as they have mine. If you wish to read more about them, look out for the rest of the books in the series as they continue to play pivotal roles in the progression towards the Apocalypse.

With my deepest gratitude!

Much love,
Jasmine

DEMONS OF THE APOCALYPSE

The world needs to reset. Heaven and Hell need to reset. The Apocalypse will decide the fate of morality.

Book 1: **Demon's Choice**
"My whole life someone, or something else has been pulling the strings… I never had a choice until I died."

Lena moved to town to disappear, but found herself drawn to a man that could do anything but…

Sacrificed to a demon she finds herself thrown into a world where she is the centre of attention, completely dependent on the man she longs for. Others now covet her and her growing power, seeking to tear her apart from the only person who has truly cared for her. The one she chose to be with.

Can she find the strength to save both her and her heart?

Book 2: **Demon's Faith** – Coming out – March 2024
"Just admit it, compared to the rest of you, I'm nothing. I'm worthless, just a waste of fucking space!"

A year after becoming the boundling to both his sister and Prince of Hell, Cyrus struggles to find his place among his fellow council members. He would do anything for his sister to trust him, to have faith in him.

"It's you… I belong with you. I belong to you. I look at you and I know you are all that is good with me."

Family has meant little to Marcus for centuries, betrayed by one he trusted. But now that he has one, he will do anything to protect it, even deny his own heart.

Book 3: **Demon's Hope** – Coming out – September 2024

Book 4: **Demon's Right** – Coming out – 2025